NEW
FEARS 2

ALSO AVAILABLE FROM TITAN BOOKS

MORE NEW HORROR STORIES
by masters of the genre

NEW FEARS 2

Edited by **Mark Morris**

TITAN BOOKS

NEW FEARS 2

Print edition ISBN: 9781785655531
Electronic edition ISBN: 9781785655593

Published by Titan Books
A division of Titan Publishing Group Ltd
144 Southwark St, London SE1 0UP

First edition: September 2018
2 4 6 8 10 9 7 5 3 1

CONTENTS

INTRODUCTION

So here we are again.

For those of you who missed out on the original volume in this series, let me explain what *New Fears* is all about. As a child I grew up reading numerous anthologies of ghost and horror stories, and back in those halcyon days they were nearly all un-themed. Each book contained a delicious blend of stories both supernatural and non-supernatural, some of which would be gory, some subtle, some surreal, some sad, some funny… In short, you never knew what kind of story you were going to be reading next, as a result of which each anthology was a leap into the unknown, a journey of twists and turns leading to a series of exhilarating destinations.

In recent years, though, market forces have dictated that if anthologies are to appeal to the reader, then they must have a *theme*. Hence we now see a proliferation of anthologies in which all the stories are about vampires, or zombies, or werewolves, or mad scientists; or anthologies in which all the stories are set in the same location; or anthologies whose stories all focus on a single, sometimes abstract concept: evolution, the dark, phobias, obsessions, dreams.

Don't get me wrong. Some of these themed anthologies are excellent. But they're also restrictive to a greater or lesser degree, and whenever I read one I find myself hankering for a bit more variety; I find myself thinking wistfully of the un-themed genre anthologies which have most influenced and excited me over the years: the annual Pan and Fontana Books of Horror and Ghost Stories; Ramsey Campbell's *New Terrors* (originally published in two volumes in 1980, and as an omnibus edition in 1985); Kirby McCauley's *Dark Voices* (1980); Douglas E. Winter's *Prime Evil* (1989); Nicholas Royle's *Darklands* (1991) and *Darklands 2* (1992); Stephen Jones and David Sutton's six-volume *Dark Terrors* series (1996–2002).

My aim with *New Fears*, therefore, is to bring back the un-themed horror anthology—and not as a one-off, but as an annual publication, with each volume acting as a showcase for the very best and most innovative fiction that this exhilarating genre has to offer. "Horror" is a catch-all term for a field that has an almost infinite variety of approaches, themes and styles, and I want *New Fears* to reflect that.

And judging by the feedback we've received for the first volume we've made an excellent start.

When *New Fears* was released in September 2017 my main hope was that the modern horror readership would buy into an old idea made new. But not only did they buy into the idea, they embraced it like a long-lost but much-loved relative, lavishing it with praise and plaudits, and even with love.

Ginger Nuts of Horror said that *New Fears* "oozes quality from an eclectic range of leading writers from the world of horror and dark fiction..." whereas Kendall Reviews described the book as "a stunning collection of nineteen tales that will both terrify and delight you. The quality of writing is brilliant... a special anthology that I hope to see run and run..." HorrorTalk, meanwhile, thought *New Fears* "...a gathering of glittering gems by some of the finest minds in the business today..." and Risingshadow simply described it as "...one of the best horror anthologies of the year..."

Additionally, *New Fears* was chosen as the only anthology on Barnes and Noble's auspicious and influential Best Horror of 2017 list.

An excellent start then, as I said.

But now it's time to look forward, not back. Which begs the question: what does *New Fears 2* have to offer?

Well, first and foremost an entirely new line-up of writers. From the outset I decided that in order to showcase the work of as many genre practitioners as possible, all of the writers who had a story in volume one would be ineligible to send me a story for volume two. What this means is that, taken together, volumes one and two of *New Fears* offer you forty brand new stories from forty of the best genre writers working today. Which doesn't mean I've now exhausted the options where new contributors are concerned—far from it. Such is the current vibrancy of the genre that if *New Fears* continues beyond volume two, there are many, *many* more writers I would love to feature within its pages. Indeed, if I wanted to, I could almost certainly fill up at least half a dozen volumes of *New Fears* before returning to writers I've used before. In fact, my only regret with editing these first two volumes has been that I've had to restrict my choices. Believe me, the hardest part of being an editor is not, as some might think, having to plough through hundreds of submissions to find the nuggets of gold; it's having to turn excellent stories and writers away because there simply isn't room to accommodate them all.

I'm delighted with the choices I've made for *New Fears 2*, though, and I hope you will be too. As in volume one, the stories featured here are from a range of established masters, such as Stephen Volk, Tim Lebbon and Steve Rasnic Tem, recent genre stars like Paul Tremblay, Benjamin Percy and Catriona Ward, and relative newcomers like Priya Sharma,

Laura Mauro, Aliya Whiteley and Kit Power.

Also, as in volume one, the stories are a dizzyingly eclectic mix of styles and approaches. Within these pages are tales of inanimate objects infused with evil; of otherworldly entities and living myths; of family curses and predators both natural and supernatural; of dread and regret and madness and outright terror.

There are stories too which may not at first seem like horror stories at all, but which nevertheless leave you with the uncomfortable notion that there is something askew, off-kilter, *not quite right* with the world.

Fears, after all, come in many shapes and sizes, and here is just a small selection of them. And who knows? Maybe one of your own fears is waiting for you right here.

Why not find out?

Just turn the page.

MARK MORRIS
January 2018

MAW
Priya Sharma

The sea brought the container in on the highest tide that Little Isle had seen in thirty years, beaching it on the rocks at the base of the cliffs.

Magnus and his sons found it first. They'd been following the trail of dead seals and fish along the beach.

The ferry had been cancelled because the sky over the other islands and the mainland was wild, but the driving wind and rain had paused over Little Isle, making it a bright spot in the darkness.

Hildy, Magnus's wife, gave him a pointed look when he suggested a day of roaming to the boys, before saying, "Back for lunchtime, okay? You have a homework box for days like this."

Days when they were cut off and they couldn't get to primary school on the next island.

The sea was now in retreat. The air smelt swept clean. Water collected in the ripples on the sand and reflected the blue sky overhead.

Donald, Magnus's younger son, saw the dead seal first. Magnus squatted beside it. Its neck was badly bruised and one of its eyes had gone. A flipper was missing.

"What happened to it, Dad?"

Magnus rolled it over. His cursory post-mortem was inconclusive.

"I don't know."

They followed the curve of the beach, and there lay mackerel, herring and ugly monkfish, dull eyes wide in surprise at their fate. Some were whole, but most were torn up, the clumsy dissection revealing guts and flesh already starting to rot.

"Shame. What a waste."

They picked their way through more seal carcasses. These had fared less well. Most were missing great chunks. Some looked bitten down to bone, the edges black and high.

"Rank." Peter covered his nose.

"It's nature." Magnus loved his sons too much to coddle them. "We all end up like this."

Magnus meant rotting, not chewed up. Donald screwed up his face.

They found pieces of oars too, beaten and worn. A rowing boat with a hole in its hull. A length of fearsome-looking chain. The ocean bed had been dredged and deposited on the shore.

After a quarter of a mile, the soft ascent of beach onto land was replaced by vertical columns of rock. The container was in the cliff's shadow.

Donald was about to run to it but Magnus grabbed the hood of his coat and hauled him back. Peter, who was ten, stayed by his father's side, frowning.

"What is it, Dad?" Peter whispered.

"A shipping container. Take Donald and go straight home. And not up the cliff path either, it'll be slippery. Go back the way we came."

Two figures approached them from the opposite direction. Magnus was relieved to see it was Jimmy and Iain. His sons walked away, looking back. Jimmy waved at them. Magnus watched them go and then turned his attention back to the container.

"They don't normally drop off ships, do they?" Iain asked.

"No, not usually."

Magnus had authority on Little Isle because of his knowledge of plumbing, plastering and mechanics, and because his grandfather was John Spence. Plus, he'd worked on the mainland port when he was younger, amid acres of decks stacked high with these identical steel boxes. That was the year before he'd married Hildy.

"That's odd." Magnus went from one end of the container to the other, kneeling to inspect it. "No twist locks."

Iain looked blank.

"There should be one at each corner. They lock each container to the one below it, or to the deck."

Jimmy picked up a pebble.

"Don't."

Iain was too late. It hit the container's side with a dull thud rather than the clang Magnus expected. The stone that had survived endless beatings by the sea shattered into jagged shards. Jimmy's gaze darted to Iain and then Magnus's face, awaiting reprimand. Iain shook his head, then turned to Magnus.

"Are they watertight?"

"Should be."

"What if it's full of bodies?" Jimmy said. "Immigrants."

"Don't be daft."

Iain's embarrassment didn't register with Jimmy, who put his ear to the container.

"What can you hear?" Magnus asked gently. Jimmy was everyone's to look out for, not just his younger brother's responsibility.

"I can't hear what they're saying." Jimmy closed his eyes.

"Oh, for God's sake."

"What?" Jimmy was on Iain, fast and fierce. "For God's sake, what?"

"Hey, hey, it's okay." Magnus soothed him. "Come and help me look for something. Can you do that?"

"Yes." Jimmy looked deflated, as if the unaccustomed anger had taken it out of him. His focus shifted to somewhere beyond Magnus.

"I'm looking for something called a CSC plate. It's a metal rectangle. So big." He held up his hands to demonstrate. "It has writing on it. Normally it's on the doors."

They circled the container, climbing up and down the rocks, or leaping from one to another. Nothing. Magnus lowered himself between two boulders to inspect the underside.

"What do you see?" Iain called.

"A load of barnacles. This hasn't come off a ship recently."

Barnacles, inside their carapaces, looked like closed eyelids or mouths. *Barnacles don't have hearts.* His father had told him that.

I must remember to teach the boys, Magnus thought.

He ran his fingers over the jagged colony that was interrupted by limpets, their shells marked with starburst ridges.

Iain reached down to help him climb out.

"Can we keep it? They found one of these on Hesketh Head. It was full of quad bikes. That would be something, wouldn't it?"

Magnus put his chin on his chest, considering Iain's suggestion. "The police called them looters."

"Didn't catch them though, did they? We don't have to keep it for ourselves. We could use it for everyone."

"Maybe you're right. We're owed a bit of luck." He lifted his eyes skyward. "Here comes his lordship. Well, that's fucked that idea then."

"Simon." Magnus gave him a curt nod.

"How's Hildy?"

"Fine."

"Give her my regards."

"Will do."

"Did that wash up this morning?" Simon gestured towards the container.

Magnus didn't reply, so neither did Iain.

"There's no CSC plate on it. We looked." Jimmy kicked at a dead fish and then wandered away when Simon gave him a bemused smile.

"Have either of you been able to get outside contact?"

"No, everything's down," Magnus replied. "The storm's still out there."

"We'll let the coastguard know when the radio's back up."

"So that's it. You've decided without a word to anyone."

Magnus willed Simon to say *It's my island* so he could have a go at him but Simon didn't oblige.

"What's there to decide?"

"You have no idea what's in there."

"Whatever it is, it isn't ours."

"Look at it. It's been in the ocean for God knows how long. The insurance will have already been paid out on it."

"It might be someone's personal things."

"Or there might be a load of laptops."

"So you're planning to sell stolen goods?"

"You can't decide for everyone."

There were distant figures on the beach. The islanders that couldn't get to work on the bigger islands were out to see what the storm had washed up.

A fish flopped around in a shallow rock pool at Magnus's feet. It was barely covered by the water. Magnus flipped the mackerel onto the sand and then seized it. He put his thumb in its mouth, snapping the head back at a sharp angle. The sudden motion ripped the gills from its throat and blood pulsed from its arteries onto its silver stripes. Magnus let it drip, holding the fish fast in its death throes.

"Was that necessary? Wouldn't hitting it on the head be kinder?"

"Ignoramus."

Bleeding kept the flesh from rotting, otherwise it clotted in the body where bacteria could breed.

Magnus flung it to Simon who fumbled with it, getting blood and brine on his jacket.

"Take it home. Make some fucking sushi or something."

Magnus left the gawping crowd that was gathering on the beach. Simon talked to them from the vantage point of a rock. Cormac had joined him. He was Simon's manager, which made him the second most important person on the island. He was also Magnus's cousin. Their shared genes were apparent in their size.

Magnus went back to where coarse grass overtook the sand and up the hill. He crossed the sodden earth and made his way to the church. It was the same path his granddad favoured. Stern John Spence transformed into historian and storyteller, just for him.

St Connaught's stood out against the scoured sky. Faith had arrived in a row boat bringing a crucifix and conviction to Little Isle. All that remained of the church was stone. Windowless, roofless, doorless, grass had sprung up within. Spiders' webs sagged with raindrops.

Magnus and Hildy had brought Simon to the ruined church when they were children.

"Posh, aren't you?" Cormac towered over Simon, who was still wearing his school uniform, even though it was the summer holidays. All the children had gathered on the makeshift football pitch at the end of the village. "Are you a frog, like your mum?"

"She's *French*." Simon's accent was cut glass.

Cormac snorted, as he'd seen the adults do when they were talking about her.

"She's a snob, that's what." Simon's mother had only visited the island once. The islanders had mistaken her shyness for snootiness and her eating disorder for Parisian chic. "And so are you, turning up for the summer and then buggering off. You don't belong here."

"Let him alone." Magnus stepped in.

"Or what?"

"You'll get another share of what I gave you last time."

The two boys squared up to one another. Simon was incidental to old enmities. The other children looked on, too scared to take sides. Except for Hildy. Strong, desirable Hildy was the only one who wielded enough power to end it. She got between them, thumping them both.

"Stop it, you idiots." Cormac laughed but Magnus still cut a fighter's pose. She pulled at his sleeve. "Let's go."

They went up to the cliffs to show Simon the puffins and the gulls' nests on the precipices. Seals basking on the rocks below. There was a whole fleet of trawlers out on the glistening water. The three of them spent the long holidays roaming. Little Isle was rough, green fields and granite hills sculpted by glaciers.

"What's that noise?"

Hildy was about to answer Simon but Magnus put a finger to his smiling lips to hush her. The roaring got louder as they approached.

Magnus stood close to Simon, enjoying his surprise. There was a whirlpool out on the calm sea. Its pull was mesmeric, the downward spiral of all that water into the depths.

"It's Maw." Magnus felt a swell of pride.

The maelstrom was a conspiracy of complex tidal flows in a narrow strait. Water forced itself up from a stone pinnacle on the seabed, opposed to the surface stream, so creating a downward vortex. The swirl was visible below the glassy surface.

"Wow."

"It's clearer when there's a high wind or standing waves. You think it's loud now. Just wait 'til the tides are right. You can hear Maw roaring from miles off."

At St Connaught's they found a nest of mice in the shadow of the stone altar. It had become nature's temple.

"I found a crow skeleton here once. And a snake's skin." Magnus had never seen Hildy so shy. She pulled a sketchbook from her rucksack and passed it to Simon. "Look."

He leafed through the pages. "These are brilliant."

She gave Simon a broad smile.

"I like drawing too, but I'm not as good as you."

"Will you show me yours?"

"Look, here." Magnus pointed to the wall above the altar. Simon squinted at the weathered markings. "What are they?"

"Fish jumping into a boat." They leapt high, pouring themselves onto the deck in an arc.

"How can you tell?"

"My grandfather said. He died last year. He knew everything. Our family have always lived here."

Simon flushed. His father had purchased the island only two years before.

"He didn't mean anything by that." Hildy nudged Simon.

Magnus hadn't finished yet. "Guess what this is."

Above the fishing boat was a figure falling into a spiral.

"A man going to hell?"

"It's Maw."

Magnus recited his granddad's teachings. "He's been given to Maw as a gift and Maw will give us the sea's bounty in return."

Magnus checked in on Mairi on his way home, just like his dad used to. Andrew Spence called her *the old woman*, even though she wasn't that much older than he was.

He would sit with her, sometimes for up to an hour at a time. Magnus would peep into the single-roomed cottage through the door that was always propped ajar to *let the weather in*. Sometimes Mairi would scream and shout at his dad, other times they'd sit in silence.

"Hello."

"I've been waiting for you." Mairi sat on a stone bench outside. "Come and sit, John."

"It's Magnus, Mairi, not John."

She turned her lined face to him. She was pushing seventy now, he reckoned. She'd been more muddled of late. He wondered whether he should talk to the doctor when the radio was back up.

"Of course you are." Her voice was strong and certain now, which unnerved him. "Have you seen it?"

"What?"

"The bloody great container down on the shore."

Her eyes were as temperamental as the sea, sometimes clear aquamarine, sometimes grey and chilly.

"Yes."

"Maw sent it."

The comment alarmed him less than her mistaking him for his granddad. Mairi was known for it. She'd lived alone from a young age. A bit touched. She'd been visited by a psychiatrist once, after which she learnt to keep her stranger pronouncements to herself.

"That bay over there"—she jabbed with her finger—"used to be full of trawlers. Everyone had work. All because of John Spence."

There'd been crops of barley, oats and potatoes that thrived on seaweed-fed beds. Lambs, sweet on salt-laden grass. There were farmers, shepherds and weavers, but the island only flourished because the fishermen were kings.

John's re-energisation of the industry brought a row of

shops, two pubs, a new church and a primary school. The only thing that remained of this golden time was the new church. The school had shut years ago, despite the protests.

"We've turned our backs on Maw. We won't be forgiven easily. To think, we have the blood of marauders and conquerors in us. We sailed to Byzantium. And now we're diminished with each generation by the milksop messiah, taxes and fishing quotas."

History marked the land. Cairns and gold torcs buried in the earth.

"I still send Maw boats."

An old tradition. The islanders once gathered on the shore at harvest festival and sent out wicker and wooden boats, laden with gifts for Maw's maelstrom. Priests came and went over the centuries, either smiling indulgently or shaking their heads.

The sea is hungry.

The sea has blue hands.

The little boats contained the choicest fish, the finest prawns, a cake, or a piece of fat-marbled lamb. A baby or man carved from soap.

"We put boats on the water last year," Magnus repeated, wondering if Mairi had heard.

"Yes," she spat, "and we were the only ones. A can of sardines and a loaf might be good for the five thousand but not Maw."

She seized Magnus's hand.

"You and I need this place. We can't survive anywhere else. Not for long. It's why you came running back with your tail between your legs. Same for your dad. You shouldn't have let them take him away."

Magnus turned his face from her. He'd looked after his dad for as long as he could after his mother died. *Poor Andrew, so young to have dementia. You've done a grand job*, the nurse had said, *but he's getting worse. He needs care from trained nurses now.*

Magnus took a job on the docks over on the mainland so that he could visit his dad's nursing home each day. The trained nurses were hard pressed and didn't have time to dab the crusted cornflakes from his dad's shirt.

His dad hated cornflakes.

Dementia stripped his father of sense, self and dignity. It took the meat from his bones and hollowed him out, as crafty and insidious as cancer.

The sea, the sea needs little boats, the sea, there are men in the water, blue hands, blue hands, blue hands. They're so hungry.

He'd gripped Magnus's wrist so hard he'd left bruises.

Hungry hands. Why did you do it, Dad?

It's Magnus, Dad, not John.

I saw you. I heard her crying. Why would Mairi give up little Brid?

Then he pushed Magnus from him, weeping into his sleeve. Magnus was relieved when his dad died and he could go home.

"How did Granddad do it, Mairi? How did he turn this place around? Were those freak years of fishing just luck?"

Her eyes were the silver of needles.

"Fool. Ingrate. All you do is complain. You're weak. Only John had what it took, the bastard. What are you willing to sacrifice for what you want?"

There was nothing to be done but leave the container. The rumble of thunder closed in. Night brought in the tide. The islanders took shelter.

Magnus watched the waves from the window until it was too dark to see out. The cottage was built from granite blocks, hunkered down against the hill to withstand the onslaught of wind and rain.

Peter and Donald lay on their bellies in front of the fire, playing cards. Hildy occupied the table, her sketchbooks spread out.

Magnus lay on his side on the sofa. He was aware of Hildy's voice but it didn't reach him. His mind drifted.

"Hild"—he rolled on to his side—"do you know if Mairi ever had a baby?"

"You're not listening."

"Sorry. What did I miss?"

"Nothing important." There was the angry clatter of pencils on the table. "I've no idea about Mairi. I've always kept clear of the spiteful old crow. When did you see her?"

"On my way back from the beach."

"I wondered why you were so long."

"I couldn't bear to listen to his lordship holding court about how we have to tell the authorities about the container."

"He's right. We can't keep it."

"Why not?"

"Because—"

The lights died. The chair creaked as Hildy got up. Husband and wife went around the room lighting candles.

"Why can't we live somewhere where the electricity always works?" Peter threw down his cards.

"Because it's much more fun here."

Quiet candlelight and their voices made the cottage timeless. When Magnus was Peter's age the power often went out. Three generations sat close, mending nets and listening to John Spence. Magnus wished such fond memories for his sons too.

"It's not fun here. It's boring."

"That's enough." Magnus's temper was a lit flare.

"Boys, I'll get the lanterns out. Early bedtime. You can read for twenty minutes."

"Mum!"

"Shift when your mum tells you." Magnus saw Donald flinch. He tried to lighten things with a joke. "Or the blue men will get you."

Magnus listened to their tread on the stairs and then the creak of floorboards above. He picked up the photo frame on the table beside him. It was of his grandfather and his crew in front of *Maw's Teeth*, the trawler named against all counsel. It was the first catch after John Spence had gone to London and insisted the Ministry of Fisheries retest the waters that had been depleted for years. He made a nuisance of himself until they did. A month later the fleet sailed after two years in dock. The sea was teeming.

It was a time of plenty. The deck was piled with fish, white in the monochrome snapshot rather than silver.

Now the fish were gone, the sea was empty and the Fisheries' team came each year to check, and left shaking their heads sadly.

When Hildy returned, Magnus was sat ramrod straight and half cast in shadow.

"Mags, don't be mad at the boys, not when it's Simon you're angry at."

"I won't be disrespected by my own sons."

"That sounds like something your grandfather would say."

"What's that mean?"

"That he was a fearsome bully."

"Don't talk about him like that."

"No, nobody can say a bad word about John Spence. How exactly was Peter being disrespectful?"

"These are my choices about our way of life."

"*Our* choices, not just yours."

That was why he'd wanted Hildy. She wouldn't be cowed. Free-spirited Hildy had been a prize.

"Peter's just a boy. He just wants to be like his friends on Big Isle."

"That bloody generator." Magnus didn't want to be reasoned with. The generator was old and unpredictable. Sam the Spark would be up there with his bag of tools.

"There never seems to be a good time for us to talk about anything any more. Promise me you won't get angry."

"Why would I get angry?"

"Because everything makes you angry."

Magnus sat back.

"Donald's been telling me about his nightmares. They're about the blue men and the Cailleach."

The blue men lived in the strait and reached for sailors with outstretched arms. The Cailleach had a list of pseudonyms and occupations but on Little Isle she was a witch who washed her linens in Maw's maelstrom.

"Why didn't he tell me?"

"Because he's scared of disappointing you. He knows how much you love the old tales."

"They're just stories. My granddad taught me them when I was younger than Donald is. And Peter wasn't bothered by them."

"Yes, he was. And just because we all learnt about them as kids it doesn't mean they have to." She shuddered. "I used to wake up screaming."

Magnus had chronicled the dreams. Only those bred from old stock had them. Magnus used to wake in a sweat after the Cailleach bundled him up with her washing and chucked him into the whirlpool. The blue men pulled him down. They were always waiting in the undertow. Their teeth were pointed. The pain of drowning was like a knife.

"I'm not trying to hurt your feelings."

"Why's everything so hard?" Magnus blurted out.

"What do you mean?"

"This place is dying. Our boys will be gone soon."

Peter would go to high school on the mainland as a

boarder. Magnus wouldn't see him from one weekend to the next. Donald would follow before he knew it. How time fleeced you.

"They're going to school, not Australia."

"They'll stay on there when they've finished to find work."

"So? They should be free to do as they please. Hell, we could even move too."

"I hate it over there. Too many bad memories." He meant the loneliness of the docks and his father's slow death.

"The world's bigger than that. We could go anywhere."

No. The boys would go and he couldn't follow. Mairi was right. He was only alive when he was on Little Isle.

The lights went back on.

When Magnus opened his eyes it was light, to his relief. He'd been waking earlier and earlier of late, the fluorescent hands of his bedside clock marking the slow progress of the night.

When Magnus slipped from the bed, Hildy rolled over, searching for him from her dreams. She snorted and settled into the warm patch on the mattress that he'd just vacated.

That one's so sharp she'll cut herself, his grandfather had said before he died. *She'll cut you, more likely. Are you sure you want a girl that's so headstrong?*

Yes, Granddaddy.

Well, just don't marry her. He cuffed Magnus's head.

Magnus pulled on the clothes he'd left on the bannister the night before. Peter's door was closed but Donald's was open. His pyjamas were rucked up to reveal spindly legs. He whimpered and shifted. Magnus knelt beside him. Donald's curls were soft and loose, the same as Magnus's were before his grandfather took the shears to them.

Girlishness. What's your dad thinking?

"Mummy?"

"Hey, little man."

Magnus waited until Donald settled and then went downstairs.

He tried the radio but all he got was static. Outside the light was still thin and grey. The storm had blown over but Magnus could see another front out on the water, waiting.

There came a tap, tap, tap.

Iain was at the kitchen window. Jimmy stood beside him, grinning.

"Mags, come quick. They're trying to get the container open."

The night had brought another massacre. The beach was littered with sea birds, flight curtailed. The tide line was thick with their carcasses.

The storm and tide had been merciless. It had thrown the birds about. Feathers were matted with blood. Heads made strange angles with their bodies. Guts were revealed, auguries that Magnus couldn't read.

He recognised the fallen, even in pieces. The black guillemot's monochrome plumage and their shocking red feet. The large angular wings of the gannet, tipped in black. The puffin, comical with its painted eyes. A variety of gulls. And his favourite, the storm petrel. His grandfather would tell him how whole flocks of these tiny birds would feed in the wake of the trawlers. Their feet would patter on the water's surface and they held their wings in a high V shape, as if trying to keep them dry.

Flies rose from the dead as gulls and corvids landed to feast on them.

Magnus stumbled on the rocks in his rush to reach the container. He could see the shower of sparks from the welding rod as he pushed through the crowd.

"Oi! What are you doing?"

Niall flipped back his visor and mopped his forehead with his sleeve. "What's it look like?"

"It's not yours."

"It's not yours either."

"It belongs to everyone."

"It belongs to whoever can get the fucking thing open."

"Check it out, Mags." Isla stepped in. "Niall's been at the same spot for twenty minutes and the paint's not even blistered. Go on, show him."

Niall pulled off his glove and slapped his palm against the spot that he'd been trying to cut. Magnus reached out with a tentative fingertip to check for himself. The metal was like ice.

"I thought I'd made myself clear." It was Simon, standing shoulder to shoulder with Cormac. "I told you all to leave it alone. We don't know what it is. It might be military. There could be something dangerous in there."

"Then it's something they'll pay to get back," Niall countered.

"The military don't pay ransoms." Cormac rolled his eyes. "They'd take it by force."

"As soon as the radio's working, we're calling it in." Simon was adamant.

"You're full of shit." Everyone turned to look at Magnus.

"Less of that." Cormac stepped forward.

"What, you and Simon are best buddies now? I remember when you picked on him every chance you got."

Cormac flushed.

"We're not fourteen any more." Simon shook his head. "Cormac had an interview, just like you. He was the better man for the role. Is that why you're so sore?"

"No, it's you. You want to be *part of the community*. *For all of us to work together.* What's in there could help fund wind turbines to replace that shitty old generator."

"I've applied for a grant for that. I told you."

"You're full of *ifs* and *when*. Nothing's guaranteed. And you're ignoring my point."

"Which is?"

"That you don't listen to any idea that runs contrary to your own. Everything's fine as long as we all do what we're told."

"You mean I ignore *you*. You're bitter because you don't get a personal invitation to meetings. Because you don't get the last word in everything. If you bothered to listen you'd understand." Simon paused. "What exactly *is* your problem with me?"

"You're blind. More and more of us leave each year. You're not one of us. You don't understand. Your rich daddy bought this place for a song. And your stuck-up mother didn't even want to live here."

Simon's face was a mask.

"My mum was painfully shy. She didn't come back here because she didn't feel welcome. She was anorexic. She spent most of her life after I was born in and out of clinics being fed through nasogastric tubes. Little Isle was all Dad and I had left. I care about it as much as you do."

"Refurbishing a few cottages and building a kiln isn't going to save us."

"And who made you the mouth of the people?" That was Cormac.

"I know the art world. My mother was a dealer. I have connections through college. I can make this happen. People will come. They'll need housing and food." Simon was talking to everyone now. "We'll bring back farming. Rare breed sheep. We can start dyeing and weaving again."

All the colours of the landscape in the warp and weft.

"That's not sustainable industry. The other islands are developing halibut farms."

"Which is exactly why we need to be different."

"What we *need* is to be rid of you. Form a community

council and a development company. Flog that big house of yours for capital. Attract people with business ideas and young families."

The sky was getting darker. The air smelt of iron. Their anger was calling in the gale. Clouds were as unreliable as the sea; they too were water, after all. Now they were in scud formation, black and loaded with rain. Magnus felt the gust front on his face, the cold downdraught a harbinger.

"And you'd be in charge, I suppose. The problem with you, Magnus, is that you need to feel important. Most of us are keen for this to work. And Hildy will be a massive draw when her book deal is announced."

"What?"

"She's not told you? Maybe you should show more interest in your wife." Simon's laugh was bitter. "You never liked me, not really. Hildy's a diamond. Did you know that I persuaded her to apply to St Martin's when I did? She turned down one of the most prestigious art schools in the country *to stay here with you.* She made me promise not to tell you. All you've done is hold her back—"

Magnus was a juggernaut. He barrelled Simon over. He felt a satisfying crunch as he landed on the man. They made a furious knot. It came down to who was bigger. At least here, in the muck and brawl, Magnus was the better man.

Hands gripped his arms. Jimmy and Iain hauled him off. Cormac pulled Simon to his feet. The rain was coming down hard.

"I'm not sleeping with your wife, you stupid sod." Simon wiped his bloodied nose. "She's too good to cheat. In fact, she's better than both of us put together."

Magnus deflated. He felt Iain's grip slacken, then he threw another punch at Simon.

"Where have you been all day?"

Hildy was sat in the hall chair, facing the front door. Magnus's hair and coat were dripping. He bristled at her tone. She threw him the towel that had been folded on her knee. He kicked off his boots and started to pat himself dry.

She followed him into the kitchen, picking up his soggy shirt and trousers and throwing them into the washing machine. He pulled warm clothes from the clothes maiden that she'd left in front of the radiator.

"Where are the boys?"

"At Jack and Helen's."

"Why?"

"So we could talk properly. Why have you been fighting with Simon?"

"He had it coming. I don't want that man in this house. I don't want you to ever see him again." Magnus sat on the kitchen stool, his mouth rucked up. "You and Simon have already done a fair bit of talking. What's this about you getting a place at a posh college when we were kids?"

"Mags, that was such a long time ago."

"Well, it's news to me."

"Your dad had just been diagnosed with Alzheimer's. Your granddad had died a few years before. I didn't want to leave you."

"Didn't stop you applying, though."

She tilted her chin at that, all remorse gone.

"My chance at that's long gone, so you've no need to worry."

"Yet here it is, another reason for Simon to insult me."

"How exactly has Simon insulted you?"

"He's robbed me of the chance to provide for my family."

The washing machine drum started to gain speed. The spiralling clothes made Magnus's stomach churn.

"Simon offered you good work on restoring the cottages and knitting."

"Men don't knit."

"Of course they do. All the men here used to. You learnt from your dad."

Knitted cables represented fishing lines and nets, knot stitches added together formed fishes. Each fisherman had a unique pattern, so that their sea-mauled corpse could be identified from their sweater if washed ashore.

"I want to make nets, not jumpers for rich boys."

"What's the difference between selling them jumpers or oysters? You heard Simon. He can get you a hundred quid for each one from a boutique in London. You have real skill. You could even teach it."

"It's not proper work!"

"There. There it is," she hissed. "That's what you *really* think of what I do. Dabbling with paints. *Not proper work.* I cook, clean and take care of the kids, and then I sit down at night and work while you stride around like a king, doing fuck all. Well, it's my dabbling that's been paying the bills and clothing our sons."

"That's not fair. And art college isn't the only thing you've been keeping secret from me." He had another reason to take the high ground. "Simon loved telling me all about your book deal. Why exactly does he know and I don't?"

"He promised not to say anything. It was him that sent my book to a friend of his in publishing. That's why he knew. They want me to write and illustrate a whole series of books. If Simon's plans work I'll have my own studio at the big house, beside the classrooms."

"I bet you will."

"You're being ridiculous. There's no room here to work properly. And I tried to tell you last night but you weren't listening. You started going on about Mairi. What is it about her and the men in your family?" Hildy didn't wait for an answer. "The worst bit is that I've been waiting for you to be in a good mood to tell you, so that I can pretend you're genuinely happy for me. If you spent as much time looking for a job as you do moaning about everything we'd all be a damn sight better off. If you don't want to work for Simon get on the ferry each day and go work somewhere else."

"Why should I? We could have a life *here*. Simon's destroying what's left of us."

"Listen to yourself. It's always about Simon. Your issue with Simon is that he went off to university and came back with new ideas that don't involve you."

Magnus stared at the floor. The words wouldn't come. Something was rising inside him.

"Sea fishing's dead. There aren't the stocks left. Get over it. Everyone laughs at you because they know all those stories you tell are hand-me-downs. You've never worked on a boat in your life and you bleat on about making nets." She followed him to the door. "And while we're at it, your grandfather was a tyrant. He trampled over everyone, including your mum and dad. He gave them a dog's life."

"He loved this place. He sacrificed everything for it."

What? What exactly had he sacrificed?

"You don't want a job or a future. You want the past."

Magnus couldn't help it. The past persisted in his blood. He craved what was lost. Lighting a candle and carrying it in a cow's skull through the byre and out into the black night of the new year. Stargazy pie. Gifts launched on the tide. A time when men ruled the seas and themselves and life was easier to navigate.

"All that crap about wanting things to be better for the boys. The problem with you is that you want them to live the life you want for yourself."

The problem with you is that you want to be important. The problem with you.

Simon and Hildy had talked behind his back. They'd talked and laughed.

"I love you, Mags. There's only ever been you, but I don't know how much more I can take. I need you to think about this. I'm telling you so that we can try and change. I'm telling you because if things don't change I'm going to leave."

"Leave? The island?"

"I'll take the boys somewhere, just until we both work things out." She started to cry. "I'm not trying to punish you. I'm trying to save our marriage."

Peter and Donald had been born at the cottage. Magnus had cut the cords tethering them to Hildy. Every inch of the squalling babies was his from the fine down on their backs to their screwed-up faces. They made him immortal. Part of an unbroken line. His heart had flipped and flopped in his chest. Fear and awe gnawed at him. It was his duty to remake the world for them.

Nothing would part him from them.

"Say something. Anything. Tell me you'll fight for us."

The swell inside him threatened to wash him away. He would pummel Hildy with his fists. He would snap her neck. This body that he promised to worship would fall before him. Beautiful Hildy. Strong Hildy. The mother of his sons. She held out her arms to him.

"I have to go out."

"Not like this—"

"No." He backed away from her, pleading on his face. "Let me be for a little while."

At the door he turned back. "I'll make it right, I promise, no matter what it takes."

The beach was clear as the tide was coming in. As Magnus approached he could see that a figure was crouched beside the container. When it stood, he could see it was Mairi.

She stood up, paint dripping from the brush as she slapped

it against the container's side. She made a clumsy spiral with a shaking hand. Red stood out against the blue paint.

"Mairi."

Her nightdress flapped around her legs. Her bare feet were covered in dark smears of paint.

"You must be freezing." He took off his coat and put it around her shoulders.

"It won't stay."

The spiral was fading. It was *sinking in*. She turned to him, crying.

"What's happened to you?" He clutched her head in his hands.

One side of her mouth drooped. She looked like a lopsided doll. He recognised it as a stroke. It wasn't paint on her feet. They were bloodied from cuts and abrasions.

"Come on, let's get you to my place."

She pulled away, intent on daubing more marks. BRID. The word faded fast.

"Who's Brid?"

"You dare ask me that, John Spence?"

"I'm Magnus, not John."

Herring gulls gathered on the rocks around the container, more and more coming in. Some of them landed on the container's top edge. A pair faced off, screaming at one another. Their wings made acute angles with their bodies in furious symmetry. Then they flew at one another, intent on blood. Red-stained grey and white feathers. The other gulls piled in, finishing off the weaker one.

"I should be young and beautiful. I used to run ahead of the lightning. Now it hurts when I get up in the morning and it's all your fault, John."

"Mairi, we need to get you inside." He reached out for her.

"No, you don't touch me. I'm not Mairi. I'm the Cailleach. You've tricked me before, you devil. I used to summon the wind and fly down to visit my brother, Maw, in the water. You, with your silky promises and kisses. Then it was too late. You made me just a woman. You stained my plaid. It'll never white again."

"What about Brid?"

"You know! Our little Brid," she keened. "I hate you. I hate you and your family, John Spence. Little Brid was the only good thing to come from you." Spittle landed on Magnus's face. "You're a damn liar. You said she wasn't real because she came from me. That she was bound for Maw. She was just a baby, and I let you do it."

"Do what?"

"You know," she wept, "you know."

Magnus did know. John Spence was a determined man.

Beneath the wind and waves there was the sound of their breathing and a click.

The container door was open.

"Will you kiss me, John?" Mairi's voice was full of self-loathing. "Will you love me, like I love you?"

Magnus leant down. Her lips were dry and withered. Her breath was sour. Her fingers fluttered around his face.

He picked her up. She was like dry kindling in his arms. The old woman's eyes were paler than he'd ever seen them. She rested her head against his chest and sighed.

She needed to be airlifted off the island to a hospital. How long would it be before the storms cleared and they could radio for help? He knew Mairi wouldn't want that. She wouldn't want to leave, not for anything.

The tide was closing in, faster than he'd ever seen, and another weather front directly behind it. Scud clouds were just the messenger. They hid the vast heights of the thunderhead above them. The air crackled with energy and the wind rose. Lightning discharged from cloud to cloud, not as a zigzag but a vein. The closing rumbling became a crack. Rain poured through.

Mairi wasn't a fallen goddess or an elemental trapped in flesh. She was an addled old woman, touched in the head. It didn't matter though. Maw had sent the container and now the tide was coming in.

THE AIRPORT GORILLA
Stephen Volk

So, this.

I see him. He sees me. Thinking these black-bead eyes unknowing, he gets an ape's grin back from the stack of cuddly toys in the bin next to the checkout at Duty Free. He fans and counts the last of his Euros, joke money to him that looks like it came with a game of Monopoly.

Boarding pass?

Certainly.

He thinks the Dutch speak better English than he does. Always felt his Aussie drawl embarrassing. Damn thing still made him self-conscious several degrees and doctorates later, called upon to talk at international conferences on matters that save lives. Still, to him, the snarl of sheep dip and hats with dangling corks, and he hates it.

Screwy-angled, I scrutinise him back.

Above his ears I see lines each side made by the arms of glasses he's not wearing. Atop, blond beach-bum waves now fading to the colour of his scalp. Aeons since he felt sand between his toes. House brick jaw he got from his dad. The twinkling eyes, his ma. Sky-coloured.

He stares down at me with something between curiosity and incipient affection.

I recognise that look.

I've watched it day in, day out, in the myriad glances that slide over me. The micro-glimmer of tears that accompany flashbacks to hearth and home.

Most turn away, not wanting to acknowledge that inner surge of sentimentality. Not him. He lets the guilt and separation anxiety rise in his chest and I feel in my complete-lack-of-bones his pang for the child he left behind.

The one he will see at the end of his journey. Soon, but not soon enough.

The one he'll sweep up in his arms. No weightier than a toy herself. Who snores now somewhere in her suburban Melbourne dreamsleep. Yet he cannot hear that. He is robbed of it, that moment, that silly, cherished everyday nothing as the flight announcements drone.

His wife and nipper, waiting for Dad to return, miss him with an indescribable ache. This is the real currency of the airport—longing.

And so. I am here to be touched, loved, adored. Made for it, and he knows it. I am the salve to the pang he feels in his heart—and I have been waiting.

He touches my plastic ear.

Air from his nostrils.

I amuse him. Hey. No problem with that.

I'm not a serious figure. My lips are too big. My mouth sticks out like an over-size bagel. I'm covered in black fur. My legs are short. Wouldn't stop a pig in a passage. Toes like fingers and thumbs. My arms reach way below my knees. I wear a T-shirt with the name of the city we're in and a logo of a tulip. I've got a comical, idiotic expression. My grin mirroring the one he dreams of seeing on his daughter's face.

He squeezes my tummy with his thumbs. Turns me over. Examines my behind.

(Ignominious, to say the least. Come on, people! Animal rights and shit!)

Made in China, he reads.

(Okay. Nobody's perfect.)

Anyway, he loves me, or knows someone who will.

So, this.

I'm face down on the counter and the tag on my ankle gets scanned. *Ping.*

Have a nice day, sir, and have a pleasant flight.

Thank you.

He lifts me up like he lifted her as a babe. A trophy, a triumph.

My face inches from his. What is he? Thirty-five, forty max. He laughs again, and though it's still soundless, it judders his whole frame in a way that's appealing.

Nice person. Good person. Come on. His kid. Gimme a break.

And here I go, under his arm now—parallel to the Famous Grouse, the overpriced chocolates, bagged and dangling from his other hand. His elbow tight across my abdomen, reassuring, protective. I feel secure.

Now he's sitting on a plastic bench, waiting for his gate to be called. Props yours truly beside him, righting me up when I droop. Some Asiatic fool chuckles. The fool would droop too if he had my legs—bandy and boneless. But I try not to get bitter. (I have a permanent fucking smile painted on, so that helps.)

The board flutters like so many call girls' eyelashes. The gate and flight number appear.

He gathers his bags. He gathers me. Flat of his hand splayed against my back, my face pressed to his chest, mashed to the buttons of his Mambo shirt, loose for travelling in, more him than the suits the conference required.

We ride the travelator. Yippee.

Children giggle. My one eye that's not mashed into Mambo psychedelic colours sees them wave and pull faces.

Fuck them. We're on our way.

I'm feeling a sense of anticipation, of excitement. A new owner and a new experience ahead. Got to be good news, when you've been in a Special Offer bin with a lumpy giraffe and a pink kangaroo for weeks on end. (Glad to see the back of that fucking giraffe, let me tell you.)

First impressions? He seems an okay guy.

I think we'll get along. Not that I'm hard to get along with. I'm adaptable. Hey, I take the path of least resistance. What can I say? It's who I am.

All right, I get attached. I know I shouldn't. I know because it always ends in tears. I can't fucking help it.

As we enter the airplane the flight attendant, orange tan and grinning (because she got fucked raw the night before) pretends to talk to me. Oh, so funny. Never heard that before. Says she hopes I'll enjoy the flight. My guy laughs out loud, like it's comic genius. He goes down in my estimation a tad.

Whoa! I think for a horrible moment I'm going up there with the hand luggage. No fucking way. What is this, some "Premature Burial" fucking bullshit?

Phew! The suitcase and the raincoat go up, but not this simian. Praise the Lord! I don't know if my man is afraid of damaging me before I even reach his precious daughter, but whatever. I'm on his lap like a baby as he leafs through the in-flight magazine.

On board, the safety demonstration. The whole Marcel Marceau.

We've got an empty seat next to us and a vastly obese person next to that. This is how vast. She even asks for an extension to her seat belt. Jesus Christ! I give thanks for that middle seat, unoccupied. I look at my man and think, you ducked a bullet there, compadre!

I end up on the floor for take-off, his Caterpillar boot on my groin. (I think orange face has a hand in this, I swear.)

I'm starting to regret he didn't choose one of those painted clogs or a bottle of advocaat.

I grin all the way up his jeans and Mambo shirt and chin to the reading light spot-lighting his chest. He isn't nervous, even when the massive weight of the plane leaves the runway, lifting like a feather. He doesn't grip the hand rests. His eyes don't leave the in-flight magazine.

I think the son of a bitch has forgotten about me, immersed as he is in first-rate journalism about foreign climes.

Then, just when I think I'm a fucking afterthought, he picks me up and I'm on his lap again like a ventriloquist's dummy and Schiphol is history.

The obese one gives a raised eyebrow. A hideous hello.

My guy flickers a smile back. Neither wants conversation. Good. There are some things these plastic ears are not built for.

As the plane levels he settles and I settle too. He's pretty comfortable, after all. Pretty well sprung as mattresses go.

Enjoy the rest of your flight, blah blah.

Melbourne-bound, he gazes down at me, thinking of his child. The idea of her expression greeting him changes his. It lightens, almost blooms. I'm thinking this is looking optimistic, but I know it's not, and can't be. That's not the nature of it. Not the nature of me.

So, this.

It's got to happen, but I'm never quite sure when it will. Sometimes it comes out of a clear blue sky, so to speak. You never can tell. Sometimes my buttocks clench and I can feel it coming. Other times, it's a sucker punch. And you know what? You never get used to it. It's never easy.

This time, I kind of know.

Kind of.

That way he looks like he is drifting off to sleep. Those heavy lids. The memories. The desire. Then it's like a big church bell chiming in my head, through my body, and it's like he's pressed a button he didn't even know existed.

I wish this flight would end quickly.

No. No, don't wish that, you fuck. You idiot. But too late—it's done. The die is fucking cast. No going back. (I fucking hate my job sometimes.)

For the technically minded, it's an SA-11 Buk surface-to-air missile system down there. A dot in a field, invisible from thirty-two thousand feet. Recently trundled over the border into Eastern Ukraine by pro-Russian rebel fighters.

I'd like to tense but my innards are cheap foam.

The missile hits.

My man's arms lift from the arm rests.

He feels the boing, the Boeing do press-ups. Everybody does, terror escaping like a puncture, a slashed tyre.

It hurtles. Dropping. Knotted stomachs in the air. Grumbling not from airline food. Not from stomach complaints. Compliant in zero-g.

Lockers spring open, clacking Jack-in-the-boxes. Oxygen masks dangle and sway in rhythm, like choreographed marionettes, kicking like the feet of can-can dancers then streaming back at the plunge.

He looks back.

Someone is horizontal like Superman, spectacular green-screen work. Outside the tilting window green fields rise to meet us at a rate of knots. Knotted loops in the bread basket, as bread baskets spin like tumbleweed from Business Class.

Blue collar, white collar, all get their top buttons undone. All get their Adam's apple freed to gasp breath and scream.

He wished for the flight to end quickly, and so it does.

Brace. Brace.

He whimpers, hunches, forearms helmeting his head. Buries his face in me the way a child might at beddie-byes. I give him warmth. I feel his pulse galloping. But I'm grinning. Always grinning. Can't stop it. Can't change.

As the metal casket dives and dives and dives he prays to God, which he never has since kindergarten, remembers the chickens they kept and fed, and how one pecked him once and he didn't think that of chickens.

Little does he know there is no God listening, just an ape.

God, please God, please God, let me see my daughter one more time before I die!

His second wish. And it's almost too easy to oblige. It has happened before I even think about it.

The locker above springs open. Luggage vomits out, spilling exuberantly across the seat backs. His coat a swirl mid-air. His mobile phone spat out of its pocket, hitting a head rest and landing randomly in the space beside him, which he misconceives as luck, snatching it up and switching it on.

It glows into life and colour, showing the child, gaps where her adult teeth haven't come through yet, freckles she always gets in warm seasons. His eyes. His wife's sarcasm.

There.

You've seen her one last time, I say to myself.

I've given you your first two wishes—what's your third?

His fingers, wrapped round the phone, tremble.

All about him reigns blasphemy and chaos. The fat one's bowels have vented. Which is only a microcosm of it.

God comes into it again, both of him and the hundreds of others, in unison and yet each alone, they call out, inwardly, to their fictions and comfort blankets.

Oh God, oh God, oh God, please let me die quickly and without pain.

And so.

Impact.

He does.

We hit the cold grey field of the Donbass and his third wish eventuates.

We spread in a million fragments over a nine-mile

43

radius, a galaxy forming of trash, belongings, chunky airport paperbacks, playing cards, letters home, old vinyl records, internal organs, hopes, and in-flight beverages. And what part, or parts, of it are him I don't even know any more. It's not my business.

Your story is over, Mambo shirt. My involvement in it, ditto.

I'm lying on broken metal, maybe wing, maybe fuselage, its heat slowly cooling like a body after sex. Nothing clinks or clanks or breathes or moves or mutters or prays any more.

I lie on this sun bed considering the musicality of distant rooks, which is non-existent and ultimately, fucking irritating. Not much I can do about that. It's always a waiting game between one host and the next and you get used to being at peace with that. But it's a fucking bore.

Passage of time I'm not great at.

I hear a tractor.

Voices. DPR insurgents, so possibly not a tractor, more likely a jeep.

Ho hum.

Military boots, the kind that lace tightly halfway up the calf, crunch through the debris. Somebody picks me up. Behind him, the devastation. Not a pretty sight.

Bodies lying everywhere, decomposed, burned, others mangled together, indistinguishable. Nobody is removing them, even touching them. Not from reverence but from indifference.

The one holding me in his fat hand wears a camouflage cap, cigarette dangling from a slug of a lower lip. Seven o'clock shadow like he just bathed in charcoal. Belt heavy with ammo and tools of war. The others wear balaclavas but him, not. The others have shaved heads. Him, no.

He turns to people with cameras. Holds me up, a soft toy gorilla, flappy-limbed, my fur coated with dust and ash.

I hear the lenses clicking. If lenses click. They probably fucking don't. I have no idea.

Ratatatatat.

He walks around with me hanging from his hand for a while. Then for a longer while I'm tucked behind the leather strap across his chest.

A toe prods this. A toe kicks that. This continues. Someone beckons. Someone shrugs. Someone yawns. One fans a wallet out, plucking cash and credit cards with crow-beak hands. Another hyena's jewellery. The radio in the jeep crackles with sibilant authority but it's unintelligible. Maybe ghosts swim between the syllables. Who knows?

In semi-slumber the paramilitaries are not good at using their own initiative. They're waiting for orders but nobody is in a hurry to give them.

As the sun sets he climbs into the back of the jeep—Land Rover, whatever the fuck it is. What do I know about cars?

Air thick with the smell of body odour and tobacco, I jostle, as he does, like we're doing a routine together as we traverse the farmland terrain. They talk, him and the others, but to me it sounds like the yapping of dogs.

I think he's forgotten about me, militia man. Oh well. I may as well sit back and enjoy the trip, because I'm thinking right now I'm going to end up in the nearest dumpster. Every day a fucking adventure.

Outskirts of a village, he leaps off onto the mud of a track.

A gate gives, and then a door into warmth.

The Kalashnikov is propped against the wall, in the manner you would an umbrella.

The burden of the belt unbuckled, divested.

He genuflects in the manner of the Moscow Patriarchate before washing his face in a bowl. I bend and rise with him, accidentally anointed. He remembers being in Slovansk when they shot a Protestant priest, needing to turn the Drobray Vest Church into an armoury, but he hates the Evangelicals even more. Spawn of the USA and the West.

But enough for today. He is home. Enough death.

He aches of it and wonders the purpose.

Then he remembers the flying of the tricolour of the Donetsk People's Republic over the police headquarters in the city. He remembers throwing that city councillor in the river.

Without touching or approaching his wife he eats from a ladle dipped into a broth on the stove. The drips sizzle where they fall. She knows better than to show affection at times like these. Finding those moments is an art beyond Michelangelo these days. Her father dug coal. She's no longer sure what this one digs.

So, this I deduce, lying splayed like spatchcock on the kitchen table, this dribbling dog of a man is too preoccupied to have wishes. Too untroubled to have dreams, because dreams open doors.

He's too tarred and withered to allow imagination. He leaves that to others, the leaders, men wiser than him. Those with a vision for the future. Something he cannot create, but can cling to in his desperation for certainty and purpose. He's a lightning-struck tree that no longer sucks in the light, but he can do that.

He can build a house or knock it down. For the cause, for the flag, he will be told more things to do and he will do them because he knows in his heart they are right. The meat on the table, the gasoline in the car, the roof over their heads, the angry fire in his guts that won't be put out—that is what matters. Beyond that, there is nothing. You might as well think what is beyond the stars.

The oil and filth under his fingernails negate the need for optional extras. His fear sneers at the possibility.

But to have no wishes—none? That's something.

A first, for this hairy ape, who thinks himself unshockable.

So now I'm picked up and he regards me in the glow of the fire, as his other hand delivers three mouthfuls of vodka, then a fourth, more from habit than requirement.

He takes me to another room and in the flickering almost-darkness crouches beside a small bed.

He wiggles me in the air. Nods my head using his index finger behind my neck. Dances me on the edge of the mattress.

I'm being introduced to her, and her, me.

She emerges, so.

Tiny, elfin concoction, itchy blanket tucked under her chin. Under the blonde fringe, scissor-cut by her mama, the too-tired eyes of a five-year-old unable to close until her father gets home, now wide and sparkling. Mouth agog, half in delight, half in disbelief, as she beholds me.

I'm adorable. I can't help it.

He holds me out, closer. He smells of onion broth and aviation fuel and burnt plastic.

The stupid grin, she loves to bits.

She takes me in her arms, snug as a bug in a rug. Then it's my chin that pokes over the blanket. And I love it that she kisses the back of my furry head. Especially as she doesn't know where I've been.

Seriously? The softness of me, it's a slam dunk.

I'm hers now. Official. I tell ya, this one is an impressive hugger. From one who knows. If I had a spine it would be broken. The hell. Spines are overrated.

From the first cuddle, I'm a keeper. I know it.

When her father has diminished and the light is lesser then lost, and she's alone with me before sleep, she looks at what's in her little hands.

Monkey's been in the wars. Monkey has blood on him, look.

I can say nothing.

Monkey needs a wash. Monkey needs to be clean.

I have no doubt she'll wash me in the morning. I'll have a good old wash, old Monkey will. Old friendly, funny Monkey will. She'll see to that. I like this one already. Then again, I'm easy to please.

And I'm waiting.

As Papa says his prayers by his piss-pot.

It may not be tonight, and it may not be tomorrow, but I'm waiting.

It might not be while she sleeps, and it might not be when she wakes, but it will come.

And I'm here for when she makes those three wishes. The ones that come with love and trust and pain and life and primates.

She's a child. She is the future. She will have wishes. I know that for sure. Children do.

All I have to do is lie in wait and enjoy the hugs.

What does she really want and desire, this babe in arms? I have no clue. I never do. It's a mystery. It's a wink from a stranger. A stiletto in the ribs. It's a monkey up a tree. It's a painted grin.

Her mind is roaming. In her dreams she swings from branch to branch on the back of glee, clinging to her saviour, this circumstantial cousin, pink-eared, long-limbed, one of her evolutionary brethren, button-eyed, holding it together as buttons do, then tearing them apart. The way the universe does.

What will her first wish be, I wonder?

So, this.

THUMBSUCKER
Robert Shearman

My father has become a thumbsucker. I know, it took me by surprise too. I'd taken him out to dinner, and it had been a fine dinner—my father and I always try to have dinner together once a month or so, but sometimes I get busy, I have to cancel and he always understands—but I'd made the time, we'd been out and had this most excellent steak in a restaurant I'd seen reviewed quite favourably in one of the Sunday supplements. We were talking about something inconsequential—cricket probably, or which Wodehouse novel he was re-reading—and the plates were being cleared. And he sighed contentedly, he smiled, he folded his hand into a fist, tapped it gently a couple of times to make the thumb pop out—and then, without any embarrassment or explanation, proceeded to put the thumb into his mouth and hold it between his teeth like the stem of a pipe.

I made no comment on it. And we continued our conversation: "What about that Bertie Wooster?" he'd say, or maybe, "What about that test match?" Puffing on the thumb as he listened to me, then removing it from his mouth and jabbing it in the air to emphasise a point in reply.

The waiter had been attentive all evening, checking that we were enjoying our meal and keeping our wine glasses filled. And when he approached we assumed it was to offer us dessert—Father had decided upon the tiramisu, and I thought I'd plump for a crème brûlée.

The waiter spoke quietly, but firmly. "I'm sorry, sir," he said to my father. "But would you please put that away?"

Father turned about, as if looking for whomever else the waiter was addressing, then narrowing his enquiry upon his own offending digit. "I'm sorry," Father said at last. "But I'm sure I'm doing it quietly. I'm not slurping."

"It's not a question of volume, sir. It's our policy. And there have been complaints."

"Indeed?" And my father looked around again, and this time I did too—but there were no other diners watching us, they were all staring intently down at their food.

"It's policy," said the waiter again. "We don't seek to discriminate…"

"No, no," said Father. "Well, then. Well." And he lowered his thumb, tucked it back deliberately into the palm of his hand.

"Thank you. Now, may I fetch you gentlemen some dessert?"

"I'll have the crème brûlée," I said.

"He's my son," said Father.

"I'm sorry, sir?"

"I said he's my son. Don't go thinking otherwise."

"I'm sure he is whatever you say he is. Dessert?"

"I'll have the crème brûlée," I said.

"No," said Father. "The bill. Just the bill, please."

"Just the bill, sir. Probably for the best." The waiter nodded, smiled perfectly politely, and was gone.

I started on some new conversation, but it was hard because Father wasn't joining in, and the restaurant seemed so much quieter somehow and I thought everyone was listening. I was relieved when the waiter returned. He put a little silver plate between us; on it were the bill and two very small mints. "When you're ready, gentlemen," he said, and this time confirmed it, there was a slight edge to the "gentlemen" and emphasis upon the word that seemed ironic.

"I'll get this," muttered Father.

"Dad, no, I invited you out for dinner…"

"I said, I'll get this." He took out his credit card and said to the waiter, "How much of a tip do you usually expect?"

"Tipping is at the customer's discretion, and in the circumstances…"

"No, no, I want to do it properly. I want to be proper, I want it to be above board. How much?"

"Fifteen per cent," said the waiter. "Usually."

"Usually, eh? Well, my maths isn't very good. Perhaps you could look at this and tell me how much I should add." He handed the waiter the bill, making it very clear he was keeping his thumb as far away from the sheet of paper as possible.

The waiter calculated, told him. My father gave him his credit card, thumb pointedly still angled away, and all the while he stared at him, he never took his eyes off him—and the waiter grew uncomfortable, he made a mistake with the card machine, tutted under his breath, had to start again.

"I don't judge," the waiter said quietly.

"What was that?"

"I don't judge." No louder than before. "I'm just doing my job." He put the credit card and the receipt down on to the table, far from my father, as far from my father as he could manage. And then he hurried off. Father and I put on our coats, and it was only as we reached the exit that the hubbub of conversation behind us seemed to return to normal.

Out on the street, and it was already dark, and I was pleased because this meant the evening was nearly over. "Let's get you to the tube," I said, and on the way I spoke brightly about the weather and things. And eventually my father said, "Are we really not going to discuss what just happened?" And he didn't sound cross, and I honestly thought he was going to apologise to me.

But instead he said, "I've lived a long time, and I've made mistakes. I've done things I'm not proud of. But they're my mistakes. Okay? What I am, it's up to me."

"Well, yes," I said. "If you like."

"You're my son," he said. "I'd have stood by you, whatever. If you'd ever been caught shoplifting. If you'd got on drugs."

"I don't do drugs," I said.

"Oh, what's the point?" Again, he wasn't angry, he just sounded tired. Sometimes it's easy to forget how old a man my father is.

We walked all the way back to the tube station in silence.

"Well, then," he said, when we reached the entrance.

"Well!" I said. I'd normally have offered him my hand, but I wasn't sure what he'd do with it.

"You think that waiter was right, don't you? Come on."

"Well," I said. "You've got to admit, it's a posh restaurant. I mean! It's not like Kentucky Fried Chicken. Finger lickin' good, I mean!" I laughed, and I thought he might laugh too.

"A man needs a hobby," he said. "What have you got that's so special?"

When I got back home, Peggy was watching television. I settled down on the sofa next to her. When the commercials came on, she said, "How's your dad?"

"He's okay, I think."

"Good."

"We had steak."

"Did you give him my love?"

"I did, yeah."

I did consider discussing the thumbsucking incident, but I couldn't be sure how to express it as a funny anecdote or as something that should be of concern, and I wasn't sure, moreover, that either approach could be comfortably confined within the length of a commercial break. And I didn't know how Peggy would react to thumbsucking; thumbsucking was one of the many areas of the conversational no man's land into which we no longer strayed.

We finished that programme, and then we watched another. At some point I suggested to Peggy that she'd be welcome to join me and my father for dinner some time, and she said that might be nice; at another point, she came up with the idea that maybe we should invite him over to ours for a home-cooked meal. Not now. Not soon. But some time.

And after a while, we went to bed.

The next day I phoned my mother. A man I didn't recognise answered.

"Who was that?" I asked her, when finally she got put on. "Was that Jim?"

"There is no Jim any more," she said. "That's Frank. Anyway. How are you?"

I told her I was fine. Peggy, fine. How was she? She was fine too.

"I wondered if you'd spoken to Dad recently?"

She gave it some thought. "I don't think so, no. There was Christmas, I think. I spoke to him then."

"Right."

"But whether it was this Christmas or the Christmas before, I really couldn't say. What's the matter? Is he ill? Is he dying?"

"No, no, nothing like that. He's fine. He's absolutely fine."

"Fine is good," she said, and to her credit, she did actually sound relieved.

"I'm just worried about him," I said. "He doesn't seem his usual self. I think maybe he's lonely."

And at that Mother gave a little hollow laugh. "Well," she said, "we're all bloody lonely, aren't we?"

Yes, he was lonely, and the solution was easy—I'd just

make more time to spend with him. But I didn't. I didn't call him to arrange a dinner, I didn't call him at all. And one day I realised three months had passed, and that was the longest time in my whole life I had ever spent apart from him.

His birthday was drawing near, and I knew I'd have to speak to him on his birthday, how could I not? And I knew too that I couldn't wait until the birthday itself. I'd have to call him some time before it, or the birthday would look too obvious, so I decided to call him one week before his birthday, one week before exactly. Time enough, I hoped, to break the ice, and make that dreadful birthday conversation we'd have to have a little less awkward. I phoned. My heart was pounding. I was scared. I didn't know why. This was my father, a man who had never hurt me all these years, who had never let me down, who loved me—I knew it—and deserved my love back. I clutched the receiver in my hands, and, dear God, I hoped he wouldn't pick up.

He did.

He wasn't tense, or annoyed, he didn't try to make me feel bad for the months of silence. I talked lightly about cricket for a while, and he seemed happy to join in. "I'm sorry," I said at last. "I'm really sorry, I've been very busy." He said it was all right, he had been very busy too.

I felt a rush of relief at that, and also, I think, a rush of love. "We should meet up soon," I said.

"That would be nice."

"As soon as you like! I could take you out to dinner for your birthday. Or before your birthday! I could take you out to dinner before your birthday and on your birthday. Do you fancy that? Do you fancy a pre-birthday dinner?"

And he said, and it was the first time in the whole conversation that there was an edge to his words, "You're always asking me out to eat. You think I want to eat? You think it's food that excites me?"

"Well," I said. "What would excite you?" Already dreading the response.

He told me.

He said, "I knew you wouldn't like it."

I said, "I wouldn't have to do anything, would I? I mean. I could just watch."

"Of course," he said. "A lot of people just come to watch."

"All right."

"You don't have to approve. But it'd be nice, I think, if my son understood who I really am. If you got to see me, once—the real me, I mean. Because who knows how much longer I have? I'm not getting any younger, you know."

"Don't talk like that, please," I said. "You've got years left."

"If I've got years left," my father told me, "this is what keeps me alive."

We agreed to meet the very next day after I'd finished work. He'd take me to his club. I asked if it would be a problem I'd be wearing my office suit, and he told me, no—there wasn't a dress code, and everyone liked a man who dressed smart.

Father was dressed in a suit too, nothing too formal, the jacket was a little faded. He explained that we weren't going to a real club, not as such; it was the private residence of a Mr J. C. Tuck. I asked Father who this J. C. Tuck was, and he said he had no idea—it wasn't forbidden to discuss your private lives, but it was considered a little crass. Father carried a plastic bowl full of guacamole. He said he'd brought enough for both of us, but if I chose to come again it'd be polite to get some refreshments of my own.

"This is it," Father said at last. We were standing outside a pretty semi-detached house in a quiet cul-de-sac off the main road; the front garden was neatly mown; the path to the door was a crazy paving; the curtains were drawn. Father rang the doorbell. The noise it made was reassuringly mundane.

J. C. Tuck answered the door. He wasn't wearing a suit; he looked comfortable in a sweater and slacks. "Welcome, welcome!" he said. He was about sixty, I think. He was tall and slim, and his silver hair was nicely combed; I guessed he was a solicitor, or perhaps a bank manager—he smiled with the gracious cheer of someone approving a loan. Father handed him his guacamole. "How lovely!" He introduced me, and said I was there to observe only—"How lovely, of course, you're welcome!" He stood aside and waved us into the house, and it was only then I realised he was wearing a pair of tight black gloves. "Come through, how lovely, we're about to begin!"

He led us into a large room. There was no furniture, but there were beanbags and settee cushions against the walls. Each of them was occupied—those men who weren't lucky enough to find one squatted on the floor. Most of the men looked up as we entered, some of them smiled at my father and raised a hand in greeting. And their faces grinning wide in anticipation were wrinkled, the men were white-haired, or bald, their smiles showed teeth that were cracked or missing altogether. They were all so old; and when I looked at my father, acknowledging their hellos and smiling back in easy recognition, I realised how old he was too.

J. C. Tuck placed our guacamole down in the middle of the room, one of a whole army of bowls. There was salad dressing, and soup, and soft cheese—but it wasn't all food, there was potpourri too, crushed roses and perfumes, and some liquid that looked suspiciously like urine. Tuck looked down at his collection and actually clapped his gloved hands together once in delight. Then he addressed the room.

"Welcome to you all," he said. "I want you to be happy here. I want you to feel relaxed. There is no judgement in this room, you may do whatever you wish. I only remind you to respect the boundaries of others, which may not yet extend as broadly as your own. We have dips. And this evening we welcome some newcomers." I thought he was talking about me, but he indicated a couple of elderly men in the corner of the room, and both were so excited, their eyes bulging out of shallow sockets at the thrill of it all. I thought they might have been twins. "Take care of them. Remember it was your first time once as well. Enjoy yourselves! Be happy! Have fun!"

And for all his fine words, for a moment I thought it had all gone horribly wrong. Everyone stared at him, reluctant to start. And then, around the room, I heard what sounded like faint clapping, and I thought they were giving him a rather half-hearted round of applause. And I realised instead that these old men were tapping at their fists, tapping hard until their thumbs popped out.

And then the sucking began. The men were putting their thumbs into their mouths, some of them were cramming them in so easily. There was one man opposite me who seemed to have no teeth at all and he was able to shove his whole hand in there. And then the slurping—and I realised how discreet my father had been in the restaurant those months ago, there was no need for such niceties here—there was the smacking of lips, and pops like little burps and farts, and the odd squelch as gobbets of saliva spilled out of their mouths and on to their chins.

My father sat next to me, slurping with just as much passion as the rest of them, his eyes closed to savour the experience—and then opening them and looking at me and, either disappointed by my reaction or merely disinterested, shutting them tight once again.

After the first bout of thumbsucking was over, some of the men shuffled over to the finger bowls in the middle of the room. They'd stick in thumbs still wet with spit, they'd scoop out generous portions of mayonnaise or hummus. And some of them would lick their thumbs dry, holding them up like ice-cream cones—others would thrust the whole sticky mass straight into their mouths. And then, cupping their thumbs so nothing would drip to the carpet, they'd return to the throng—they would offer their thumbs up to the other men to suck, and those men would break away from their own and instead take inside their mouths these strangers' thumbs all laden high with goodies.

And there, still standing, taking no part in the proceedings but smiling as if with love and pride, was J. C. Tuck. He caught me looking at him and winked. I looked away.

One man approached my father. He offered him a thumb covered with apricot jam. My father smiled and shook his head. I was relieved by that, at least, that there were depths to which my father would not stoop. Then the man offered him his other thumb, and it was dripping with guacamole, *our* guacamole, and my father nodded eagerly and took the thumb into his mouth in one gulp. A man to his side lifted my father's left hand, and began sucking on his thumb; my father didn't even appear to notice. A man to the other side took his right thumb—and my father was blind to it all, all he cared about was licking every trace of crushed avocado away, licking that thumb clean and then licking still further—and with his arms spread out and supported by the elderly men guzzling at his side Dad looked like a starfish or Jesus on the cross in beatific bliss.

I made myself turn from him. Politely awaiting my attention were the two elderly brothers. They didn't say a word; they smiled hopefully.

"No, thanks," I said.

I got to my feet and left the room. I went out into the back garden and took some deep breaths of air. It was spattering with rain, just a little. I didn't mind.

There was no way to leave the garden without going back

through the house; I decided to stay there for a bit.

I heard a voice behind me. "Embarrassing, isn't it? Watching other people enjoy themselves?" And I turned around, ready to meet the challenge. But there was no challenge, the words were not unkindly meant—there was J. C. Tuck, and he was smiling at me.

"I didn't see you joining in either," I said. "Is that what the gloves are for, to keep people away?"

"Ah," said Tuck, and he smiled wider, and I thought it was a sad smile. "I think my thumbsucking days are over. I have other tastes now." He reached into his pocket. "Cigarette?" he asked.

"Thanks," I said. I lit one. I had to light his too, he couldn't manage with his gloves on. He held on to my hand gently as I steadied the flame.

"You should come back inside," he said. "You might like it. What's the worst that could happen?"

"No, thank you," I said. "No, I'm not that... I have a wife."

"So? Lots of the men here have wives. You're not cheating on them, you know. You're only tasting. Are you cheating on your wife if you taste a nice sandwich?" He pulled on his cigarette. "Here you don't even have to swallow."

My own cigarette was getting damp. I tried to pull on it too, but no matter how hard I tried there was no draw to it. I threw it away. "How long has my father been coming here?"

"I don't notice such things," he said. "That he's here now is all that matters, sharing the bounty. It's a good place. Anyone can come here and be free."

"In which case, why is everyone here a man? And old? And white?"

Tuck shrugged. "I'm sure I don't know. You should ask all those young negro girls. I'm sure we don't discriminate."

"I think I would like to go now."

"Your father wanted you to see this. Why do you think that was?"

"I don't know."

"The thumb," said J. C. Tuck, "is the most remarkable part of the human body, you know."

"Actually, I'm pretty sure it isn't."

"It's the thumb which separates man from the animals," said Tuck. "The opposable digit, which allows us to wield tools, to make something better of ourselves. Without our thumbs we would be nothing. The thumb is the greatest gift God gave us. And just because he loves us so, he gave us a second one, on the other hand, as a spare!"

"I don't really believe in God."

"I can see you're not a man who believes in things." He smiled at me, to show he wasn't blaming me for this—if anything, he pitied me. "You're an individual, yes? But what gives you the *key* to your individuality? The thumb. You know your fingerprints are unique. And the thumbprint is that uniqueness writ large. Thicker and wider and prouder than any mere finger." He leaned into me, and I wanted to back away, but I didn't dare somehow, and his voice was now so calm and gentle. "Do you know why babies like to suck their thumbs?"

"Um. To feel secure?"

"Because they know. Because at the very core of us, before civilisation moulds us and corrupts us, when we're still pure and newly born, we *know*. The thumb is sacred. They tuck it away into their mouths to mother it, to comfort it and keep it safe. Why else would you think God designed the tongue so that it would fit so exactly around it?"

I looked down at my thumb. I didn't want to. I felt compelled to.

"When did you last suck your thumb?" J. C. Tuck asked me.

"I don't know."

"So long ago," whispered Tuck. "A time of comfort, so

far away." I don't know why, but I felt my eyes begin to prick with tears. "It's all right," said Tuck. "Bring your thumb home. Suck your thumb for me now."

I put my thumb in my mouth. It didn't feel especially comfortable; it certainly didn't feel like it had been brought home. My tongue lolled around the intruder awkwardly; it wasn't really sure what to do with it.

"Not like that," said Tuck. "Let me show you."

And his gloved hand reached for mine, he drew it away from my lips and towards his. "Don't worry," he said. "I won't bite." And he opened his mouth and pulled my thumb inside.

The first thing I noticed was how warm his mouth was, warm like a bed on a frosty morning, warm that was cosy and nice. And it was such a *big* mouth—mine had been all teeth and tongue, and half-chewed food most probably, there was barely room for my thumb at all—but in Tuck's mouth the thumb could roam wide and free, the plains were vast and empty and my thumb for the taking. Tuck clamped my thumb gently to his soft palate with his tongue. The soft palate yielded like a sponge, the tongue was firm and it knew its business and it brooked no argument, it kept me pressed there and then it stroked me—it didn't lick, it was nothing so uncouth, it flexed and flexed again, it seemed to pulsate.

And then, so soon, it was over. He pulled me out of his mouth, his lips pressed hard so they slid against my skin.

"Was that all right?" he asked.

"Yes," I said.

"Good," he said. "And now then. Maybe you would do a little something for me." He began to tug off his glove.

"You want me to suck your thumb?" I asked.

"No, as I say, my tastes have changed." And he lifted up his hand.

There, on the end, was now just a stump. It cut off abruptly above the knuckle. There were tooth marks, some fresh too, there were still traces of blood—I saw little specks of bone.

"I like to chew," he said.

He brought it up to my face, that stub of raw meat, and I wasn't going to open my mouth, I wasn't, but I had to breathe, and I felt my lips part. "Share the bounty."

"Let him go," said my father.

J. C. Tuck didn't take his eyes off me for a moment, his face now so close to me I could taste that warm breath once more. The warmth that was so cosy. "Get back inside," he said genially enough. "You'll get wet." And it was only then I realised that it was now raining very hard indeed.

"Let him go." Father sounded frightened. He sounded as if he would run away at any second. "He's my son. I brought him here to know me better. To understand. I…" I thought he had stopped, so did Tuck, who gave his attention back to me.

"He's my son," said my father one last time.

Tuck didn't move for a moment. Then he looked down at the ground, and he stepped back from me. "Then go home," he said softly. "Both of you." And he went indoors.

Father and I held back in the garden for a minute, we didn't dare follow. I went to my father and I smiled. He smiled back weakly. There was a line of guacamole on his chin.

It was raining heavily as we walked to the tube station, but Father was in no hurry, and I didn't feel I could rush him. I took his hand. He held on to me, but there was no grip to it. I looked down at him, and thought once more how old he was.

"What am I going to do now?" he said at last.

"There's still cricket," I said. "There's still Wodehouse."

We reached the station. And he looked so sad, and I opened my arms wide for him and took him in a hug. I kissed him. I kissed him on the top of the head, and then I kissed him on the cheek.

"I'll call you," I said.

He nodded, and he turned, and he went.

When I got back home, Peggy was watching television. I settled down on the sofa next to her. When the commercials came on, she spoke to me. "Your Dad all right?"

"I think so."

"Did you have steak?"

I realised I hadn't eaten all evening. I wasn't hungry. "Yes," I said.

We watched the programme together. And I suddenly felt a rage inside me, that this was what our lives had become, that the love I knew we still had for each other had become so passionless. There was a time we could barely keep our hands to ourselves, and now—this, just this. And I wasn't sure whether the rage was at her, or at myself. And then it passed.

I took her hand. She held on to it happily enough.

A few minutes later, I raised her hand to my lips. She let me do so. It was a dead weight. It had no will of its own. I kissed it gently. I put the hand back.

I waited until the commercial break. And then I raised her hand to my lips again. But this time I took her thumb inside my mouth. And it filled my mouth. I had never realised how large my wife's thumb was.

At last I released her. And I lowered her hand gently back to her side. She didn't say a word, she seemed a world away, a world of washing powder and furniture discount sales.

The programme ended. "Shall we watch another?" I asked.

"No," she said. "Let's go to bed." So we did.

BULB
Gemma Files

Dedicated to Stephen J. Barringer

Lucas Brennan 1:41 PM (4 hours ago)
to me ▼

Ian,
I wish you'd told me to listen to your recordings first, because
I just wasted ninety fucking minutes on editing your intro
script. There's absolutely no way we can use this interview,
Ian—this isn't what we're about, it isn't what our listeners
want, and it isn't what we sold anyone on or what our
advertisers want to be connected with! I hate being the heavy
here, but you've put the rest of us in a truly bad position—I
can either pull Jen and Oshi off the May 17 episode to try
putting together a half-assed substitute or we can screw
over our listeners with a rerun, and either way we're almost
certainly gonna lose audience clicks, which means we lose
ad clicks which means we all lose revenue.
I'll let you know which way we go. In the interim I'd do
yourself a favour and stay off line for a day or two. I'm not the
only person on the team who's pissed about this.
--L.

Sent from my iPhone
Ian Dossimer Apr 20 (1 day ago)
to Lucas ▼

Hey Luke,
I've enclosed the first whack at the intro script for the May 3 episode. Sorry it's a little late but I think we've still got time, especially given how little editing I think the interview portion's going to need. Text me or call me with any questions!—Doss

> "GRIDLOST" -- EPISODE 22 MAY 3 2018
> Proposed Title: "Leaving the Light Behind"
> *Intro Script*

Good morning, afternoon or evening, everybody, whenever you're listening. I'm your host Ian Dossimer and welcome to another episode of "GridLost", the podcast where we interview the new pioneers of the 21st century, people looking for ways to build themselves a space of privacy and safety in an increasingly technology-polluted world. We've got something of exceptional interest today, so I hope everybody has time to sit down and listen straight through, because, I can promise you, this story isn't like anything you've heard on "GridLost" before. It isn't like anything we've *done* on "GridLost" before.

The first and most important thing I have to tell you today is about our guest. Because her name is... not something we know, in fact. That's right, for the first time in our show's history we're conducting an anonymous interview. The only contact information I have for this woman is an Internet forum handle and a phone number that I was assured belongs to a burner phone she plans to discard pretty much the moment she hangs up on us.

Some of our more devoted fans may recognize this handle if they frequent the right websites: she goes by the alias "Harmony6893", and she's posted on Prepperforums.net and Survivalistboards.com, among others.

If you do recognize that alias, you'll also probably know why this is something of a coup for us: unlike a lot of our subjects, Harmony6893 hasn't just disconnected from the central North American power network, she has (so she claims) completely abandoned the use of *any* kind of electrical technology or telecommunications device. She has no cable, no Wi-Fi, no smartphone, no solar panels, batteries or wind turbines, not even an emergency generator—in fact, she only posts to the Net every two weeks when she visits a not-exactly-nearby town to use their Internet cafe. More controversially, some say dangerously, she's doing this all completely alone; she has no family or housemates in her property, wherever it is. If there is an ultimate off-the-grid story, this woman is it.

The next thing I have to warn you about is the nature of Harmony6893's story. As you'll know from our other episodes, the reasons people choose to unplug are as varied as the people themselves. Some want to recapture a childhood that modern technology is destroying, some are preparing for an EMP attack or any of half a dozen other kinds of disaster, some want to help bring about political decentralization by creating the infrastructure for social decentralization. But in my first phone call, when I asked Harmony6893 to explain the reasons for her self-imposed isolation, she told me that it wasn't any of that. Rather it was something utterly unique to her, something she was utterly sure nobody else would understand or believe. And after listening to what she has to say... well, I'm not sure she's wrong. But I do think it's something that our listeners deserve the chance to make up their own minds about.

Harmony is, in fact, so cautious that during our interview, she was obviously using some sort of commercial sound distorter on her phone to disguise her voice—just to explain why it sounds so odd. Please don't blame our tech guys! Without further ado, then, let us introduce you... to Harmony6893.

harmony-interview-apr-18.mp3

INTERVIEW TRANSCRIPT
Q: I. DOSSIMER, "GRIDLOST", 2018-04-18
A: "HARMONY6893"

Q: I want to thank you again for being willing to take the time to do this.

A: (PAUSE) "Willing" might be a strong word. "Attack of conscience" is probably more accurate.

Q: Well, *that* sounds ominous.

A: If you're not going to take this seriously, I'm hanging up.

Q: No, yes, of course, you're right, I do apologize. Let's begin with the standard introduction: So... you're currently known only as Harmony6893 on a number of Internet forums.

A: You already know that.

Q: And your real name is...?

A: None of your business.

Q: Well, that creates just a bit of a problem for us, especially in terms of, you know, fact-checking whatever it is you're going to—

A: Mmm-hmh, yeah, I don't care. If that's some kind of deal-breaker for you, then I guess we're...

Q: No, no, it's okay, it's all right! How would you prefer we refer to you, then?

A: Um. (PAUSES) Bronwyn, that's always been a name I liked. Call me that.

Q: All right, Bronwyn. How long have you been off the grid, at this point?

A: Almost a year and four months. Since January of last year.

Q: And you've gone completely non-technological? Like, back to the nineteenth century?

A: Hardly. When I need to buy tools and supplies, I buy modern machine-shop versions. I don't hand-carve my own butter churns. (BEAT) But I do *have* a butter churn. (CHUCKLES) That's one of the reasons I started posting to prepper sites in the first place—I had to learn a lot of the old techniques just to stay afloat, and people in the survivalist community put big value on skill-sharing.

Q: And yet you also live completely by yourself as well, we hear. One thing a lot of our other interviewees have said is that total isolation is actually dangerous—not just in case you find yourself hurt and without help, but because humans aren't really meant to live that way. Community's a key part of sanity. Why forgo it?

A: (PAUSE) I'd have to call that a matter of conscience as well.

Q: Meaning you don't want to tell us? It's all right if you don't. We always respect the defined spaces of our guests' privacy.

A: No, I'm *going* to tell you. It's just that explaining it is going to take a while. And enough of your listeners are going to think I'm a psycho by the end of this anyway.

Q: You might be surprised. We're pretty open-minded around here.

A: We'll see.

(PAUSE)

Q: So we may as well start from the beginning. Had you always been interested in disconnection as a lifestyle, or was it a sudden change?

A: You could call it "sudden".

(BEAT)

A: The truth is, up until last January, you would probably have pegged me as the last person you'd have imagined doing this. I was a stockbroker—or, as I liked to tell people I thought would think it was charming, I tricked suckers into throwing away their money trying to cheat the system out of more for a living. I was one of those people you see power walking along Bay Street with a Bluetooth in her ear and her nose in her smartphone, checking on Bloomberg and the TSE[1] for the latest buying and selling movements. That's how it all started, in fact—I got a promotion and a pay raise that meant I'd finally be able to live downtown on my own salary, so I started looking around for a condo within walking distance of my office. And in December, I thought I'd finally found it.

It wasn't a new unit, just a one-bedroom plus den job belonging to a guy who flew back and forth every week between Hong Kong and... and where I used to live, so when his job suddenly changed and he didn't need to be there any more, he was more interested in unloading it fast than in gauging potential buyers. Not a lot of room, but all the space I needed for my office, plus a lot of shelving and a really nice northern view with lots of natural light. And there was this beautiful line of track-lighting in the main room, one of the best I'd ever seen—bright bulbs, understated fixtures, on a dimmer switch. I remember looking up at it while the realtor was nattering on and thinking, "Wow, that's *really nice*."

---

[1] The references to "Bay Street" and the "TSE" make it likely that Harmony/Bronwyn is Canadian, specifically from Toronto, Ontario; "TSE" in context almost certainly stands for the Toronto Stock Exchange, and Bay Street runs through the downtown finance core of the city, making it the Canadian equivalent of Wall Street in Manhattan.

Q: So what you're saying is, it was really nice.

A: Yeah, well, I think ultimately, that lighting might've been the primary reason I agreed to buy the place. So I go through all the paperwork, wait for buddy to move out and head back to Hong Kong, and I move in three weeks later and… the lighting is gone. He took it with him.

Q: You mean he actually removed the entire fixture? Not just took out the bulbs?

A: Yeah, that's what I mean. There wasn't anything left in the ceiling except this S-shaped row of plastic nodules where it must have been attached. I don't mind telling you I was really pissed off about that, especially when the realtor said she couldn't do anything—if the guy put it in he had the right to take it out.

Q: Was this some kind of unique hand-made brand or something? I wouldn't think it'd be that impossible to replace a set of lights.

A: You wouldn't, right? But no. I mean… getting a new track and bulbs wasn't the problem—didn't look exactly like what'd been there before, but at this point, I was willing to settle. The *problem* was when I got the lighting tech in to hook everything up, and he just couldn't get it to work.

Q: How do you mean?

A: I mean he couldn't get a current out of any of the wires running into those sockets. And even weirder? He couldn't even find the goddam *switch* that worked that particular fixture. The dimmer and all that shit? Well, my realtor couldn't remember where it was supposed to be, and neither I nor the lighting guy could find anything like it. Sure, there was a switch inside the door for the hall light, one for the kitchen—guy-o didn't take *that*. A switch inside the john, for the vanity lights above the sink. But no switches anywhere else except right next to the en-suite washer-dryer unit built-in, and you know what *that* turned out to run?

Q: The washer-dryer?

A: Got it in one.

Q: Okay, I admit it, that's a little weird... You're sure you saw these lights actually working when you were first looking at the apartment? When the realtor was there?

A: *Yes*, for fuck's sake.

Q: Uh, we'd really rather you didn't—

A: Whatever. (ANOTHER PAUSE) And then I went downstairs, talked to the concierge, wanted to know what the lighting set-up was in all the other apartments with the same layout—they wouldn't tell me. Cited privacy, can you believe that? So I tell them what's happened, and how I just want to figure out how to put in lights that'll turn on so I don't have to light the whole place with floor lamps, and they're like: well, we can't help, can't even get in touch with the Hong Kong dude because he changed his phone number and it turns out they never even had his email. And my mortgage agreement says I'm the one who's basically responsible for everything that happens inside my walls, anyhow.

Q: So it was the, um... annoying, frustrating, no doubt expensive unreliability of this system which prompted your eventual... lifestyle change?

A: No. Not that.

(ANOTHER, LONGER PAUSE)

Have you ever thought—I mean, I guess you kind of must have, considering this show you run—but have you ever *really* thought, like in *detail*, about just how much we all rely on things these days that almost *none* of us actually understand?

Q: You mean, technologically? Like—

A: Yeah, that too, of course. But... not just that.

Q: Well, a lot of the people we interview do make a big deal out of how much we take for granted. How our whole society runs on these... tides of energy going back and forth: electricity, cellular signals, microwaves. Invisible presences that we all work with constantly, and only a tiny minority of people actually know how to build, or control, or fix. I remember one bloke talking about how he'd taught himself practical electrician's skills as part of getting his lodge set up, and he did some handyman work for his friends and neighbours in the meantime; what always amazed him, he said, was how mind-boggled everybody he helped was. "It really was like I was some kind of wizard or magician," he told me. "Wave my screwdriver, say stuff that made no sense, then everything works again. I mean, it felt good, but it was also kind of unnerving, you know?"

A: Wow, it's like you do this for a living. Though I guess it's probably not much of one, right?

Q: Well, we get to do what we enjoy; most of us think that's worth the trade-off.

A: Yeah. Well, my way of dealing with stuff like that was always to pay other people, like your friend, to do it for me. As it happened, I was dating a guy at the time, who was—lucky for me—both an engineering student and *not* a dickhead, surprisingly. It was early days, we'd met in a club and liked each other, I brought him home, and he looked around and said, "Why do you have all these floor lamps?" So I told him the story, or a truncated version thereof, and he said, "Oh, I can fix that for you." I didn't say, *I doubt it*, largely because I still wanted to sleep with him, but his pitch was that he'd had a light meter at home, which he'd used before for similar things, so it would be cheap and we could enjoy each other's company while he did it.

Q: He was well fit I take it?

A: Very. Very… well fit. (PAUSE) So a couple of days later, he comes over to my place and I buzz him in. He's got his toolbox with him, and a vest on with all these pockets where you can stick things, like he's dressed to go into battle, and he's got what look like bandoliers of shotgun shells slung across his chest. They weren't, obviously; they were batteries and light bulbs, all the different kinds he thought he'd be likely to need. I say, "Great," show him the empty fixture sockets, the light switch and where everything is, including the fuse box, and he gets to work.

Well, he can't get anything out of the wires either, any more than the other guy did. I'm standing by this stepladder he also brought holding the light meter up over my head, and he keeps asking me, "Did you see it jump? Is it jumping now?" to which I just kept saying, "Nope." I honestly thought the meter was broken, and for a minute so did he, until he tested it with one of the floor lamps and proved that it wasn't. Then he gets into the fuse box, and manages to turn everything else in the apartment on and off at least once, but still can't find anything that looks like a working light circuit in the ceiling outside the kitchen and the front hallway. And he's like, "Well, *that's* weird." And it *was* weird. To be frank, it was kind of starting to freak me out at this point, and I was perfectly willing to tell him to stop. But you know how guys get; he had this look on his face like he was taking it personally. Like "This is pissing me off, and I'm gonna *beat* it."

So he took the light meter from me—he was a tall guy—and he stuck it right up near the ceiling, maybe ten centimetres[2] away, started going back and forth across the ceiling from the fixture, doing this sort of—like he was sweeping a field for mines, you know? Or using a

---

2 *Four inches.*

metal detector to look for treasure, and I was like, *Oh, this is ridiculous.* But eventually, he was almost to the main window, and he was making a sweep to his left, and suddenly... the pointer on the meter twitched. He stops, says: "Look at this!" Further he went towards the corner, meanwhile, the more reaction he got, until finally it was reading as though there was an active socket there.

Q: But there couldn't have been, was there? Or you'd have seen it.

A: Correct. There wasn't even a power point. I never even put a floor lamp in that corner.

Q: Why not?

A: Because... I didn't like that corner. It was always cold there. I mean, it was always going to be a little cold, because it was winter; plus, an additional downside to floor-to-ceiling windows that slide open is that if you want to be *able* to open them you can't caulk them up. But this was—colder. Off-puttingly so. So I just avoided putting anything in there, because I didn't want to *be* there.

Q: What was it like in summer?

A: I never made it to summer. (PAUSE) So he asks me, "Was there *ever* a fixture here?" and I tell him I have no idea. And he looked at me and I looked at him, and then he said, "I'm gonna try something." Gave me the light meter, and took out one of the light bulbs by the—what do you call the metal part on the bottom, the part that screws in?

Q: That's the cap.

A: Right, yeah. So he held it by the cap, just this standard 100-watt incandescent, and lifted it up closer and closer to the ceiling... and as he got further and further up, the filament began to glow, and then, suddenly, it turned on. Full brightness. It was... it was horrible. Unnatural. I mean, anything unnatural is horrible, right? Like a preaching dog or a singing rose, that kind of shit? Somebody said that.[3]

Q: I guess. And, uh, your boyfriend—how did he react?

A: Oh, he was delighted. Very impressed with himself. He started to laugh. He had his arm straight out at shoulder height, and he was moving it all around watching the light brighten and dim, like it was the coolest toy in the world. It must have been really hot, but he didn't seem to notice; maybe he had calluses on his fingers. And then, basically just by accident, he brushed the wall with the metal base of the bulb—and it *stuck* there. Like, it actually pulled out of his fingers and stayed behind on the wall, sticking right out like a, I don't know, like a fucking *tumour* or something. A fucking glowing tumour.

And he shook his hand, fingers snapping like he'd just figured out how close he'd come to almost burning them, and he goes: "Whoo! *That* was something!" Me, I just stand there with my mouth open, not knowing what the hell to say. But then he's peering closer at it, until finally I can't stand it any more, and I just tell him, "Pull it off. I don't want it there." He starts going on about how there must be something magnetized in the wall, and this is a complete cock-up that I could probably sue the building over, and I say, "I don't *care*, I want you to *get it off my wall, please!*" So because he'd have to grab it by the hot part of the bulb this time, he put on a pair of work gloves and took hold of it— very gently—and starts trying to pull it off the wall.

And it won't come off.

Q: Was he right? Had something been magnetized in the walls?

A: I have no fucking idea, but I *really* don't think so. Anyway, he's like, "I don't know what to do at this point, I don't want to break it," and I'm like, "*Break* it, man!" So he tries

---

[3] *Arthur Machen, in the prologue to "The White People." Paraphrased.*

to pull it from the cap this time, hauling on it harder and harder, and then he slips a little and the bulb *slides up* the wall, and we both suddenly realize he can move it *upwards*. Towards where the reading is coming from.

Q: The cold spot.

A: Yeah. I hadn't thought about it like that, but—that's what it was, wasn't it?

Q: Like in a haunted house?

A: You tell me. (PAUSE) So he keeps pushing it up the wall, closer and closer to the cold spot—the "source", he's calling it—and it gets brighter and brighter. And I didn't really realize this at first, but it was as if, while the bulb was getting brighter, the rest of the apartment seemed to be getting... dimmer. Like it was about to flicker; I'd seen that before, plenty of times. Normal stuff. Even brand new, very expensive condos have power fluctuations.

Q: Well, if the bulb was that bright, it would have made everything else *look* dim, wouldn't it?

A: Exactly. Brighter, and brighter, and then—it popped. Not just burnt out, I mean the whole bulb actually exploded, and it was only because my guy already had one hand up shielding his eyes against the light that he didn't get hurt. And we both jump back, and we're left with nothing except the cap and a little jagged rim of broken glass around it stuck almost right in the top corner of my ceiling. And we look at each other, and I tell him, "Okay, I think we're done with this tonight," and I go to get the broom and dustpan and start sweeping up the broken glass off my lovingly installed hardwood floors.

But, you know, there's gotta be more to it. So he takes out the highest-wattage bulb he has—spotlight-quality halogen, it looks like—puts on a pair of fricking polarized safety glasses, for fuck's sake, and says: "Let me just try one more thing." Well, how was I gonna stop him? He holds up the bulb, pointing it away from me, and the same thing happens as he lifts it closer and closer to the cold spot: Filament starts glowing, ramps up as he lifts, until the cone of light it's throwing is so bright the colours on that side of the apartment look almost completely washed out. And I turn away, shielding my face, which is the only reason I see it happening.

Q: See... what happening?

A: How every other bulb in the place really *is* dimming down now, *very* visibly: kitchen, hallway, bathroom—and before you ask, this isn't just my vision adjusting to one bright light source, I can *see* them browning out. And it's getting *colder* in the place, too, like the window and front door have both been thrown open and a cross breeze is sucking out all the heat. Except everything's still closed. And then Joe—my... my friend—I hear him yelp, like the sound you'd make if somebody startled you by slapping your hand. He staggers back from the corner, and he's just staring at the bulb hovering there, and the look on his face is finally about as freaked out as I've been for the last fifteen minutes. So I hurry over to him, asking what's wrong, and he pulls me almost right against the window so I can see what he's seeing.

The bulb isn't stuck to the wall. It's floating there right in mid-fucking-*air*. And smoke is curling and hissing off the plaster overhead, except the stain spilling across it isn't black, it's... "white" isn't strong enough. It was like someone photographed a heat-scorch and then flipped it into negative, so black becomes white, except it's this blinding purplish-UV glow that—I can't describe it; staring at it *hurt*, like someone was squeezing my eyeballs, like the world's worst case of glaucoma, and after a second I had to hunch over with my palms in my eye sockets. But Joe, he's got his glasses on so I guess it wasn't hurting him to look at, and he was just staring up at it, his mouth open a little, almost smiling—like he was so amazed, he was happy. Like he was seeing God.

Then, under the sizzling sound of my ceiling cooking, there's this rippling wave of sharp cracking, banging sounds, and the plaster splits open all around the bulb, shooting out in all directions from the corner—along the ceiling, down the wall, towards the windows. And more glowing shit spills out through all these cracks, except this isn't light or smoke or fire; it's more like...

Ever seen one of those phosphorescent jellyfish they have in aquariums? Like the wall at Ripley's Aquarium, the one they shot part of *The Handmaid's Tale* pilot episode in front of? They're all made of, um, goo, right, even the biggest ones... transparent, like slime, or mucus that isn't infected. Invisible, really. Until you shine a light behind them.

(PAUSE) I'll assume you have. Anyway, imagine that, but with the wall's brightness amped up to eleven, almost as hard to look at as the bulb itself. And I can't even *see* the bulb, any more, only the place in the corner where the light is brightest. And this horrid blinding incandescent shit coming in through the cracks, that fizzling, spitting sparkler of a fissure between here and—somewhere else starts... *weaving* itself out in all directions, dropping these wet viscous tendrils onto the floor, throwing them out at the walls like the support lines on a spider web. Oh God, and just the way it *sounded* made me want to puke, and the smell was like ozone and rotten seaweed and rancid fat. But even while it's doing all this—making itself *manifest* like somebody fucking cutting themselves apart so their entrails fall out, or whatever—it's still cycling through every colour you can think of, and it's fucking *beautiful*, like staring into a ten-foot-tall kaleidoscope.

The bell forms, then filaments, then tentacles. Mucus and spines spread all over Joe, cocooning him—he's up to his waist in this swamp of oozing, spiny tendrils, and I'm standing in a puddle of oil-slick glowing crap that's inching its way up my ankles, like I'm sinking into the floor. If I hadn't already had the broom in my hand I really don't think I would have gotten out of there, but thank Christ, I did.

I don't even remember being angry, or frightened, just… wired. Like I was buzzing. Like a signal going through me.

So I stumble forwards with my eyes closed and start flailing with the broom at the corner of the ceiling, the cold spot. And I can feel the sickening, wet way all this slimy guck gives way under it when I'm swinging and jabbing, but then—somehow—there's this solid *crunch*, and the light goes out, with this… it isn't a *sound*. It's like a feeling in the air. This silent, agonizing trembling all along my skin, like a thousand dog whistles all screaming at once.

I broke the bulb, and that's all it took. Right then, anyhow.

So. All the shit that's wrapping up Joe falls apart with this disgusting squelching noise, and Joe goes over on his side, which is when I grab him up with both hands, trying to haul him to the door—where I thought the door used to be. Because it was *dark* in there, man, super-dark; dark plus. I've never seen dark like that, before or after.

Must've looked pretty funny, in retrospect: there I am, dragging—attempting to drag—this huge, cute young dude twice my size, slapping his face and yelling hysterically at him, desperate to get him to wake up. Couldn't see much, but I remember his arms felt slimy, and patches of his skin almost seemed… *soft*, like if I squeezed too hard it would just slide right off his arm. Overcooked meat, that was the feel. (SOFTER) God, I wish I hadn't remembered that.

(PAUSE, THEN NORMAL TONE) Okay, so. I get him past the kitchen counter into the vestibule, still fumbling around, and my hand falls on the door handle, at fucking *last*. Jesus! It was like a miracle. And I open the main door, so I can finally *see* again in the light coming in from the hallway—

—which is exactly when the thing in the apartment suddenly bursts into blazing light again, even brighter, but I can *still see what it's doing*. It kind of... *pulses*, first inward and then outward, and opens up like a gigantic umbrella, a vampire fucking squid, with red and purple teeth all ringed round inside and dripping. Tendrils shoot out and they wrap round Joe and haul him back in, so fast and hard I don't have time to let go. Next thing I know, it snaps shut on us both: all of him, me just to the wrist, the right one. Joe's just—gone, swallowed. And my hand is stuck inside the peak of the thing, and it's *burning*, like I stuck it in a beehive, or a vat full of acid. Like I'd stuck it through a hole, right into somebody else's stomach.

I must've been screaming, but I don't remember. Just hauling as hard as I could till my hand peeled free and throwing myself back out that door, slamming it shut behind me.

Q: (AFTER A MOMENT) ...Joe?

A: (SOFT) No.

I didn't—I don't... I don't *feel* good about it. But... I didn't...

Q: You didn't know him well enough to die for him.

A: Thank you for saying it.

(ANOTHER LONG PAUSE)

By the way, when I say "peeled", I mean literally. Large patches of skin on my hand just—melted away, exposing layered patches of fat, visible veins and tendons. Nauseating, and painful as *shit*. I wound up having to have most of the rest of the epidermis debrided so the skin would grow back evenly, and I still don't have any mobility in my right ring or little fingers.

By the time I got to the nearest ER, I'd been making a fist so long they had to sort of prise, sort of cut it open, because it'd already started healing shut. Human body's an amazing thing, man. When they got my fingers uncurled, a bunch of stuff fell out: goo, pulp, faintly pinkish. Things that looked like bones, but soft—bendy. Like they'd been digested and shit back out. And something else.

It was a Ryerson University Engineering Department ring.

So yeah, nobody ever found much else of Joe. Just this... layer of sludge all over the apartment, unidentifiable, biological in origin. Just cracks in the ceiling and two broken bulbs lying in the far left corner, right by the window.

Adding insult to injury, the condo corporation tried like hell to blame *me* for the damage. They only gave up when I got a lawyer smart enough to point out that just publicizing the legal battle would tank sales in the entire building. That's how I got out of my mortgage with enough money to do whatever I wanted after that.

But by that point I already knew what I had to do.

See, after that day? I couldn't turn on an electric light anywhere—couldn't even get near one—without hearing this... *buzzing*. Incandescent, CFL, LED, doesn't matter. If I listen hard enough, like really, *really* hard, I can even hear it coming from computer screens or smartphones. And the buzzing... once you listen long enough, it sounds like—a voice. Whispering. I can't ever make out *what* it's saying, but I know it's saying something. You know, how you can always tell?

And once it starts sounding like a voice, I know whose voice it is.

Has to be.

So.

(LONG PAUSE)

I quit my job. I bought a farmhouse—all stone and wood, not a bit of metal in it. I took up growing my own vegetables, raising my own chickens—they really are amazingly stupid birds, by the way. I made goddam sure they ripped out every piece of wiring in the building. I cut my own firewood, I buy oil supplies for lanterns and candles. Reading is the only entertainment I have. And when I'm too tired to read, I shut off the lantern and I sit in the dark, and the quiet, until I can fall asleep.

Because the grid is a web, a network of energies. Of ghosts. And things live in it, waiting for food. Hunting. Like spiders.

I mean, maybe I'm being paranoid. Maybe that thing was as ass-dumb as a chicken itself. But if it wasn't... if it remembers there's stuff here to eat, and at least one meal escaped... it might come looking. And I don't want anybody else to die like Joe, eaten just because I wasn't fast enough to get him to safety in time. That's why I live alone. That's the "conscience" part.

That's why I'm telling you this story now. Because if it happened to me, it might happen again. To someone else.

(LONG, LONG PAUSE)

Hey. Did I lose you there, Doss?

Q: No. No, I just... um... I'm not sure what to say to all that. (PAUSE) I mean, I assume this is the reason for the anonymity and the alias. And the burner phone, too.

A: Bingo. (PAUSE) So how crazy do you think I am, now? C'mon. Scale of one to ten.

Q: Bronwyn, we don't... look, that's not...

A: Relax. I've heard your show before. You did an interview last year with those guys who're waiting for the shape-shifting space lizards to reveal they control the world, remember?

Q: Well—yeah, but as long as they stuck to talking about building shelters and hunting schedules, they *sounded* sane. Maybe… maybe you could tell us a little more about your daily routine, the skills you use as part of your off-grid life…

A: Nope. I've already been on this phone too long.

Q: Wait, Bronwyn—one last question. If you're afraid that this—thing, whatever—that it might come after whoever talks about it… should *we* be careful? What kind of… of risk would we be taking if we release this interview?

A: If you *do* think I'm crazy, then obviously none. Right?

Q: Bronwyn—

(DIAL TONE)

Oshi Takamura 4:53 PM (1 hour ago)
to me, Jen ▼

Hi Lucas,
Listened to Doss's file, and I have to say I agree—don't care about people's crazy reasons for living off-grid, but our shows have to talk about actually *living off grid*, because that's what people tune in for. It's also not long enough—we'd need at least another twenty minutes to round out a full episode. Try not to be too hard on Doss, BTW. I'll have to pull an all-nighter to catch up, but it's still a couple of weeks before exams.

Oshi

Lucas Brennan 5:21 PM (30 minutes ago)
to Oshi, Jen ▼

Hey Oshi,
Dude, you're way too forgiving. Doss should have damn well known better before he wasted all our time on this. This is not the same as spending three out of forty-two minutes on a conspiracy theory, this is Stephen King nightmare crap. If Doss wasn't our biggest audience draw I'd be seriously tempted to fire his ass. I'm deleting that file and I'd strongly recommend you do too.
If you're OK with the all-nighters, Oshi, then I'm going to go ahead and pull the May 17th episode material forward to the 3rd—make sure you update the home page sidebars to match. Jen, I've reworked the interstitial scripts to pad them out a little. If you could review the attached files and do a couple of rehearsals on your own, then be ready to go for a recording session on the afternoon of April 25th, that'd be great. Let me know if either of you have any problems.
--L.

From Reddit.com, posted May 13th 2018:

Lost episode of "GridLost"
submitted 11 hours ago by DossalFinn
74 commentssharesavehidereport
harmony–interview–apr–18.mp3

[-] **offbroadwaychaos**
anyone got a screenshot of the GridLost home page? i wanna see if this was ever scheduled.
permalinkembedsavereply
[-] **HyperJoan**

I've attached a .gif from Wayback but it just says "Special Guest Star coming". Which could be this Harmony chick, I suppose.
permalinkembedsavereply

[–] **svalbard43**

Don't get it. Is this supposed to be a late April Fool's joke or what?
permalinkembedsavereply

[–] **MichaelTwyla50**

No, I listen to GL all the time and this is the guy, this is Doss. + on the May 3rd show the producer did come on and apologize for a shorter-than-usual episode, which would completely make sense if they chickened out of releasing this. + Harmony6893's a real person, I've read some of her posts on prepperforums.net
permalinkembedsavereply

[–] **ChocoBot14**

I've posted a transcript of the file here if anyone's interested, with a few annotations.
permalinkembedsavereply

[–] **RagingManticore**

Okay guys: read transcript and phoned up the Toronto police department. theyve got a missing persons case still on the books from January 2017 for a ryerson engineering student age 22 named joseph macklay, last seen near a condo off adelaide west, fifteen minutes from downtown bay street. local real estate records say theres a corner one bed plus den unit still listed hasnt sold since. sooooo either a *really* well-researched creepypasta or ???????!!!!!?????
permalinkembedsavereply

[–] **KevlarTuxedo**

lol youre a tool—links or its bullshit
permalinkembedsavereply

From a subforum on www.prepperforums.net, *posted June 5, 2018:*

Hello everyone.

I've been drafting this post for a couple of weeks now, after my last trip into town, when I realized that my interview with the "GridLost" people had gone viral. Honestly, I never expected them to release it in any form. I just wanted to tell myself I'd told *somebody*. I still don't know if I haven't made a really big mistake. But there's nothing I can do about it now.

That's why this is going to be my last post to these forums, or any other. I'm cutting the last cord. I want to thank everyone for everything I've learned here, and I hope I've given as much as I've gained. If I came into this community out of fear, I think I've found something like peace, and I couldn't be more grateful.

Some of you are probably going to ask why I'm not trying to make more out of this. I mean, if you believe me, then you accept I saw something that proves everything people think they know about the world is wrong, or at the very least horrifically incomplete—and when there are millions desperate for *any* reason to believe there's something out there beyond the 9-to-5, beyond iPhone line-ups and Netflix, why would I not trumpet everywhere I could? Some people would say even a universe full of horrors is better than a universe full of nothing but us.

To that, I say: Wait until *you* meet one.

If we do live in the bubble I think we do, then the single best thing I can do is not poke more holes in it than I have to. Maybe it's temporary and futile; maybe the bubble's going to collapse anyway, one day. Maybe we'll all become nothing more than parts of the same EM spectrum we're living off of, energy reduced to its lowest thermodynamic denominator, constantly preyed upon, consumed without ever being destroyed. And in that endlessness will be our end, an ouroboros knot, forever tied and untying—no heaven, no hell. Just the circuit, eternally casting off energy, the sparks that move this awful world.

But not today. Not if I have anything to... *not* say... about it.

This is Harmony6893, signing off.

FISH HOOKS
Kit Power

Sarah was buying a coffee in the train station when she first saw the fish hooks.

She was reaching for her change, mind already on the journey and the meetings that would follow it, when she saw the single trickle of blood running down the man's hand and onto the coins he was holding out to her.

She froze, her own arm extended, fist half opened, and watched as the dark-red fluid rolled over the man's knuckles before beading on his fingertips. Her mind was blank in that moment—devoid of any sense of place, of self. *He's bleeding*, she thought. Just that, as the droplet grew fat and pregnant. Her eyes, moving apparently independently of her brain, tracked up the fingers to the hand holding the money.

There, she saw the two-pronged fish hook.

It was stuck in the back of the man's hand, piercing the flesh either side of a prominent vein. There was no line or wire on the end of it, but the skin around it was taut, as though the hook were pulling the hand towards her, and she saw—with a cool, detached clarity born of profound shock—that the skin between the hook's entrance and exit wounds was puckered and open, causing fresh blood to well up in the holes and stream down the pink skin.

She stared at the hook in the man's hand, thinking nothing

at all. The moment stretched and stretched. She wondered vaguely what would happen when it snapped.

The small eternity ended when the man grunted. The skin puckered more widely, the curve of the hook clearly visible beneath his flesh, as his hand moved closer to hers and his fingers opened.

Blood splashed onto her palm; the coins bounced off her hand and fell from her nerveless fingers, scattering across the floor. It sounded like hailstones on canvas.

"Oh, I'm sorry, miss."

She looked up then—the polite response so ingrained that it operated independently of the sudden roaring blankness in her mind.

It was the man who worked at the drinks counter, who took her order and handed her coffee most mornings. A young guy with a thin goatee, earrings, long black hair in a ponytail, and an easy smile that often reached his eyes.

The hooks were in his face too.

He was frowning with concern as she stared at him. The two hooks in his eyebrows pulled them down, causing the skin beneath to wrinkle. The blood ran from the holes down either side of his nose like red tears. There were hooks in his cheeks too, pulling his mouth down in dismay, leaving running red lines to his chin.

As he opened his mouth to speak, the hooks in his upper and lower lip tugged his mouth open, dribbling blood over his teeth.

The paralysis broke then, and her fist clenched over the coins left in her hand as she turned and ran from the station.

She had a moment of peace outside. The autumn sun was dazzling enough that she couldn't see clearly. She shut her eyes against the glare, not caring at the crowd jostling around her, past her, into the station. She felt like an island in the middle of a busy stream, and in the moment she embraced her stillness, relishing the feeling.

Then she opened her eyes.

The hooks were everywhere.

She was looking down at the pavement, at the parade of legs in smart trousers and business skirts. The hooks were in thighs, in shins—red blotches on tights, crimson and clotted, like obscene poppies. Everywhere the hooks pulled flesh, stretched skin, dragging people into motion. Glancing up, panic rising, she saw more: a woman's hand tugged to her face, brushing the hair from her eyes, droplets of blood falling onto her white blouse; a young man, ear buds in, the hooks pulling his eyebrows hard enough to almost tear, blood streaming down his face.

She saw more, and more, her mind a series of impressions of spiked bent metal and open wounds, and always the pulling, the stretching, and the pounding of her heart became a piston beat in her ears, and her mind filled with one thought, one impulse, to be *away*, and she started to sprint, fleeing blindly across the road, past a blare of horns and a screech of tyres, and up the street.

Eventually the pain in her chest got too much, and Sarah stopped running. She slowed to a walk, and then all but fell onto a bench. Her heart was punching a hard, heavy rhythm, and her lungs burned with each ragged breath. She gingerly stretched her legs out, wincing at the pain the movement caused in her thighs and calves.

She closed her eyes briefly, intending to focus on her breathing, to count, but when she did the image of fish hooks in skin came into her mind. She quickly pulled them open again.

She took in the park around her. The spring sunlight played through the leaves of the tree whose branches overhung the bench, dappling her skin with spots of light and shade. A cool breeze set those spots dancing over her and the tarmac of the footpath in front of her. Further away, the path sloped down through the middle of the grass, towards the edge of the park. She could just make out the shape of the archway above the train station entrance, and suddenly the cool breeze made her shudder violently. Her jaw began to judder, her teeth clattering together, goosebumps rippling under her cardigan. She let the shakes come, hugging herself and tilting her face up, looking through the branches and leaves into the lush blue sky.

Time passed. The shakes tapered off gradually, resolving into a tremble in her hands. She closed them into fists, gently, looking at the unmarked skin, wondering. Watching the trembles stutter and finally stop. She closed her eyes, and this time there was only blessed darkness. She took a deep breath, slowly pulling in air from her diaphragm, feeling her lungs swell. Held it. Exhaled.

Then she opened her eyes. Turned her fists over.

"Okay, here we go."

Unaware that she'd spoken out loud, she opened her left fist.

In the centre of her palm was a dark, almost black stain, tapering to a smear of red. Blood, from the coins.

"Okay, well… okay," she said.

Then she started to cry.

She walked home. All six miles. There was a bus that went straight to her door, but the thought repelled her. She briefly considered phoning a cab, but couldn't face the idea of being in an enclosed space, especially if the driver…

So she walked, head down, eyes fixed on her feet, following

the path through the park, back to the streets. There were other people, but she refused to look up, knowing what she would see. Even then, just looking at the ground, she knew. The dark splotches on the pavement were everywhere, some baked black in the warm light, others fresh red.

She passed several people. She didn't look up once.

She let herself into her house, shut the door behind her, and slid down it, curling into a ball. She held her head and stared at the bristles on the door mat.

Sometime later the phone rang, and she gingerly rose to her feet, wincing anew as her leg muscles protested. She let the phone ring—work probably, wondering where the hell she'd got to—and went into the kitchen to make a cup of tea. She took it to the living room and sat on the sofa, sipping it and wondering what to do next.

When she got to the bottom of the cup, she still didn't have any answers. So she went into the spare room, made the bed up, and climbed into it.

The knocking woke her.

"Love?"

Tim's voice was muffled by the door, but even so she could hear the note of concern. By common consent the spare room was reserved for when one or the other was ill, or had got in too late and was courting a hangover. They had learned early on that unbroken sleep was a must have for both of them, and acted accordingly. They'd barely had a disagreement since introducing the policy.

"Don't come in!" An image sprung to her mind—of Tim's face, pierced by thin metal hooks, pulling his features into what she sometimes laughingly called his "concerned face", the wounds bleeding... she thought if she saw that she might not come back to herself.

"Okay, love. What's wrong?"

She felt a laugh threatening to bubble up in her throat, and she clenched her jaw hard until the feeling subsided.

"Not sure. Some kind of… bug. Came on very sudden. At the station."

"So you didn't make it in?"

"Nah, had to come home."

"God, I'm sorry. You throwing up?"

"No, I'm… no."

"Okay. Well, can I get you anything?"

"No, love, I just really need to rest up, okay?"

"Sure, no problem. I love you. Text me if you need anything."

She smiled at that, briefly.

"I will. Love you."

She heard him take a step, pause, then head back downstairs. Shortly after, the sound of the television came through the floorboards, loud, then muted to a mumble.

Sarah dug out her phone. At some point, either on the walk home or after she'd had her tea, she'd set it on silent. The conversation with Tim made her think of it. Six missed calls, over a dozen texts; all from work. Shit.

She replied to the last text from her boss, not bothering to read the message.

Sorry. Really unwell. Running a fever, totally out of it. Unlikely to be in for the rest of the week. She hit send. It was after 7 pm, but the reply came back within a minute. *Get well soon. If you're going to be off more than 4 days, you'll need a doctor's note.*

Sarah lobbed the phone to the end of the bed with an almost silent snarl, then pulled the duvet around her. Snuggling into the warmth and comfort, she slipped into an uneasy, restless sleep.

That had been Monday. Now it was Friday, and nothing had changed.

Sarah had quickly fallen into a new routine. It consisted of feigning sleep until Tim left in the morning, then shuffling down to the living room to eat and drink tea. On the first morning, she'd tried watching the television, only to turn it off in horror after a few seconds, the mutilated faces and hands of the breakfast TV hosts and the blood-soaked sofas repelling her.

The cartoon channels seemed safer initially, but after the first advert featuring a young girl with blood-soaked hooks in her cheeks came on, the TV stayed off.

Instead, she read. Not the magazines she'd previously devoured—the bleeding faces of the smiling models on the covers turned her stomach—but books. They became an escape, a window back into a world she'd known, lived in, understood.

Whatever was going on was still going on. Even with her isolation and media avoidance, the clues were all over the house—literally. Every morning there were fresh drops of blood in the sink, on the bathroom floor, the kettle. She could track Tim's movements by the red dots on the floor and smears on surfaces, like some grisly dance-step diagram. Each day, after getting up, she spent the best part of an hour cleaning the surfaces and floors, trying not to think about what she was doing and why.

Managing Tim through the door was increasingly hard. She'd claimed fever for forty-eight hours, until he started sounding scared, threatening to call an ambulance. Wednesday night, he'd begged to be let in to see her, wept when she'd denied him access. It had been a horrible scene, but she'd promised him that she loved him and that she needed the space and that she wasn't seriously hurt, just ill, and eventually he'd left her alone. She texted him more after that, to let him know she still cared—and, most importantly, to keep him away from her.

On Thursday morning her door handle was caked with

dried blood, his palm print stark on the white plastic, and she'd done some weeping of her own.

And now it was Friday. And she had to leave the house.

She'd arranged the doctor's appointment the previous day, having promised Tim she'd do so. She had to, anyway. Work would need a sick note, or they'd stop her pay—she'd seen it happen before, it was the kind of thing the firm was really strict on. Of course, she wasn't running the fever she'd been feigning for the last week. But: "There *is* something wrong with me," she said ruefully to the empty house.

She spent most of the cab ride to the surgery with her eyes closed behind her dark glasses, trying to shut out her brief glimpse of the driver's wounded face and hands, attempting instead to rehearse what she was going to say to the doctor. She'd been working on the problem since she'd made the appointment yesterday morning. It would have to be mental health, obviously; there simply weren't any physical symptoms. That worried her. Officially the firm was as supportive around mental health issues as other illnesses, but in practice she suspected *that* kind of sick note—especially one with the dread word "stress" anywhere near it—would probably put a damper on any further career progression.

The sound of her own laugh surprised her, her underused vocal cords producing a noise somewhere between a cough and a bark. Her concerns about retaining her job, when she could not bring herself to leave the house without battling waves of panic, seemed pitiful, bleakly comic.

The realisation hit her then, in the back of the cab, the conclusion she'd avoided all week as she devoured paperback after paperback and slept too long and wiped drops of blood from door handles, sinks and floors, absorbed in her new normal.

There was no going back to work.

She tried to picture it, tried to imagine the office, her colleagues; faces torn, bleeding, the thin sharp metal pulling, twisting…

Her sob did not sound much different to her laugh.

She let the cabbie keep the change from the tenner—anything to avoid more bloody coins in her hand. There was a self-service check-in system at the waiting room (good), but it was a touchscreen (bad). She used a paper napkin she'd found in her coat pocket to wipe the surface before using it, but even so, a thin film of rusty brown coated the screen and stuck to her fingertips. She went straight to the bathroom after signing herself in to wash her hands, but there was blood, dried and fresh, on the taps, in the sink basin, and all over the door handles.

She rinsed her hands, pulling her sleeve over her fingers to operate the sink, and again to pull the door open to leave. Back in the foyer, she glanced through the glass into the waiting room proper.

It was a charnel house. There were maybe fifteen people in there, mostly old, but a few her age, and a couple of young mothers with toddlers. The blood was everywhere—on the chairs, soaking into the clothes. It darkened the carpeted floor, the blackened trail of footprints reminding her of dirty melting snow. She felt a strange sensation in her head, behind her eyes, as though the world she was seeing was flattening, becoming distant. It was disorientating, but not entirely unpleasant. The distance allowed her to watch without flinching as the hooks tugged, flexed, moving a hand over a mouth here, crossing a leg there. She wondered if this glassy bubble she was in would hold, allow her to rejoin the world somehow, live with this new reality. She suspected not. It felt both insubstantial and brittle.

Still, for now, she watched. And because she watched, she finally saw the toddler. It was a boy, to judge by the haircut and clothing, and it was playing near another child, moving coloured wooden squares from one end of a wire path to another. The other child was older, and Sarah could see the hooks in the back of its hands as it ran a toy car back and forth across the floor.

But the first child, the one playing with the blocks, had no hooks at all.

She stared at the child, without thought, mesmerised by its undamaged skin.

"Sarah Meld to Room Seven, Room Seven for Sarah Meld, thank you."

Sarah blinked, attempted to swallow, but produced only a dry click. The announcement from inside the waiting room had been muffled but clear enough. She pulled open the door (the habit of using the sleeve of her coat to cover her hand already almost instinctive) and stalked through the room and into the corridor that held the doctors' offices.

The corridor was in some ways the worst part so far; the harshness of the overhead strip lights gave the bloody tracks on the linoleum a garish glare, especially where the darker puddles had been smeared by a dragged foot. She walked as close to the wall as she could, carefully placing each footstep as clear of the blood as possible, like a child solemnly avoiding the cracks in the pavement.

The door to Room Seven stood open.

The doctor was in profile as Sarah entered, but even a quick glance showed the redness and telltale flashes of metal in his face and hands. Blood pattered on the keyboard and corner desk as he typed into his computer. She got an impression of blue eyes under bushy salt-and-pepper brows and a bald head, wrinkles and laugh lines, a long clean-shaven jawline.

"Sarah, is it? Come and take a seat." His Welsh accent was soft, his voice smooth and kind. The chair he indicated was against the wall next to his desk. She would be facing his direction, but not directly opposite him. She sat hesitantly, making sure her long coat covered the bloodstains on the seat. More blood was pooled at her feet, so she stared straight ahead, at the wall above the examination couch in the corner. She hoped the sunglasses would hide the fact that she wasn't looking at him.

"So, I understand you've been poorly—running a temperature, headaches, that kind of thing. Can you tell me how you're feeling now?"

She was relieved to find the rehearsed words came to her lips easily enough, as she stared at the wall.

"I wasn't honest with my work about what's been wrong with me."

"I see."

The silence sat, punctuated by a slow, quiet dripping. She quickly started talking, raising her voice slightly to smother the sound. "I've been feeling afraid. Afraid to leave the house. To talk to anyone."

"Can you remember when you first started feeling like this?"

"Monday."

"Did anything happen on Monday that made you feel this way?"

She felt her voice catch in her throat, the prepared lines momentarily refusing to come. "It... I... no. I was just..." The hooked, bleeding hand holding her money flashed into her mind, and she swallowed. "...I was just getting coffee. At the station."

He shifted in his seat, and through her peripheral vision she could see he was now looking straight at her. She continued to stare at the wall.

"At the station?"

"Train station. I was on my way to work."

"I see. And has the feeling been constant, or does it come and go?"

"Constant. I mean, if I read it's not so bad. But even watching telly, I can't… I get scared." She'd thought about it carefully. Stay close to the truth. As close as she could without sounding crazy.

The doctor leaned forward, and all of a sudden the dripping became a steady patter, and she looked before she could help herself. The hooks in his face were making the skin bulge out, in his brows, his cheeks. The blood was running down his face in a small stream, almost flowing off his chin onto the floor.

Her jaw clenched against a sob. Trying to look away, but unable to, her eyes darted from wound to wound.

"Sarah, I have to…" The smaller hooks pulled and twisted his lips, and as his mouth opened there was a flash of silver behind his teeth, tugging at his tongue, and the shock of it was powerful enough that she lost most of what he'd said, the words senseless syllables which fell around her, empty noise.

"…glasses off, please?"

Numbly, trembling, she folded the glasses and placed them in her lap, keeping her eyes on them. She couldn't look back into that kindly, ruined face. She could not.

"Sarah, are you feeling scared now?"

"Yes. Yes, very."

"Is it… Would you prefer to see a woman doctor?"

"No. It wouldn't make any difference."

"Okay, Sarah."

He went on with the questions. How well was she sleeping, on a scale of one to five? How anxious was she? Was work especially stressful? How were her relationships? Had she ever had anxiety or depression before? She answered them all carefully, quietly, staring at her sunglasses and trying to ignore the dripping sounds.

At length the doctor sighed, and his chair creaked as he moved away from his desk, closer to her.

"Sarah, I can tell this is making you feel very uncomfortable, and I'm sorry about that. Can you tell me why you think it is that you've suddenly started feeling like this, this past week? What is it about being around other people that makes you anxious?"

Drip. Drip. Drip.

"…hooks."

She couldn't help it. The sound put the image in her head. Sharp, thin hooks piercing skin. It was all she could see.

She heard him shift in his chair.

"Hooks?"

Drip, drip, drip.

"Sarah…"

Drip.

"Nothing you tell me in here has to go any further if…"

Drip.

"…you want it to. It's called…"

Drip.

"…confidentiality. You really can tell me…"

Drip.

"I see hooks. Fish hooks. In people's skin." The words came out in a monotone. She stared at her glasses, willing her mouth to stop, but it didn't. "In hands. Legs. Faces. I see them pulling. Every time someone moves, I see a hook in them pulling them, making them move. Everyone. Even the people on the TV. I see blood everywhere. I can't stop seeing it. It's horrible. I can't stand to look at anyone, be around anyone." She took another breath, to say more, and then realised there was nothing more to say, and let it out in a long, shaky sigh.

"I see." The doctor spoke gently, kindly. Sarah could feel herself trembling, but the sensation was distant, indifferent. Dislocated. "Is that why you won't look at me? You can see hooks in me?"

"Yes, in…" She thought of the child in the waiting room,

then dismissed the image. "...everyone."

"But not in yourself."

It wasn't a question. She felt a hollowness in her stomach. "No, I... no."

"Well, that must be horrible. I hope I don't sound patronising, but I think you're very brave to tell me about this. You must have been petrified, this last week."

She nodded, as the hollowness in her stomach spread to her legs and chest, bringing a numbness that was chilling, yet also vaguely comforting.

"Luckily..." He opened a drawer in his desk, and took out a small plastic container. "...we've got just the ticket here. We'll have you right as rain in no time."

She watched his bloody hand open the box and saw the set of silvery hooks twinkling on a bed of cotton wool. She felt the numbness creep into her mind, filling up behind her eyes. Her scalp prickled.

"It'll only take a few minutes, and then it'll all be over. I promise." The doctor took her right hand, and she felt it move, something attached but distant. The warmth of his touch felt insubstantial. A single tear welled up in her eye. She blinked and barely felt it roll down her cheek.

"Just a small pinch..." He slid the hook into the back of her hand. There was a momentary tug, the welling of blood, and then the hook and wound both vanished.

The doctor held up his own right hand, and she saw his hook had vanished too.

His ruined face wrenched into a smile. "See?"

She nodded.

"Ready for the next one?"

She gave no reply, only offered her right hand and turned her head away.

The pinch of the second hook was even fainter than the first.

EMERGENCE
Tim Lebbon

Sometimes it's turning left or right that changes your life. Sometimes it's staring straight ahead, not paying attention to what's around you in case it's dangerous, or unpleasant, or something you wouldn't want to go to sleep that night remembering. On occasion closing your eyes and just standing still will alter everything, because as the world parts and flows around you, you cannot help but feel its tides.

Sometimes, it's recognising that a place you once thought of as normal really, really isn't.

That was why I went closer to the tunnel. I'm naturally curious, and hidden places fascinate me as much as paths that lead away from the beaten track. I like to explore. I don't know why it was that particular day and hour, but something about it drew me when I passed. It could be that I glimpsed the skull from the corner of my eye. Maybe it was the smell.

I'd climbed this steep path and run back down it thirty or forty times. It was a favourite run of mine, starting with a solid, unrelenting thousand-foot climb from the small car park to the top of the mountain, then a good trail run around the summit until I descended back down to the car. I'd cover seven or eight miles and spend two hours on my own, just me and the wild and the breeze, the views and the sheep, the sense that I was alone in a wilderness only barely touched by humankind. It was glorious.

Halfway down the heavily wooded lower portion of the slope, I skidded to a stop and stood staring at the tunnel mouth. I was panting, sweating, and I couldn't quite explain the draw it had over me. I'd glanced at it a dozen times before but never gone closer than this. It was little more than an arch of rough brickwork, partly broken away by years of plant growth and frost damage, half-buried by leaf falls and tumbled tree branches, and enclosing a half-moon of deep darkness that seemed to lead nowhere. I'd often wondered why it was there and who had built it. I assumed it was the remains of an old drainage culvert constructed by some farmer or landowner long ago. The hillsides were scattered with such remnants, evidence of past labours that seemed to serve little or no purpose. It was something else that attracted me to places like this.

I climbed the small bank and moved closer. The darkness inside didn't feel intimidating, I wasn't afraid, but it was deep and heavy, like a weight luring me down. In the shadow of the brick overhang was a skull, picked clean by birds and insects. It sat on a carpet of old leaves and twigs. Scattered around were smaller bones, the shattered remains of whatever creature had come there to die. A sheep, probably. I'd seen them before, corpses taken apart amongst the heathers and ferns of the wild hillsides. The skull was smallish, and there were scraps of wool snagged on brambles and rolled into dirty clumps. A lamb, then. I wondered what had killed the poor creature.

I edged closer and saw more of the tunnel mouth. It was strange seeing such skilled brickwork in this wild place, and I tried to imagine the people who had worked there. It must have been an effort lugging bricks and mortar up the steep slope, and the purposes of the tunnel still eluded me. It was set deep into a steep bank, trees growing above it. I could see heavy roots dangling down inside, and dislodged bricks littered the ground.

The entrance was half-buried by years of leaf falls, much of it turned to mulch and providing home to ferns and on one side a bramble bush.

I dug into the hip pocket of my rucksack and pulled out my head torch. The batteries were new, but I paused just for a second before turning it on, wondering how long it had been since the tunnel's interior had been touched by light.

I looked down at the skull close to my left knee. "So what were you doing here?" I asked. For a second afterwards, the silence was loaded. I laughed and turned on the torch.

It revealed no surprises inside. The curved ceiling sloped down, as did the floor, the tunnel burrowing gently beneath the bank. There were more fallen bricks, plants, dead leaves, a few pieces of lonely litter either dropped there by snacking hikers or blown by the wind. I played the light around, crouching in an effort to see further. I already knew I was going to venture inside.

When I was a kid, two friends and I found the remains of an old air-raid shelter close to some allotments, left over from when a row of houses had been demolished. We'd all got cuts and bruises from going down there, and Gavin had ended up in hospital having a gashed thigh sewn up. But we'd all come out with something too. I still had the old gas mask I'd found in its cloth bag, tucked away in the attic at home where plenty of old memories withered and faded.

Faded until something like this brought them crashing back again.

I remembered Jimmy's taunting when the three of us were egging each other on, all afraid, all trying to be brave enough to go first. Gavin had been the brash one, but his fear of the dark had made itself apparent. We'd gone exploring down there three times before Gavin slashed his leg open on a ragged shard of metal protruding from the old brick wall. They were good times. I hadn't seen either of them in over fifteen years.

"Not worth it," I said, glancing down at the sheep's skull one more time. It grinned up at me. Maybe I'd seen this creature alive on an earlier run that year. A memory of me might once have resided within its now-empty cranium.

I put the head torch around my head to free up both hands, then slipped feet-first into the low tunnel.

Enveloped by the tunnel's darkness, everything felt very different. The smells of the hillside changed, becoming wet and dank, the scent of old things and decay. As I made my way down the gentle slope, my boots dislodged clumps of mud and rocks, and the rich fug of darkness rose around me. The cool, wet ground soaked through my long-sleeved T-shirt, and my shorts were soon heavy with mud.

I shone the torch all around, moving slowly, checking the tunnel structure above and around me, and the floor ahead. I probed with my boot, digging at the ground in case any holes had been covered over with detritus. Fall in, break a bone, shatter my torch, and over time my bones would join those of the dead sheep guarding the entrance.

Soon the tunnel levelled and the ceiling grew a little higher. The floor was comprised of damp, hard silt rather than leaves and loose soil, and I guessed the leaves would not have been blown in this deep.

I turned and crawled on head first. It would have been easy to lose track of time down there. I checked my watch and realised it was still ticking along recording my run, although it had lost satellite reception so the GPS would no longer be working. I paused it and switched it back to showing the time. 11:18. I'd been in the tunnel for maybe five minutes.

It felt longer.

I should turn around and go back, I thought. *There's nothing down here. It's just an old drainage tunnel or something. Goes nowhere. I should go back.*

But I didn't go back, because that old curiosity drew me on. Though there was still a vague light behind me from the entrance, my main source of illumination was now the head torch, and I played it around as I continued to crawl. The walls were wet and slick with moss, the ceiling broken here and there where tree roots had grown through. I had to push some of them aside and they trailed cool fingers across my skin.

The tunnel seemed to be growing wider and deeper. I crawled on all fours, careful where I placed my hands, watching every move. Glancing left and right, I saw hollows in the vaulted walls that might once have led elsewhere, but each one was blocked from a cave-in, bricks and soil forming solid barriers.

This tunnel will cave in one day, I thought. I was moving deeper on trust, hoping that my being there didn't cause a fault, a tumble, a roar of old frost-shattered bricks, soil and rock thumping down from above to trap me there forever. Jayne knew where I'd gone, but there was no phone or GPS reception this deep. If a search party did come looking and eventually found me, it would likely be way too late.

The danger was something like a thrill.

Next time I glanced at my watch, twenty minutes had passed. I paused at that, staring at the illuminated digital time blinking back at me. It hadn't felt like more than a couple of minutes, but I couldn't doubt what I saw. I'd reached a place in the tunnel where the walls were slick and wet, the floor increasingly boggy, and the roots protruding through the joints between bricks in the ceiling were pale and fine, hanging still like an upside-down forest. Some of them snapped as I brushed by, as if dead and petrified. Others caressed the back of my head and neck.

"Time to turn around," I whispered. My words carried,

and as I glanced ahead—imagining my voice winging its way deeper, into a darkness that might not have heard a human voice since this place was built—I saw the faint glow of daylight.

Excitement took me once again. The idea of seeing where this tunnel ended gripped me, and I felt like a true explorer. Maybe I'd emerge wet and muddied, and surprise someone looking into the far entrance and wondering where it went.

I scrambled onwards, and this lowest part of the tunnel was also the wettest. I slopped through mud, shaking my hands and spattering it up the walls. It was thick and black, and it smelled of forgotten places and age. I hurried on towards the glow, and soon the ground sloped up enough for me to see daylight.

Minutes later I approached the opposite end of the tunnel. I could see that it was somewhere still within the woods, and for a moment I was disappointed. I'd imagined emerging into an old tumbled building, or perhaps on to part of the barren hillside where I had never been. In truth, it was probably only a hundred feet from where I'd gone underground.

As the daylight grew stronger, so I anticipated its touch even more. I had no wish to go back into that gloom. There was nothing down there to concern me, but something about the darkness I was leaving behind started to repulse me, urging me onwards into the light.

Close to the entrance I saw the pale gleam of a skull.

I frowned. I was convinced that I'd crawled into the tunnel at one end and out the other. I moved closer, and as the sun touched my skin I realised that it was the same lamb's skull.

Weird.

The sun felt good, dappling down through the tree canopy to speckle my arms and face. I stood and stretched, shaking mud from my hands, brushing it from my knees and bare legs, hearing the slosh of water in my backpack's water bladder. I hadn't taken a single drink while I'd been underground, and now thirst burnt in with a vengeance across my throat and tongue.

I sucked at the nozzle. The water was warm but welcome. I blinked and sighed, then looked up.

The sky past the trees was a blazing blue, scorched by sunlight. Wispy clouds streaked the heavens high above. Closer, the trees swayed in a gentle breeze, leaning back and forth as if whispering to one another about me. I looked up as they looked down.

I shivered. It was an unsettling thought.

Dropping back onto the path leading down through the woods to the road, I pushed through a spread of nettles. They kissed against my bare legs and fire tingled there, spiky, almost pleasant in its low burn. I didn't recall the nettles being there a couple of hours before when I'd climbed towards the summit. Their leaves were speckled with some sort of fungus, making them hang heavy and low. I crouched down to look. Maybe being underground in the dark had made me so much more receptive to detail.

The fungus was pale grey in colour, each growth the thickness of a matchstick and just a few millimetres long, topped with a darker, globular speck. There were perhaps a hundred stems on each leaf, all of them curved and pointed in the same direction like miniature soldiers stood to attention. Although the nettles were still a rich, healthy green, I couldn't help thinking that the fungal growths were parasitic.

Energised by my unexpected mini-adventure, I scanned the ground ahead as I started running downhill, dodging rocks, leaping down some of the steps that had been built into the path by local scouts a few years before. I always enjoyed running downhill, even though I was heading towards fifty and becoming more concerned about my knees. I needed to look after my joints if I was going to continue doing what I loved into my old age. But every time I thought that, I countered with, *But this* is *looking after myself.*

Something about my visit down into the tunnel niggled at me, like a whisper behind a door I couldn't quite make out. It worried and scratched, and as I glanced around I felt unsettled in this, one of my favourite places, for the very first time.

The path followed a wide gulley carved into the mountainside over millennia by a stream. There were a few small waterfalls along its course, and now I noticed that the pool at the base of one was dammed with several fallen trees and debris accumulated against their trunks and branches. It formed an expanded lake where water gathered before slinking its way past or through the blockage. I briefly considered stripping off and taking a dip. The water looked cool and inviting.

It also looked dangerous.

I paused and frowned, catching my breath and trying to open the door on those niggles and whispers. Being below ground had unsettled me more than I'd believed, and I'd brought that feeling up with me, carrying it down towards the road, car park, and the car where a fresh change of clothes and a flask of coffee awaited.

I haven't seen this pool before, I thought. I had no recollection of the falls being dammed like this, but then I always climbed the hill with my head down, checking the uneven path for trip hazards, pushing down on my knees so that I could achieve the best climb possible. My record so far was a little under half an hour. Maybe today I'd have broken it.

I glanced at my watch. It was still searching for a satellite signal.

Passing the pool I carried on, and it was only as I approached the bottom of the winding path that I acknowledged what was worrying me. The door opened and the truth roared in.

Everything was different. Only slightly, but there was a rough edge to things, like a sheen of wilderness smothering my surroundings.

The trees above me were heavier with leaves. A few had fallen, with several lying across the path and forcing me to squeeze underneath or climb over them. They had not been there before my ascent, and I could tell from one of their exposed root balls—the hole filled with a swathe of nettles, no bare soil showing, and the cracked timber pale from weathering—that it had not happened recently.

The path emerged onto a gravelled area beside the canal, the wide driveway and parking area attached to a low wooden house. There was a narrow tunnel leading beneath the canal and down to the car park beyond, but this side was a private residence, the public footpath running across the gravel to the tunnel. I'd seen the elderly owners of the house several times, and they always spared a wave or nod for those passing across their land to or from the steep path up the mountain.

The gravel was churned, and in places overgrown with weeds. The house looked abandoned, with smashed windows and paint flaking from its previously pristine woodwork. A Range Rover rested on flat tyres beside the house, its windows misted with a hazing layer of moss on the insides.

"What the hell?"

I stopped and looked around. Birds flitted from branch to branch, a few of them landing in the long grass of the canal's towpath on the opposite bank. The towpath was overgrown. I could just make out a bike leaning against a wall. Plant tendrils had curled around its spokes and uprights.

"Hello?" I called. Some birds took flight at my shout, but they quickly landed again and started singing as if I wasn't there. I frowned and shook my head. Maybe I was dehydrated. I took a drink and suddenly the taste of my water had changed, from warm but clean to stale and dirty, as if I was sucking up water from the canal.

This was all wrong. There was so much I hadn't noticed on the way up the mountain, so much that I'd been certain of but which now was being proved less certain. When had the old couple moved out of their home and left it to decay? Why leave their vehicle behind?

I took a few steps towards the tunnel beneath the canal, and paused.

It had caved in. The steps down to it were piled with tumbled stones, and the tunnel itself was filled with dried mud and rocks, blocking it completely. If I hadn't known it was there, it would not have been at all obvious.

"That's just not right," I said. "I came up through there two hours ago. Just a couple of hours." I checked my watch. It was still searching for a satellite signal. *Not right.* "Hello?" I shouted louder, the sound of my voice the only thing pinning me to the world. Birds took flight again, but I didn't seem to trouble them unduly. If I remained silent, if I did not interact with the world, I might as well not be there at all.

The canal bridge was fenced off, meant for exclusive use by the owners of the dilapidated house and enclosed within their garden and land. The tunnel was the public access, but now that it was blocked there was no other way across the canal. I skirted around the garden, pushing through waist-high undergrowth until I passed the garden area and stood close to the canal.

The water level was vastly reduced. *That's what's happened*, I thought. *Maybe there's been a breach and everything has changed.* But a breach in the canal wouldn't have changed so much in such a short time.

And this damage had been wrought a long, long time ago. There were still pools of water across the canal bed, but most of it had gone, perhaps flowing downhill from the fracture that had filled the tunnel. The pools remaining looked surprisingly clear, reflecting the blue sky and fluffy clouds as if presenting a memory of better times. Weeds grew across the rest of the canal's uneven, dried-silt bed.

I climbed down, walked across, and scrambled out onto the towpath. It was deep with knee-high weeds.

It was impossible, yet the evidence was there before my eyes. *Everything has changed.*

I made my way to the steps that led down to where the tunnel emerged on the other side, at the top of the gentle slope that descended to the car park where I'd left my car. I needed to be there. I had to reach the comfortable Mazda, to see whether it was new and clean from the polish I'd given it last weekend, or old and rusting, wheels flat, windows grimy, metalwork fading from so long sitting unused and exposed to the harsh sunlight.

While I'd been down in the tunnel the world, and time, had moved on. All I could hear was the chatter of birds and the conspiratorial whispering of the trees as they observed my growing panic, laughing amongst themselves.

I climbed down the steps and saw that much of the landscape on this side of the canal had changed. The breach must have caused the cave-in, and tens of thousands of gallons of water had cascaded down the slope, carrying silt and rocks with it and washing away the gravelled road, hedges, and many tonnes of soil. The resulting slick had spread wide, and in the time since the breach had provided fertile ground for new plant growth. I ran through the low shrubs and long grasses, hearing creatures scurrying from my path, kicking my way from the canal and down what was left of the path to the car park. I heard no traffic. I smelled no fumes, and I realised just how clear and clean the air seemed, untainted by humankind.

I'm still underground, I thought. *I fell and banged my head. I'm semi-conscious in that tunnel, and unless I wake and move I'll be there until dusk, and then I might never find my way out.*

The grasses felt cool and sharp against my bare legs. Seeds carried on the air tickled my face. Sweat ran down my back. Everything looked lush and rich, as if the plants were relishing this new-found freedom. And yet many plants were also home to that strange fungus I'd seen on the nettles back up the slope. It provided a haze across everything that seemed to knock my vision out of focus.

If I was still beneath the ground, my imagination was running riot.

I reached the road and ran straight across. The buildings to my right were familiar, but I barely glanced at them. I knew what I would see.

I knew because I could see my car. It might have been there forever.

I ran the three miles home. It was the strangest journey of my life, but running gave me the rhythm, pace and room to try and rationalise what was happening. It didn't work, but just as concentrating on my breathing and footfalls helped occupy my mind, the attempt to make sense of what I was seeing, hearing and smelling diluted some of the terror that was settling over me.

I'd tried starting the car, of course, but the battery was flat. It was strange sticking the clean, shiny key into a vehicle so obviously degraded by time.

I was worried about Jayne. If everyone and everything had gone, then what about her? Where was she? *On the other side of the tunnel*, I thought, but I tried to silence that idea.

I lived three miles from the bottom of the hill. Usually I would have run that distance in a little under half an hour, but today I was faster. Everything I saw gave me energy, fear driving my legs and muscles.

Strange, faded red circles decorated the doors of at least half the homes, hints at something terrible. And although the town was empty of people, it was far from dead. By the Indian restaurant where we had celebrated our tenth anniversary I saw a small herd of deer, milling in the overgrown car park, wary as they watched me pass. A pack of half a dozen feral dogs stalked from an alley a few minutes later, and the hairs on the back of my neck bristled as they growled. I threw stones at them and they stalked away. Squirrels sat on rooftops and window ledges, rabbits frolicked across roads where weeds grew through cracked tarmac, and what might have been a big cat flowed through the shadows beneath a bridge. Nature had made this place of people its own now that the people were gone.

If I wasn't so terrified, so confused and frightened, it might have been beautiful.

Just past an old car showroom, now displaying a score of vehicles resting on flat tyres and with rust eating at bodywork, I drew level with the local park. It had once contained a playing field, a bandstand and a play area for children, but now all that was gone. Close to the park gates and fence were three JCBs, motionless and dead. Beyond them, the park had been excavated in several long, wide strips. Some of these massive trenches were partly filled in, but most remained open to view. One was filled with rough timber coffins, piled in without any real care, like a tumble of giant Jenga blocks. The next trench along was filled with skeletons. They had run out of time to box up the dead.

I stopped and leaned against the cast-iron fence at the park's boundary. I felt a deep, cool shock settling in me, a sickness of the soul as similar images from history sprung to mind. But these were no murder pits. Piled beside one trench were hundreds of simple wooden crosses, unplanted. I wondered if each of them bore a name, and my eyes were drawn back to the countless skeletons settled in the open excavation, staring at the sky with hollow eyes as they waited forever to be hidden away from this cruel, dead world.

I tore myself away from the dreadful sight and moved on. I saw no other mass burials, but the memory remained with me, an awful visual echo to everything else I witnessed.

When I reached my house there were no surprises to be found. It was the same as everywhere else. My home, the place where I lived and loved and felt safe, had fallen into ruin.

Seeing a place I knew so well in such a state was shattering, hitting home much harder than anything else I had seen. The house name Jayne and I had screwed to the front wall together was broken in two, half of it fallen away. She'd cut her thumb while we were fixing the plaque to the brickwork, and I'd put it in my mouth to ease her pain. The garish red paintwork she had chosen for the front door was faded, much of it peeled away to the bare wood beneath. The hawthorn tree we had planted in the front garden, and which had become so much work to keep under control, had grown wild, its spiked branches reaching forward for the street and back towards the house as if to embrace the place for itself. I remembered clipping those branches one by one, while Jayne snipped them small enough to feed carefully into the garden-waste bags. We'd both suffered pricks and wounds that day. She'd laughed at my pin-cushion hand that evening, and I'd rolled her onto the sofa and silenced her with a kiss.

I sobbed, standing in the street and staring at the place I had once called home.

I'd only left three hours earlier.

"Somebody!" I shouted. "Jayne! Anybody!" My cries echoed from buildings close by, but were soon swallowed by the wild trees and shrubs along our street. I reckoned that within another ten years much of this place would resemble an infant forest. Twenty years after that, new trees would be higher than the house roofs. And a century later, the houses would be little more than piles of rubble subsumed by undergrowth, hugged to the land's embrace by brambly limbs.

I shouted again, the only reply my despairing and muffled cry echoing back at me. I took a step towards the house. It was desolate, silent and dead, and I dreaded what I might find inside. Nothing would be bad. The bones of my wife would be so much worse.

And then, as I pushed past the rotten front fence and the clasping plants that held it upright, movement. A shadow shifted in one of my home's upper windows. Sunlight glinted from fractured glass. A pale face appeared at the window, still too far inside to make out properly, but definitely there.

Jayne, I thought, and took a step forward.

But it was not Jayne.

The face that appeared at the window was wild, heavy with beard and framed with long, straggly hair, thin and sunburned, eyes staring and mad. I felt a moment of rage at the man who had made my house his own.

Then I realised that this was the only person I had seen since leaving the tunnel, and my rage became confused. Tears came to my eyes, and I felt a pang of deep loneliness. I wanted to rush in and hug this man, speak to him, and hopefully understand that this strange situation was not merely my own personal madness. I wished it was.

"Hello!" I called. I took another step forward into the front garden, edging around the clasping thorns of the hawthorn. "What happened here? I went for a run and when I came back—"

He lifted an object and pointed it at me. I heard a low *twang*, and something sliced across my right bicep.

Shock rooted me to the spot as the man fumbled with the object and raised it again. I fell to the left just as another arrow whispered by, bouncing off the road behind me. Then I stood and ran.

Another arrow struck my bare left thigh, and I felt the piercing cool kiss of the tip slicing into my skin. I yelped and reached back, but the arrow had fallen away. Its head had merely cut my flesh, and when I brought my hand up it was smeared with blood. The pain was keen and sharp, the wound superficial. It didn't seem to have affected my ability to move.

I did not stop running. I could not. I had to run as fast as I could, back across that strange town I had once known and over the drained canal, up the hillside, into the tunnel where everything had changed. There was no discernible thought process leading to this action, no consideration. It was the only thing to do, and it felt like the only way I might find my way back to normality.

From the house I had once lived in came a dreadful, guttural roar, a scream of such hopelessness that my blood ran cold and every hair on my body stood on end. I sprinted back the way I had come, fearing another arrow. The buildings around me now loomed, and every dark window or open doorway might have been the source of another deadly shot. But no more came, and it seemed that the person in my old house might have been the only one. I glanced back when I felt it safe, and for a second—just as I checked the ground ahead before twisting around to look behind me—I knew that he would be there with me, a ragged, wild shape so close behind that I could smell his breath, feel his body heat as he ran after me in complete, monstrous silence.

I was alone. I reached the bottom of the hill and retraced my steps, crossing the drained canal, climbing, arriving at last at the tunnel mouth beneath the steep bank. Panting hard, sweating, I hesitated only for a second before ducking inside. I glanced at the skull as I did so, suddenly certain that it would not be a sheep's skull at all, but a human's. Buried there at the tunnel entrance, it was one of the few things about my world that had not changed.

I moved much faster than I had the first time. The tunnel seemed smaller, the floor higher. My head torch lit the way and I ducked to avoid banging my skull on the low ceiling.

He's behind me, I thought, crawling, hands clawed, so quiet that my own gasps and scramblings covered his sound. I looked back but I was alone.

Every shadow was danger. Only the small splash of light ahead offered any hope of freedom and salvation, but the sinking conviction came that I would emerge into that desolate landscape once again.

The first time I'd come in here I had somehow turned around, exiting the way I had entered even though I had continued through the tunnel towards daylight at the other end. I had no wish to do that again. Reaching into my backpack's hip pocket I pulled out the small penknife I always carried with me. Jayne had given it to me for my eighteenth birthday, our first year together.

I opened the blade and crawled to the tunnel wall, ready to carve in a simple arrow to show me the direction I was taking. When I aimed my head torch at the old brickwork, at first I thought it was laced with a network of thin white strands, roots from one of the trees growing above. Then I saw the arrows.

There must have been fifty of them, maybe more, carved into the brickwork and all pointing in the same direction. A few of them were recent, their edges sharp and clear. Others appeared older, with moss dulling their clarity. Some were faded almost to nothing.

I stopped, gasping as I tried to catch my breath. *Not my arrows*, I thought, because they could not have been. I'd only been inside this tunnel once before and I hadn't taken out my penknife.

I carved in a new arrow nonetheless, finding a bare spread of pitted brick and leaving my mark. I tried not to touch any of the others as I worked. Touching might link me to them, draw me in and make me part of the experience that had etched them there. All I wanted now was to find my way home.

It was like waking from a bad dream.

When I emerged from the tunnel at the same location where I'd entered—even though I *knew* I had not turned around down there—I could sense that everything had changed once again. Birds were singing a more familiar song. The light was softer and less threatening. Trees no longer whispered in the breeze. The skull close to the tunnel entrance was more exposed, and when I ran downhill and approached the canal, the old man who lived in the house there gave me a gruff nod.

I drove home faster than I should have, to find a jug of coffee on the warmer and Jayne in the shower. I stripped and got into the shower with her, and she reached for me as I started to cry, shivering uncontrollably even though she turned up the heat and hugged me to her, confused at my reaction and almost crying herself. I welcomed her touch and smell. I never wanted to let go.

By the time we went to one of our favourite riverside pubs for lunch, the things I had seen and experienced were starting to feel like a dream. The memories were woolly, although they did not fade. I drove so that Jayne could drink, but the real reason was that I did not want to muddy my thoughts and allow back in the fears and confusion.

Later, with Jayne snoring softly in bed beside me, moonlight passed through the curtains and cast uneasy patterns across the ceiling, shapes in which I perceived uncertain truths. But they were only shapes in my imagination, it was only moonlight, and I eased into a comfortable sleep listening to my wife's breathing and feeling the weight of night as a comfort rather than a threat.

Upon waking, the previous day's events had faded even more into that place where bad dreams inevitably dissolve.

Two days later I started climbing the hill to fill in the tunnel. Jayne knew that something had changed within me on that early morning run, and she did her best to draw it out and help me move on. But she also acknowledged my need to return on my own. The first time, I sat twenty feet from the tunnel and just stared, tempting the darkness to reveal to me what had happened. *Something in there*, I thought, and I imagined old discarded canisters of degraded gas, natural fumes from an unknown cavern system, tainted water dripping from the tunnel ceiling and entering my mouth. Something had taken me and edged me towards a terrifying madness, holding me over the edge of a deep and awful ravine. Only my determination had prevented me from falling.

That first day I kicked the sheep's skull into the tunnel and piled a few rocks into the entrance, sweating and panting with the effort. When a family climbing up for a walk on the mountain gave me a strange look, I paused in my efforts and smiled at them. I offered no explanation. There was none that made any sense.

From then on I returned in the early mornings, telling Jayne I was going for a run up and around my familiar route. I halted every time at the tunnel, and after five days I'd piled in enough scattered rocks and fallen bricks to clog the entrance. On day six I used a heavy block to loosen more bricks, encouraging heavy falls of damp dirt from the banking above the tunnel, pushing it into hollows to bind and seal, testing the new barrier by standing and jumping on it.

Still it was not enough. At night the bad dreams lurked, and sometimes they came fully fledged, pursuing me like that mad, raving shape from my own ruined house as I thrashed and groaned myself awake and submitted to Jayne's concerned hugs. She suggested I see someone. I agreed. I never kept the appointments, instead climbing the slope with bags of sand and cement in my rucksack. When there were enough I mixed the concrete, and probed it deep between rocks and bricks, filling hollows and smearing it across the filled-in tunnel entrance until I could see no holes at all leading inside.

Once dried, I covered the rough structure with mud and leaves and fallen branches. I planted several fast-growing shrubs around the area. By the time winter came, all evidence of the tunnel entrance was gone. Some people might have remembered it being there, but soon they would forget.

Sometimes I had nightmares about being buried alive, following a thousand arrows to an entrance that no longer existed. Often I believed that my waking life was the dream, and the tunnel was my dark, damp reality.

Jayne became tired of my nightmares. She found out that I had never gone to any appointments with the doctor or therapist. She left, accusing me of not doing anything to help myself.

In truth, I'd done everything I possibly could.

I've become one of *those* people. You know the type. People talk about me behind my back, sometimes in pity, more often with humour. Part of me wishes it was all back to the way it was before, but another part of me knows that I'm doing the right thing. This isn't madness. I left madness down there in the tunnel, scratched on the wall and shut away with tons of stones and bricks, soil and cement. This is the exact opposite of madness. This is clarity. This is being prepared.

People have started to die. I'd been expecting it, and I've always been certain of who would go first—the closest person to me, though that closeness has changed. At least Jayne welcomed me to her bedside as she was ailing, and when I told her I loved her she smiled and said she loved me too. That means an awful lot and such knowledge will, I hope, give me courage in the times to come.

Times of plague and death, confusion and chaos. Times of silence. Times of decay.

I still go running every day, sometimes covering upwards of twenty miles. I pass by the hidden tunnel mouth occasionally, but I have no worries about anyone emerging from there. It's solidly plugged. Besides, there are countless other places. Manholes and culverts, drains and caverns, riverbank hollows and old, forgotten tunnels under churches and castles, car parks and hotels.

I'm collecting as many weapons as I can find. I target houses where people have died, and it's easy because the authorities have started painting these places with red circles. So far I have seven bows, three crossbows and two shotguns. Hardly a stockpile, but it will only be one man, and it will only take one shot.

I brought something back with me through that tunnel. A disease that is making this world its own, and which does not touch me. Thinking about why that is will send me mad, because I've heard no evidence of anyone else being immune. I'm cursed with a terrible purpose. I saw evidence of the contagion on the plants over there, the strange fungal-like growths, and perhaps I should have thought more of it when I found the empty town, the dilapidation, the mass graves. But I'm not in the business of regret.

Today, the traumatised authorities started digging a huge trench in the local park.

One day soon, when the world is dead and I'm one of the last left alive—perhaps the only one left—he will emerge from somewhere else and come to pay me a visit. He'll know where to come because home is an important place. It's somewhere you're meant to feel safe. Once here, there's no way I can let him return and take the infection back to where he came from. It's a heavy responsibility, but one which I know I was destined to shoulder.

I have no idea what shooting myself will feel like.

This time I will not miss.

ON CUTLER STREET
Benjamin Percy

This isn't a neighbourhood where bad things happen. You can tell just by looking at it. The 1920s bungalows have been lovingly refurbished. Flowered pots hang from porches. The gardens are freshly mulched. Lush, knuckly oak trees reach their branches across the street and create a sun-dappled archway. A sprinkler hisses. An American flag ripples with the warm breeze. A boy with a soccer ball chases around his yard, dodging imaginary opponents, and a girl on a bike with pink streamers pumps her little legs and calls out, "Pumpkin? Pumpkin, where are you?"

Her name is Sadie and Pumpkin is her cat. That's how she thinks of the cat anyway—as *hers*—even though her parents haven't officially said yes. Yet. The cat showed up yesterday, pawing at the screen door with a plaintive meow. The cat didn't wear a collar, but it was clean and purred when scratched behind the ears, and Sadie begged, "Please, please, please, can we keep her?" This is the kind of neighbourhood, after all, where everybody has a pet—dogs and cats and turtles and even one African grey parrot—everybody except Sadie. So it was only fair.

When her parents put out a saucer of milk and a plate of tuna, the cat would only sniff it. "She must not be hungry," Sadie said, scooping up the cat so that it dangled pendulously from her arms. "Or maybe my kitty only eats mouse lasagne."

She played with the cat the rest of the day, kneading her fingers into the orange fur of its belly, rolling a tennis ball across the living room for it to pounce on. When it was time for bed, she begged to sleep with Pumpkin, and though her parents tried to refuse her, saying the cat wasn't a stuffed animal, Sadie kept up her argument.

"What if she has a disease?" her parents said, and Sadie said, "Then I already have it."

"What if the cat is dangerous," her parents said, and Sadie rolled the cat around and flopped its tail and squished the fur around its face and said, "See? She's perfectly friendly. She loves me."

It is easy to believe in love on Cutler Street. Whatever war or crime or monstrousness afflicts the rest of the world, you are safe from it here. You can leave your doors unlocked and your windows open. You keep the weeds picked and you keep an eye out for each other.

The Petersons sometimes grill out with the Jacobsons. And the Whites sometimes have the Lordans over for cocktails. And the Bergmeyers don't really like the Stotts, but their children are friends, so they tolerate each other. During the winters, everyone strings coloured lights from their gutters and keeps their sidewalks shovelled and salted—and during the summers, everyone washes their cars in their driveways and fertilizes their lawns, mowing the grass into tidy stripes.

Even now, a mower growls, the only sound. Herb Adams is pushing it. He wears a white undershirt and gym shorts and flip-flops, his feet stained green from the clippings. Something catches his eye and he looks toward the end of the street.

An orange tabby cat scurries along, and then pauses in the road, looking back the way it came.

Something is there. Something is coming.

The lawn is only half finished, but Herb releases the handle and the mower engine powers off. "What in the name of—"

That is when the gunshot cracks. Herb startles back and nearly trips over the mower, burning his calf against the exhaust. A chunk of asphalt dislodges from the street, and the cat leaps and goes running again.

Herb holds out his arms and says, "No, no, no," and rushes toward the source of the gunfire, toward the heavy old woman in the floral-patterned nightie with the pink bathrobe flapping around her. One foot wears a slipper; the other foot is bare. No makeup. No dentures. Her hair sleep-mussed, white filaments floating behind her. She is the picture of vulnerability. Except for the rifle she carries.

This is Mrs Flanders. Over the past few years most of the neighbourhood has turned over to younger families, but she and her husband have been living here since the sixties. Now she is trying, with some difficulty, to eject the casing of the round fired and load another bullet.

She manages to blast off another shot—once again missing, the cat now dodging off into a hedgerow.

And then Herb intercepts her, wrestling the rifle away. She barely seems to recognize he is there. She is determined to kill the cat, continuing her pursuit of it. And when Herb holds her back, she lets out a desperate, keening wail.

A sound that ten minutes later warps into the noise of an ambulance. The vehicle comes to a jerking stop outside a small blue house with a hydrangea bush skirting the porch.

The front door is open. Like a gaping shadowed mouth. Mrs Flanders's other bedroom slipper lies on the stoop, abandoned there.

When the EMTs hump into the house, hefting their equipment, they move uncertainly through the shadowed interior. Past a living room with a box TV and an afghan thrown over a La-Z-Boy recliner. Past a hallway staggered with family photos in wooden frames. To the bedroom.

In the doorway they pause. They don't say anything. Because they don't need to. The siren—wailing, wailing—speaks for them.

They don't notice the crocheted pillows and beige drapes and porcelain figurines. Their eyes are on the bed. Here lies an old man, Mr Flanders. His body has been rent and bent in so many unnatural angles that he seems like a puzzle pulled apart and fitted together incorrectly. One of his legs has been hurled against the wall, leaving behind a sunburst of blood.

Everyone on Cutler Street is standing on their flowered porches or on the swept sidewalks or on their deep-green lawns, holding up their hands to shade their eyes from the sun, calling out to each other, "Do you know what's going on?" Their faces wrinkle in confusion. This sort of thing isn't supposed to happen here.

Everyone except for Sadie. She has finally found her kitty, her stray, her little Pumpkin. The cat lounges in a sunbeam in the living room, flicking her tail and purring, and Sadie curls up beside her and licks her thumb and cleans off a stain of blood on her muzzle and says, "Did you find a mouse? I bet there are lots of mices here. I bet you'll like it here. Yes, you will. You're the best thing that ever happened to this boring old neighbourhood."

LETTERS FROM ELODIE
Laura Mauro

I went home with Sean the night Elodie died. I remember glancing in her direction as we turned to leave; she was dancing barefoot in the incoming tide, and the pebbles were bright with moonlight, her legs glistening. The beautiful Swedish boys were singing and clapping a rhythm and she danced for them. Her smile was luminous. I'd never liked men but I went home with Sean anyway, because I was angry, and because I was lonely, and because he'd slept with Elodie a few times before and by my bitter, drunken logic it was the closest I would ever come to being with her.

I remember the way she moved, loose-limbed, keeping time not to the rhythm of their clapping but to the beat in her head; Elodie had always been out of sync with the rest of the world. There was laughter on her lips as they sang to her, bliss in her half-closed eyes. The Swedish boys were tall, white-gold, like angels. She caught my eye as I turned to leave, paused a moment—arms held high above her head as though in rapturous sky worship—and her mouth formed two silent words: *Bye, Ruth.*

The next morning, I woke alone, and she was dead.

I met Elodie on New Year's Eve, at the house party of an

artist friend whose opulent basement flat looked out onto Palmeira Square. Elodie sat alone in the courtyard garden as the clock struck midnight, chain-smoking rollups. She had blunt-bobbed hair, like a silent movie star; she wore a dove-grey silk dress, her legs bare, face pink with cold. I thought she was ridiculous. I thought she was beautiful. I brought her a flute of champagne and offered her my coat and she smiled. We shared rollups stained scarlet with the imprint of her lipstick and when morning came—red sun rising sluggish over the rooftops—I walked her home just to be with her for a little longer. We walked slowly along the seafront, her shoes dangling from her fingers, the sharp salt air scouring my smoke-heavy lungs clean. She knew all the homeless people by name, and wished them all a happy New Year. "I've been homeless more than once," she told me, though she'd known me only a few hours. She used to say that if no one person could claim to know her better than the rest of the world, then nobody could ever own her.

She always was full of shit.

Her flat was a top-floor conversion on a shabby street near Hove station, the kind of place artists and loners lived; the kind of place people died alone, surrounded by empty vodka bottles and the black-scorched bowls of misused spoons. She didn't ask me in for coffee, and I didn't ask for her number. I thought I'd never see her again. I hoped that I would.

The next time I saw her she was a face in the crowd, dancing to the beat of a local indie band while I worked the bar. The band were regulars, and their fan base was small and loyal. I was sure I'd never seen her there before, but she knew all the words, whooped for joy when they announced her favourite song. She was breathless when she came to me at last, black hair plastered to her face with sweat. She smiled, greeted me with warmth, and even though her voice was half-swallowed by the din my name had never sounded sweeter in anyone else's mouth.

She was one of the stragglers who stayed behind as the band packed up. It seemed that everyone knew her, that I had been stumbling around Brighton all these years oblivious to her influence. She sipped black rum through a straw and told me about herself. She was so bright, so effervescent that I felt shabby in comparison, embarrassed by the mundanity of my life. She frequently broke off mid-conversation to introduce me to her friends. Everyone was Elodie's friend. She invited people into her life with such ease and yet, for those few hours, bathed in the spotlight of her attention, it seemed that I was the most important person in her world.

Elodie talked about herself like her entire life was a story in the midst of unfolding, and it ought to have sounded terribly pretentious but she was magnetic: she'd hitchhiked solo across Australia, lived on a boat in Amsterdam with a trio of sex workers who barely spoke English. She'd taken acid on a beach in Greece and seen the face of God in the water. She delivered this last anecdote with such sincerity that the incredulous laughter never made it past my lips. Her dark cat-eyes were trained intently on mine as though she could share her experience telepathically. As though she could show me God.

"What did He look like?" I asked, half-joking.

She smelled like cigarettes and sweat and rum. Her lips were silk against my ear.

"Everything," she whispered.

They found Elodie's body washed up on the beach. The Swedish boys had been the last people to see her alive. They'd parted ways with her at two in the morning. She'd seemed happy, they said. They had alibis, all of them. The only thing they'd done wrong was to leave her alone that night, but stupidity wasn't a criminal offence. They could have saved her. They would carry that mistake with them for the rest of their lives.

Her pockets had been full of stones, the police said. She'd walked out into the water, under the pier, where nobody would see her in the dark. There had been no drugs in her blood, no alcohol. No signs of a struggle. The pieces came together: Elodie had walked into the sea, and Elodie had drowned.

I didn't believe any of it.

Her parents must have come to collect her body, though there was no word of a funeral. Elodie spoke about her parents sometimes, but they seemed distant, and faintly sketched, as though they were purely hypothetical. She'd said they'd disapproved of her decision to stay in Brighton, where—they had opined—*we* would drag her down. *We*, the "druggies and dropouts and perverts", who gathered on the beach six nights after her death to celebrate her short, vibrant life, who shed tears at the cruelty of it all; *we*, her legion of friends and acquaintances and ex-lovers, who built a bonfire and told stories of her: how special she had been, how rare and bright a jewel. It was bullshit. A grotesque pantomime in which Elodie, even in death, was the star. It was exactly what she would have wanted.

"It doesn't feel like she's gone," Sean said, as we hunched side by side next to the dying fire and shared a cigarette. I trusted Sean as I trusted few other men; he and I operated under the unspoken agreement that what happened between us on the night of Elodie's death was a one-off, and I knew his sudden appearance was not by virtue of scouting for exploitable weakness. "Sometimes I wonder if she was ever really there. You know? Like she was a dream we all had. She never felt *real*."

I turned to Sean. He hadn't shaved since Elodie's death. His eyes were cow-large and sad. I chewed the inside of my cheek until the taste of iron flooded across my tongue.

"She was, though," I said. Of all the lies I might have told, it was a lesser transgression. I could sense by the loosening of his shoulders that he was grateful for it. He lit another cigarette, and said nothing more.

I walked away from the fire, away from everyone else, bitter-mouthed and nauseous with stories of her. I stared out at the sea that had stolen her from me, and I pictured her: water spilling from between bruise-dark lips, eyes wide and sightless; skin blue-marbled, hair wet and glossy against her face like black blood. Exquisite dead girl, long-limbed and balletic on her mortuary slab. My beautiful narcissist. I'd known her more intimately than any of her lovers. I knew that she would never have chosen to die so quietly, so secretly, her pockets full of stones. I wondered why she'd put them there. Why she'd walked out into the water that night and let herself drown.

She rejected me gently, the way I imagine she'd rejected countless others. She explained that I met every single one of her criteria. I was as perfect a partner as she might hope for except for one very significant thing.

"I'm not gay," she said, apologetic, as though what I kept between my legs was the sole obstacle to a great and profound love affair. I did not know what her criteria were. In all the time I loved her, I could never pare down her extensive list of partners to a common set of characteristics. The only hard and fast rule, it seemed, was that a cunt was a deal-breaker.

I burned with shame. I should have read her better. She was unselfconscious; she held herself with the easy confidence of one who has never learned to be ashamed, who has never had to repress and hide away. She was dressed as David Bowie that night. Another party, another performance. Bare skin beneath her jumpsuit. A beautiful boy under black light, a handsome girl in the glow of the streetlamps. And in the dark, a black-eyed angel; a long-limbed, perfect creature for whom binary notions of sex seemed quaint and inadequate. Strange, that someone so straight should wear queer so well.

"But I hope we can still be friends," she added, and the smile in her eyes was so sweet; the promise in there of some nebulous closeness that I knew in my heart would amount to Elodie's emotional table scraps, but I was so hungry, so desperate. She kissed me on the cheek, wound an arm around my shoulders. "You're very special to me, Ruth," she murmured, though we had barely known one another six months. Her warm, soft body felt like heaven. I greedily drank up her affection and despised myself for every last drop.

I walked along the beach towards the bright lights and noisy chaos of the Palace Pier, where life had not stopped for Elodie. Against the gathering dark the pier shone gold, a gaudy ersatz sun. She'd always hated that pier, though she herself had only lived in Brighton for a few years, scarcely enough time to consider herself rooted. She hated the noise of it, the quaint seaside tackiness—bingo halls and funfairs and sticks of rock, a monument to an era which, she contended, ought to have died out with the new millennium. She used to say that Brighton was for artists and outcasts, and it didn't seem to matter to her that she was neither of those things because she was so good at pretending to be; so good that even when she was dead, people talked about the "free spirit" she had been, as though there'd been any truth in it at all.

She played the part well. She would commit to no one, to nothing. Plan would supersede hazy, unrealised plan as though they had only ever been suggestions: *I'll move to New Zealand. I'll learn sign language. I'll open up my own bar.* She flitted between jobs, subsisted off borrowed money, which she solemnly promised she would pay back someday. It was an adventure, she used to say, to never know, to be at the mercy of the future. Nobody else could make meandering through near-poverty sound quite so romantic.

Cold water engulfed my shoes, a sudden shock. I'd wandered off towards the incoming tide. Above me, the pier stretched out, consuming the sky. The sea lapped at my ankles. Alone in that empty, liminal space, waves hissing like blood in my ears, I heard a voice calling out from the darkness.

She'd leave me voicemails. She knew I had an aversion to talking on the phone, even to her. She knew I would switch my phone to "silent" overnight because I valued my sleep far more than I valued human interaction. Elodie was a forest fire, burning through men, consuming hearts and leaving them in ashes, but it was never about love, or sex. She was Narcissus, and she beheld her own reflection in the eyes of her lovers.

I called them her "letters", as though it were an intimate correspondence, something we had both consented to. I told her I threw them away, "unread". She smiled at the metaphor, at my compliance, and we never spoke of it again. She knew I was lying, but that was okay. I was so good at keeping her secrets.

More often than not, she'd be drunk when she called. The persona she had so carefully put together would lie tattered, her crisp accent slurred; all the things she hated, all the people who had disappointed her. All the lies she had told. With each letter I pieced her together until she was no longer a patchwork of wild stories and daydreams and wispy, far-off ambitions but something else entirely. Something sadder, smaller. Threadbare at the edges and bitter at the core. Still vibrant; she could be no other way.

I'd lie alone in the dark at 3 am listening to her messages over and over, revelling in her vulnerability. I'd run her entrails gently through my fingers, press my tongue against her raw, exposed skin. I'd savour the anger and loneliness in her voice, feel a warm thrill in my heart at every barely suppressed sob. She disgusted me. I adored her. She would not love me, but she gave herself to me all the same. I held the truth of her in the palm of my hand. At any moment I might have exposed her, shown all her acolytes what they were really worshipping. She gave me the means to destroy her and trusted that I would never do it. That's all love is, when you strip it down to the bare bones. A loaded gun to the temple with someone else's finger on the trigger.

The salt stung my nostrils, the rich smell of wet decay. Thick moss grew where the struts met the water, damp and glossy. The space beneath the pier stretched out before me like a long, lightless corridor, framed on either side by deepening dusk. She was out there, beneath the water. I heard her whispering in the dark, though she couldn't have been; her lungs had been reservoirs, her mouth filled with sand. And yet it was her voice, her cadence. I'd listened to her messages enough times that I remembered entire monologues by heart, could quote her the way other people quoted beloved films.

I pulled my phone out of my pocket and laid it on the shingle. Peeled off my shoes and placed them beside it. The pebbles were cold, wet with brine. She'd filled her pockets with stones. Walked out into the water. She'd died alone. She'd died without telling me.

The sea swallowed my ankles, tugging at the hems of my jeans. I walked into the incoming tide, and though the sharp chill gnawed at my skin, my bones, I felt the rhythm of her words like a pulse. Like sonar, rising to meet me as I turned to face the empty beach, sinking back into the sea. Cold water rushed to embrace me. I let it take my weight, cradling my skull, gentle as a lover. Filling my mouth and ears so that I might taste her, so that I might hear her. Her words carried on the current as clear and as eerie as whale song. Her voice in the water. Elodie's last letter.

Eight days before she died Elodie and I went to a club, because a band she loved was playing, and because she didn't want to go alone. I stood at the bar and watched her dance, though I hated the music: lo-fi indie bullshit, guitars scrawling out derivative riffs, narcoleptic vocals. I watched her pick her victim. He was tall and pretty, like they always were: long blond hair, a sick-skinny boy in tight jeans and pristine white T-shirt. She smiled like a sunrise, radiant. She leaned up and whispered in his ear, pressing her body *just so* against his so that there could be no ambiguity, but her coy smile was a play to his ego. She liked to let them believe they were in control.

I downed vodka tonics until the dancers began to blend into one another, an amorphous mass of arms and blissed-out faces moving ceaselessly. I drank until I couldn't see Elodie anymore and so it didn't matter when she disappeared, inevitably, her prize in tow. Always his place; nobody was allowed inside her flat, not even in the name of conquest. I drank until I could barely string a thought together so I wouldn't picture them, so that the images (skin against skin, limbs sinuous, his eyes pale and glassy and her face, there, in the black of his pupils) would be lost in a sea of drunken non sequiturs. So that they couldn't hurt me.

When the lights came up, I staggered out into the cold blue dawn, and the streets were full of us: the dishevelled and the desolate, grey-faced, haunting the seafront. Avoiding one another's empty gazes as we navigated the slow crash of the comedown.

(I saw her flat for the first time a few days after she died. I asked the landlord for the spare keys. I stood in the doorway holding an empty suitcase, watching dust motes dance in the sunlight. There was a mattress on the floor, a holdall with clothes in. Nothing else. No signs of a life. As though she had only ever been visiting.)

There was a message from her when I woke up. The sun was high and bright, like a pickaxe to the skull. I crawled to the bathroom, pressed my face against the cool tiles. I lay there until the rotten-tooth throb of my head began to subside. I felt empty. Her voice echoed in the small space, omnipresent.

"I suppose I could keep doing this forever," she said, her voice quiet, and I knew he must be there, somewhere, just out of earshot; asleep, perhaps, blissfully unaware that she would be gone before he woke, and that he would never have her again. "What's that poem, you know... the one where she eats men like air? It's so easy, Ruth. They make it so easy. The world will never run dry of gullible men."

The slow drip of the toilet cistern, like water torture. *Press "2" to repeat. Press "3" to delete.*

"I suppose I could keep doing this forever," she said.
Press "2" to repeat.

"It kills them when they realise they can't have me," she said. "Only it's not really *me* they want. That's the thing. They want the *idea* of me, the one they've built in their heads. I give them so little to work with, and when they fill in the blanks the Elodie they come up with never looks like me. It's only you, Ruth. You're the only one who knows me at all."
Press "2" to repeat.

"It's only you, Ruth."

Slack face pressed against cold tiles. Mouthing her words like an incantation.

Press "2" to repeat.

"It's only you."

"It just felt right," she said. "It felt like it was time. Like a voice, somewhere inside. Calling me back. I had a good run this time, I think."

I drew air into disembodied lungs, breathing on blind faith. I was numb meat. I might not have existed at all but for the dull fire of my fingertips, my toes, cold-bitten and burning as I kicked feebly against the current, struggling to stay afloat.

Her voice cut through the cold blood-rush of the water, an arrow to the brain: "It tires you out, always having to pretend. And of all the places I've been, of all the people I've met, you were the only one who ever got it right. You were the only one who thought to look inside."

Hands light on my shoulders. Skin so cold the breath caught in my lungs. Above me, moonlight seared through the gaps in the pier, stark as bleached ribs. I'd looked inside of her and seen nothing at all but bones couched in black rot; her magpie soul, pieced together out of the fragments she stole from other people, other lives, like a ransom note assembled from newsprint. I could have destroyed her, if I'd wanted to. I could have ruined her. I could have.

"Remember when I told you I'd seen the face of God?"

Arms around me, firm. A lover's embrace. Drifting together out into that dark, quiet space, away from the shore. Numb feet free-floating in the cold, black water. Gently, she lifted my head.

"Nobody believed me but you. Nobody knows me like you do, Ruth. Nobody loves me like you do."

I remembered Sean on the beach, staring fretfully at the blood-red embers. *She never felt real,* he'd said, and he'd been right. Elodie wasn't real. She was better than real. She was an act nobody could follow. How could you love a flesh-and-blood human after being exposed to such a perfect cipher?

Her teeth against my skin, anaesthetised with cold as she tore away the flesh, swallowed without chewing. Her tongue was so warm, lapping catlike at my blood. I had dreamed of this, of her tongue and her mouth and her hands, fingers sliding between my teeth. I bit down, tasted the bitter salt of her the way she had tasted me.

Perhaps, when she returned—decades later, somewhere far from here, wearing someone else's face, someone else's name—there would still be something of me inside of her. A fragment lodged deep in that black, empty cavity; woven into the tapestry of her salvage-yard persona, a series of anecdotes here, a personality quirk there. Perhaps she might even remember me.

"It's only you, Ruth." Skin shearing as her mouth opened wide, hot and cavernous, the wet tear of muscle fibre, of flesh; like birth in reverse, the silk of her pulsing throat hot against my skull. The exquisite agony of teeth splintering bone. Down into the black water, where she was lithe and strong, legs tight around my ribcage, squeezing out the last tightly held breath. Silvery bubbles rose, broke on the surface. Her lips eclipsed me.

It's only you.

Her mouth, like a black hole. Like the end of everything.

STEEL BODIES
Ray Cluley

With a subtle turn of the outboard, Abesh steered them towards a narrow gap between the two nearest vessels. Before they slipped into the dark channel, Samir cast another glance along the coast, taking in all of the tankers and container ships beached there. Some of the vessels were still very much intact, and if they did not look as good as new they at least looked functional. Others were merely skeletal outlines of steel, stripped down to holds empty of all but shadows. Or so they seemed.

The ship Abesh was taking him to was in a state of only partial decay. Several attempts had been made to take it apart, but work was now far behind schedule. It usually took three to six months to break a ship, but the *Karen May* had been sitting in the mud for nearly a year.

They passed massive propeller blades that sat only half submerged, huge fans of rusty red-brown metal hanging mud-crusted over seawater they had once twisted into currents, churned into froth. And then man and boy were past them and between ships, moving through the shadows of giants.

A sudden chill enveloped Samir as they left the sun behind, its warmth and light eclipsed by the ships either side. The metal walls channelled a cool breeze between them as Abesh steered them in and through with the tide, bump-bumping over the small waves that swelled in the reduced straight space of the sea. The shadows here were deep, deep as the cavities exposed in the steel, the metal skins of the ships pockmarked and stripped of material. Enormous superstructures, rising out of the water, they threw a vast darkness that seemed to leak from their hulls, casting them into premature dusk until there, suddenly, from high above, a shower of shooting stars that were gone before they could reach the water. Sparks from an acetylene torch somewhere nearby. Someone was working late.

Abesh muttered something, his Chittagonian fast and clipped with urgency. He put a finger to his lips to hush Samir, though he wasn't the one to have spoken.

"They will tell us it is dangerous," Abesh said, his voice low.

"It is," said Samir.

Abesh cut the engine and they drifted, carried by their momentum. It was the same way Samir had travelled for years now. Momentum. All that had ever happened drove him towards all that was yet to occur.

"Listen," said Abesh.

Samir could hear the waves slapping against the sides of their own small boat and the enormous ships to their left and right. From somewhere hidden within one of them came some deep gurgling, the throaty rumble of an ocean contained, longing to escape. He heard the resounding clank of something heavy, its echo swallowed by other settling noises.

"Can you hear them?"

Abesh was joking, or trying to, but Samir said, "Not yet."

The boy shrugged. "This is it." He pulled their drifting boat closer to the structure beside them. The sea lapped into an exposed corridor or hold, Samir couldn't tell, and a set of steps led deeper into the vessel. "This is a good place," Abesh said as he roped them to the framework.

"That's not what I was told."

Abesh laughed. "Are you scared?"

Samir shook his head. "No," he said, but he was lying.

Samir had come to Chittagong three days ago. More specifically, he had come to a single stretch of coastline where ships came to die. Not so many years ago, it was a part of Bangladesh that would have been dense with mangroves. Now it held more than a hundred ship-breaking yards, the mangroves cleared to make way for the ever-expanding and always-profitable business of destruction.

For Samir's first visit to one of those yards, he'd arrived at low tide and watched as a line of men and boys—too many boys—dragged heavy lengths of cable through the mud towards a row of beached liners. The mud that sucked at their legs and caked their skin was loaded with all sort of toxins—poisoned blood from the beached vessels dying on the mud flats—but all they wore for protection were shorts and T-shirts. It was exhausting even to watch. The cable would be used to heave pieces of ship inland, vast sections of steel excised from vessels that had once known the glory of the open water but now stood mired in mud. They had been tourist attractions once, even in their ruin; there was little else this region had to offer. Now each yard was fenced off. Some were even patrolled, or so Samir had been told, though he had seen no guards. Only signs that promised danger. Signs warning against trespass. Signs forbidding photos. Samir had looked at one of those signs and had taken a picture of it because it would have amused Kamala. She would have admonished him, laughing or shaking her head.

Samir shook his head now, watching the men at work. Danger, said the signs, and yet beyond the fences people worked. The rest of the world had strict health and safety regulations, Samir had no doubt. In Bangladesh, safety precautions ranged from optional to non-existent, and there would always be plenty of men in the local shanty towns desperate enough for the dangerous work that paid so little. If it meant they could feed themselves and their families then they'd face the physical hazards of injury and fatality, risk poisoning from a range of toxic materials Samir could only guess at. Ship-breaking was big business, and almost all of the local men worked in one yard or another. Children, too, like Abesh. They were cheaper. All of the ones Samir spoke to said they were fourteen years old, but most of them were lying; it was the minimum age for ship-breaking work. Children or not, they were no less aware of the dangers and difficulties. They wore the same slack expressions of exhaustion as the men. It was what they had for a uniform, along with their filthy T-shirts and grubby shorts and the mud they wore up their legs and arms. Some already had their own "Chittagong tattoos". That's what they called work-related scars. The shanty towns were filled with men carrying such marks. Many of them were missing fingers. Some were missing entire limbs, or were disfigured in other ways, bent and crippled. More than few carried the clean smooth scars of burnt skin. But still they worked the yards, and the children followed their example. They had little choice.

"Our bodies are made of steel," one of boys had said, flexing his scrawny biceps. "Strong."

One of the other boys had pointed to Samir's face and said, "Tattoo," for the scar that cut a line through his beard. When Samir tried to smile it twisted like a broken snake.

"Tattoo," he agreed. It was work-related, so he supposed it counted.

A foreman of some kind, or someone who wanted to be, came over and yelled at the boys, his Bengali quick to emphasise the hurry. He clapped his hands once, and children who thought they were men rose to their feet to get back to work. They trudged through the mud towards a line of waiting vessels. *Boys against giants*, Samir thought. *Every ship a Goliath waiting to fall.*

"They're very young," Samir said.

The man looked at Samir. "You here to work?" He clearly didn't think so, not the way Samir was dressed.

Samir nodded. "Yes."

The man shook his head. Said, "There is nothing here for you."

The ground reverberated beneath their feet at that moment and thunder roared, shaking the beach. The enormous noise of fallen metal as a huge section of ship collapsed down the shore. Many days of cutting through deck after deck after deck had cleaved a massive section from the main body and it crashed to the ground in a shower of sparks and sharp metal, slapping hard enough into the mud to reshape it. None of the boys walking away were startled by the noise, but Samir had ducked and the foreman had laughed at him. The thunder lingered in Samir's feet and charged his legs with a quickening tingle.

"I'm here to work," he said.

The man sighed his laughter to an end and shook his head again. "Follow me."

A crowd of workers gathered down the beach at the section of fallen hull. The metal plate would be dragged across the mud to a waiting truck, dragged using chains and rollers and the flagging strength of malnourished men and boys. Thousands of pounds of metal moved by skinny people in tattered shorts and sandals. *Sandals.* Some of them even barefoot, risking tetanus at the very least. And there, clinging to the framework of what remained like fiery barnacles, were the cuttermen who sliced the ship into pieces. Samir saw how they leaned for hard to reach places, an assistant paired with each to hold not only the trailing hose of the acetylene torch but also the cutterman's free hand as he suspended himself over a fatal drop.

Samir said a prayer for them, and as he concluded he saw the ship he had come for. It loomed over the other vessels from further down the beach, as if creeping slowly back out to sea. A hulk of steel, rusted red like some scabbed wound. The *Karen May*.

Brine and diesel. The smell of it seemed to cling to Samir's skin even just sitting close to the ship. Abesh stood and leaned to clutch at one of the exposed struts of the *Karen May* and pulled them closer.

Samir tipped away what was left of his water and refilled his bottle from the sea. He fastened the lid tight and tucked it away in his bag as Abesh tied the boat secure.

Samir looked inside the exposed section of ship and saw only shadows and absences where once there was steel and substance. It was disorientating, so many missing walls and floors in this section of the ship, and each missing floor a missing ceiling. Samir leaned to look further in and up. There was a rectangle of sky above where a stairwell used to be. The sky was tinged orange, with hues of pink turning red, a fire suspended above him that shed little of its light into the ship.

"Tell me about your brother again," Samir said as he eased himself into a standing position in the small boat. He'd made a list of those killed in various accidents over the last year in the ship-breaking yard, and of those he'd made a second list that he'd brought with him of those killed or otherwise lost on the *Karen May*. Abesh's brother was on that list.

"Ibrahim?" Abesh asked. He was little more than a dusky shape in the shadows of the ship, a grubby baseball cap and thin limbs and, incongruous with Samir's question, a bright smile. He made the sound of a blast, miming an explosion with his hands. *Bravado*, Samir thought. *As I walk through the valley of the shadow of death, I shall fear no evil*, performed with a simple gesture and sound effect.

Abesh's brother had been a cutterman, slicing up sections of the ship when his torch ignited a gas pocket. He was killed in the explosion. His assistant too. Abesh had seen it happen from the beach, he'd said. Saw them both thrown hard against metal and engulfed in sudden flames. He'd told the story like it was a film he'd seen. Like a story he'd heard from someone else and hadn't been a part of himself. "It's okay," he'd said. "I have lots of brothers."

He was looking into the ship now as if his brother might still be in there.

Perhaps he was.

"How old are you, Abesh?"

"Fourteen," the boy said, and grinned.

Samir climbed from the boat into the remains of the far larger vessel they'd anchored themselves to. "I never had any brothers," he said. "Just a sister. Kamala."

Abesh made a sympathetic noise.

"I lost her when I was just a little older than you claim to be."

Abesh had no additional sympathy for that. Perhaps he thought it was worse to have a sister than to have lost one. The only sound was the boat knocking against the ship and the water lapping.

"We were living in Munshiganj when Aila hit. Do you remember Aila?"

"One of the storms?"

Aila had not been a simple storm. Aila had been a cyclone, killing hundreds, leaving thousands homeless. But Samir agreed.

"Yes, one of the storms."

Abesh shrugged. "I remember lots of storms. They are all the same storm."

All the same storm.

Samir remembered how the water had rushed into their home. How it had filled the rooms and toppled the mud walls. Remembered how his sister had reached for him before the water took her away. He told Abesh some of this, staring into the *Karen May*. What remained of his family had fled to Dhaka, already crowded with those running from other floods. Other storms.

All the same storm.

Samir had often looked for Kamala in those crowds.

"Why are you telling me this?" Abesh asked. He had stopped looking into the ship's shadows and instead looked set to follow Samir.

"Wait here," Samir told him.

Abesh looked disappointed, but he sat down.

"I'm the only one left," Samir told him. "I told you about Kamala so that you can remember her."

He shrugged his bag into a more comfortable position on his shoulder and pulled his way deeper into the *Karen May*.

The foreman had taken Samir to an office made from an old cargo container. It sat on short stilts of recovered scrap but still it sank into the mud at one end. The lean was even more obvious inside thanks to the papers, maps, and notices pinned to the walls.

"Wait here," the man said.

Samir waited.

The paperwork on the walls all concerned the ship-breaking, of course. Each vessel had its own hanging clipboard of papers, and a large map of the beach illustrated where they were located with barely legible script, circled numbers, and shorthand symbols, like some mystical chart. The trappings of a spell that summoned wealth. Samir read some of the details, though he'd already done his research. Ships were bought by an international broker, and a suitable captain—a *good* captain—was hired to beach it properly on the narrow strip of mud-beach like someone else might park a car. Then more people were paid to take the thing apart. A ship had a lifespan of only thirty years or so and then they became too expensive to maintain, too costly to insure. With profits dwindling, each ship became more valuable as scrap, with more than ninety per cent of each vessel recyclable. A lot of the material was resold right away: the liquids, machinery, the easily removed fixtures; it all got sold on to salvage dealers. Engines, wiring. Everything. Samir saw a list detailing all the copper pulled from one of the vessels, and the sum beside it amazed him. The steel would be converted into building materials like rebar, tension devices to reinforce larger constructs. Samir thought of the workers standing in bent shapes or taut with the strain of some heavy task, sticking from the mud; they were like exposed rebar themselves, holding the yards together. Profits in excess of eighty-three million taka, depending on the price of steel, were built upon their strength, and at great cost. He had a list of dead men who knew the truth of that.

He turned from the records when the door behind him opened. A large man stepped into the office. Samir knew already that this would be Mabud Kibria. He barely glanced at Samir, making his way to a heavily loaded desk and rifling through the papers piled there. The foreman who had escorted Samir earlier followed.

"This is the man looking for work."

Judging by the number of clipboards and the red underlines on the map, there would be plenty of work for those who wanted it. India may have dismantled more ships each year, but here in Bangladesh they recycled more deadweight tonnage than anywhere else in the world.

"I'm not *looking* for work," Samir reminded the foreman.

Mabud gave Samir more than a glance this time, clearly annoyed that whatever little time he was going to spare had already been wasted.

"I am here *to* work," Samir told him. "Rokeya Begum sent me."

Samir fumbled for a handrail he'd forgotten was no longer there as he climbed. He would start from the top and work his way down. He had to be careful; the handrail was missing, but so were some of the steps themselves. The portholes had been taken from the walls, and in many places the walls were gone as well. Inside the ship was an absence that expanded. Samir walked within a steady decomposing of steel. There were no railings on the deck either. Samir passed mounts for missing cranes. Saw signs for lifeboats that weren't there.

Out to sea, in the fading light of the setting sun, children were playing in the dieselled waters. They swam around a raft of wreckage, clambering up only to throw their young careless bodies at toxic water and whatever scrap metal might lurk submerged there. Despite what they might have thought, their bodies were not made of steel. Each was susceptible to breakage, all too easily opened up and spilt empty, or filled with fluid instead of breath. Samir had to look away from their play, unable to stop imagining the worst.

Port and starboard, the Bangladeshi beach was an open graveyard. The ships here did not sink, they slumped; rotting, rusting corpses alive only by day with the men who took them apart reducing them to rivetless pieces. But in the dark they looked almost whole again. It was easy to imagine each as it might have once been. Their slow progress across the world's oceans; the sudden climb and plunging fall over waves the size of mountains. Leviathan, each of them, forging paths that disappeared almost immediately behind them as they fell and rose again. These were cruise liners and tankers and container ships from all over the world. Who had sailed them? What had brought them to the ships, and where had each ship taken them? And what else had each ship carried? Here they were now, these amazing constructions, at their journey's end. Waiting to be torn apart, they spilled silent stories into the mud, into the sea, like slicks of oil, each sinking or getting dragged away with every outgoing tide.

In the bridge, every monitor and machine, every button, every wire, had all been taken. Samir stood where the windows used to be, imagining himself the captain looking out at a vast ocean and a sky full of stars. Now windows empty of glass framed a landscape that was all mud and lights coming on in the city inland, or from the fires on the beach where workers kept the evening chill away burning unsalvageable materials in old oil drums. Burning asbestos and worse, probably.

Samir retrieved a small bound bundle of sage from his bag and wedged it into a tight corner of metal. He lit it and wafted the aromatic smoke with his hands as he recited a prayer. He was combining his faith with "smudging", a Native American ritual which cleansed a space of negative energy, and with science; sage cleared the air of bacteria.

He would descend now and wind his way through the corridors until he found the "dark heart" of the ship. It was a suitable metaphor. Much of what Samir did was couched in metaphor. That was how faith worked, and it made the supernatural easier to understand. He had grown up Christian in a Muslim country but he knew all the faiths now. He liked the stories. Stories were useful. Powerful, sometimes.

Inside the ship again, it was difficult to remember the noble majesty he'd imagined from the bridge. What he saw here, in the beam of his torch, was decrepit. There was no engine thrumming life through the body of this giant, and no rhythmic movement of tide around it that he could feel. Yet there was something. Some vibration of life inside, something more than silence. Sounds that rose from its own depths. The sudden clank-spank echo from some unseen place as something fell. The metallic groan of steel grinding on steel, like the drawn-out inhalation of a final breath. From somewhere deep came a steady ticking, like a swinging chain striking a wall in a hidden chamber. And always, everywhere, dripping. Wherever Samir touched, his hand came away wet, red-brown with rust.

Throughout the ship, Samir inhaled the thick smell of the saltwater mud sump it sat in, breathing in the sharp odours of steel and copper and whatever else remained to oxidise. He could smell oil and some pungent chemical that wasn't altogether unpleasant. He fancied he could feel the odours on his skin, and the dark he moved through, too. He rolled his sleeves down against it.

Samir explored. He found a galley stripped of its sinks, seeing only rectangles in the metal where they used to be. He cast the beam of his torch over holes where once there were pipes. He found sockets and vents in a long line—a laundry room, maybe, or somewhere for computers or some other kinds of machines, all of it gone now. Yet for all the absences, the atmosphere was still oppressive. The passages were tight, and stepping through doorways stripped of their hatches seemed to take Samir into closer confines instead of opening up into empty vacant spaces. He was walking a labyrinth of steel that seemed to narrow around him.

He needed some air. What he was breathing was thin, like others had exhaled it countless times before, leaving little for him. It was metallic and sharp like blood. And though what he breathed in seemed thin, the air around him seemed dense. A thickening of atmosphere that pressed against him. He had experienced such contrasts before, such oppressiveness and shortness of breath, but even in Dhaka it had never been as severe as this. He took a small canister from his bag, fixed a plastic piece that would cover his mouth, and pumped a deep fresh breath from it. Another.

Stepping aboard the *Karen May* had been like stepping into the inhalation before a scream. Some had told him the ship was brooding, waiting for someone to come aboard, and he'd felt that. Now he felt like he walked poised on a pendulum at the highest point of its swing, waiting to plummet.

He descended walkways that hadn't felt footsteps for months, maybe a year. The sound each step made was strangely muted, stifled before it could echo fully. Surprised to find a handrail at one section, he had taken it, only for it to come away from the cancerous sheet metal. He dropped it in surprise and it made only the briefest noise in falling. Even with the torch beam cutting a way ahead of him, Samir felt like he barely had any presence of his own. Like his passage through the dark was a temporary unseaming of the shadows he walked through, shadows that sealed up again behind him, and for a moment he couldn't shake the impression of having been swallowed whole. Like Jonah in the body of Leviathan.

The thought brought him comfort. The whale had swallowed Jonah to protect him from a storm.

All the same storm.

As if to mock Samir's train of thought, the ship released a sudden low groan and, on the tail of it came a soft stuttered sound. Like someone sobbing in the dark.

"Peace be with you," Samir called. It came back to him only in part, a repetition of peaces—

Pieces?

—and then a sudden scream. Shrill, and brief, like wrenched metal.

"Samir?"

The voice came quietly.

"I'm here," Samir said. He set his bag down and swept his torch behind, and up, and down. It showed him only narrow passageways like ventricles and walls red with rust, and he thought again of being held inside the body of a beast, only now he thought of the other Jonah, the one sailors thought bad luck. He took another puff of air from the canister and flinched at the hiss of it. Thought he heard it come back to him, closer than it should have been, and sharper. A gasp of sound. He swept the torch behind again and was startled when a shape pulled away from the wall. A body peeled from the gloom, dark but for the wide eyes and the teeth suddenly grinning.

"You frightened me!" said the boy.

"Abesh!"

The boy spoke again before Samir could admonish him fully.

"I want to see my brother."

Samir sighed. "He's not here."

"Then where is he?"

"He's with you."

"But what if he's here as well? Like the others?"

Previously, Abesh had feigned to not believe the stories. He had scoffed at the idea of a haunted wreck and, according to Mabud, was not only unafraid but actually keen to work the ship, though nobody would work it with him. Now, though, it seemed the stories had convinced him, at least partially. Only partially, because still the boy was unafraid.

"Will you help him?"

Samir nodded. "I will help him. Now go. Back to the boat. It's dangerous here."

Abesh did as he was told. Samir only stopped him when he heard a quick rasp and saw the sudden flare of flame that came with a lit match. The boy held it aloft to light his way but dropped it, startled, when Samir yelled at him.

"Dangerous!" he repeated, and handed the boy his torch. He had another.

"You'll help him?" Abesh said again, shining the beam close enough to Samir to see his face. "You promise?"

"I'll do all I can," Samir said.

He watched the child carry the light away until it was gone.

Rokeya Begum had served Samir *choddo shaak* almost as soon as he'd arrived at her house. It was a vast dish, made up of fourteen different vegetables, but he was hungry and thankful for the meal and did not care that this was not the right time to eat it, that this was not *Bhoot Chaturdashi*. She had prepared it thinking of how it might help him, but he ate only to satisfy his hunger. He would welcome the protection, but he had other wards, other charms. Symbols of his faiths, which were all the stronger for being plural.

He had in his bag a selection of photographs he'd taken of the ship after speaking with Mabud Kibria at the breaking yard. He'd zoomed in on the vessel after downloading the pictures to his laptop, and had printed several copies of what he'd found. He retrieved them now, as he ate.

"Please, look at these. I took these this morning. What do you see?"

Even enlarged, the pictures showed little more than the ship. Presented in a state of partial deterioration, it held shadows like blemishes, and looked in places as if the picture had not developed fully. There were many dark spaces. But if you looked long enough…

"Faces," Rokeya said. "I see faces." She pointed. "There. And there. And—there are so many of them."

Samir noted how she would not touch the photograph. Didn't poke them when she pointed, hadn't picked up a single one, just looked at where they lay on the table amongst the dishes of food. "Are they all…?" But she didn't finish her question. She looked at Samir and said again instead, "So many."

"Your son?"

She nodded.

"Where?" He tried to hand her one of the pictures but she recoiled, albeit subtly; she half-stood and leaned across the table to fetch him more water.

"Will you help them?" she said, refilling his glass.

Samir gathered up the photos.

"I'll do all I can."

"Muhammed Goswami said you helped him. In Dhaka?"

Samir touched the scar on his face but turned the gesture into a rub of his beard, remembering. "Yes."

It had been difficult, but yes, he had helped.

"You are Christian?"

"I am."

Less than one percent were in this country, but Samir had been taken in by missionaries after Aila and though they hadn't forced any of their teachings on him, he'd learned from them anyway.

"Christian," she said. "Not Muslim."

"Muslim too."

What did it matter, he felt like asking. God is the ocean, and religions are the ships that carry us.

But of course, it did matter.

He drank some of his water. It tasted salty. "I can help."

Rokeya sighed. She had little choice but to let him try, at least. They always had little choice by the time they were requesting his help.

"I want you to free my son's spirit," Rokeya told him. Samir knew this already; she was only saying it to hear it herself. "Release him from that terrible place."

It was likely that the only ones he would be setting free

were those left behind. Those who grieved and held on so hard that it hurt. Like squeezing a handful of keys. He would ease them of that, at least.

He looked around the room as he closed his bag on the photographs. There were many pictures of her son. He was well-remembered. This was good. It would help him more than the *choddo shaak*.

"Tell me about him."

She nodded again, but said nothing for a long time. "There was an accident..." she managed eventually.

"I know. Tell me about him before then."

She found that much easier.

The Bengali word for ghost is *bhoot* or *bhut*. It is also the word for past. So Samir listened to all of her stories, and he ate all of the vegetables she gave him, and he hoped it would be enough.

Samir had been told once, by a man in Jamalpur, that ghosts could only exist for as long as it took their body to decompose. Samir could understand how such a belief might be born, how it could stand as a metaphor for the grieving process. He could see, too, how it might appeal to those who'd had little time to prepare for a great loss. A transition period in which loved ones could linger but not be trapped, able, still, to pass on to whatever it was that came next. For the brief time he had known Dr Shahid, a missionary he'd met in Dhaka, he had come to recognise a different belief. That the dead remained, in some form or another, for as long as there was someone else to remember them. This was how Christ could still be with us, she'd explained, and Samir had nodded like he was supposed to, and stored the story away with all the others that made up the different faiths he carried with him.

When it came to the *Karen May*, he was more inclined

to believe Dr Shahid's version than what he'd heard in Jamalpur. He thought of Abesh's brother, incinerated in a blast; what had remained to decompose in a case like that? He thought of Nasir, Rokeya's son. He'd fallen through a hatch, plummeting deep into the vessel's hold. Enough water had flooded the wreck that the fall didn't kill him, but he broke so many bones on the way down hitting struts and part-walls that he couldn't keep afloat or swim and the man had drowned before anyone could help him. His body had been recovered. It had been cleaned, shrouded, and buried, as according to Islam. No doubt something of him still remained in his grave, though for many he was already forgotten. Rokeya remembered him for who he had been, Rokeya and Abdul, but Mabud Kibria in the ship-breaking office hadn't even remembered the name, was reminded only when Samir explained how the man had died. That's all he was now. A death. Like all the others. Every dead worker had become the method of their ending: the one who fell, the one who burned, the one who suffocated. The one crushed flat beneath tonnes of freed steel. The one thrown and broken by an unexpected blast. Each of them united in that their work had killed them.

And that this ship had taken them.

The ship wanted him too; Samir could feel it. Not Samir specifically, just someone; it had been so long. Nobody would work the vessel anymore. It was the only reason he had been allowed to even take a look. Often Samir would need to convince people to allow him to complete his work, persuade them with a mix of cajoling or something spiritual if they seemed that way inclined—he knew various faiths well enough to talk about them with authority. This time, though, he had been granted permission with little hesitation or reservation. The men in charge were more interested in profits than prophets and didn't care what had to be done, so long as people would work the ship again. Whether Samir could cleanse the ship or not didn't matter. So long as they had been seen to try, the workers would be less afraid.

Samir found a suitable spot for his purpose and stopped. He estimated he was near the middle of the ship, both regarding its length and his position between decks. Where he stood, the passage branched off in two directions. Taken with a missing wall opposite, he was positioned at an improvised crossroads. Not exactly the points of the compass, but it would do.

"This is it, Kamala," he said. He took a final puff from the oxygen canister and readied other items from his bag. "You ready?"

Of all his faiths, his sister was the one Samir believed in most of all. Reciting her name was as much a part of any of his rituals as any sacred text or practised gesture. She looked after him still, just as he cared for her in carrying her with him. She—

From the dark ahead, the opened room, came the tiny scrape of furtive movement. As if a sandal had trodden rust underfoot.

"Abesh?"

But Abesh would be behind him, would be back at the boat by now, and the boy had been barefoot.

From the dark again, another sound. Someone panting, like the breaths between hard sobs. Or the noise someone might make as they suffocated.

Whimpering.

And from over there, a muttering he couldn't make out. A trailing of words he couldn't quite hear, quick but quiet, like a desperate prayer or the hasty promises someone made when in trouble.

Samir set his torch down on the floor, leant it within the loop of his bag's strap, opened both arms to all he heard, and spoke so they might hear him.

He told them about his sister. He told them she liked ice

cream and the way birds flew in patterns and how she hated to be called Kami. He told them about how she died too, and how she was forever with him.

This was how he always started.

A standing shape came into the corridor, rolling in from behind a door frame as if detaching itself from the wall there. It was a man. He had a shredded face. His skin was hanging in thin wet ribbons from his brow, cheeks, and from his jowls where the front of his throat was open. Lower, and Samir saw the chest was open too.

"My name is Samir Zakir Hamid," he told him, and his voice wavered. He could see the broken bones of an exposed ribcage protruding from the man. He nudged his torch so the grisly sight was illuminated clearly and saw amongst those bloody bones rows of metal struts curving from the flesh. Rusted bars, like railings or corroded pipes.

From deep below, beneath his feet, a wallowing groan swallowed its own echo in rising through the decks. It engulfed Samir, heavy but brief, and faded like some distant whale song.

The sudden stench of charred meat announced a second presence. Emerging from further away, clambering up from the floor as if it had knelt there all this time, a red-black man scorched featureless of all but wet glistening limbs and a blackened nub where a face used to be. It took faltering steps towards Samir, guiding itself by bumping into one wall and then the other as it stumbled forward.

"You don't have to—"

And now there, from between the legs of the first, came another. Drawing itself across the floor with torn arms. A man whose torso marked the end of his body, save for what trailed out of it. He reached for Samir with the hand that wasn't pulling him forward, the left, then the right, in some tortured dry-swimming crawl.

Samir looked back the way he had come and saw more shadows than had been there before. He nudged the torch with his foot and saw others of those who'd perished here. Brought them into life by seeing them. They had changed, forced into new shapes by what had killed them and wearing scars that disfigured them beyond any Chittagong tattoo, each carrying some aspect of the ship. This one rusted where it should have rotted. This one with struts like splints, another with rivets where eyes should be, or a gaping porthole for a face.

Their stories were mingling. All who died here found their identities bound together and bound to the ship.

Samir talked about each of the men who had died on this ship, knowing those who approached were some of those same men. And as corrupted as they had been, as disfigured and reduced, they recognised something of themselves in what Samir said. He had a notebook filled with what their families had told him, and he had photographs too, but he relied on his memory, speaking in a rush not because he was afraid—though he was—but as a sort of litany, a tribute given not to appease but to convince. I can keep you alive, his stories said. I will remember you, and you can live on in me. Not here, in this rusting hulk of cold metal. In the flesh and blood of me, where my own spirit is anchored. Where my sister lives. And Christ. And Allah. Ninety-nine gods, and more. Replace this vessel with me. Let me carry you.

"Nasir?"

The nearest dark passenger of the *Karen May* made a guttural sound, a thick growl that bubbled from a throat choked with water. It reached for Samir with hands black and slick with oil.

"Your name is Nasir. You fell and you drowned."

He saw it happen in more detail than he had been told, saw it more vividly than was contained in any written report. He saw how quickly and quietly the man plummeted, and how he landed across a beam as yet untaken. Saw him fold over it, heard the crack of spine and the way his feet kicked against metal as he flipped around it, and fell. Saw him face down in the filthy water, drowning in the ship's black dregs.

The man pulled a fistful of Samir's shirt, yanking buttons from their threads and tearing one half of the garment almost entirely free. It exposed the crucifix he wore. The blue peacock eye of a *nazar boncuğu* amulet. The scriptures he'd tattooed across his chest. Whether from one or the sum total of all, Nasir recoiled vampire-like, though perhaps it was simply the momentum of his violence as he staggered back with a wet handful of Samir's clothing.

"Your name is Nasir, and you lived with your mother, Rokeya, and your father, Abdul, who is too old for physical work but loved to hear about yours. Your mother told me. She remembers your life well."

What had once been a man came again at Samir, pushed him hard to the wall and went in quick to meet him and—

Was gone.

"And which one are you?" Samir said to the next. "Did you fall, did you explode, did you burn or bleed? Because I remember all of you, now. I wasn't there when you died, but I've heard how you lived and I'm here now; I can take you away with me when I go."

There was a sharp, high grinding whine of metal from somewhere within the ship. Sheet metal torn and folded. A deep wailing came up from the bowels of the vessel as a foul-smelling wind. A fetid stench, channelled to Samir through empty chambers and corridors stripped down to metal bones. It passed over him like breath, sour and dank. With the buffeting of his clothes, the tousling of his hair, some of those Samir had come to see collapsed back into the steel that had taken them. One fell, and burst into red flakes of rust that were dispersed by that same air. Another staggered into a wall, then a second wall, ricocheting in frantic spinning turmoil before falling against a space where a wall only used to be and tumbling into a dark that swallowed him whole. The ship would regurgitate him when it needed, unless...

"There's more to remember you by than how you died," Samir told those who gathered to him, moths to his flame of hope. "There are others who remember you better than this."

The crowd was dispersing and growing and dispersing, all in flux. Some were taken by shadows, others birthed by them, but there were those who flared, consumed suddenly not by fire but some bright burning light.

"Yes," said Samir. Memories and ghosts. Each so easily became the other.

Still, many remained. Those whose families Samir could not find or would not speak to him. Those who had no one but those they worked with, who knew them now only as ghost stories.

"Tell me who you were," Samir said. "Before this place."

One by one, they came to him. They held him tight in desperation, pulling him hard to support their listing forms as they breathed their stories into his ear. They smelled of rust and oil and mud, burnt flesh, blood, and the bilge of old flooded compartments. Their words fluttered like scraps of wind-blown tarpaulin, and with the last whispered one, so did they.

Samir, exhausted, lowered himself to sit when they were done. His breath came in thin bursts, like he'd run some long race, so he took another full blast from the mask and canister he'd brought with him. Then he began unpacking other items from his bag.

He wasn't finished.

Some had called the *Karen May* haunted, and others had called it cursed, when in fact it was merely dying and trying not to. The *Karen May* had slowed her own demise by creating a new identity. Rather than suffer an undignified death at foreign hands on a dirty shore, she would make others suffer, and she would live.

"You've sailed every ocean," Samir said, fumbling at the clasps in his bag, "sailed all of them so often to know there is only really one. We give it different names. The Atlantic. The Pacific. The Bay of Bengal. We recognise the strength that comes with a name. The containment."

Samir grabbed handfuls of paper and cast them about the floor in front of him. Maps and charts and travel records.

"You are the *Karen May*, and you have known the power of the sea."

He spread rolls of paper and weighted them at the corners with piles of salt, lined the edges with it to hold them. It was used in many rituals, but this was the first time he'd used it to represent the sea. He cast photographs of the *Karen May* upon them, none of the ones he'd taken, nor those from the ship-breaking office, but pictures of her in harbour, at sea, loaded with crew, with passengers, containers. He splashed water over them, anointed them as if with something holy but using the sea he'd brought in with him in his water bottle. There was an article from a newspaper he read aloud before adding it to the pile, an itinerary, a manifest of documents and statistics and records that he shared, though he mentioned nothing of money or of costs, said nothing of profits. He did not reduce her to that.

Her. Like all ships, she had been given a name and personified. Given life. Why would she not be bitter about seeing it end?

These ocean-going giants were never meant to be broken. They had withstood the world's most ferocious conditions, crossing oceans that rose like mountains and dropped like valleys, burdened with cargo or passengers and taking them safely to wherever they needed to go. And now they sank only in mud, with the sea behind them. Sliced into sections and repurposed, more savaged than salvaged, and all they'd ever done before was forgotten.

The *Karen May* was not a graveyard, haunted by those who had died within her. She was a corpse, haunting the shore and doing all she could to be remembered. That was the problem. She was a ghost, existing only for as long as it took to decompose but no one willing to take her apart anymore. Or existing only for as long as she was remembered, but being remembered wrong. Every life she took became a new story and built her anew, created a cursed or haunted ship none would dare venture aboard, prolonging her own destruction by building her into something terrifying.

"We are each of us vessels in the same turbulent sea."

Samir thought of all people did to stave off their gradual collapse into irrelevance and insignificance. Whenever Samir's faith faltered, he found another to cling to. And another. That was their beauty, that was their strength. Surely it didn't matter to God?

The salt piles shifted in a gentle trembling. The papers moved askew and some were picked up in a new breeze. The torch fell from where it nestled in the bag strap and began to roll, turning half-circles this way and that and jittering with the new vibrations that were passing through the ship.

Samir stood. He clutched at the nearest support.

The lost engine, and all the ghost machinery of the vessel, was making itself heard for a final time. From somewhere distant came the sound of water churning. For a brief moment Samir wondered if it was his turn to be taken and was glad there were few to remember him. Then the ship listed and Samir staggered with it. He clutched at a frame where a hatch used to be and his legs kicked out into open air as the vessel suddenly slumped violently to one side. Pieces of it fell. Lots of them. A thunderous succession of crashes, metal clattering on metal. Samir felt a wash of heat, and for a moment shadows were cast into dancing shapes by some blooming flare of orange somewhere distant in the ship's belly.

The echo of whatever blast that had been faded like a sigh.

Samir found his feet again, though the floor he stood on now was angled and it groaned as if the weight of him was too much to bear.

Samir scooped up his torch and ran.

He'd done it. What he hadn't expected, though, was the quick disintegration of the ship once it had let go. Now metal buckled beneath his feet and he stomped boot prints into each panel as he fled. Each step of the stairs bowed in the middle as he climbed, the last few giving way entirely under him just as he set foot on the next. He stumbled onto the deck and rolled, got back to his feet. The entire ship was leaning, as if pitched in some slow violent sea, and Samir was disorientated. His torch still worked but he might as well have been in darkness; he did not recognise where he was. Until there, on the ground, a spent match. This was the way Abesh had come. And there—another. He followed them quickly, found more stairs, and hauled himself up as parts of them crashed away beneath him.

He burst out of the ship's confines into the free fresh air of its uppermost deck and saw they were being swept out in a rush to sea. Pulled from the shore that no longer held them, water washing in and around them as the land receded, receded—

Samir threw himself overboard. For a moment he held a graceful dive, like he'd seen the boys doing at dusk, and he panicked, recognising how he had been tricked. He had been expelled, jettisoned like spray from a cresting whale, and he had a moment to worry that he had flung himself from a great height towards mud flats that would smack him dead. But there was tide enough to catch him after all, and though it was so shallow that he felt the seabed in his kick to resurface, it held him safe.

Beside him, looming huge where it had always been, was the mud-mired steel-picked wreck of the *Karen May*, hollow and unhallowed. Sullen and spiteful, and silent now, but for the quiet hush of the shallows around it, and the bumping of the boat in which Abesh had brought them, still tethered to its hull and empty of all but shadows.

THE MIGRANTS
Tim Lucas

It was an unusual hour for anyone unbidden to be knocking at my door. Night had fallen and the porch light was off, extending no further invitations. I couldn't see through the slats of the blinds who was out there and felt some hesitation about turning the light on, but inside my house the lights were burning brightly, so my caller could certainly see me. I illuminated my porch and did not recognize with the middle-aged male face looking back at me with its hat-in-hand expression.

I could tell at once that he wasn't a salesman. There was something kindly and enquiring about his countenance that eased any concerns I might have had about undoing the locks.

"Good evening," he said in a voice ripe with character. "You don't know me, but I live a block over, on Angora Path." He half-turned and pointed across my street to the second house on the left. "Over there, behind the Sturdivants."

I could see no house behind the Sturdivants, only trees, but this was not to say there might not be a house there, somewhere beyond them.

I was already calculating, in the back of my mind, the possibilities awaiting me behind this obliquely neighbourly approach. This fellow had mentioned the name of a family, the Sturdivants, but in the more than thirty years that Cosima and I had lived on Locust Lane, I had never known them as anything more than a whisper of rumour, a passing blur. Of course, we kept to ourselves, by and large, though we had always been friendly with our immediate neighbours, those on either side of us, and responsive to their needs when required. In all the time we had lived here, we had seen the ramshackle house two doors down and across run down, refurbished, sold and run down again several times before the Sturdivants involved themselves in its trading of hands. But where was all this leading?

"Excuse me," I said, closing the storm door and—in the same movement—sliding the upper window down to permit continued conversation. "I'm sorry," I explained, "but we have a cat that likes to dart out."

"No offence taken. That's quite all right."

"Was a package of ours delivered to you by accident?" I asked, hazarding a guess. "The delivery people are always doing that. I'm afraid the only time I ever get over to Angora Path is when I have someone else's mail under my arm."

"Well, as you see, I don't," my visitor said, showing his arms upraised and empty-handed. "I've actually come to you about another matter. It's about..." He lowered his voice. "It's concerning someone in the neighbourhood."

"The drummer? I know what you mean. We can hear him clear over here when he's practising. I can't imagine the hell it must be for you, living right next to him."

"No, no, that's not what this is about."

"All right then"—I hurried him along as politely as I could—"what *is* this about?"

"I don't mean... to disturb you," he said, showing sensitivity to my feelings and pausing every few words to weigh and squeeze those next to be spoken, "but there are... some things in place... for which we all must... assume some responsibility. It's simply the way things work. We only involve people when they absolutely need to be and… well, now… you need to be."

What the—? "I'm listening."

"There is a neighbour of ours… a certain neighbour who requires, shall we say, a nightly escort."

"An escort."

"I assure you," he pressed, detecting a hard coloration of suspicion in my tone, "this is nothing sinister nor unwholesome. But it *is*," he continued, after a slow peer over each shoulder, "hush-hush. A kind of privilege, you might say. All that I mean is precisely what I said." He leaned closer to the door and lowered his voice. "We have a special neighbour, who keeps a very low profile. This neighbour moves around a lot and needs to be accompanied when the time comes for them to move… from place to place. It's as simple as that, really. It may sound strange, but the fact is, each and every night, this neighbour packs up all their belongings in a single suitcase and moves house. And we of the neighbourhood have inherited this arrangement that this business is always conducted on our watch, under our protection."

"This person… packs up. All of their belongings… and moves house. Every night."

"Well, yes," my visitor confirmed. "You know how some people are about walking around after dark."

"But ours has always been a good, safe neighbourhood."

"Oh, I agree," my visitor enthused, though his words conveyed a worrisome undertone that this might, could, somehow change at any moment.

"My wife and I have lived here for most of our lives," I reasoned. "If the neighbourhood has always had this arrangement, why have you not come to us before now?"

"This is the first time I have spoken to you," the man on the porch allowed, "but on those occasions I have spoken with your wife, she was always most accommodating."

I turned my sight internally. Cosima did sometimes enjoy an evening walk. Unaccompanied, I thought.

"My wife is away on a business trip," I admitted.

"She communicated to us that she might be. But the fact remains," he continued with some urgency, "we need someone, rather badly, to serve as our neighbour's escort tomorrow night. You seemed to be a good bet."

"And why is that?"

"Well, we know that you're a night owl and, being a writer, the hours you keep must be your own."

"How do you know I'm a night owl?"

"I sometimes have difficulty sleeping. I look out the window. Your upstairs lights are always burning."

"You can see that from your place?"

"In the autumn and winter, when the trees clear."

"And how do you know I'm a writer? Do you also have a view of my desk?"

"Not at all, my friend. It's just that, you know… your good wife is very proud."

"Not to my face, she isn't." I smiled. "If you don't mind, so that I might have the comfort of equal footing, what exactly is it that *you* do?"

His expression turned suppositional. "I go knocking."

"I see. Well, just so we understand each other… Is this to be a one-time thing, or an on-going… obligation?"

Standing out there on my porch, a jacket draped over his arm, its hand sunk deep into his trouser pocket, he shrugged from a place I had clearly never been.

"I believe, when all is said and done, you will consider it something of a privilege."

I was now too intrigued to refuse him. "Very well then, shall I get my jacket?"

"You aren't needed tonight. I'm actually on my way back home from tonight's duty."

"And you're not available tomorrow night?"

"That's not it. I really can't tell you why. Our neighbour likes variety among the escorts."

"And accommodations, apparently."

"Indeed." The word hovered in the air between us, as if somehow etched in elemental stone.

"Right. Where shall I meet this person—and when?"

My evening caller once again leaned toward me, lowering his voice conspiratorially. "696 Murdock Avenue. It's the third house from the corner where Locust meets Murdock. You must be there tomorrow night at precisely seven twenty."

"And if I can't?" There was no reason I couldn't, but it seemed worth testing the waters, if only to better define them.

"Then these pages were never written." I took his strange comment in the manner of spontaneous poetry rather than as a threat.

"No worries," I assured him. "As you surmised earlier, my time is my own."

"Now this is very important," my visitor told me. "When you get to—what is it?"

"696 Murdock Avenue."

"Flying colours. When you get to 696 Murdock Avenue, you will see there is a gate. Do not pass through the gate. Do not come to the porch. Do not knock or ring the bell. You won't have to. Our neighbour is very punctual."

"I'll be there." The man looked at me a bit timorously until I added, "You have my word."

At this he smiled meekly, nodded appreciatively and turned to step down from my porch.

"Hold on a minute," I called out, opening the door a crack and placing one foot on my porch. "How will I know this person? You haven't even told me their sex."

"That's not how it works." He smiled over his shoulder, and receded into the night, shrinking and shrinking until he became one with the darkness surrounding the nearest street lamp.

It was true what I'd said about Cosima being away on business. That night, I was alone in the house with Honouria our haughty Scottish fold. I had recently finished the novel I was reading and, needing something new, I went looking through the vertical stacks of the recent incoming on the floor of my library before climbing into bed. A full moon was shining directly through the window; there was no need for electrical light to guide me. As I perused the horizontal spines, I was startled by a sudden sound in the room. At first I saw nothing but then something black flapped out from the alphabetic filings on one of the higher shelves and flailed to the floor. I was fearful at first that a bat had got into the house, having an irrational fear of bats, but it turned out to be a small, young blackbird. Much as with mice, I had no problem with birds in their own element but I could not welcome them indoors. I watched it with apprehension. It seemed fairly docile. After gaining its bearings and shaking out its feathers a bit, it flew towards me! I crossed my arms guardedly over my face… and felt it perch on my pyjama sleeve. I carried it to the window so bright with lunar light and found another bird like it stationed on the sill. I unlatched the window and opened it outward, at which point the bird on my sleeve hopped outside, joining its mate. I closed the window but remained there watching as the two of them tilted their heads, their black eyes sparking in mysterious awareness of one another, a prelude to their taking off together into the night.

I still hadn't settled on a new novel to read. To be honest, I was feeling a bit too distracted to choose wisely, so I brought to bed my trusty *Dream Dictionary*, a very old volume that smelled of tea and had originated from China.

It was in its acid-browned pages that I learned that dreaming of a blackbird in your house signifies a lack of motivation and lingering concerns that one isn't realizing their fullest potential—or it may alternately represent feelings of jealousy, lust or temptation. I went to sleep that night wondering why I didn't find more blackbirds in the rooms of my house.

At 7:19 the following evening, I was keeping my word, standing on the sidewalk outside the house at 696 Murdock Avenue. There was a chill out, so I had worn my wool-lined jacket to the appointment. No active rain or drizzle, but the evening air around me twinkled wetly as though a rain cloud had descended to ground level.

There was nothing at all auspicious about the residence. Frankly, it was a bit on the dumpy side. I looked at my watch and counted the seconds.

At exactly 7:20, its front door popped open—with almost supernatural alacrity. It did so silently; had it made a sound, I imagine it would have been a hydraulic hiss, like the sound a bus makes when it drops off a passenger. Framed inside the doorway, silhouetted against a bright-yellow interior wall, was a squat black figure. For a moment I thought the shape might be that of the mysterious neighbour's baggage, but then it leapt forward—almost merrily, half walking and half hopping the way a child might toward a beloved uncle. The closer this figure came to me, the better I could see that it was adorned in a woollen, hooded mackintosh, carrying a small overnight bag and what appeared to be a violin case in unseen hands.

I had been strongly forewarned not to pass through the gate; but, seeing my charge's hands full of belongings, I felt obliged to open it, so this strange, migratory creature could pass through without inconvenience. I couldn't see a face, well-recessed inside the hood as it was, but as the figure waddled to a standstill beside me on the sidewalk, I intuited that the truth underlying this concealment had to be much older than I. Indeed, I felt an almost supernatural intuition that here was someone infinitely old, vulnerable and precious, whose security during this passage was both my great responsibility and my honour. I volunteered to carry the overnight bag and did so, finding it somewhat heavier than its size indicated, but under no circumstances would the violin case be relinquished. I had been given no indication of our destination, so I trailed behind their gnomic trailblazing—tailgating, really—like a guardian shadow.

After we had walked the distance of a block, I noticed that, while it was not a very late hour, our entire neighbourhood had fallen into a most peculiar silence. All the streets were empty, yet behind the façades of the homes we passed there were no muffled sounds of stereos or televisions or even children at play indoors. As we stepped from one corner to the next as if from one ice floe to another, I would sometimes look up from this bobbing, incessantly restless hobgoblin of a figure to the darkened fronts of the houses falling behind us on either side. I could see no watchful eyes peering out, no hands or faces pressed to glass, neither openly nor covertly. There was not so much as the whisper of another living soul, and the quality of the silence was unusual; it was that special, tucked-in silence that is ordinarily experienced only during heavy, blanketing snowfalls. Though the air was cold and crisp, there was no snow, and the only sounds to be heard were those of our footsteps, mine trailing those in front, and the lively murmur of a soliloquy in a language unknown to me.

Before I knew it, we arrived at our destination. It was numbered 969, I took no note of the street. It was one of those apartment buildings composed of four residences, two on each floor, each side mirroring the other. There was a piece of ornamental stone framed in brick above the main entrance, inscribed with a woman's name. Someone beloved by the architect, I imagined. As I write these words, I very much doubt I could ever find my way back there, wherever it was, though it could not be more than a five-minute walk from my own home. My neighbourhood is rife with buildings just like it.

My charge scurried ahead of me, pushing through the building's front door. I hurried in pursuit, feeling my responsibility, and trailed a happily chattering voice to the second floor, where I found an open door, numbered 3. It offered ingress to an apartment with another bright-yellow interior. It had green wall-to-wall carpeting like the blades of a well-manicured lawn and no furnishing other than a single wooden chair, into which I sank—as I say—with intuition.

Once I had time to settle, the figure then solemnly, respectfully, removed from the violin case a stringed instrument of indescribable beauty, of such exquisite refinement and delicacy that its wooden parts were wholly translucent, as clear as glass. Even so, it was unquestionably made of wood, albeit wood curbed to the will of an inconceivable level of high craftsmanship.

Without removing its hood, the migrant raised the butt of the instrument and nestled it shoulder-wise under the clamp of a chin, a golden cleft and sacred chin, the only aspect of identity made available to my sight. Fingers of similar hue curled around the strings of its neck and then—gently, tentatively—the other hand lowered a magnificent bow to hover just above them. From my close vantage, I could see that the instrument was strung with four taut filaments of subtly different colours. They seemed to ripple up and down their full length as though they contained the rapids of a great river, alive with untapped sound even before they were touched.

My squat charge held this intent, disciplined, tentative

pose for so long that I began to wonder if the divine instrument might produce its music somehow other than by direct contact—if it had to come about through some more inscrutable form of conductivity. Its celestial makeup did seem to argue against the involvement of anything so coarse as the frenzied scratching of horsehair upon catgut, however skilled, however impassioned might be the bow's guiding hand.

Then, as if zooming inward from the outer reaches of my suspense, the figure suddenly upraised its bow and struck, with violence and panache, a galvanizing pose. From that pose arose a single note—and from that note radiated each of the world's wonders, and from the next its horrors; in the summoned melody could be experienced each of the world's defining revolutions, each of the world's enlarging calculations, its decapitations and abominations, each of the world's great declarations of love—each and every god-damned eureka—all symmetrically ordered and then fanned and arrayed as in a peacock's tail, a gleaming spectrum of refulgent miracles, shames and intrigues. I found my senses dialling into them, my spinning form that of a weightless cosmonaut, visiting, inhabiting, becoming each place, each moment, each instance, each shaded evil and proud passion with perfect attenuation and detachment. I could stop wherever I chose.

Somewhere between the Taj Mahal and the Great Pyramid of Giza, I disentangled myself from the cartwheeling of the Khajuraho Monuments in Madhya Pradesh to find myself once again walking along Locust Lane. Each step, I knew, was taking me farther away from a feeling of wanting to remain, but I could not help but move forward. Had I turned on my heel, I knew there would be no finding my way back—which would only condemn me to a greater loss. This fate had been woven into my opportunity, and the point of it all was not what had happened, or where, or even with whom, but what still lay ahead.

There was a notable difference in the feeling of my homeward journey. The crystalline chill in the night air began to subside, the cloud now lifting. Here and there I could hear the muffled sounds of courtroom testimonies and criminal investigations being played out on different televisions tuned to different channels. I saw hands and faces pressed to glass, observing me in transit. I saw fear. I saw impatience. I saw the cold sweat of envy.

My jacket was beginning to feel a bit too warm, so I took it off and draped it through the handle of my arm, my hand sunk deep in my pants pocket. A shiver of sense memory, like a feeling of exposure, caused the hairs on the back of my neck to stand up.

I turned and saw the vague outline of a man, watching me intently and curiously as I made my way home. He stood with one foot inside his house, the other planted on his porch. Honouria ran through his legs onto the porch, her back arching and bristling at the receding sight of me.

After I had moved some distance beyond the streetlamp, I looked back once again and found that page had turned.

RUT SEASONS
Brian Hodge

It was somewhere between the tenth and twentieth heap of roadkill Casey passed that the irony of their demises declared itself to her. These heaps of meat and smears of blood were white-tailed deer, mostly, and deer most obviously. It was early November, the start of rut season, and they were on the move and on the make, so desperate to propagate the species they forgot to look both ways before crossing the street.

Did their mothers not teach them, or did they just not listen?

Simmer down, boys. I know what drives you. I know it's all you can think about right now. It drove your father too, the horny old rogue. But take a little care, for buck's sakes. You have to watch yourselves on these hard grey rivers. A little pause here and there isn't going to hurt anything. You'll be haunches-deep in some nice perky doe soon enough, but not if you're a big splattered tangle of antlers and legs and—oh, god, not again, I can't keep watching this happen.

They were distributed in wide clusters, bunched in the crossing regions where the woods and the lonelier fields edged close to the interstate. A few nauseating miles as messy as a deregulated slaughterhouse, then nothing for a long while, and then she'd be back in another kill zone.

It weighed on a person. It grew nerve-wracking. It made her more watchful, not a bad thing in itself, but driving a few hundred miles under that level of tension was exhausting. Things would be exhausting enough once she got there.

How many more Saturdays of this to look forward to? She really wanted to know, like right now, but dared not take a hand off the wheel to grab her phone from the console, much less take her eyes off the road. Plan B, then:

"Hey Siri, how long does rut season last this year?"

"Sorry, Casey, I don't know the answer to that one."

"Hey Siri, what the fuck good are you?"

"Your language!"

"Hey Siri, you sound like my mother."

"You're certainly entitled to that opinion."

Brought that on herself, hadn't she? The wiring was old and the roots went deep.

There was a time, when she'd left home twenty-odd years ago, that three hundred miles away sounded like the optimal distance. She could drive it in a few hours when she had to. Fly it in less, in case of emergency. Still far enough away, though. No drop-in visits, endured or expected. No "I was just in the neighbourhood." Yet it was close enough that it didn't look like she was trying too hard. It wasn't a thousand miles. It wasn't the nuclear option of clear across the country, on the coast. It wasn't Seattle, or LA, I'd keep on going west but there's this ocean in the way.

Now, though? Now it was starting to feel like a trap she'd set for herself without realizing it, one that didn't snap shut until it was too late. Yes, three hundred miles was a haul. But it was a doable haul, so there really were no excuses.

If you'd get up early for a change, you could be here before lunchtime. That would give us most of the weekend. We don't know how many more weekends we have left, do we?

No, Mom. We don't.

Proof? Just ask the deer. These poor, single-minded deer.

As always, she stopped to see her father first, because it was on the way in, practically right there as soon as you took the off-ramp from the highway. When she'd moved away, after college, there was hardly anything out here, just gas and greasy food, but the town had gradually shed its oldest, northernmost skin and oozed south to straddle the interstate.

The place they'd moved him to was nice, as assisted-living facilities went, but even here he was under an extra degree of sequestration. The memory care unit was... not solitary confinement exactly; more like Death Row to a prison's gen pop. Dementia, Alzheimer's... nobody here was going to get parole. Just getting in to visit family took a staffer with keys. These were the folks at risk of wandering off, who might keep going until tragedy found them.

While they were under twenty-four-hour lockdown, they at least had TV. That kept some of them occupied. The rest contorted themselves into chairs, at strange angles for reasons even they wouldn't know, staring into space without seeming to see a thing.

"How are you doing, Daddy?"

He was one of the occupieds, watching TV, sort of. He knew it was on but appeared not to care, knowing only that he was supposed to watch it. And he knew her, once it penetrated that *Daddy* meant him. As the recognition swam up to register in his eyes, he broke into a big, slow smile. Just the sweetest man, still, now that he'd run out of reasons for anger. Something about him had begun to look soft, sexless.

She hugged him, and he smelled okay, better than before he moved out here. They reminded him to wash and kept his clothes clean. They helped dress him, although he still looked like a ragamuffin, dishevelled and diminished, forty pounds lighter than the man who used to pilot the family car and yell for quiet from the back seat.

He asked her how she was. He said he was doing well when she asked him. He spoke with a lisp now, four of his top front teeth gone, having darkened and chipped away after he started neglecting to brush.

"How's David doing?" he asked.

Casey patted his hand. "David's fine. He's keeping as busy as ever."

Daddy told her he was getting on well here, that there were friends to have coffee with in the morning but they were asleep now.

"How's David doing?" he asked when the next commercials came on.

He remembered David, had always liked him. He never remembered the divorce.

"He's doing great," she said. "He's training for another marathon."

That made her father happy to hear.

It was easier, making this visit first, like a warm-up act. It came with fewer expectations. Daddy just seemed happy to see her, and while the past was all he had, he didn't seem inclined to dig around in the worst of it. The past was all he had, but he lived in the moment, because the prior moments kept crumbling behind him.

"How's David doing?"

He asked about David eight times while she was there, and each was like the first. Until she kissed him on the cheek and told him she'd see him again soon, and it made him happy to hear that, and when she left, the countdown started again, how long it would take to slip his mind that she'd been there at all.

That was what it was like now, with both of them. Her parents' existence had become a series of loops. There was no such thing as forward motion any more. Their health had banked into a downward spiral, while the rest of their lives circled back and back again to the same territories whether they liked it there or not. Her father's loops were smaller, tighter—that was all.

Her mother? Still in the house, under the same old roof, after a few brief detours. She'd tried the ACF route as well, three times, but it never lasted for longer than seventeen days. She had standards, you know, and once she got somewhere, always found reasons why the place didn't measure up to them. The people weren't nice. The food was bland. The apartment was too small. The shower curtain wasn't pretty.

There was no place like home.

Casey had the keys so she could let herself in. Every time, it hit her anew that 3,500 square feet was a tremendous amount of house for one person. The atmosphere still felt as brittle as it ever did when Mom was getting around normally, able to infuse each room and hallway by direct contact. The vibe was a lesser version of wartime killing grounds: *People once fought here.*

Maybe it was sustained indefinitely by the same looping mechanism that regulated so much of what her mother had to say.

Innocuous Opening #1: "Hi, Mom. How are you getting along?"

"Ohhh… it just goes from bad to worse here."

Thirty-eight times for that one, word-for-word, since Casey started keeping a tally. Phone calls counted.

Casey said she was sorry to hear that. She was always sorry to hear that.

Mom spent most of her waking hours in a single room now. As went the house, so went the family room, far more square footage than she needed. She interacted with the TV, the sofa, the coffee table… and that was about it. Everything else, from paintings to candle sconces, was just there, stored in place for some eventual estate sale.

Her mother struggled first to sit upright, then to get comfortable. She'd gained the weight Daddy had lost, and then some.

She'd never exercised. Casey couldn't think of a single time she'd seen her mother exert herself for the sake of exertion. Some gardening, but even that was leisurely. She never so much as went for walks. *A lady doesn't sweat*—that was her credo. She meant it, and lived by it. She'd drive around a parking lot for ten minutes to find a spot close enough to spare herself two minutes of walking. And that was when she was thirty-five. A lady didn't sweat.

Well, now a lady could barely stand up straight. Now a lady was more bulbous than she'd ever been in her life—a neat trick for someone who claimed to go days without eating because there was never any food in the house.

"What would you say about getting you moving a little this weekend?" Casey asked, not for the first time. "Not far. Just to the end of the driveway."

"And *back*," Mom said, as if that was the deal-breaker. She put on her sceptical face, like: Why don't you just ask me to climb Mount Everest? "And you'd expect the same thing tomorrow, I suppose?"

"Probably."

From sceptical to dismissive, in one practised swipe. "Pssh. Are you trying to turn me into a crazy person like you? No thanks." And, just as quickly, from dismissive to omniscient. "With that ring off your finger and you back on the market, maybe you'll finally admit I was right all along. I kept telling you, 'til I was blue in the face, men don't like girls who are muscly."

You couldn't get too irritated with her, not when that tremor in her jaw was getting worse.

"Mom. That isn't what happens ninety-nine per cent of

the time." And if it did, then, yes, actually there *were* men who went for that sort of look. Not a thing Mom would ever let herself understand. "Most women don't get big muscles. We mostly get really fit-looking."

"Pssh. I never had to put myself through that. It came naturally to me. I didn't have to work at it. I just had to *be*. I used to be pretty. As pretty as you."

Prettier, she figured her mother was thinking, but for the moment her diplomacy gyroscope was operational. Until it wasn't. What a difference eight seconds could make.

Start loop.

Mom stared at her as if they hadn't seen each other for years, and what the hell happened, anyway.

"*You* used to be so pretty," she said.

End loop. Running tally, nineteen.

She'd added a new one to the playlist in the past months. It would usually take her awhile to get to it, something she held in reserve for later.

"I'm at that age where I don't know why I'm alive anymore," she said. "I wish I wasn't."

It would've been callous to tell her that a lot of people felt the same, and it didn't take all those birthdays to bring it on. Purpose could abandon you at any age. You were never too young for the future to look meaningless. But maybe after a certain point in life this outlook was a guarantee. You crossed it like a finish line that was nothing of the sort, a cruel hoax, because there was so much left to go. So Casey said nothing.

"I wish a heart attack or a stroke would come along and finish me off. I go to bed and pray for that every night. God never answers."

The good news was he was bound to eventually. She couldn't say that either.

Now, though, finally, something new: "You could help me. Would you help me? Just get me some pills. They won't give them to me anymore, not the good kind. All the doctors around here know me from when…"

She didn't finish. She didn't have to.

"I'm not getting you pills, Mom."

"I could tell you what to say. It would be easy for you. You were always a good liar anyway, it came so natural you hardly had to put your mind to it."

"Mom! I am *not* getting you pills! If you were to do something bad with them, they're going to know somebody else had to bring them to you. Who do you think the first person they're going to come looking for is?"

Her mother sat a little straighter and swapped faces again: the poor-me face.

"Isn't that just typical," she said. "Never thinking about anybody but yourself."

Her old bike was still in the garage and the hand-pump still on a shelf, and for now the tyres held air, so she went for it. The last thing that mattered was how silly she felt, a middle-aged woman astride a dorky-looking relic from another era, painted a mauve that only a teenage girl could love. Ten minutes of good, hard riding—that's all she asked of it.

Maybe fifteen.

Twenty, tops.

The reasons why could change but the therapeutics didn't, and if a lady didn't sweat, then let it be known—she was no lady.

She whizzed along the streets of her childhood, then the roads of her youth, the old byways along the edges of town where she and her friends had learned to drink and smoke and barf and fumble under one another's clothes. Most of it looked remarkably unchanged, as if she might round one of the more dangerous curves and collide with an old ghost, stuck in the amber of time.

Here, where a carful of friends she'd almost joined had steered into a massive oak that had become known as Dead Man's Tree.

Here, where she'd met to engage in single combat with another girl over some slight that seemed gargantuan at the time, both of them backed by teams of jeering friends, and prevailed, because only one of them had a father who'd taught her how to fight.

Here, the turnoff to the cemetery where young immortals once gathered to look at the night sky and confess their worst fears, how maybe they weren't immortal after all.

It was early November but she'd worked up a sweat worthy of August when the front tyre gave out. Maybe this was it, the real reason she drove herself so hard. She'd always thought it was the most direct thing she could do to not be like her mother, but maybe the truth was more fundamental than that.

When the time came, *this* was how she wanted to go: like a tyre blowing out. No lingering, no hobbling, no complaining and no warning... just whup-whup-whup over to the side of the road.

Mid-November was peak rut season and the highway all the worse for it—that much bloodier, that much chunkier. That much more relentless striving for life jumping straight to the messy end. Casey navigated the carnage and considered it a small victory that she didn't add to it, as she again looped back to where she had begun and hit PLAY one more time.

"How's David doing?"

"He's fine. He found a co-worker he really, really likes.

They're spending a lot of time together, so I don't see him as much."

And at home, the old home, the once-and-dear-god-please-not-future home, the fourteenth occurrence of some variant of this: The young woman from the home care agency was in, not one of Natalia's usual days. She'd swapped Thursday for Saturday because of a paediatrician appointment. But one day was about as good as another when $22 an hour was buying you all the shopping, cooking, cleaning, and light nursing needed to keep you living at home.

Which made today floor day, but as soon as Natalia made some quip about mopping away the scuffs from all the dancing, Casey knew it was a terrible mistake.

"Did you hear that?" her mother said. "Do you hear how she talks to me?"

"It was just a joke, Mom. It sounded pretty light-hearted to me."

Now came the face of wrath and condemnation. "Pay attention, clean your ears out if you can't hear any better than that. She talks that way to me all the time. I'm supposed to sit here and take it? No ma'am. I won't."

Mom looked to make sure there was no eavesdropping going on, and switched to her conspirators face.

"You tell her to not come back. You'll have to find somebody else. What kind of home did she come from? We brought *you* up better than that."

"We're not firing another one, Mom. Not for a harmless joke. If you keep this up you're going to end up on a blacklist, and you won't be able to get *anybody* in."

The funny thing? Casey didn't mind this one. Instead of being wearying, it was… validating. Every so often something like this popped up, another saving grace about being here, that reframed more of the past and put it into a context that made a reconfigured sense.

It wasn't age, it wasn't the Parkinson's, nor anything else in her mother's mind that had degenerated to bring this on. It was *her*. Just her. She'd always been this way, only by this point she was off her game, no longer the least bit convincing in prosecuting her case.

So think of all those whippings that hadn't needed to be administered after all. Casey had never counted, but by the time she'd advanced to middle school—too big to spank now, and needing to be punished in other ways, because privileges had come to mean more than pain—it must have happened two hundred times or more. A conversation going off the rails and she hadn't even known how, other than that she must not have rolled over in complete submission like a dog baring her throat to the alpha bitch. Maybe she'd asked to do some chore later, rather than sooner. Maybe she'd protested some minor domestic injustice. Even if she had been a smart-mouthed kid at the very beginning, she was a quick learner, and figured out how to neutralize her voice for the sake of peacekeeping.

For all the good that did. Matters always ended up at the same go-to: "Just wait until your father gets home."

Protests and seeking clarification—*What? What did I say?*—only made things worse. Okay, she'd been slow to learn that.

"It wasn't what you said," her mother would tell her, "it's how you said it."

Come evening, though, the replay never sounded anything like the original. As for Dad, well, who was he going to believe, beyond his belief in the power of the belt to set things right?

So thanks, Mom. Thanks for teaching me dread. Thanks for showing me how a master works, to really sell the lie. Thanks for teaching me self-doubt, that no matter how much care I'd taken with each and every syllable, decibel and inflection, I still got it all wrong, but surely that was to be expected from somebody who couldn't do anything right. That's how we roll.

And thanks, most of all, for teaching me to mistrust my own memory, my reality.

You can't imagine what an asset that's been over the years.

Occurrence tally, only four, but emerging as the hot new trend: "I don't know why I've made it this far. Nobody needs to make it this far."

She might have had a valid point there, actually. Maybe the human species wasn't supposed to, and medical science had gotten overzealous to the point of godhood. All that hardy pioneer stock you heard about, from whom they supposedly descended? Those folks were done in long before now:

Here lies the body of Jedediah McGee
Died at the ripened age of 50 and 3

Maybe cholera and bear attacks were overdue for a big comeback.

Mom was wearing her pleading face. "Why can't you help me with this? Just hold a pillow over my face. They do it on TV all the time. It shouldn't take long. I won't fight it."

"I'm not smothering you, Mom." Casey huffed a sigh. "It won't look like you died in your sleep. Can you promise me you won't rupture the capillaries in your eyes?"

"Yourself yourself yourself, that's all you ever think about."

"You're goddamn right I'm thinking of myself! It's called matricide. I don't want to spend the rest of my life in prison for it. But if I did, I'd have a lot of friends there, because ninety per cent of the other women on the cell block would understand."

Of course she hated herself for it, and would for the rest of the night. Maybe all day tomorrow too. Self-loathing was a strange way to keep yourself sane, but better the verbal outbursts than an aneurysm on the inside.

Sometimes she could almost have fun with it, once she let herself start playing with the contradictions.

Loop tally, twenty-nine: "He's trying to kill me," her mother would confide. "You have to stop him."

"Who?" Even though Casey knew damn well who. There was only one root of all evil under this roof.

"Your father. Who else? Your father's trying to kill me."

"Mom, you don't have to worry about him. He's been in the memory care unit for a year and a half. They don't get out. So he can't be trying to hurt you."

The aggrieved face. "I know that. Don't treat me like I don't know what I'm talking about."

Mom directed her to the chair across the room and had her run her fingers along the back edge until, *ow*, she drew back with a slice gouged into the pad of her finger. She wrestled the chair around for a look and found the culprit: an upholstery staple that had worked itself loose.

"He set booby traps before he went. How am I supposed to sleep, not knowing what else he may have done around here? And if you think he doesn't sneak out, you're just being naive."

Early on, Casey could never decide which would be the better way to handle things like this. To play along, so her mother felt heard? Or try to set the record straight so she wasn't reinforcing the delusions? Eventually she realized it didn't matter. Either way, her mother had achieved master level status in taking whatever was there and using it to paint everyone involved as the worst human beings in the world.

"Mom, he's not trying to kill you. He's always loved you. You're going to have to trust me on this."

"You don't know your father. You've never known who

he really is. He's a liar and a cheat. Even if the truth would save his life, he'd lie just to see if he could get away with it. He's cheated half this town. There are all kinds of things I could've told you, but I never did. I didn't want to hurt you. But you should hear the truth for a change. He wants to kill me for what I know."

Fun times? Why not: "Then why are you endangering me by bringing me in on this? What's to stop him from coming after me, too?"

Wrong tone, as usual. It wasn't what she'd said. Must've been how she said it.

"You're doing it again. Treating me like I don't know what I'm talking about."

Fun times, option two: "Listen, if you're this tired of living, why not let him do it. Then you both get what you want."

"I don't want to let him win. My terms. I want to die on my terms."

And who could argue with that? The sad thing was, there didn't seem to be any such thing as *my terms* left anymore. She proved it every day.

"Mom… it's not Dad. It's the Parkinson's. It's just…" *Delusions*, she stopped short of saying. It was such a cruel word, a hard-edged word. "Remember the doctor telling you how it might put funny thoughts in your head?"

Mom sat with this awhile, staring straight ahead and down, seeming to try to process it, as though there was enough of a rational side in there to grapple with the matter, push back, assert some dominance. After a couple minutes, she turned back with a sidelong look that curdled into a sweet-and-sour smirk.

"Parkinson's *is* hereditary," she said.

At last the carnage along the highway began to wane. The end of rut season was near, plus maybe the stupid, reckless deer had all been killed off by now. Midway through the trip, Casey spotted a highway crew scraping up another godawful mess into the back of a truck, and wondered how the guys felt about the end of November. If they were relieved, sick of the blood, or if there was job security in it and they missed the overtime.

You could miss anything.

For sure, she missed making this trip in her own car. But in this instance it was safer to borrow from a friend, in case anyone checked later. Her license plate wouldn't show up anywhere on surveillance video for the weekend, and with a big enough hat and sunglasses and coat, neither would her likeness. Whatever she bought, she would pay for with cash, so forget about a debit card trail.

You could miss anything. But she didn't think she would.

There had been good times, too, beyond counting, but the longer this went on, the harder they got to recognize through the growing cataract of now.

The infinity loop: It always came down to not measuring up. There were so many ways to fail someone, so many iterations, it went on and on, and there was no outrunning it. You could drive until the tyres blew out, then discover you'd been carrying the baggage in your trunk all along.

Sometimes the reminders came from people who meant no harm.

"How's David doing?"

"He's got the world by the tail, Daddy. He's got a new lease on life. It must feel amazing to be so admired by someone that much younger. It's hard to compete with that."

And sometimes the reminders came from people who knew exactly where to stick the daggers. Their aim would be the last thing they ever forgot.

"When your grandmother was going through this, I took

care of her. I took *care* of *my* mother."

Although Mom didn't come right out and say so, the implied contrast couldn't have been more apparent. It wasn't what she didn't say, it was how she didn't say it.

"I did her laundry. I did the vacuuming and dusting once a week. I made sure she didn't lack for anything. *Anything.* And I visited her. I sat with her like it wasn't an imposition, unlike some people I know. And I was glad to do it, every time, because we never knew if that might be the last."

So many answers, so many combinations. Like a slot machine, pull the lever and see what comes up.

[A] Yes, you did. You absolutely did, and I admire you for that. It can't have been easy. It's only now that I can appreciate how hard it must've been.

[B] Remember when you yelled at her and made her cry and said you hoped somebody would shoot you if you ever got like her? That time you didn't sound very glad.

[C] Uh huh. Because you could. Because Daddy made sure you had the freedom to do it. He worked full-time in insurance with a side-gig in real estate to make sure you never had to work outside the home if you didn't want to.

[D] The reason you could do that is because you pulled her out of her home and moved her seventy miles to an assisted living facility three miles from your garage door. And guess who won't hear of that for herself?

[E] None of the above. Because sometimes, if you didn't find a way to break the loop, get out of the rut, the loop would break you.

"Okay, I'll help you," Casey said instead. "What you've been asking for? I'll help you. I just have to know one thing. Has it only been talk from you, all this time, or is it what you really want?"

For a change, her mother didn't scurry back from being offered exactly what she said she wanted. So Casey told her how it had to be to work.

She'd once heard it said that success in life could be correlated with the number of uncomfortable conversations you were willing to have. Well, this was uncomfortable, profoundly uncomfortable, but nothing about it felt like success. A conversation like this reeked of failure. This was a conversation of last resort.

At least they'd only have to have it once.

What got to her most was hearing her mother murmur about being cold. A thing like that hurt to hear and nearly made her get them back in the car and turn around, because it didn't arise from looking for something to complain about. A thing like that was real. It was primal. Because it was late November and the air promised winter, so of course her mother was cold. Anybody would be.

She'd worn her coat for as long as she could, for as long as Casey dared let her. But the town was never that big, so the drive was short, through the streets of her childhood and the roads of her youth, and the old byways along the edges where she and her friends had learned to live and lurk beneath the notice of adults.

She knew where to drive to. Knew where to park so the car would never be seen, not as long as it was night. The trees were thirty years taller, and the old woodland paths still the same. It just took longer to walk them this time.

"I have to take your coat now, Mom. I told you back at the house, it'll look better if you're not wearing a coat."

She needed some coaxing, but finally complied. Housecoat, slippers... she looked the part. It would work. Tragic. This happened more than people realized.

"I can't go with you past here, Mom. I'm sorry. But all you have to do is keep going a little farther. The walk isn't that long. The highway's right through there."

And as Casey watched her go, she thought of the rumours she'd heard all her life, of women who enjoyed lifelong good relationships with their mothers. *My mom's my best friend. I want you to meet my daughter, the best thing that ever happened to me.* She was pretty sure she had never encountered one.

Squabbles? Sure. Nattering? Naturally. Blow-ups? On occasion, but never bad, and five minutes later everything was forgotten.

These women had to exist, but there was a measure of relief in suspecting they didn't. They were tricks of light and swamp gas. They were cryptids, creatures that had gone extinct fifty thousand years ago, that someone thought they'd seen. They were mythological, avatars of an ideal worth striving for, but impossible to attain in the real world.

She'd done the best she could. Maybe they both had.

What a horrible thought.

And as she drove back in the darkest depths of the night, to wait for the phone call in the morning, it went okay for an hour. Until she came to the first of the blood-smeared crossings where the last of the season's deer had come to die.

Mile after mile, she thought she saw them from the corner of her eye, emerging from the darkness into the edge of her headlights, and she swerved to miss them. But there was always another one ahead, until she realized no, these weren't deer, they were her mother, tottering out of the night, so in time she stopped swerving, because if she was ever going to get home, she'd have to keep driving through the woman, every chance she got.

SENTINEL
Catriona Ward

Anna droops in the green wing chair, black skirts spread about her. Night comes in through the open doors, warm and speaking. Wisteria, oleander, flowers that bloom as briefly as a gasp. The distant road is quiet. No neighbours but the dark and the trees. She thinks of the afternoons she spent as a child under the spreading reaches of those woods. She swore she'd get away from here and she did. But death has hurtled her back, the pendulum swinging over the fixed point.

Ma died the day after Anna came home, as if that had been the signal. By the end her faculties were blunted into nothing by stroke. She stared ahead or inwards. You could raise her arm and it would stay there. Her face was a carnival mask. Her lip drew up over her yellow teeth in a gunslinger's snarl. Her body seemed barely tenanted. There was no sign of her passing. It was the nurse who told Anna that she held the hand of a corpse.

Sweat prickles on Anna's brow, her palms. She should put out the lights, go upstairs and sleep. But she does not. If she sleeps now, her mother is truly dead and buried. When she next opens her eyes it will be to a world without Ma.

Her legs ache. Funerals require so much standing. Images flicker through Anna's mind like sparks from bad circuitry. The Reverend's red, sore nose, dripping. Soft rain on black umbrellas. Fresh-turned earth. Curling sandwiches, picked over by many fingers. The slight *clunk,* like a turnstile, as the coffin settled into the ground. Anna had hoped to feel lighter afterwards—that one burial might serve for all the past. She had wondered if she might feel free. She feels tired.

Boxes are piled high against the walls. Her mother's possessions sit eyeless in the cardboard dark. Anna feels that they are judging her or planning something. The tiny glass figurines, each requiring careful individual wrapping. The collections of commemorative spoons and tea towels. The hundreds of plastic bags tucked into every crevice. Under cushions, behind radiators, at the back of cupboards. How can there be so many? What emergency would require them?

A thin wail trickles down the stairs. Pearl.

Anna starts, shivers, and goes to her daughter with relief. It is good to busy herself with life.

The tiny box room is hot, full of Pearl's breath. They both sleep here. Next door is the dark bedroom where the apparatus of illness still stands; an IV drip swaying gently on an unfelt breeze.

Pearl is a small resentful shape curled on the inflatable mattress on the floor. Her head is silken under Anna's hand. How can anything be so soft? The pyjamas with dragons on them, the plump, perfect limbs—Anna lets herself feel the animal joy in her daughter's physical being. "You were so good today," Anna says. "Such a brave girl."

"I want to go home," Pearl says. "I don't like it here."

"We will," Anna says. "But now you sleep."

Pearl clutches at Anna, tugs her hair. "I don't like him. The boy. He was dirty. His teeth were brown. He said that he would take me. Tell him to go away." She watches her mother for the effect of her words. Pearl's imagination has begun to take flight. She is at that age.

"No one will take you," Anna says. "Hush now."

"It was the reekling," Pearl says.

Anna's blood cools so quickly that her ears sing. She strokes Pearl's silken head. But the touch has lost its power. "Where did you hear that word?"

"He told me," says Pearl.

"Don't fib," says Anna sharply. But who did? Her mother must have come to her senses when Anna left the room or as she dozed... recovered clarity just long enough to slip this old fear into Pearl's mind, like a coin into a slot. Anna is savagely glad that her mother is dead. "That was just Granny's story," she says.

Pearl's face goes pink. "I saw him."

"Well," Anna says, "I am a tiger and I will protect you from—everything." She cannot bring herself to say "*the reekling*". She makes her fingers claws, bares her teeth.

Her mother's very own monster. It is different for everyone, taking the form of what you most fear. A beastie, or a scuttling thing... Perhaps it has long dangling arms like a chimpanzee and no eyes. Perhaps it curls about you softly, beneath the water, with its eight suckered arms. Perhaps it looks like the man at the deserted grocery store where Anna bought candy that summer when she was eleven. He slipped his cold hand up under her skirt as he gave her change. Whatever it looks like, it is the reekling and you know it when it comes.

Ma's warm voice is in Anna's ear now, shot through with the lilt of the old country. *It takes you from the world and puts you behind a wall of glass. You are forever outside in the dark, your palms pressed against the lighted window. You feel the breath heavy on the back of your neck.* You and I, alone together, *the reekling says soft in your ear.*

The hairs on Anna's forearms lift like spiders' legs and she scolds herself. "Do you want a drink?" she asks, nose buried in Pearl's fine hair.

"I want hot chocolate," Pearl says.

Anna wipes a fine sheen of sweat from her brow. "Surely not."

"I do, I do, I do!" Each *do* rises higher.

In the kitchen Anna lights the stove. A breeze ruffles the curtains. Through the open window, the scent of flowers opening in the dark. She puts a drop of vanilla essence in the pan with the milk. It sits warm in the air, mingling with wisteria and moonflower. Anna thinks of her mother's dark eyes, her dark mind. She curses her, wherever she is. And she feels the ache of loss.

Sometimes she thinks her mother began dying the day she stepped off the boat forty years ago. Ma never accustomed herself to this country, to its high clean horizons. The land here had no memory, she said. But Ma brought something with her from the old world.

"I led it here," she said. "But I won't let it get us. I know its tricks." Ma took Anna tightly in her arms and the long brown skein of her hair fell over them both.

Anna stirs cocoa powder and sugar into a paste, takes the pan off the heat, pours in more milk. A little cinnamon, more vanilla. Anna puts the pan back on the stove now, just as Ma taught her. Not all the memories are bad. In the early days Ma cooked. Childhood was full of the grainy scent of scones, cauliflower cheese soup, tipsy cake which took a little bite out of the back of Anna's throat and made her head sing pleasantly. Perhaps the reekling was just a story then, to frighten Anna into obedience. But imagination can be an unpredictable guest. The reekling took up residence.

Anna does not recall exactly when Ma stopped sleeping. She began to sit up nights, drinking coffee thick as syrup. Later it was laced with whiskey and then with ground-up Benzedrine. "I will stop it coming in."

There was no more cooking. Or there should have been no more. Anna found pieces of glass in mouthfuls of potato. She spat the shards out carefully and said nothing. She was afraid but she could not say of whom. It was not possible that she should fear her mother.

Eventually Ma just stayed in her chair at the window. She watched for the reekling at all hours, her trembling hand parting the curtains in the dawn. "I guard this house," she said to no one.

Anna taught herself to drive the truck. Each day she drove most of the way to school, parked down a track in the woods and walked the rest. She would have rather died than let anyone know about Ma.

Later they gave it a name. A soft-sounding word, *schizophrenia*, the *s* and *z* sounds slithering after one another, the plump landing of the *ph*. But all that came afterwards. For years it was just Anna and Ma, watching for the reekling.

Everyone has a secret that lies at the heart of them. This is Anna's. No matter where she goes or how many years pass, it is nested within her. Her mother's wide eyes fixed on the middle distance, her frame shaking after six wakeful days.

The hot chocolate steams in the pan. Anna tastes it. It is perfect. Sweet, homelike in a way this home never was. Anna shakes her head, irritable. She has fought to give Pearl a life different from her own. But the past is everywhere tonight, wreathed about like smoke.

Anna does not see the boy until he is almost upon her.

He comes out of the store cupboard like a shadow, face dead-pale above his ragged shirt, brown teeth bared, eyes deep whorls into nothing. An iron bar whistles by her head as she ducks, the air hums with its passage.

Anna seizes the pan from the stove and swings it at his face. She hears it connect with cartilage and bone. The boy screams. Steaming milk spatters, runs down his acne-scarred cheeks in rivulets. He falls to the floor, moaning through bubbles of milky blood.

Anna looks at him for what feels like an age but is probably no more than a moment. His lank black hair, his broken fingernails. Dark lashes, long on plump cheeks. Arms mottled with purple scars. Face dusted with acne. He is small, slight. He looks hungry. She takes in everything, each detail of the boy who has come into the house where her child is.

Anna seizes the phone from the shelf above the stove. She runs from the kitchen. She has been preparing for this moment since Pearl first opened her dim baby eyes.

Pearl stands on the half-landing. Her face is open, her mouth a soft questioning O. Anna seizes her daughter in her arms, throws open the front door and they are out. It feels like a single smooth movement. The world is rendered in the sheerest clarity, the edges of everything are apparent. They are held by the night.

Anna runs, stumbling, dialling with her thumb. She does not stop until she reaches the moonlit rise of the hill. She speaks into the phone. *Yes, no*, gives directions for how to get there from the highway, *It's ok, we're outside*. She is impressed by how calm she sounds. Below, the house is lit, windows blazing in the dark.

She ends the call. Her foot crunches on something. A can. It could have come from anywhere. But an image comes to Anna now, of the boy standing in the night, watching, drinking soda in the long wait. She looks at the house, at the room where she sat minutes ago. The books, the green wing chair. A fragile world in a bright box. She feels sick.

A shadow moves at the corner of the brightly lit living room. A slight, dark curve by the curtains. A head. He is crouching by the window, trying to keep out of sight, looking into the night. Looking for them. Anna laughs a little to herself. She was never great at science, but she knows you can't see out of a lit window into the dark.

The lights go out. The house vanishes, black into black.

Timeless fear pours into her. She thinks for the first time that there might be others. How did he come here? There is no sign of a car. *Breathe*, she tells herself.

"Get on my shoulders, Pearl," she says. "Up you come. Pony ride." Small, hot palms on her neck. Pearl's silence is wrong too. Pearl is never quiet. She seizes her daughter's legs where they hang over her shoulders and runs.

The forest is full of night whistles and petrichor leaks from the earth. As Anna runs she pants, looks behind her at intervals. She feels beasts and old things trotting beside her in the shadows of the trees.

The gas station is a mile distant, off the highway. The man there is tall, quiet. He gives Pearl a juice box even though they have no money. He lets them wait for the police in the back room. He lets them watch his little TV. There is nothing playing this time of night but a biography of a Prime Minister. The man closes the front and sits with them. Either he feels sorry for them or he does not want to leave them alone in his shop.

"She's a good girl," he says, nodding at Pearl, who kicks her legs. There are twigs in her dark hair. Anna begins to pick them out.

Red and blue light flares on the glass. The eerie squawk of a siren.

The policeman is the most exhausted person Anna has ever seen. He is composed of a series of pouches: under his eyes, around his mouth, about his midriff. There is no one at the house, the officer says. He searched. He found the saucepan in the kitchen, leaking a bay of brown milk across the floor. There was no blood. No sign of forced entry. Most of the windows were open, the front door swinging gently in the night air. No trace of a vehicle. No trace of anyone for miles about. Where could he be, or have gone? What more was there to be done?

Anna says, "I can't take my daughter back to that house unless you find him."

The tired policeman says, "You should get a dog. They're good company if you live alone."

She sees what is happening with the slow grace of a nightmare. "Listen," she says. "He was in the house. He went into my little girl's room. He tried to hit me with an iron bar. Pearl saw him, I saw him…"

"I wouldn't tell her scary stories before bed either," says the policeman. He mops his forehead with his handkerchief. The hot night is not kind to him. "Children imagine things." She hears what he leaves unspoken. *Women and children.* He asks her what medication she is taking. She tells the truth and sees his face harden to certainty.

"I didn't imagine it." The pitch of her voice rises. She sounds like Pearl denied a story. "Is there someone else I can speak to?"

The policeman shrugs. "Come to town in the morning." He rubs his face hard, leaving a flaming trail on his cheek. "Take you home," he says. "Been a long day for all of us."

Back at the house thin greenish dawn is leaking into the east.

"Bed, now," she says to Pearl.

Pearl yawns and rolls her new fire engine across the coverlet. "*Brrrrrm,*" she says. The man at the gas station gave it to her. Anna was flustered by his kindness.

"If you have trouble," he said as she got into the police car, "you call me. Here's the number. I'm closer than they are. Get there faster." In his eyes she saw weary acceptance. He knows that the law is only for some. She despises him for his weakness, she is grateful for the offer.

Her eyes have the grainy, burning feeling that comes of no sleep. Her body is toxic; the chemicals of high alert swill uneasily around, riding in her blood.

Pearl *broom-brooms* the fire engine over the coverlet.

"The bad boy won't come back," Anna says. "He's gone."

Pearl gazes at her truck with loving, unfocused eyes.

"Do you want anything?" Anna stops herself from asking, "*Hot chocolate?*"

Pearl shakes her head and yawns. She will sleep soon.

Anna goes downstairs. She mops the kitchen floor. Then she puts the pan back on the stove. She makes more chocolate, steaming and hot. She puts three heaped tablespoons of sugar in it. Then she brews coffee thick as syrup. She adds the coffee to the hot chocolate. She takes the whiskey bottle from the shelf.

She sits in the green wing chair in the dawn. This was Ma's favourite chair, of course. How had she forgotten that? Anna thinks of the long nights her mother watched as she slept upstairs. How alone she must have felt.

Anna drinks. Her eyes water at the fumes. The alcohol, sugar and caffeine are good. She needs something more. She gets pills from her handbag and crushes two under a saucer. They make the coffee mouth-numbing.

We will leave here, she promises Pearl silently. *Perhaps it will not follow us.* But she knows in her heart that what's done is done.

She hears the rustle in the wisteria outside. Morning birds

explode into the air in the wake of something's passage.

When Anna looks it is there, in the grey light beyond the window. It wears her mother's face, eyes sewn shut for the grave. Ma's nightdress flutters about its chalky ankles. The reekling sways, sensing Anna. The blind head seeks her, yearning. Its dead lips stretch to show yellow teeth.

Anna comes close to the glass. "You may not come in," she whispers. Her breath leaves white clouds on the pane. "I guard this house."

ALMOST AUREATE
V.H. Leslie

Eamon saw the bronzed man as soon as they arrived at Casa del Sol. Laden with luggage and shepherding two toddlers on Trunki Ride-On suitcases away from the ornamental fountain and toward the entrance, he could see the man leaning against the railings of the uppermost balcony, watching the new arrivals with apparent interest. He was shirtless, thin and wizened, the colour of Hawaiian Tropic. Eamon followed the stream of holidaymakers into the foyer, pausing at the entrance just long enough for the twins to wave goodbye to the coach and the holiday rep who'd accompanied them for the brief journey from the airport and whose only job had appeared to be apprising them of the temperature: 36 degrees, set to rise. It certainly felt hot, hotter still as Eamon passed beneath the bronzed man's gaze and into the welcome relief of the air-conditioned foyer.

The hotel could have been any hotel on the resort, though Sherry had spent a great deal of time agonising over the choice in the brochure. A stucco complex edged with bougainvillea, it had the added bonus of a poolside crèche, so they could entrust the twins to someone else and still keep a watchful eye on proceedings. Eamon had initially cautioned against this arrangement, fearing that either the twins or Sherry would be distressed at being separated from one another though in such close proximity; far better out of sight, out of mind. But he knew that Sherry would never agree to hotel babysitters or to placing the children in a *kidz* club—the post-trendy spelling now as old and worn as many of the regular holiday guests who passed through the doors. It was a miracle they were even having a holiday with Sherry's new-found maternal cautiousness, so it seemed wise to concede to all of her whims and preferences.

Sherry trailed behind Eamon and the twins with the rest of their suitcases, having opted to retrieve the remaining luggage from the underside of the coach rather than convey the children into the hotel. Eamon remembered a time when he did all the heavy lifting in their relationship; now the more arduous task was supervising the twins. He watched the children circle the foyer on their wheeled cases while he moved slowly along the check-in queue, their orbits getting wider and more energetic with each revolution. He ignored the tuts he could hear further back in the line, even when they threatened to collide with a baggage carrier. It was easy to observe them in this detached way, from this distance, as if they were nothing to do with him, moving excitably along their elliptical paths while he stayed rooted to one spot.

Eventually his eldest—by approximately fifteen minutes—Alex, came to settle at his side, screeching the sound of imaginary brakes so there was no doubt whose child he was. Annabelle, less accurate, bumped into her brother and sent him toppling. Sherry called them the *Two As*, a hangover from her time as a teacher, coupled with the iteration *Top of the class* whenever they did so much as smile, poo, or eat what was placed in front of them. Eamon had observed nothing in their brief lives that set them out as being particularly remarkable, save their ability to cry for protracted periods of time, which they started up in earnest now over their mini-collision. Eamon tried to appease them whilst handing over their passports to the receptionist, knowing it was part of their twin nature to goad and outdo each other in all things. Only when Sherry picked them up in turn was calm restored and Eamon fell back behind them, dragging their cases and bags as they headed towards their room.

It was not the kind of holiday he and Sherry had ever envisioned taking. They were the kind of people who went travelling, who were fundamentally opposed to the package holiday mentality and who avoided tourist locations. But since the twins had come along, many of the things he felt were defining to their identity as a couple were being slowly undermined. He thought of this almost always as a betrayal on Sherry's part, though he had to admit, as he reclined on a sunlounger, beer in hand, that he hadn't given a thought to the lack of historical hotspots they would be visiting, or the authentic Spanish cuisine they'd be forfeiting for burgers and full Englishes.

He was, in truth, relieved not to have to learn the local lingo or spend weeks researching the best restaurants and cultural sites to tick off from an array of guidebooks. Here, he was just one of the anonymous horde of English holidaymakers, pale and pasty or sunburnt and peeling depending on how far into their holiday they were, sporting beer bellies and football shirts with equal pride. Just once, he could allow himself permission to disappear into the stereotype.

Sherry smiled across at him, two pina coladas lined up on the plastic drinks tray while the *Two As* napped in the shade of a parasol. The hotel complex enhanced this feeling of concealment, the pool area having been built deep into the earth, the accommodation blocks clustered around the circumference giving the impression of a beautified council estate. Eamon imagined the process of digging the foundations, of excavating all that dry red earth to make way for fun pools and slides. It was like lying at the foot of an enormous amphitheatre, a cavernous tiered hollow, decorated with terracotta planters of bougainvillea and orange blossom.

At the summit of all this, on the uppermost balcony above the reception, he spied a solitary figure. He knew instinctively that it was the man he'd seen upon his arrival. He observed the bronzed man's bleached hair, which contrasted so discernibly with his dark skin, both testament to a lifetime of sun-worship. Though his frame was diminutive and skeletal, he stood at the apex with such command and authority, like a prince surveying his kingdom.

Eamon found himself thinking about what the view would be like from up there and was reminded of the pictures he had seen in the holiday brochure. Parasols of coconut husk, clay-coloured orbs from such a height, encircled the pool, alongside neat rows of sunbeds arranged like seating at an auditorium. Eamon's view of the complex in comparison was obscured by the poolside bar and the imitation waterfall which cascaded down from manmade boulders, severing the kids' side of the pool from that of the adults'.

He wondered whether the bronzed man could hear the inane chitchat from the group of teenagers at the water's edge or the shrieks of children as they splashed in the shallows. For a moment, Eamon was transported to the top, to the blissful quietude beside the bronzed man, away from the commotion and noise of the day to day and all the burdens and stresses at the very bottom.

He felt a prodding at his side and turned to see Sherry staring at him, her sunglasses pulled down against her nose. She nudged him again and pointed firmly toward the twins who had begun to stir in their pushchair. He stood at her silent bidding, creeping across the hot ground in the hope they might fall back asleep. But a chorus started up behind him as a group of children practised their cannonballs and the *Two As* burst into stuttering wails. He tried to glance up at the bronzed man as he rocked the pushchair, but the angles were all wrong and he was unable to see beyond the façade of the reception. From across the pool, he did see another man, however, a young father wearing a baseball cap, bouncing a gurgling baby on his knee, and he recognised a similar worn expression that spoke of sleep deprivation and regret. But the young man didn't return his glance for he was looking up.

Eamon rose early the next morning and as quietly as possible gathered his swimming trunks and towel and snuck out of the hotel room and down to the pool. A brigade of hotel staff were lining up the sunbeds and opening parasols, one man kneeling studiously at the pool's edge, taking samples. The water was an expanse of smooth, unbroken turquoise, the scent of citrus and chlorine mingled together in open invitation. It was too early for a swim really, the sun still low, the water not yet warmed, but Eamon wanted the pool all to himself, to not have to swim under the scrutiny of the bikini-clad teenagers who flirted at the water's edge or weave between elderly women blindly backstroking their way along speculated trajectories. Eamon draped his towel over a sunlounger and waited for the hotel staff to disperse.

Even at such an early hour, the bronzed man was there. Eamon wondered if he was watching the sun rise between the mountains, but his line of sight seemed directed irrefutably down. Eamon took off his T-shirt and felt the warmth of the bronzed man's gaze as he stepped into the tepid water.

He found himself contemplating the colour of the bronzed man's tan as he swam. Perhaps it was the morning light, but he appeared almost aureate, shimmering on high like a statue or idol. If it weren't for the occasional movement as he shifted position or extended his grasp along the balcony railing, it would have been easy to take him for the gilded figure of a man.

The hotel complex was coming alive, guests emerging bleary-eyed on their way to breakfast, pausing to reserve clusters of sunbeds, the circumference now littered with emblems of footballs clubs and Disney characters in terrycloth. Eamon heard the familiar shrieks of the *Two As*, spotting Sherry in the distance with the pushchair and he stopped mid-stroke to rise onto his back. He stretched out his limbs to float, his ears beneath the surface so he was deaf to everything except the sound of water. And he watched the bronzed man at the summit stretch upwards in imitation, reaching toward the sky.

After breakfast, Eamon decided to take a walk around the complex. He wanted to see how high he could get. He took the elevator to the top floor, but came out beside a conference room full of stacked chairs and trestle tables. He leant against the glass and looked down at the pool, spying Sherry asleep in the sun, but it wasn't nearly as high as the bronzed man's platform. The only staircase descended back to the foyer, so he made his way down, taking another set of elevators to a parallel accommodation block. Though he emerged at a roof terrace, he couldn't find a way across to the bronzed man's balcony. Chancing upon a cleaner, he tried to ask in broken Spanish for a way up to the topmost floor. But without the bronzed man there it merely looked like part of the roof and the cleaner shook her head blankly, whether in answer to his question or due to misunderstanding he was unsure.

Making his way back down and resuming his place poolside, Eamon saw that the bronzed man had likewise returned to his station. But his arms were folded as if he were displeased by Eamon's wandering. Eamon sank into his sunbed, lifting his book to block out the bronzed man's gaze. He forced himself to read, though the words held no gravity and he glanced up every few pages to check if the bronzed man was still there.

He felt better in the water. Despite the fear of colliding bodies, he began to swim with more dexterity, weaving between children crowded on lilos and novice swimmers lacking spatial awareness. In the afternoon, he took turns pushing the twins across the water in their swimming rings and taught them to jump off the edge into his waiting arms, making a big show of lifting them into the air as he caught them. It would have been easier with one, instead of having to partition his attention between each child, but eventually Sherry rose from her sunbed to join in their game and they were able to all play together.

The bronzed man continued his vigil into the peak of the day. Even when Eamon wasn't looking directly at him, he seemed to cast a golden light over the complex. Eamon's hippie sister practised Reiki and was always talking of auras and mystic energies. *Aura* was not a word he would typically use but the bronzed man did seem to radiate an ochroid glow that extended beyond the mere colour of his tan. Looking at him for too long was like staring at the sun; you had to blink away while the afterimage blurred on your retina.

The *Two As* cried at being returned to the crèche after so much fun in the water. They gripped the safety rails as if they were prison bars. Sherry turned her sunbed round, hoping they would calm down if they couldn't make eye contact. Their whimpering increased when the *kidz* club mascot tried to pacify them.

"Ignore them," Sherry said. But Eamon was watching the way the gold light fell across the play area and trickled onto Annabelle's face.

Back home the twins were Eamon's usual alarm clock, but here he woke before them and made his way down to the pool. He liked this nascent hour before the hotel was overrun with people, when he could swim in the adults' side of the pool instead of being stationed opposite the crèche, before he was called upon to change nappies and placate tantrums. It also meant getting out of dressing the twins and the tedious process of covering them both in a milky film of suntan lotion, and he would continue to swim until he was summoned away for breakfast. Of course, there would be a reckoning for enjoying so much free time, but he didn't care how many jobs and errands Sherry devised when they got home to satisfy her sense of fairness, to atone for being an unrepentant sun-worshipper.

The bronzed man was always in his customary position when Eamon arrived, leaning over the balcony railing, presiding over the complex. Eamon had considered getting up even earlier to see if he could be at the pool before the bronzed man, but he felt intuitively that the bronzed man wouldn't approve and was reminded of the defensive posture he'd assumed when Eamon had tried to make his way to the top of the complex. The bronzed man clearly did not want to share his dais.

Eamon assessed his own tan as he took off his T-shirt, literally pale in comparison to the bronzed man's, though certainly possessing a healthier glow than when he'd arrived. He wondered what kind of spectacle he made. He was overweight for sure, but he felt better moving through the water, becoming more proficient with his swimming each day. He wondered if the bronzed man had noticed the improvement; keen to be more than just another idle holidaymaker.

Why the bronzed man never deigned to come down to

the pool often occupied Eamon's thoughts as he swam. Surely, he would want to cool off, to dip his feet at the very least as the day drew on. The roof terrace offered no shade, and in all this time Eamon had not seen the bronzed man pause to apply sunblock or to take a drink. He just remained at his post, apparently without fear of sunstroke or melanoma, as the sun beat relentlessly down.

With a flourish, Eamon dived underwater, surprised at his own confidence. He emerged seeking the gaze of the bronzed man and his inward applause. But the bronzed man was looking into the distance, beyond the arc of patio umbrellas, the coconut fibres like witches' tresses. They cast shadows on the ground, knotted mounds resembling bonfires. Eamon heard the cry of a baby before he saw the young man in the baseball cap, rocking the infant in his arms. He watched him walk toward the edge of the pool whilst trying to hush the child. The man nodded at Eamon when he caught his eye and, as Eamon returned the greeting, he noted that in all this time he had never exchanged such a simple courtesy with the bronzed man.

Eamon tried to continue swimming but the young father pacing beside the pool put him off his stride. The sound of his flip-flops against the paving, the whimpering of the baby, all served to distract him. Eamon observed how tired the young man was; the way he rocked the baby with his eyes closed as if encouraging the child to do the same. The young father tried lying back against the sunbed whilst maintaining a cradling position, but whenever he got comfortable the infant would stir up. The child sought movement and the man rose again, rocking with renewed conviction.

Eamon had little sympathy. Though the *Two As* were better sleepers now, he was not out of the woods yet and he had two to contend with, after all. *Try having twins*, he wanted to shout at the young man. But he sank into a breaststroke instead, swimming toward the pool ladder, not wanting to advertise the fact he could devote a portion of his day to leisure.

But the man was too preoccupied with the baby to notice Eamon. He walked and rocked, walked and rocked. He came closer to the water, stepping into a stream of light peeling down from the mountains and the baby's crying became louder. The young man didn't step back into the shade, however, but looked up towards the bronzed man, lifting the peak of his cap so he could see more clearly. It was then Eamon saw the flash of understanding across the young man's face, the expression so transparent it was as if he were mouthing his intentions. He began to rock more vigorously, gaining momentum, and for a moment Eamon was sure he was about to release the baby into the water.

"Eamon!" He heard his name called from across the complex, saw Sherry waving impatiently from behind the pushchair, beckoning him to breakfast. When he looked back, the young man was walking away from the pool, cooing softly to his child.

It seemed ridiculously early to be eating such a big lunch. They'd not long finished breakfast when they were back in the dining hall, lining up at the buffet. Sherry had insisted, since it was nearing the end of their holiday, that they should experience the luxury of full board. It was no different really to their evening meal, the counters full of typical English fare, a tokenistic corner reserved for paella and an untouched urn of gazpacho. Eamon had managed to skirt Sherry's entreaties to go down to the beach, citing the difficulty with the pushchair, the irritation of sand, but he had to concede something. He much preferred grabbing a bite at the poolside bar, where he could keep an eye on the bronzed man and he felt strangely disloyal being sat at a linen-covered table and not by the pool, where he was supposed to be.

The *Two As* seemed similarly frustrated at being indoors and force fed, snivelling in their highchairs as Sherry tried to tempt them with coils of pasta. Eamon found a CBeebies clip they liked and placed his phone in front of them.

"This is the future," he heard an elderly woman say to her companion, "devices with dinner."

Sherry smiled apologetically but returned to the buffet so that Eamon was alone in feeling their disdain. He tried to call after Sherry to get more bread rolls, but she'd woven her way along the dessert aisle and out of earshot. He stood to get her attention and it was then that he saw the bronzed man making his way through the canteen. He looked smaller among the other diners than he did perched at his summit, his tan less golden and more rust-coloured; clearly not as immune to the ravages of the sun as Eamon had first thought.

The bronzed man walked past the laminated notice which banned swimwear from the dining hall, dressed only in yellow Lycra trunks. His flip-flops squeaked against the terracotta tiles as he approached Eamon, but no one seemed to notice; his attire seemingly less offensive than the presence of an iPhone displaying cartoons. Eamon sat upright, expecting a nod of acknowledgement, an exchange of words, but the bronzed man walked straight past and Eamon was left to observe the leathery quality of his flesh, the skin folded like vellum above the band of his swimming shorts.

The incident at the pool with the young father had left Eamon unsettled, along with the bronzed man's uncharacteristic venture into the dining hall. But he was determined to have one last swim on this, the final day of the holiday, before he was expected to begin the tedious task of packing. But the twins were already stirring before Eamon was awake, as if they could sense the impending departure. Annabelle sat upright in her cot as Eamon dressed, reaching upwards to be released from her prison.

"You can't leave me with both," Sherry said, pulling the bed sheet around her tighter. "You'll have to take one."

Alex still squirmed under the weight of sleep, so Eamon reached for Annabelle, dressing her hastily, his morning solitude now shattered with the encumbrance of a toddler and changing bag. But he wasn't about to forgo his swim and approaching the poolside he placed Annabelle in the crèche, scattering a selection of toys across the crash mats. He stepped into the kids' side of the pool, realising how inferior it was for swimming, the waterfall partially obscuring his view of the bronzed man. Annabelle seemed content enough, so he swam beneath the cascade, a feat he wouldn't have contemplated earlier in the week, and emerged in the deep end.

He was able to swim a couple of lengths, feeling the appraisal of the bronzed man as he moved through the water, before he heard Annabelle crying with the realisation she was abandoned and alone. Somehow, he knew it was a sound that would please the bronzed man.

The hotel was busier than normal with new arrivals, their body clocks out of kilter with the early hour. They gravitated to the pool, pale satellites encircling the radiance of the bronzed man. A group of teenagers ran beside the water, pretending to push one another in before disappearing out of sight, their voices carrying across the complex. Eamon plunged beneath the surface, imagining himself at the top beside the bronzed man, watching the suffusion of golden light drift down from the mountains.

When he resurfaced, he saw Annabelle toddling along the periphery of the pool. Had he not closed the gate of the crèche? Had it been opened? Her pace quickened when she saw him in the water, the tiles underfoot slippery from the splashing of the waterfall.

Stop, he said in his mind, but he continued to tread water, knowing the bronzed man was watching, knowing what he craved. And he saw Annabelle's awkward gait, her mismatched clothes that he'd selected, as she made her way closer to the edge. Eamon found himself watching the situation as if from a height, as if through a bronze haze, all the while thinking how much easier it would all be with just one.

Amid the hum of cicadas, he hardly perceived Sherry emerging from the lift, Alex on her hip, the quickening patter of her flip-flops against the ground as she ran toward the pool. His name called in a vague, far-off way, but resounding through the complex, like a nagging light at the edge of slumber.

Suddenly, life starts up. Annabelle crouches to jump and spurred into action Eamon swims across the pool with uncharacteristic speed, as if he had been practising all week for such a moment. Between his strokes, he sees the fear in his daughter's eyes as she leaps, as she begins to fall, the shock of the water against her chubby legs, replaced with a breathless smile as he manages, just in time, to reclaim her from the water. She squirms safely in her daddy's arms. Again. Again. But Eamon clutches her tightly, rocks her gently and feels the cold breeze against his skin as a shadow passes overhead.

He would live that moment again and again as he lay alone, or in the arms of various girlfriends who came in and out of his life in the future, Sherry having filed for divorce a few years after the holiday, unable to forgive his negligence that day. The recollection resurfaced with increasing vibrancy the night Annabelle missed her curfew and he found her slumped outside a kebab house, one shoe lost to the gaiety of the night, and the time she broke her wrist playing basketball; these brushes with danger all lent a golden aura that he could see as clearly as his daughter's younger self, hovering beside the water's edge. He forgot all about the bronzed man, of how close he came to his sulphurous glow. All that endured was a dull patina that formed over the memory, reddish gold, like scales of rust.

THE TYPEWRITER
Rio Youers

Thursday 16th January 1964

So frightfully cold outside. Watkins says it's going to snow overnight, and Watkins is usually right about such things. He has uncanny knowledge. Ask him about the Purley contract and he'll chase his tail like a dog. Ask him about dowsing or the healing properties of certain minerals and he'll talk for hours. A most peculiar individual.

I told the children to expect snow, and how their little faces glowed. Patricia danced up and down the hallway, and Christopher has already set aside his coat and gloves. They won't sleep tonight, I'm sure. It warms me to see them so full of glee. After tea, Christopher asked if he could put a log on the fire and I permitted him, watching as he removed the guard from the hearth and gently laid the log amongst the flames. He gave it a couple of manly prods with the poker, then replaced the guard and turned to me with an expression of boundless pride. We then sat as a family and talked for a full hour, mostly nonsense, but with a measure of love and understanding I so miss when I'm not with them... and sometimes when I am. It was a precious moment, and it didn't matter that the windows rattled in their draughty way, or that the chimney sometimes howled and made the single log hiss as if it were alive.

At eight o'clock we sent the children to their beds, and

Evelyn and I curled in front of the fire, she with her head on my shoulder, me with my fingers in her hair. I smiled and watched the flames, listening to the window rattle, believing myself the luckiest man alive.

Friday 17th January 1964

A strange day, all told. Watkins was right about the snow. My goodness! I woke to a different world, with everything draped in a white so clean it hurt your eyes to look at it. When I left for work, Christopher and Patricia were playing in the front garden, their noses red and their gloves wet from snowballing.

There were no buses running, so I had to walk, and thus arrived late. I wasn't the only one, of course, so Drummond couldn't reprimand me, although I could tell he wanted to. I appeased him by completing the Worthington contract ahead of schedule, and starting on Blackwell-Wright. I occasionally glanced up at our single office window, watching the snow fall, sometimes in dusty swirls, often in delicate clusters. The drifts were knee-deep by the time I collected my wages and left. Still no buses, so I walked with my coat tugged close and my scarf wrapped about my face. I trudged down the Old Kent Road, desperately cold and bleak, until I passed Temple's Bric-à-Brac, where the light spilled onto the pavement in a most inviting fashion. I was drawn to look at the window display and saw there an item that immediately took my fancy: an old typewriter, an Oliver No. 6, with a ridge of dust along its platen and its green paint in places scorched away as if it had been recovered from a fire. The price tag propped between the second and third row of keys read: £1/5s. Rather pricy for a thing so neglected. Nevertheless, it had a distinct appeal, like a mongrel dog or a worn pair of slippers, and I was moved to enquire within.

The shop itself is quite fabulous: a cornucopia of wondrous

artefacts in various states of disrepair. Muskets spotted with corrosion, gramophones with tarnished horns, spinning tops that have lost the will to whistle. Temple himself is equally threadbare, a chameleon amongst his wares, to the point that I thought the shop empty when I first entered, and in calling his name was startled to see him rise from the camouflage of a cluttered desk.

"Temple, my good man," I said as he shuffled towards me. "The typewriter in the window... What can you tell me about it?"

"One pound, five shillings," he replied.

"Yes, I can see the price tag," I said. "But does the machine work? It looks in questionable condition."

Temple shrugged his dusty shoulders. "It's not meant to work, is it? It's an antique. A display piece."

"A display piece?" I barked, aghast. "Where would you display such a monstrosity? Other than in your window?"

"Obviously, it needs to be restored." Temple took a packet of Embassy Regal from his shirt pocket, but didn't offer me one. He lit the fag with a box of matches plucked from a nearby table of oddments and blew his smoke into the air above us. "Think of it as a project. You clean it up, replace a few parts, tighten some screws, and Bob's your uncle. Display in pride of place or sell to a collector. You might even make a few nicker."

The idea had appeal. Not for fiscal gain, but to take a thing so untended and make it kind on the eye. It seemed the opposite of what we do with our lives—everything being worn to nothing: our possessions, our bodies, our state of mind. Here was an opportunity to reverse the process.

Temple, as I have mentioned, is a dishevelled individual. His skull consists of three teeth, brown as ale and unkindly spaced. His left eye is perpetually closed. It works fine, to the best of my knowledge, but he keeps it screwed shut, regardless. This gives him the appearance of a pirate, which makes bartering with him easier.

"I'll give you fifteen shillings," I offered.

Temple blew a string of smoke into the air, which bloomed like a peacock's tail. "You saw the price tag." He cracked an unsightly grin. "I'll take a pound even."

"Codswallop," I said. "Seventeen shillings. I'll not go higher."

"Nineteen," he said. "And six."

"Eighteen," I countered brashly. "And not a penny more."

He considered in histrionic fashion, rubbing his chin and shaking his head, and then agreed with a greasy handshake. I subtracted the total from my wage packet of £15, and then left with the typewriter—a deceptively heavy beast—in my arms.

It made the walk home longer, and harder.

I could write several pages more in regard to Evelyn's reaction to my purchase, but suffice it to say that she was not best pleased, and the atmosphere in the house tonight was decidedly icier than that of yesterday. Indeed, it was less frosty outside, standing next to the snowman built lovingly by my children. At one point his carrot nose fell off, and I popped it back into place, thinking, with a wry smile, that I had better get used to restoring things.

Sunday 19th January 1964

The typewriter is in the shed, sitting on my workbench. It is an ugly little thing, and I can see why Evelyn does not want it in the house. It smells dreadful too. A sickly, back-of-the-throat stench I can only liken to a dead puppy I once discovered in a drift of fallen leaves. Yes… the typewriter smells like a dead puppy.

But not for long. I shall strip it and clean its individual components with cotton buds, fine brushes and turpentine. Broken parts will be either fixed or replaced. Once reassembled, I dare say it will be fine enough for a museum.

Wednesday January 22nd 1964

Spent the entire evening in the shed with my typewriter—or what used to be my typewriter, but is now a sprawl of levers, wheels, bars, and various other pieces I have no name for. Had a blanket wrapped around me, but still so cold, my fingers numb as I painstakingly cleaned each piece. Got about 1/8th of them done. Will continue tomorrow.

Monday 27th January 1964

Repainted the typewriter's body today. Found the exact shade of olive green in a model shop. It took me hours to sand away the old paint and scorch marks, and I used a spray gun to apply the new coat evenly. I must say, it looks rather splendid.

Wednesday 29th January 1964

An altercation this evening. Evelyn says I am spending far too much time in the shed with my typewriter, to which I replied that a working man is entitled to his small pleasures, and I would not be in the shed at all if the machine were permitted in the house. Voices were raised and the children wept. Evelyn dashed to the bedroom and locked the door. I could hear her crying into the pillows, the foolish woman, so removed to the shed where I lovingly polished the typebars F through to U.

Thursday 30th January 1964

On the way home I bought some carnations from Cheeky Dave's stall and presented them to Evelyn. It softened the edges, somewhat. By the time we'd finished tea, she could look me in the eye again. She even managed a smile. We then gathered about the fire and listened to the wireless. Patricia showed me her new dance. An imperfect tap dance, of sorts, but then she is only eight. Christopher showed me the book he had borrowed from the library: an illustrated abridgment of *Treasure Island*. He turned to a picture of Long John Silver, and this made me think of Temple, which in turn made me think of the typewriter. Suddenly I yearned to be in the shed, cleaning ink from the typebars and listening to the comforting click of the ribbon spools. I even stood up, quite distracted from Christopher's enthusiasm, and took two steps towards the door. Then I stopped. That I would rather be in a cold shed than spend time with my wonderful family filled me with shame. I dropped to one knee, pulled my children close, and whispered that I loved them.

As deep as my obsession with the typewriter runs, it will not come between me and my family. When convenient, I shall tinker. Until then, I shall not.

Saturday 1st February 1964
Ordered: 1 x carriage release lever, 1 x backspace lever, 1 x replacement rubber for platen, 1 x space bar, 1 x shift key, 1 x type guide, 2 x paper guides, 4 x typebars (G, O, T, M), 6 x face keys (B, E, H, O, R, W), 1 x ribbon, 1 x bell.

I spent all day looking around specialist shops in London. Evelyn was in a foul mood when I returned home.

Sunday 22nd March 1964
It is done. After more than two months of fastidious cleaning, fiddling, adjusting, and waiting for parts, the typewriter is now in working order. Not quite as polished as I had hoped, but a vast improvement on the eyesore I brought home from Temple's Bric-à-Brac. Even Evelyn stated that I did a splendid job and has allowed me to bring it into the house (although a whiff of dead puppy remains; try as I have, I simply cannot eradicate it). I set it on a table in the back room, where we keep all manner of items too cumbersome to transfer to the loft: the children's old cot, a wardrobe with

a cracked mirror in the door, Auntie Mabel's mangle, which we inherited after a rather unfortunate mishap. I must admit to a wonderful feeling of achievement, to have breathed new life into something so fractured... so pitiable. I wonder if heart surgeons feel the same way after a successful operation. Needless to say, I was as happy as a sandboy this evening, singing along to the BBC Light Programme, dancing with Patricia, and play-wrestling with Christopher on the living room floor.

"You're in good spirits, Arthur," Evelyn remarked. "Perhaps we should get you to fix some things around the house."

To which I laughed, twirled her in my arms, and planted a kiss on her lips.

Later, with the children in bed and Evelyn listening to her favourite show, I retired to the back room with a sheaf of foolscap, thinking I would compose a brief poem on my restored machine, one pertinent to my good mood. I pulled a chair to the table and sat for a moment, admiring my handiwork, and then fed a sheet of paper into the carriage. Before beginning, I thought I should test the quality of each letter, but no sooner had I set my fingers upon the keys than a dire sensation gripped me. It was like nothing I'd felt before, and I lost all sense of myself. My fingers rattled upon the keys with a will of their own. I heard the typebars strike the page and the carriage judder to the left. With a gasp I pulled—yes, pulled: an act of force—my hands from the keytop and stood up quickly. The chair toppled over but I barely noticed; my attention was on the page. Whereas I had intended to type, "The quick brown fox jumps over the lazy dog," what I had actually typed was, "Kill the cunt. Cut her in half."

I took a quick, sharp breath, then pulled the page from the carriage and crumpled it in my hands. I was shocked beyond measure, and my heart raced in my chest. I cast a distrustful eye upon the typewriter and stepped away from it, but not before catching my reflection in the cracked mirror on the wardrobe door. I'm sure it was a device of the mirror's imperfection, but I was certain I saw two reflections: my own, and that of a distorted figure looming not behind, but *within* me, like a blurred photograph.

I hurried from the back room, disposed of the offensive sheet of paper (I pushed it to the bottom of the dustbin, where Evelyn would not find it), then washed my hands and joined my wife in the living room.

She was too absorbed in her show to notice my strained smile.

Monday 23rd March 1964

Couldn't concentrate at work today. Thinking about the typewriter, more particularly about the odd sensation that overcame me, and the words—those shocking words—that had jumped unbidden across the page.

I returned home subdued and confused. Evelyn asked what was wrong and I told her only half the truth—that I'd had a long and stressful day. The lamb chops and mint sauce cheered me up a little, although the mashed potatoes were cold and lumpy.

Avoided the back room, but felt the typewriter calling to me.

This is all very disturbing.

Tuesday 24th March 1964

Called in sick today after a night of terrible dreams. In the most vivid of them I stood in the living room with a human kidney in my hands. The wireless played, not the BBC Light Programme, but a melody of clicks, clacks and bells. I turned to the fire, then laid the kidney gently amongst the flames. It hissed and sizzled. I gave it a couple of prods with the poker, then turned around, my chest swelling with pride.

I awoke in a dishevelled state, dripping with perspiration, my heart pounding in my chest.

I think I'm coming down with something.

Friday 27th March 1964

Feverish for… I don't know how long. Days? Yes, days. In bed writing this. The room is spinning and the sheets smell of sickness. I can barely read my own writing. Think I'll sleep for a while.

Monday 30th March 1964

The fever continues and every sound hurts. I need a shave. I'm a whiskery chap. Like a sailor. No, like a pirate. Arrrrggh! Did you hear that the quick brown fox jumped over the dead puppy? What a terrible smell. Arrrrrrrggggghhh!

Tuesday 14th April 1964

It is illogical to fear an inanimate object (unless the object happens to be a Nazi V-1 Doodlebug, as my dear grandmother discovered—God rest her soul). After three weeks of avoiding the typewriter, I decided to confront it, having attributed the previous aberration to the fledgling stages of my illness.

And so, after tea, I entered the back room and found the typewriter as I had left it, sitting on the table, its U-shaped typebars resembling the wings of an insect about to take flight. I pulled up a seat and wiped sweat from my brow, then grabbed a sheet of foolscap and rolled it into position.

I placed my fingers on the keytop and typed, "Cut their juglars very quiet with a razer and use an ax to lop off their fucken limbs."

So, nothing to worry about, then. And all the letters in fine working order.

Jolly good.

Wednesday 22nd April 1964
Writing diary entry on typewriter for first
time. Why not, eh? Will cut out her kidne and
snip off her fingurs and staple it into the
diary proper.

   Rather a long day at work. Drummond still
giving me flack for taking two weeks off sick,
but I had a doctor's note so I don't know what
his problem is I'll kil him too cut his fucken
throat the toad.

   The family was in fine form tonight. Jollity
all around. Nothing I lik more than to watch
someon bleed.

   Sausage, egg and chips for tea.

Thursday 23rd April 1964
Wrote a poem tonight on my typewriter. A rather beautiful
piece, reminiscent of Coleridge. I may try to get it published.

Friday 24th April 1964
My reflection in the cracked mirror is a peculiar thing.
The defect runs directly down the middle of my face.
On one side I appear quite normal. On the other I am
distorted. My mouth is twisted, my eye dripping, and the
air around me is dank with shadow. However, when I
move away from the table upon which the typewriter sits,
my reflection snaps back into something more familiar. It
is simply me again, on both sides of the crack. A handsome
devil, it has to be said.

Saturday 9th May 1964
Received a rather stern rejection from *Ambit* magazine,
requesting I never sully their slush pile with my filth again. A
perplexing response.

Sunday 10th May 1964

Another quarrel with Evelyn. Been happening a lot of late. She suggests that I haven't been myself, and that our relationship is fractured. I of course told her that she was being downright silly, but I wonder...

She is sleeping now. I have spent the last twenty minutes or so standing by her bedside, staring at her. Moonlight spills through the window and her skin seems so pale, and so breakable. I think how vulnerable her eyes are, and how soft her lips. It amazes me how easily she would shatter.

We are such fragile creatures.

Wednesday 20th May 1964

Tried my hand at some traditional Japanese haiku. I have stapled one into the diary:

```
Slyce the bitch open
Krimson petals stane the floor
Her eyes close slowly.
```

Will submit to *Ambit*. Reject that, you buggers!

Tuesday 23rd June 1964

The last month or so has been extremely trying. Diary entries have been sporadic, at best, but I'll try to cover the important things here.

I'll begin by saying that Evelyn has threatened to take the children and leave. She has called my behaviour damnable and believes I need psychiatric help. She doesn't like my beard either. She says it makes me look like a Russian. The beard (which I think looks rather dashing) is a problem that can be solved with a pair of scissors and a sharp razor. I am more concerned with other issues.

Namely, the typewriter.

I began to suspect a deviance about the little machine, something—dare I say it?—*paranormal*. Not simply because of the dead-puppy smell, or my deformed reflection when I'm typing. There is a disquieting presence about it... a dismalness to the clacking of the keys and the peal of the tiny bell, and I believe some small measure of it has leaked into me. And so I hastened to the one man who would know about such things: Watkins. I cornered him on his lunch break. He was eating marmalade sandwiches, like Paddington Bear, and reading a book on radiesthesia.

"Watkins," I said. "I need your expertise."

"The Purley contract?" he enquired worriedly.

"No," I said. "Something even more inexplicable."

He raised an eyebrow.

"Is it possible," I began, "for a non-living object to be spiritually possessed?"

"You mean like a house?"

"No," I replied. "Something smaller."

"A packet of fags?"

"Don't be an imbecile."

"Well, what do you mean, Arthur? Spit it out."

I told him about the typewriter. I thought, prior to our conversation, that I would share only the relevant details, but found myself divulging everything, from the dead-puppy smell to the fact that my wife now sleeps in a separate bed. He listened, munching his marmalade sandwiches, nodding occasionally, and when I finished he took a pen from a pot on his desk and wrote down the name and telephone number of someone who could help.

"Kingsley Pringle?" I asked, eyeing the piece of paper suspiciously. "Is this a psychiatrist, Watkins? Do you think I'm bananas?"

"Not at all," he said. "Pringle is the most renowned

psychometrist in the UK, and luckily for you, he's right here in Bermondsey."

"Psychometrist?" I said.

Watkins nodded. "It is believed that all things—be they animal, vegetable, or mineral—have a unique vibratory signature. The psychometrist, through touch, is able to channel this energy and divine aspects of the subject's history. For instance, he or she might touch an item of clothing and be able to tell you to whom it belonged. Pringle is particularly remarkable, and has several times been employed by Scotland Yard. He has touched murder victims, weapons, etcetera, and provided the police with vital information."

"Fascinating," I said.

"Quite," Watkins agreed. A blob of marmalade dripped onto his tie. "Take your typewriter to Pringle, and he'll be able to tell you more about it than you probably want to know."

I thanked Watkins, went to my own desk, and called the number at once. Pringle answered. Our conversation was brisk. I told him about the typewriter and made an appointment for the following evening.

Pringle lives in a gloomy block of flats on The Grange. I took the bus to Tower Bridge Road (feeling somewhat odd with the typewriter perched on my lap) and walked from there. He lives on the top floor, of course, which meant I had to lug the beast up four flights of stairs. I was out of breath when I reached his door.

"Clayworth?"

"A pleasure to meet you, Mr Pringle."

"Come in," he said.

I had expected a bright, fox-faced man in wire-framed spectacles, but Pringle was a dour-looking oldster with a plumage of silver hair and dandruff on his shoulders. He asked for payment of one pound up front, then led me to a room furnished only with a table and chair. At his request, I set the typewriter on the table and stepped back.

"An Oliver number 6," he said, looking at it carefully, but not touching.

"Yes," I replied. "It was in terrible con——"

"Shh." He waved one porky digit in the air. "Don't tell me anything."

I bit my lip and nodded mutely.

"Partially restored."

I wasn't sure if it was a question or not, so remained silent.

"1909, I believe."

I shrugged.

"And an ugly mite, if ever there was one."

"It has a certain charm," I said, having become used to defending the typewriter. Evelyn calls it the cockroach, and has begged me to get rid of it. But I cannot bring myself to discard something I worked so hard to restore. With my hands I made it comely (to my eye, at least), working in a cold shed to bring it to life. It feels like a part of me.

"Charm," Pringle repeated. He shook his head and took a seat at the table. "Now, I ask that you remain quiet, Clayworth. I require absolute silence when scrying."

"Scrying?"

"Shh." The porky digit again.

I have since learned that Pringle has "scried" over a thousand objects, many of them with huge degrees of success. Smaller objects he places against his forehead. Those too heavy to lift are touched with hand position aligned with certain celestial energies. His usual reaction is a light fluttering of the eyelids and perhaps a few mumbled phrases. Then he will break contact and reveal what he has learned.

On this occasion, he assumed the position, placed his hands on either side of the typewriter, and immediately started to tremble—and quite violently too, as if several thousand volts of electricity were passing through his body.

I, of course, thought this a normal aspect of the scrying process, along with the frothing at the corners of his mouth, so simply stood and watched, silently, as requested. However, I suspected something was awry when I smelled his silver plumage burning and noticed blood trickling from his ears.

"I say... Pringle?"

Pringle shrieked. He pulled his hands from the machine and flew backwards in his chair, spilling to the floor in a most ungainly manner.

"My dear man," I said. "Is this quite normal?"

"Evil," he said, holding his head. Tears sparkled in the corners of his eyes. "I've never known such evil. And it's restless... looking for—"

"What are you talking about?" I took a step backward.

"Blood... screaming."

I shook my head. The sight of Pringle so distressed, and the smell of his burning hair, was extremely unsettling.

"Go," he pleaded, waving at the door. "And take that infernal machine with you."

"Go?" I asked, gathering the typewriter to my chest. "But I gave you a pound."

Pringle drew a long breath that sounded like the wind rattling my windows. Tendrils of smoke rippled from his scalp.

"What do you mean by evil?" I asked. "I shan't leave without answers."

The psychometrist regarded me with his small, wet eyes. "That typewriter belonged to Emory Grist. That's all I can tell you. Now please... leave!"

That name, Emory Grist, was familiar to me. I pondered it on the bus ride home, but couldn't place it—one of those annoying tip-of-the-tongue things. Evelyn would know, but she was sleeping by the time I arrived home, so I didn't disturb her. I waited until the following day at work and asked Watkins.

"Leather Apron strikes again," Watkins said.

"What do you mean?" I asked.

"That was the headline in the *Evening Standard*," Watkins said. "April of 1910, I believe. Emory Grist killed six women in Whitechapel in the space of three weeks. Cut their throats in two places, from left to right, and disembowelled them too. The similarities to Leather Apron—also known as Jack the Ripper—were so remarkable that many people believed Grist and the Ripper were one and the same."

My heart dropped in my chest. I shook my head and took a deep breath.

"Grist killed himself in a house fire as the police were closing in," Watkins continued. "To this day nobody knows if he truly was the Ripper."

"House fire," I said vaguely, recalling the scorch marks on the typewriter's body.

"Then there were the letters," Watkins said.

"The letters?"

"From Hell." Watkins grinned and rubbed his chin. "In 1888 someone purporting to be Jack the Ripper sent a letter to the head of the Whitechapel Vigilance Committee. The communication was badly misspelled—deliberately, some scholars believe—and accompanied by a portion of human kidney. The address in the top corner read simply, 'From Hell.' Twenty-two years later, Emory Grist did something eerily similar. The only notable differences were that his letters were sent to Scotland Yard, and they weren't handwritten… they were typed."

Watkins made typing gestures with his fingers.

"Of course," I said, feeling woozy.

"Which reminds me," Watkins said. "What did old Pringle say about your—" And then his mouth closed with a little snap and his eyebrows knitted neatly in the middle of his forehead. I could almost hear the proverbial penny drop.

I walked away from his desk and avoided him for the rest of the day.

Returning home that evening, I brimmed with resolve to jettison the typewriter. My plan was to put it in a sack and throw it in the Thames. However, when I walked into the back room and laid my hands on the machine, I had a sudden change of heart. I found myself caressing its keytop and platen. Same the following evening, and the evening after that. Much as I knew I should, I just couldn't bring myself to part with it.

It would appear that it has quite a hold on me.

Wednesday 24th June 1964

So many bad dreams. Click–clack–ding! Click–clack–ding! Last night was the worst yet, and the violent imagery still pours through my head. Far too disturbing to commit to paper. I'll keep it in my head and hope it fades.

Thursday 25th June 1964

Drummond has requested I shave. And bathe. He insists my shabby-genteel image is not appropriate for the workplace. I imagined plunging my dividers into his left eye. Ding!

Monday 29th June 1964

I stopped at Temple's Bric-à-Brac on the way home, fully intending to ask if he would take the typewriter off my hands. He could have it for free, if he was willing to come and collect it.

I couldn't do it, though. I stammered like a moron and Temple looked at me through one eye, but the offer wouldn't spill from my lips. Instead I purchased a ceremonial Japanese samurai sword. The blade is a little rusty, but I'm sure it'll sharpen nicely.

Tuesday 30th June 1964

Many tears tonight. Not from me, but from Evelyn and the children. They are all sleeping now and their bags are packed. They leave for Liverpool tomorrow.

The window rattles, but the sound of the whetstone along the blade is very comforting.

Wenzday 1st Juli 1964

I mad some poetry for a whil and lookd in mirror and saw the crack. Then I got my samri sord and went upstares and there was Evelyn sleping in the bed like an angel. I thoht I could kep her and stop her from leeving if I cut her into peeses and put her in a nise littel box. Then the windo ratteld a sound like clik and clack and clik and Evelyn waked up and saw me and screemed. I tryed to cut her in half with the sord. I think I cut somethin bekuase there was some blood but not much and Evelyn throw the lamp at me the fucken bitch. She run from the bedroom and down the landin and I chayse her with my sord. She gos to kiddys bedroom and slams the door and bloks it with somethin I think a chare. I could here them all cryin and screeming. I try to brake down the door and evn used my nise sord but I couldnt brake it. I needed somethin hevvy so went downstares and got my typewryter which I luv. I carry it back upstares and use it on the door wam and bam and crak and yes the door brake open but wen I lok inside the windo is open and Evelyn the fucken bitch is gone and tak the kiddles with her. I think she gos to Livrpol but she

```
left her bags. Mayb she come bak. The windos
still rattel and I lik the way they go clik
and clak and ding.
```

Friday 3rd July 1964

The police are looking for me. My picture adorns the *Evening Standard*, along with a warning that I am extremely danjerous and not to be approached. I think they will be looking for some time, though. I have effected a disguise by shaving my hed bald and trimming my beard into a neat goatee. I look very different from the man I used to be.

I feel different, two.

I write this—my final dire entry—from the Ten Bells in Whitechapel. It is late, and the pub is crowded with merrymakers. Some rabblesome men, and a bounty of young women—pale and frajile, all.

So many shadows outside. So many places untouched by streetlight.

I think I'll linger here a whil, with my samri sord conceeled inside my long koat. I rather like these crooked streets. It feels like hell.

In fact, it feels lik coming home.

LEAKING OUT

Brian Evenson

I

It was abandoned, the clapboard peeling and splintered, but practically a mansion. And surely, thought Lars, warmer than the outside. No wind anyway. The front door was padlocked and the windows boarded, but it didn't take long to find the place where the boards only looked nailed down and the shards of glass had been picked out of a window frame. The place where, with a minimum of effort, he could wriggle his way through and inside.

But of course that place meant that someone had arrived before him, and might still be inside. *He* didn't mind sharing—it was a big enough house that there was plenty of it to go around—but would *they*?

"Hello?" he called softly into the darkened building. When there was no answer, he pushed his duffle bag through the gap and wormed his way in after it.

He waited for his eyes to adjust, but even after a few minutes had passed all he saw were odd thin grey stripes, floating in the air around him. Eventually, he divined these to be the joins between the boards nailed over the windows, letting the slightest hint of light in.

He felt around with one gloved hand, but the floor seemed bare. No rubbish, no sign of habitation—which meant that whoever had been here hadn't stayed long or perhaps, like him, had just arrived.

"Hello?" he called again, louder this time, then listened. No answer.

Just me, then, he told himself. Though he wasn't entirely sure it *was* just him. He groped for the top of his duffle bag and unzipped it, then took his glove off with his teeth so he could root around by touch inside. Lumps of cloth that were wadded dirty clothing, the squat cylinders of batteries, the thin length of a knife, a dented tin plate, a can of food. There it was, deep in the bag: a hard, long cylinder with a pebbled grip. He took it out, fiddled with it until he found the switch.

The flashlight beam came on, the glow low, battery nearly dead or the contacts corroded. He shook the flashlight a little and it brightened enough to cut through the dark.

He shined it about him, walking around. Ordinary room, it seemed. The only odd thing was how clean it was: no debris, no dust. The pine floors shone as if they had just been waxed. Immaculate. Had he been wrong in thinking the house deserted? But no, it had appeared ruined from the outside, and the windows were boarded.

Strange, he thought. And then the flashlight flickered and went out.

He shook it, slapped it with the heel of his hand, but it didn't come on again. He cursed himself for having left his duffle bag near the window. He returned slowly backward in what he hoped was the direction he had come from, but darkness was making the space change, becoming uncertain, vast. He kept backing up anyway.

The back of his heel struck something. Feeling behind

him he found a wall. Where was the window he had entered through? He couldn't find it, there was just solid wall.

It's just a house, he told himself. *No need to worry. Just a house.*

But he'd never been able to bear the dark. He hadn't liked it when he was a boy and he didn't like it now. He felt along the wall again. Still no window. He was hyperventilating, he realized. *Take a breath*, he told himself. *Calm down.*

He passed out.

When he woke up he was calm somehow, almost as if he were another person. He had none of the disorientation that comes with waking in a strange place. It was almost as if the place wasn't strange after all—as if he'd been there a very long time, perhaps forever.

The stripes, he thought. And immediately he began to see them, the lines of grey that marked the windows. There were none near him—the wall he had been touching must have been an interior wall, he must have taken a wrong turn somewhere. How had he gotten so turned around?

He stood and made his way to them. Halfway there, he stumbled over something and went down in a heap. His duffle bag, he thought at first, but when he groped around on the floor for it, he found nothing at all. What had he tripped on?

He climbed to his feet. Once he'd touched the wall with the window in it, he swept his foot over the floor looking for his duffle bag, still not finding it. He tugged on the slats of wood over the window, but none were loose.

Wrong window, he thought. *Wrong wall.* He did his best not to panic.

Turning away from it, he peered into the darkness. He could just make out, at what seemed a great distance, another set of lines defining another set of windows. He made his way toward it.

The duffle bag was there this time—he stumbled on it, and when he felt around for it, it had the decency not to vanish. It felt just slightly wrong beneath his fingers, but that no doubt had come when he had forced it through the gap in the boards and let it drop. He shouldn't worry, it was his duffle bag: what else could it possibly be?

Sitting cross-legged on the floor, he searched through it for the spare batteries and in a moment had them. He unscrewed the cap at the end of the flashlight. Shaking out the old batteries, he dropped them onto the floor with a clunk, then pushed the new ones in, screwing the cap back into place.

Carefully he pressed the switch, and this time the beam came on bright and strong. The room became a room again, boundaries clean and distinct. Nothing to be afraid of, just an ordinary room, empty except for him and his duffle bag.

He slung the bag over his shoulder and started toward the door that led deeper into the house. Halfway there, he stopped and, turning, swept the light across the floor behind him. The dead batteries, he wondered, where could they possibly have gone? They simply weren't there.

The adjoining room offered a stairway and then narrowed into a passageway that led to the remainder of the ground floor. Here too everything appeared immaculate, the floor and stairs dustless, as if they had just been cleaned.

He shined the light up the stairway but didn't climb it, instead following the passage back. After openings leading to a dining room, a kitchen, and a storeroom, the passage terminated in a series of three doors, one directly before him and one to either side. He tried the door to his right and found it locked. The one on the left was locked as well. But the door in front of him opened smoothly. He went through.

A fireplace dominated the room, a large ornate affair faced in porcelain tile. The grate and firebox were as clean as the rest of the house: spotless, as if a fire had never been made. There was a perfectly symmetrical stack of wood to one side, a box of kindling in front of it. On the other side was a poker in its stand, also seemingly unused. The porcelain of the tiles had been painted with what at first struck him as birds but which, as he drew closer, he realized were not birds at all but a series of gesticulating disembodied hands.

And there, on the wall above the mantel, what he took at first for a curious work of art: something seemingly scribbled directly on the plaster. Upon closer inspection, it proved to be a stain—the only blemish he had seen in the whole house. And then he came closer, and closer still, and recoiled: it was not just any stain, he realized, but the remnants of a great cloud of blood.

There were two armchairs here and a bearskin on the floor. He could light a fire and get warm. Did he dare start one? What if someone saw smoke coming up from the chimney? Would they cause trouble for him?

But his batteries wouldn't last forever and the last thing he wanted was to be left in the dark again. No, he needed a fire. If he was caught, so what: it would mean a night in jail and then they'd let him go. And the jail would be warm.

He balanced the flashlight on its end so that the light fountained up toward the ceiling, then rummaged through his bag until he found his book of matches.

It was bent and crumpled, the striking pad worn along the middle of the strip through to the paper backing. Most of the matches were torn out and gone.

Carefully he arranged the split logs in a crosshatched stack, and then on top of this built a little mound of tinder. The mound looked, he realized, like a star, and once he'd noticed this he found his fingers working to make it even more of one.

The first match he struck fizzled out. The second did a little better, but the tinder didn't catch. With the third, once the match was alight he lit the matchbook as well, pushing both into the tinder.

He blew on the flame until the tinder caught, watched it blacken and curl, charring its mark onto the pale wood below, and then that catching too. He stared into the flames. Soon he felt the warmth radiating from the fire. Soon after that, it was too hot to be so near.

He made his way back to one of the armchairs, but before he could sit in it realized there was something already there. A rubberized blanket perhaps, strangely shaped and nearly see-through. An odd colour, a dirty pink—pigskin maybe, cured in a way that gave it a translucency or stretched thin. It was soft to the touch, and warm—no doubt from the fire. He grasped it in both hands and lifted it, found it to be more a sheath than a blanket, something you could crawl into, as large as a man, roughly the shape of a man as well.

He dropped it as if stung, took a few steps away from the chair. His first impulse was to flee, but with each step away from the sheath he felt safer, more secure. *Somebody's idea of a joke*, he told himself. *An odd costume.* Nothing to worry about.

He settled into the other chair, still shaken. He would rest for a few minutes, warm up, and then leave.

A moment later, he was sound asleep.

He dreamt that he was in an operating theatre, much like the one his father had performed surgery in back when he was still alive. There was a chair on the upper tier just for him, his name on a brass plate set in the back of the chair. When he entered the theatre, everyone turned and faced him, and stared. It was crowded, every chair taken but his own, and to reach his spot he had to force his way down the aisle and to the centre of the row, stepping with apologies over the legs of the others. Down below, the surgeon stood with his gloved hands held motionless and awkwardly raised, his face mostly hidden by his surgical mask. He seemed to be waiting for Lars to take his seat.

Lars sat and then, when the surgeon still continued to stare at him, motioned for him to proceed. The surgeon nodded sharply and turned toward the only other man on the theatre floor: a tall elderly gentleman, stripped nude and standing just beside the operating table.

The surgeon ran his hand across a tray of instruments and took up a scalpel. He made a continuous incision along the man's clavicle, from one shoulder to the other. The elderly man didn't seem to mind or even to feel it. He remained standing, smiling absently. The surgeon set the bloody scalpel down on the edge of the operating table. Carefully, he worked his gloved fingers into the incision he had created and then, once he had a firm grasp on the skin, began very slowly to pull it down, gradually stripping the man's flesh off his chest in a single slick sheet, from time to time looking back at Lars, as if for approval.

Lars awoke gasping, unsure of where he was. He was sweating, the room warmer than when he'd fallen asleep, the fire glowing a deep red, the heat making the air in front of the fireplace shimmer.

"Bad dream?" asked a voice.

He turned, startled. There in the other armchair was a

man. Something was wrong with his skin: it hung strangely on him, too loose in the fingers and elbows, too tight in other places. There was something wrong too with his face, as if the skin didn't quite align with the bones beneath. One eye was oddly stretched so that it was open too wide, the other bunched and all but shut.

"Bad dream?" asked the malformed man again.

"Yes, it is," said Lars.

"*Was*, you mean," said the malformed man. But Lars had not meant *was* but *is*. *I'm dreaming*, thought Lars. *I'm still asleep and dreaming.*

"What are you staring at?" asked the man. "Is it me?" He reached up and touched his face, and then began to tug on it, sliding the skin slightly over with a wet sucking sound. The eye that had been bloated began to shrink back, the other eye opening up. Lars, sickened, had to look away.

"There we are," said the man. "You see? Nothing to be concerned over." When Lars still stared into the fire, he added, "Look at me."

Reluctantly Lars did. It was just, he saw, a normal man now, not malformed at all.

"What was wrong with you?" he couldn't stop himself from asking.

"Wrong?" asked the man. He smoothed back his hair. "Nothing. Why would you think anything is wrong?"

Lars opened his mouth, then closed it again. From the other chair, the man watched him.

"I hadn't realized someone else was here," Lars finally managed. "I didn't mean to intrude. I'll go."

"Nonsense," said the man. "It's a big house. A mansion of sorts. I don't mind sharing."

"It's just—"

"Don't worry," said the man. "I've already eaten."

What the hell? wondered Lars. Had the man thought he

wasn't going to stay because he had no food to offer? Was that a custom around these parts? Confused, he started to rise from the chair.

But the other man was already up, patting the air in front of him with his hands. *Sit, sit*, he was saying. To get past him, Lars would have to touch him, and that was something he felt he did not want to do.

He let himself fall back into the chair. Impossibly, the man was already back in his own chair as well, sitting down. The skin on one side of his face seemed to be growing loose again, or maybe that was just the flickering of the firelight.

"I didn't mean to wake you," said the man. "Though perhaps it wasn't I who woke you."

"I... don't know," said Lars.

The man uncrossed his legs and then crossed them in the other direction. "Will you tell it to me?" he asked.

"Tell you what?"

"Your dream? Will you share it with me?"

"I don't think that's a good idea."

The man smiled, gave a little laugh. "No? Then the least I can do is try to help you fall back to sleep."

"There was once a man who was not a man," the man began. He was frowning, or perhaps it was just that his face was slipping. "He acted like a man, but he was not, in fact, a man after all. Then why, you might wonder, did he live with men or among them?

"Why indeed?

"But this is not that kind of story, the kind meant to explain things. It just tells things as they are, and as you know there is no explanation for how things are, at least none that would make any difference and allow them to be something else.

"He acted like a man and in many respects he *was* a man,

but he was not a man as well, and sometimes he would forget this and allow himself to relax a little and leak out."

"What?" said Lars, his voice rising.

"Leak out," said the man. He had pulled his chair a little closer, or at least it seemed that way to Lars.

"But what," said Lars. "How—"

"Leak out," said the man with finality. "I already told you this is not that kind of story, the kind that explains things. Be quiet and listen.

"He would relax a little and leak out, and sometimes it was hard for him to make his way back in again. Sometimes people would come along while he was this way, humans, and he'd have to decide what to do with them. Or perhaps *to* them. Sometimes if he couldn't get back in to where he had been, he could at least get into one of them."

The man suddenly reached out and touched his cheek. Lars felt warmth spreading through his face. Or maybe it was cold, but so cold it felt warm. He found he could not move.

"Sometimes," said the man, "once he got into one of them, he would stay for a while. But other times, he would just swallow them up and be done with them."

II

When he woke up it was late in the day, enough sunlight seeping through the gaps between boards to fill the house with a pale light. He was lying on the floor, on the bearskin, and had slept in such a way that he was stiff all along one side, his shoulder tingling, his jaw tight. The other man was nowhere to be seen.

Had anything really happened? Perhaps he had dreamt it all.

The ashes in the grate were still warm. The room, which had seemed to him so immaculate in his flashlight beam the night before, clearly wasn't: the floor was dusty. There was litter and garbage as well and a faint sour smell. The bearskin he had slept on was moth-eaten and tattered, as were the two chairs. The only place that was immaculate was the wall above the fireplace: there wasn't a stain there after all.

He quickly packed his duffle bag and made for the door. He wouldn't come back, he told himself. He was, after all, just passing through. He'd never stayed in the same place more than a day or two, not since his father's death.

He searched the house, found nothing of value. The dead batteries still weren't anywhere.

It was late afternoon by the time he walked the half-mile into town. The town was smaller than he'd hoped, the business district little more than one main street, with a diner, a general store with a lunch counter in back, a drugstore, a feed and grain supply and a hardware store. He spent some time in the hardware store, but there weren't enough other customers and the clerk was paying too much attention to him for him to lift anything. So he left and went down to the general store.

He walked down the aisles, considering. One clerk here too, seemingly the identical twin of the fellow in the hardware store, but less attentive. In the candy aisle he slipped a pair of energy bars into his coat pocket as he bent down to pretend to examine something on the bottom shelf. Batteries were on an endcap and a little trickier to pocket unobserved, but when he stood just right he got his body between the display and the clerk and managed to slip a set down his pants.

He wandered a little more, just to throw off the scent. By the time he was turning again toward the front of the store, prepared to leave without buying anything, it was beginning to grow dark outside, snow just beginning to fall. The clerk seemed to have doubled, having been joined by his brother or cousin or whatever the fuck he was from the hardware store next door. Unless there was a third one floating around. They were whispering back and forth, watching him.

He considered briefly putting everything back. But he needed the food—it had been well over a day since he had had anything to eat—and he needed the batteries too, particularly if he was going to spend the night outdoors. He needed to be certain his flashlight wouldn't go out. *Matches, too*, he thought, *otherwise no fire*. He found a box of them, slipped them into his duffle bag.

The clerk from the hardware store was heading toward him, his lips in a tight line. The other clerk, the one who actually worked there, had moved to block the front door.

Lars headed quickly up the aisle and toward the back of the store. Behind him, the man closest to him gave a shout, and Lars burst into a run, darting through the door marked *Employees Only*. He swerved around boxes and metal shelves until he reached the back wall. He chose a direction and ran along it until he hit the door, a metal bar slung about waist-level. He pushed on the bar and the door opened to a blast of cold and an alarm went off. And then he was out in an alley, the light fading, snow drifting slowly down. He ran, his feet slipping on the ice, hearing the sounds of the two clerks in pursuit behind him.

He ran until he no longer heard them, then stopped, listened. It was all but dark out now. He walked for a while, catching his breath. Where was he? He wasn't sure exactly—one of the roads leading out of town, fields on all sides. And then he heard something, a cry from behind him. He began to run again.

And then in the darkness he heard voices even closer, as if he had not run away from the two men but toward them. He cut quickly off the road and into the field beside it—only it wasn't a field but a house and its grounds. Almost a mansion from what he could see of it, he found himself idly thinking. And then he realized exactly what house it was.

But he hadn't been anywhere near it. How could that house be here?

The voices drew closer. Would they see him if he just stood still in the yard? It was already dark, but was it dark enough? Would they see his face shining like a buoy in the darkness?

It's just a house, he tried to tell himself. *Just an ordinary house. Nothing to worry about.* Before the voices came any closer, he forced himself to walk toward it, find the loose boards over the window, and squirm in.

Later he wondered if he'd heard voices after all. Or, rather, wondered if the voices he'd heard had been connected to the two clerks, if they were still chasing him. That was, he told himself as he waited in the house, the heart of the matter. Either the voices were the clerks' or they weren't. But if they weren't, what were they?

I'll just wait a little, he told himself once inside, *just until I'm sure they're gone.* But each time he thought he was safe and made for the window, he'd hear them again. Or hear something like them anyway.

How much time passed? He wasn't sure. Had he slept? He didn't think so, but it was much darker in the house now, so dark he couldn't see at all save for the pale lines of light marking the joins between the window boards.

He got out his flashlight. It wasn't wise, not if the two men were still outside looking for him, but he couldn't help himself—he couldn't stand the dark, not in here. He turned it on, pointed it at the ground.

The room, he saw, looked just as it had the night before: clean, immaculately so, the floor itself freshly polished. As if it were not a deserted house after all. Having the flashlight on made him feel better, but seeing this made him feel worse.

He listened. The voices came and went for a while and then dissolved into wind, a lonely sound with nothing human to it at all. He pulled on the boards to look out and see if they were still there—or tried to anyway: the boards wouldn't give. It was as if they had been nailed back in place since he had entered. He pulled at them, hammered on them with his flashlight. Disoriented, he looked around, tried the boards on the other windows, but they were all tightly nailed in place.

He went to the front door, unlocked it, rattled the handle, but something held the door shut from the other side. He hit it with his shoulder, then stopped. It had been padlocked, he remembered. Of course it wouldn't open.

All he needed was something to pry the boards away from the window. It didn't matter how they had gotten stuck—it was not worth thinking about. All that mattered was to get them off and get out.

But there was nothing in the room—the room was empty: he knew that already. He hit one of the boards with the butt of his flashlight, but when its beam began to flicker, he stopped. He couldn't bear to be without a light. Not here. He needed to find something he could pry with. He would have to find something else.

He found himself going back and forth between the entrance hall and the hallway, but stopping shy of opening the door at the end of the hallway. He looked in the kitchen, found nothing but empty cabinets. The dining room was empty too. He tried the doors to either side at the end of the passage, discovered them both still locked. He kept searching the same empty rooms and finding nothing. *I won't go*, he was telling himself, *not in there*.

But in the end he did go. He could see the poker in his mind, leaning in its stand just beside the fireplace. He would, he told himself, rush in, take the poker, leave. He would look at nothing, no one. He would think about nothing, no one. He would just come and go. He wouldn't stay.

But when he finally opened the door, a fire was already lit, roaring in the fireplace. He couldn't help but see that. And he couldn't help but see that the spray of blood was there again on the wall above the mantel, looking even larger than before. Just as he couldn't help but see the creature in the chair, struggling into, or perhaps out of, its skin. The skin was still on the bottom half of its body, but not the top half.

It looked at him and perhaps smiled. Moved its face anyway in a way that frightened him.

"Back for more?" it said.

"I was just leaving," said Lars.

The creature ignored him. "You wanted another story?" it said. "Is that what you came for?" And it reached out toward his face.

It didn't touch him, but his face still felt warm. He could not, he suddenly found, move.

It reached down and wormed further into the sheath. What had not been a hand became a hand. It flexed the fingers experimentally, settling the skin deeper around them.

"No story," it said. "I haven't eaten."

Lars felt the flashlight slip from his fingers. It struck the floor with a clunk, then began to roll away, the sound abruptly cut off as if, suddenly, it was no longer there.

"Well," it said. "What am I to do with you?"

The fire roared and then suddenly fell silent, the rest of

the room too. In the silence, the creature came closer. First it touched Lars with its hand, then with the thing that was not a hand, and finally it wrapped what remained of the loose, empty skin around him and drew him in.

THANATRAUMA
Steve Rasnic Tem

The limitless sky outside Andrew's bedroom window was the hue of soured milk and mushrooms. It wasn't an unusual sky for a cold, late autumn day, with the fallen leaves dark and shredded, streaking the lawns, turned into a decaying filth encrusting the edges of things.

Last night someone had turned over the trashcans put out for this morning's collection. Up and down the street the large green cans lay on their sides, garbage spilling over the sidewalks and out into the lanes. He wondered who could have been so angry, or in these times was it a sign of the carefree? Everyone would think a gang of young people did it, but sightings of sick raccoons had been reported in the neighbourhood the past few weeks. Wasn't it more likely to be one of them? A flyer stuck in his door had provided a phone number to call in case of a sighting, and a warning not to approach, as raccoons were known carriers of rabies.

To make matters worse, vehicles had driven through this cold variegated sludge and dragged the trash everywhere. Some of his neighbours were already out there vigorously trying to make things right. He'd neglected to put his own trash out; it slipped his mind regularly. Still, he needed to lend a hand.

But he hadn't talked to any of these people since his wife's passing. And now, several years later, how could he even begin? There was far too much that should have been said.

On such days he longed for snow to cover everything, to provide some semblance that the world had been made fresh. But more often than not the snow did not come, and he'd choose to close the curtains rather than look outside. Which he did now, in case one of his neighbours looked up at the window and saw him spying on all their efforts.

From inside his body came a soft noise like something breaking. He could feel his deadened flesh falling away, bones slipping and sour organs spilling out. Still, he managed to move forward despite his demise.

It bothered him, how sensitive he was to changes in the weather, to colours, to atmosphere and mood. It was hard to say how he really felt about anything.

He'd rearranged his bedroom several times in the years since Marge's death. He'd first gotten rid of the bed and all the bedding. He'd given their daughters the chest of drawers, the twin nightstands, her armoire, her clothes and jewellery. They'd been happy to receive them, although they didn't understand why he'd wanted to let her things go so quickly. He didn't know how to explain, but he felt his life depended on it.

Later he'd removed key pieces from the living and dining rooms—the ones she'd liked the most—and given them to various thrift shops. He and his wife had had similar tastes so it was necessary to replace some of the furniture with styles not at all to his liking. He wanted no reminders. As a result, some mornings it felt as if he had awakened in a random hotel. Who had chosen such bland artwork? He must have ordered it online, although he couldn't remember actually doing so. Desert scenes, mostly, a fried-egg sun over plains of crumbling whites. The American Southwest, or perhaps Australia, or some alien world.

Andrew went over to his dresser and sorted his prescriptions and supplements. He re-read the yellowing paper specifying the proper amounts. He had no idea why he couldn't remember them, but he could not. He dutifully consumed his pills with three full glasses of water. He had no idea what might happen if he neglected to take them. He doubted that there would be anything dramatic, but he wouldn't take the chance. His primary focus of late was to avoid suffering. His ancient physician had told him, "You're actually pretty healthy, considering. Hell, you're in better shape than me!"

His eyes began their involuntary flutter. He clutched the edges of the dresser as anxiety grabbed onto him and shook. Several bottles fell over, a half-empty glass. He would have a mess to clean up. "Nerves," the physician called it. One of these bottles was supposed to take care of his nerves, but often did not. Of course, Andrew had never revealed to his doctor all his symptoms.

His hands appeared claw-like, the skin stretched. When had his wrists gotten so skinny? He'd been trying to lose weight, but feared that some of his weight loss might be involuntary. How could you tell the difference? He supposed if he suddenly died he would have his answer.

His vision blurred slightly. Great hunks of flesh began to disappear from his arms and legs. They looked like partially eaten chicken wings and drumsticks. It was enough to put one off meat, but he figured he needed the protein. He gazed down at his naked body. Numerous bits were missing, others dripping. He felt the beginnings of nausea, made his hands let go of the dresser, and ran to the bathroom.

Once he'd emptied his system sufficiently the visions disappeared. He stared at himself in the mirror. Mirrors had become largely useless. They rarely showed him anyone he could recognize.

He went back into the bedroom and sat on the edge of the bed. He'd have to do something about the smell. He hated how his body smelled even at the best of times. He was tempted to crawl back under the covers but would not allow himself that escape. Again, he sensed that his life depended on it.

He should eat something, although he couldn't think of anything he was hungry for. Something pre-packaged perhaps. Something processed to the point that it was no longer recognizable. Anything that didn't look as if it had once been alive.

Marge had been unable to eat the last month of her life. Not crackers, not even gelatine. She'd put something in her mouth and chew but her throat would not permit her to swallow it down. She had simply lost all desire for it. Similarly, she lost all desire for his touches, his stories, his speech, their daughters' speech. Marge could no longer bear to listen, and eventually, to talk. She began to live in a world where such activities no longer had meaning.

He struggled to understand and accept. They'd always talked things through, and when he'd promised to be with her until the very end, he'd assumed he would do so as they talked about this, about everything.

In the hospital they fed her this cream-coloured liquid in plastic bags through a tube leading into a vein above her heart. They'd sent her home with a supply of these refrigerated bags and shown him how to prepare and administer them once daily, how to attach the tubing and how to disinfect. They told him the bags contained a mixture of nutrients and chemicals. It filled their bedroom with a grainy smell. He recalled a similar smell when he'd been a young man working near a dog food factory.

Every day he would talk to Marge and tell her what he was doing as he prepared her daily meal: the steps required to reduce the chances of infection, the attachment of the tubes, the readying of the pump. Marge still had nothing to say, but periodically she would say "yes"—whether out of politeness or as some part of her own internal process he did not know. He was terrified, of course, of making a mistake, of doing something that would make it worse for her, but each day he still did what he'd been instructed to do. And her belly did swell over time, although he wasn't sure that it was from nourishment.

Eventually Andrew dressed, got in his car, and obtained a burger and some fries via a drive-thru. Once home he pulled the meal apart and examined it: the bun had a plastic sheen and the perfectly circular patty resembled no meat he'd ever seen before. He gobbled everything greedily. The accompanying soda burned down his throat gratifyingly.

Although retirement required no scheduling on his part, no necessary destination or progress toward any sort of goal, no need to ever leave the house really, Andrew had still instituted a regular routine as a way of giving some minimal structure and meaning to his life. Meals and sleep occurred at the same times every day, as did reading the newspaper or a book, as did brooding, as did panic.

As it did every day following lunch the wallpaper in the living and dining rooms began to peel from the top, long curling bits dropping down to reveal great patches of black mould underneath. Wall board began to buckle and dark insects crawled out of the resulting gaps. There were drips everywhere as paste and paint began to liquefy. There were other things as well: vermin and tiny creatures he had no name for living in the walls, coming out to reveal themselves. But he never looked at these too closely as a previous glance had shown they bore the faces of dead friends and relatives.

Andrew made some coffee—hard to think of it even remotely as food—and carried it out into the backyard. He sat in an ancient wooden chair beneath a naked maple and drank it while gazing at the mass of wreckage the yard had become.

Marge used to spend an enormous amount of time out here; he had not. He'd hired a man to rake the bulk of the leaves and haul them away. Dead flower heads bent the grey stems of the ravaged beds leaving jagged ends pointing at the sky. A stiff breeze lifted wire-like branches and made them rattle, broken bits joining the debris piles beneath the bushes. He regretted not paying the man enough to simply take everything away.

Nature made its own trash, and it used to be Marge's chosen role to deal with it. Andrew had become accustomed to letting it lay. Since her death the backyard had accumulated a collection of broken pots, ice-cracked plaster statuary, rusted garden implements, rotted cushions, and objects whose names and functions had escaped his memory. Marge would have been ashamed, and he was ashamed to realize her opinions were no longer relevant to him. She should have managed to stay alive if she'd wanted some say.

But was it really so bad? Andrew felt both drawn and repelled. Some day he might just take a nap out here, and whatever crawled his way was welcome to anything it could grab.

But he supposed it would be bad if his daughters found him that way. Perhaps he would pass away peacefully in his sleep. That's what everyone hoped for, wasn't it? No suffering, and a little bit of dignity?

When the visiting nurse first met Marge lying so quietly, making such a small shape in the bed, she'd said, "Your mother…" and both alarmed and angered Andrew had interrupted, "My *wife*." Another time he might have been flattered, although now he could not imagine when.

After several weeks at home Marge entered a period of even more intense silence, and no longer replied "yes" to his recitation of her food preparation, nor did she ask him to adjust her pillows or apply ointment to her lips. She slept, or he assumed she slept. Sometimes he would ask her questions and she would reward him with a vague nod. Frequently he studied her for signs of breathing, and he changed her adult diapers as necessary, although she gave him only minimal cooperation. The nurse on her daily visits reassured him this was to be expected with the increase in her pain medications.

Eventually there came a day when the sounds of her breathing returned, but they were laboured, occasionally violent, and frightening. The nurse came to the house after he called, and let him know that again, this was normal, she wasn't in any distress. This was to be expected as the body shuts down. The end would be relatively soon, so perhaps he wanted to call their daughters for a final visit?

Their daughters came, and cried, and left again and Andrew was left with Marge and her body and her breathing.

Andrew had gone downstairs to eat something. A can of tuna fish, which thankfully did not look like fish, but more like very soft, flavourful wood chips, like mulch for the neglected flower beds.

When he returned to their bedroom he discovered that everything was silent, back to where it had been before this last stage, and he felt almost relieved. He stared at her for a while, and unable to find those vague indications of breath, he approached, and lay down beside her, and touched her, and tried to gently shake her awake. He knew she wouldn't come awake, but he still felt that was what he was supposed to do.

He needed to call his daughters, and then he would lie with her for a while until they came, but there was this stench, and he didn't want his daughters to have to deal with that on their final visit. Marge would have hated that, and he thought he needed to do something, or else what kind of husband had he been, what kind of father?

He readied a clean diaper and some wipes, and he gently turned her, but hadn't anticipated the imbalance she possessed now, or her inability to participate, and she flopped over onto her face and a kind of sludge flowed out of her mouth, the rank contents of her stomach he supposed, but he really had no idea. He was completely ignorant, and here he had made this terrible mistake, and it had broken him, what he had done, how he had let her down, and he cried out in pained confusion, and tried to roll her back as gently as he could, but nothing about her felt right or normal, and her chin went down, and now he had more to clean. So he grabbed every rag and towel he could find to soak it all up, blotting and wiping it away, crying and cursing himself, and what he could not wipe away he tried to find ways to hide by folding and bunching the bed clothes and towels around her, all of which he knew he must throw out once they'd taken her away.

Andrew must have dozed off outside in the yard, because suddenly he was blinking his eyes against the changing sunlight. The sky appeared to be melting, great gobs of it dropping away like soaked tissue wherever the sun broke through the clouds. But he was just tired. He never seemed to get enough sleep. He'd even forgotten how much he was supposed to get. What had his physician said? "As much as you can." That old man was useless, but perhaps the appropriate physician for Andrew in this phase of his life.

It had been years since he'd had his eyes checked. No doubt his prescription needed updating, or did you reach a point where very little improvement was possible? Perhaps he simply needed more sugar. He looked at his wrist but he must have left his watch by the bed. Was that his hand with all the skin hanging from every finger, as if he had forced his way through a mass of cobwebs? He looked away and gazed at the lawn, where great masses of dirt were churning. At any moment he expected an arm to pop out of the soil.

He looked at his hand again. It was an ugly, emaciated thing, this old man's appendage, but at least its covering of skin was more or less intact again. But he was alarmed at the apparent thinness of its skin—he could see almost every vein and joint. Sometimes as the body declines it breaks our sense of time. Had he read this, or simply experienced it?

Marge had always loved his body, or at least that was what she had said. Now he could not imagine how that was possible—he couldn't stand the look of it, the smell of it. Did everyone else smell their own stink the way he did? He considered that perhaps they didn't, otherwise they'd be unable to show themselves in public.

He heard a murmuring beyond the bushes from where his neighbours had their lawns, and lives. He tried to put down his coffee cup and climb out of the chair but the cup was no longer in his hand. He searched the ground around him but found only mushrooms, hundreds of them showing their dirty faces to the sky. Of course it was their season, but he hadn't noticed them when he first sat down.

He stood and made his way across the lawn, walking carefully because he didn't want to step on any of the mushrooms. Although he couldn't imagine there being any danger in it the prospect repelled him. He almost stumbled over an old log by one of the dead flowerbeds. He remembered how he had placed it there under Marge's instructions. Now it had dark, spongy pieces falling away and a spread of moss over one end. Moss crept up the bases of several other trees in the yard—some of it a bright, almost phosphorescent green, and some of it dark and dry-looking, like spreading patches of dead skin. The sight made him want to rub his arms, but when he tried it hurt, as if the skin were loose and detaching itself from the muscle underneath.

He thought of Marge, and how in her last days she had seemed this old, rotted log, and he hated himself for it. She had been his beautiful wife. Should he call the man back to remove this log, or would that only make him feel worse? Suddenly he was at a loss as to where he should step. A tumble of bleached flesh and internals had spilled from one of the flowerbeds, gummed together with translucent membrane. It smelled both sweet and sour. It alarmed him that he suddenly felt hungry, thinking of seafood, which at one time he had loved. He had an impulse to drop to his knees, bend and fill his mouth with its rankness. It was like leaping off a cliff, not caring at all.

He looked again. It was ordinary dead vegetation; how could he have thought otherwise? Nothing here that reminded him of human flesh, although there in one corner, sunlight stirring some cobweb, some network of filament, seemed vaguely familiar. He immediately looked away.

A sharp pain on the back of his right hand. He raised it, making a fist. Some sort of wasp was stinging the same place again and again, aggressive in its attack. Odd—he hadn't seen any wasps in a few months—weren't they out of season? It turned its tiny head and appeared to glare at him, its multifaceted eyes far bigger than they should have been. He shouted and shook the thing away. Now in terrible pain he stumbled toward the back door.

One of the outdoor lamps had separated from the wall and now lay in pieces to one side of the back door. Broken glass scattered like a spray of ice. When had that happened and why hadn't he noticed it before? At one shattered end a pile of crushed insects—moths and mayflies and the like—lay with their bodies roasted by the bulb. More invisible flying things buzzed at him. He cried out and struggled with the knob, finally jerked the door open, slamming it shut behind him.

Both daughters stayed at the house until the hearse arrived. The nurse had given him some names of funeral homes, and once he'd made his selection she made the initial call. While his girls cried over their mother's body he waited in his study. He thought he simply wanted to honour their privacy, but in a moment of clarity realized he couldn't bear to witness that moment. He had no idea if this made him a bad person or not.

When the men arrived he went downstairs and let them

in. He was surprised to see their black suits and ties, and the long black vehicle parked in his driveway. Andrew wasn't sure exactly what he'd expected, but he hadn't expected this TV-like scene. They were quite circumspect, and one practically whispered that they needed his signature before they could come inside. He signed, but did not read the paper on the man's clipboard. He showed them upstairs, and they said hello to his daughters. The one who had done all the talking said the family might not want to be in the room as they removed the body. His daughters insisted on staying, while he retreated into the room next door. He stood there, waiting, unable to sit down. He heard a sliding sound coming from the bed, and one of his daughters made a sudden, soft sob. He did not know what she had seen, and would never ask.

It had been explained to him that the transporters would take the body to a central place, a "hub," where it would wait with other bodies until picked up by the designated funeral home. He could not imagine such a place, and he knew that Marge would have hated the very idea.

In his bathroom Andrew poured disinfectant over the sting, and then waited there cradling the injured hand with the other until it stopped burning. Then he took a long shower. He'd started taking multiple showers every day after Marge died. He wondered if that was bad for the skin. He really should look it up. It wasn't that he felt dirty, or in any way unclean. He simply liked the release it gave him. There seemed to be a kind of exchange, the heat, the liquid passing into his flesh even as some aspect of his flesh—some tension, some secret—passed into the water, striking the tiles beneath his feet and disappearing down the drain. He wondered if it were possible to stay under the water for so long the body eventually disappeared. He would have to look that up as well.

When the snow finally did come it was almost a surprise. It filled the sky rapidly with bits of white—as if the world were rapidly disintegrating to reveal the blank backdrop beneath. Andrew wandered from window to window, opening all the curtains, eager for some new view. Snow quickly packed the lawns, piled up against the fences, gathered along the edges of limbs, highlighting then weighing them down. By the time it stopped late in the day there was at least a foot of heavy, wet snow, maybe more. The world lay hushed and lifeless beneath its sheets.

Inside the house the rooms filled with brilliant snow-glare. There was nothing flattering in its revelations of dust and grime accumulated since his wife's death, the spaces left empty from furniture removed, the aging stacks of laundry and unopened mail. Had he really been living this way?

He glanced out an upstairs window into the back yard. Snow had erased almost everything, an emptiness bounded by fence. But there, a man was climbing over his fence, his face turned up defiantly in Andrew's direction.

He pulled on his slippers and raced down the stairs. He grabbed the poker from the fireplace and went through the porch and the door and into the backyard. He kept the poker raised, stepping awkwardly through the snow, watching for the man's footprints. The snow was churned by the fence, but Andrew could find no distinct trail.

His feet were completely swallowed up by the white, but he didn't really feel that cold. There was a chill, certainly, stiffening his skin and making him blush, but nothing that he couldn't handle. He'd handled so much already, and he was doing just fine, wasn't he?

The old chair under the maple had finally collapsed, pieces of it protruding above the snow.

He wasn't sure where to go. He heard a terrible sound of breathing behind him and swung, throwing him off balance, sprawling into the snow. Something dark and furious leapt over him, attaching itself to the fence. Andrew jerked his head up. An old man was perched on the top of the fence, staring at him. It didn't seem possible—surely that fence was too flimsy to support the weight of a man. And yet there he was, staring at him wide-eyed and shaking. Andrew felt suddenly weak and dizzy and struggled for breath. His chest felt as if it might erupt.

Then the old man turned his head, changing into a raccoon, its long tongue hanging out. Was it ill? Andrew didn't even know what he was supposed to look for.

The raccoon bounded from the fence and landed beside him. Andrew covered his face, but the raccoon didn't touch him. He heard it race across the snow, scramble over something, and then nothing. But Andrew still kept his face covered, listening, refusing to move until he'd heard something more.

"Sweetheart," he said after some time had passed. "Please."

There were the sounds of distant traffic, the soft whisper of wind across the snow, a dripping suggestive of an imminent thaw, and then, possibly, *yes*.

PACK YOUR COAT
Aliya Whiteley

It swept through our school at a ferocious rate. By the time first bell had sounded for break everyone already knew it, and it was busily mutating in the playground to appeal even more to the children that shared it.

Such stories are viruses. They have a life of their own. They breathe, and move, and infect us.

This one was about an orange coat.

I didn't realise how much it had a hold on me until I came across it again, twenty years later, in my office.

"My sister's friend," said Katie.

"Your sister's friend saw him?" Tyler leaned forward, over his desk, his attention fully diverted from his computer.

"What's this?" I said. I'd just finished a call with a potential buyer for the business. It was the first sniff in an age, and I had been indulging myself in the dream of leaving town for good, starting over somewhere else, as I emerged from the back room to get a coffee.

"Tell her," said Tyler. "Start at the beginning."

She walks along the top of the cliffs, with eyes cast down,

attention reserved only for the sea. It is unpredictable where the rocks jut out the waves bulge and then spray erupts over the jagged peaks. But this is all happening far below her, and there is no path down. The cliffs have been marked as unsafe, and wire nets have been stapled over the barefaced slabs that threaten to fall. It feels like containment to her; if they should crash, let them go.

There isn't much daylight left. The tide is coming in fast. The waves have a ferocity to them that excites her. Soon the rocks will be covered, and then the small lip of the beach below.

The dog is having a fine time, capering ahead of her, stopping, sniffing, running on. She doesn't call him back. He'll come when he's ready.

The path diverges from the cliff, turning inwards, and gorse bushes spring up on either side, but she ignores it and sticks to the edge instead. It's her usual route. A faint track has established itself through footfall over the years. She's not sure whether it's been made only by her own walking, or if she's just one of many locals who come this way.

The wind shifts direction to blow her hair straight back, bringing tears to her eyes and new sounds to her ears. Seagulls. The shush and crash of water. The dog, barking.

She calls for him, and he doesn't come.

She speeds up, scanning for him, and finally spots him in the distance. He's very close to the edge, dodging forwards, barking, chasing around in a circle to start again. Shouting at him does no good. She runs the remaining distance, the cold wind stabbing at her face, into her lungs, and grabs his collar to clip on the lead.

His attention is still on the edge. She looks over and sees, on the rocks, an orange coat.

It takes her a moment to work out that it's not just a coat, flapping. A man wears it. He is waving.

She waves back. He does not stop waving, using both

arms over his head. The spray of the waves is soaking him in regular bursts. He slips to one knee, then struggles to stand.

There's no boat, no sign of how he got there. Did he climb down? How can he climb back up?

The waves are breaking so close to him. For a moment he is hidden from view by a fierce uprush of the sea, and she holds her breath. But he's still there when it recedes. He is looking at her.

She takes out her phone and dials the emergency number. She asks for the coastguard, and describes where he is. She feels calm, even though the dog is pulling at the lead, still barking. She can't hear what the voice is saying. "What was that?" she asks.

"Hold on," says the voice. "Hold on." It's not really a message for her, but for the man on the rocks, so she shouts it down to him, knowing that he can't possibly hear her.

He continues to wave. She can't wave back any more, with one hand holding the lead and the other holding the phone. "Hold on," she calls again.

She feels the big wave coming. There's a pattern to the sea. The smaller waves clashing over the rocks can only lead to a larger swell. The sea pulls back, exposing more of the rock on which he stands, and then the water surges over him entirely, like a sheet being thrown into the air to settle on a bed.

When it recedes, he's gone.

She scans for a sign of him. The orange coat. Surely that will be visible? Her eyes will find the orange coat. But she does not see it, and the coastguard does not find it, even though they search for hours, well into the night.

Later on, an official suggests delicately to her that maybe the man was a product of her imagination. Not there at all.

"That's an old one," I say. It has made some more changes to itself since the first time I heard it, but I'd know it anywhere.

It's the coat that gives it away; the coat is always the same.

"It just happened last week," says Katie. "To my sister's friend."

"Friend of a friend of a friend," adds Tyler, and smiles at me.

I try to think of something managerial to say, but the best I can come up with is some old cliché about time being money, and then I retreat to my office, abandoning my plans for coffee in my desire to get away from the same old conversations, the usual crowd. The story that never ends

I meet Sarah in the Ship and Anchor. She's already ordered two white wines. Large ones. It's been a bad week for her too, then.

We sit in the back room. It was once called the Ladies' Lounge, and is always quieter than the main bar, as if memories of those times continue to permeate the atmosphere.

"Here's to Fridays."

"Fridays," I echo. She starts talking, and I listen. She's not from here originally, so even when she's moaning about life I find it more bearable than talking to the people I grew up amongst. She brings a fresh perspective to it all, which makes me feel better for a while.

I tell her about the possible buyer for the firm.

"That's brilliant! I know it's taken a while, but I've always said someone was going to come along. That place is a goldmine. Solar panels are the future."

"Not my future, hopefully."

She knows this story too. I inherited a business from my father, gave it a few tweaks to bring it up to the present day, and have been tied to it ever since. And she's wrong: it's not a goldmine. It's a life support machine. It sustains me and ties me to itself. Being connected to it, and this town, is almost like living, and nothing like a life at all.

"Are they offering enough?" says Sarah.

"Just about." I have a whole year of travel planned. I've had my route marked on a map above my bed for years. I used to trace it with my finger. "There's a long way to go yet, though."

She doesn't say *good luck* or *fingers crossed* or anything along those lines, which is another reason why I like her. She tips her glass to touch mine, and we both drink.

"Why do you hate this town so much?" she asks. "It's really not so bad. There are worse places to live."

This is something I've never explained to her, no matter how many times she asks the question. I suspect she'd think me crazy if I told her that it is the act of belonging here that makes me hate it. It claims me as its property, and the more I struggle, the more it presents reasons to stay. Financial, emotional. The business, my mother. Love, fear. So many things that it should not be possible to leave behind, and I resent every one of them. Fear—that's the one I hate the most.

So I shrug and say, "All I want is the opportunity to find that out for myself."

"Listen," she says. "The strangest thing happened to my neighbour's uncle when he was walking the coastal path a while back. Apparently—"

Up high, walking free: it's the daily routine. A stroll along the cliffs. Every day the hills to the path get harder to climb, but he has it in his head now: miss a day and that's the start of the end. He's become attached to routines, that's how he phrases it to the cleaner who comes in twice a week, paid for by his nephew, who's a good lad.

Lad. He's in his forties, with children of his own, but the passage of time never quite seems to take. It's like this walk. He's done it so many times, and it's new to him every day.

The sea is unique, of course, so perhaps that's the reason. What's that quote? About never being able to stand in the same river twice. Down below, at the base of the cliffs, the sea is alive, twisting and dragging, rumbling over the spit of rocks that stretches out to form part of the natural harbour of the town. The tide is rushing in, along with the stronger light of late morning. Unstoppable.

He ignores the official path and follows the lighter trail for local feet, hugging the cliff edge. There's talk of it being dangerous, but if he's going to go in a rock fall then so be it. Nature itself, snatching away the ground from under you; you can't argue with that.

There's a girl on the rocks.

That can't be right. There's no path that leads down that way, never has been. But there she is, clear as day, in an orange coat with the hood up and her brown hair spilling out around the sides. The white spray is fierce about her as the waves dance. She has her legs planted wide, no doubt to try to keep her balance, but they are such very thin legs, sticking out from the frill of a dark dress, just visible beneath the coat.

She is waving to him.

He waves back.

She's in danger. Can't she see it? Maybe she could swim for it. Her face is very small, and his eyesight is not what it used to be, but he thinks she's smiling.

He shouts, but his voice is snatched away by the wind. Useless. If only he had one of those phones—his nephew offered to get him one, and he said he'd never use it. What a stupid thing to say. Arrogant, really, to assume there'd never be a need for such a thing.

He shouts that he'll get help.

A big wave hits, one of those that can reach far up the cliff side and make you think it can even come over the top in the worst weather, and he steps back from the edge, and catches his breath. When he looks for her again, she's not there. No sign of her, not even a flash of that bright coat.

He looks and looks, wishing for better eyes, and eventually forces himself to look away and start a shambling pace home, to find help, to reach a phone, wishing for faster legs this time. For youth. For anything that could make a difference to the day.

"The weirdest part is, the coastguard searched for hours and—"

"Didn't find a thing?" I supply smoothly.

"They found an orange coat. For a girl. But it was really old. An antique. They couldn't understand how it had survived for that long, and then to stay intact in the water, too…"

"That's a good twist," I tell her.

"No, it's true! My neighbour told me directly. Seriously, he wouldn't lie." She looks so earnest. I think she really wants to believe it.

This is how it survives. This is how it spreads.

The negotiations of the sale progress, and I try to focus on that alone, but my mind keeps returning to the first time I heard the story. I was very young; was *it* young too? I doubt it. It had a power to it, even then, that suggested a certain maturity.

I ran home after school that day and found my mother in the kitchen, as usual, looking out of the window towards the harbour. We lived high up in the hills, close to the old church building and the temporary cabins that constituted the school. Behind us a new estate was being built at a frightening speed. We were a growing town.

I told her about the young girl on the rocks, in her orange coat. To me, she was the friend of the Headmaster's niece, or some such string of relationships. My grasp of how people were connected was tenuous. Like many people, it still is: when others talk of their husband's brother's friend's wife's daughter's uncle's and so on and so on, I soon lose interest. Where do all these paths intersect? The story is always complete, encapsulated, no matter how many degrees of separation it involves. The walker on the cliffs and how they are connected to the town—that remains incidental. We should all be focusing on that orange coat. That's what the story wants.

The orange coat was the part I wanted to tell my mother about in particular. I could see it so clearly in my mind.

"That old chestnut," said my mother.

She returned her calm gaze to the sea.

Then the story disappeared as quickly as it had arrived. I wonder where it moved on to. Down the coast to Cornwall, perhaps.

I hated every small alteration that came along as it continued its impregnation of the playground. I had thought it was true. Some part of me wanted it to be true.

"Did they find the girl?" I asked my mother one night as she sat with me after one of the nightmares that started at around that time. "The one with the orange coat?"

She kissed my forehead and squeezed my hand. Her palm was warm and solid. "Best take it all with a pinch of salt," she said.

Years later I looked up where that phrase came from. There are a few variations. The one I remember is that the Roman general Pompey ingested a little poison every night to try to make himself immune to it; in order to make it palatable he took it with a grain of salt.

My mother likes her sayings. I wonder if she realises that they all have old stories attached to them too.

"It's a beautiful part of the world," says Simon. He has balanced his brown leather briefcase against the leg of his chair. It looks expensive and shiny and new. Possibly it was made in China, and then displayed in a shop that's part of a chain. There's no story lurking behind it.

It will become part of this office. My father occupied this space for so many years, struggling to keep the business afloat, and now I will sell it and be gone, and Simon and his briefcase can take my place.

"It is stunning in the summer," I say. "Bleak in the winter, if I'm honest. But some people prefer it that way."

"Fewer tourists," says Simon with a smile. "I'm sure there are lots of local customs I'm not aware of. I'll stand out by a mile at first."

"You'll get to know them. Everyone's very friendly. Katie and Tyler are keen to take you on a night out once you're settled, and they'll tell you everything you need to know."

"They seem very capable. It's a real shame you can't hang around for a bit so I can pick your brain, but—"

"My flight leaves tonight," I tell him. Saying such words brings on a spasm of terror every single time. It's tempting fate, surely. This is where he says *I've changed my mind*. But no. He doesn't. He nods.

"Very exciting," he says. I can tell from his face that he thinks he's got the best deal here. I'm the fool who sold a goldmine to get away from a beautiful place. Surely there can't be any place in the world as wonderful as this.

"The best thing about living here is the sea," says my mother.

"There's sea in other places," I hear myself saying, ridiculously. "Seventy per cent of the world is water."

"It's not the same."

She's been positioned next to the window that looks out

over the harbour. Her favourite spot. A crocheted blanket has been tucked around her knees by one of the workers. I feel grateful for their ongoing care of her, and their sympathetic looks on the bad days, but today is a good day.

"You're right," I say. "It's not the same."

Is it even worth saying goodbye, when she won't remember it? Maybe she will. I have constructed versions of her, leading up to this moment. There is a version that calls out my name every night, and one of the workers phones my mobile and tells me I have to return. And there is a version that forgets me as soon as I'm gone, sits peaceably in this spot, and looks blankly at me if I ever return. I honestly don't know which version I'd prefer.

"You look like that lady," she says.

So it's not such a good day, after all.

"Which one, Mum?"

"The one on the rocks that time."

"When?"

She can't answer this. I shouldn't have asked the question. She moves her head from side to side, searching, and then returns her vision to the view.

I could ask—was it by the cliffs? What was the woman wearing?

In truth, I don't know if the story follows me, or if I search it out. It's like the fear of the dark I developed after the nightmares started. At first, a small bedside light kept it at bay. Then it wasn't enough. I needed the overhead light on, to try to banish all shadows, and what might lurk in them. Then the dark was a strip of black, under the door, ready to creep in if I let it. I had my eyes fixed on it every night until sleep overcame me.

Once you are afraid of something, you see it, for just a moment, every time you close your eyes. You hear the echo of it between each breath.

I said goodbye in the end, and she looked confused and shook her head. But she did not make a fuss, and now it's done, and the last thing before I take a taxi to the train station is a slow walk up the cliffs to look out over a view from a vantage point I've not dared to visit since I was a child.

It's approaching sunset, and it's going to be an unspectacular one, not worthy of a picture postcard; the clouds are low on the horizon, and the sea is choppy. There's a light, stinging rain starting up. The tide is coming in. It roars and crashes below, and then gathers itself back for another assault upon the rocks.

I take the path that only locals use, skirting around the gorse bushes to stick close to the crumbling edge. I refuse to lift my eyes from my feet; I will not look over the edge. Not until I'm ready. I'll know when I'm ready.

I wondered if I would know the spot, but a voice inside me tells me when to stop walking. I've arrived. I will see it. If I dare to look over the edge, it will be there.

I blink. I breathe.

The line of rocks stretches out to sea, and the tide is rushing in fast, churning and writhing around the peaks. The rain is intensifying; it is hard and cold against my face. It makes it difficult to see, and I have to stand there for a long time before I'm certain.

There's nobody down there.

No man, no woman. No little girl. No apparition, no mermaid, no creature of the deep. No ghost, no spirit.

No orange coat.

It was never waiting for me in this place. And that means I cannot leave it, and my fear of it, behind.

Will I find it on the other side of the world? It might not be set on a cliff top, or hinge on the threat of a relentless tide. It might have replaced the police or the coastguard with other officials, or done away with the dog barking at the waves. But it will manifest again.

Wherever I go, I'll take it with me.

HAAK
John Langan

Today Mr Haringa was wearing a scarlet waistcoat with gold trim and gold buttons under his usual tweed jacket and over his usual shirt and tie. A gold watch chain looped out of the waistcoat's right pocket, through which the outline of a large pocket watch was visible. While Mr Haringa was required to dress professionally, as were all staff and students at Quinsigamond Academy, he did so without the irony and even mockery evident in the wardrobe choices of many students and not a few of his colleagues: cartoon-character ties, movie-print blouses, black Doc Martens. His jackets and trousers were in dark, muted colours, his white button-down shirts equally unassuming, and his half-Windsor-knotted ties tended to blue and forest-green tartans. If he added a sweater vest to the day's ensemble, which he did as fall crisped and stripped the leaves of the school's oaks, then that garment matched the day's colour scheme. "It's like he *likes* dressing this way," the occasional student muttered, and though delivered disparagingly, the remark sounded fundamentally accurate.

For Mr Haringa to appear in so extravagant, so ornate an article of clothing was worthy of commentary from the majority of the student body and a significant minority of his fellow teachers; although the conversation only circled, and did not veer toward, him. Aside from the scarlet-and-gold waistcoat, whose material had the dull shine of age, Mr Haringa behaved in typical fashion, returning essays crowded with stringent corrections and unsparing comments, lecturing on the connection between Coleridge's *Rime of the Ancient Mariner* and Robert Bloch's "Yours Truly, Jack the Ripper" to his two morning sections, and discussing the possible impact of Maturin's *Melmoth the Wanderer* on Browning's "Childe Roland to the Dark Tower Came" with the first of his afternoon classes. By his second class, the change in his attire had receded in the students' notice.

A few in the final session wondered if the waistcoat was related to that date on the course syllabus, which had been left uncharacteristically blank. They had completed two weeks of exhaustive analysis of Conrad's *Heart of Darkness*, during which they had lingered at each stop on Marlow's journey into the interior of the African continent to meet the elusive and terrible Kurtz, examining sentences, symbols, and allusions with the care of naturalists cataloguing a biosphere. Ahead lay a selection of Yeats's poetry, including "Second Coming," which several students had mentioned they knew already but which Mr Haringa assured them they did not. This afternoon, however, was a white space, unmapped terrain. As the rest of the syllabus was a study in meticulous planning, it seemed impossible for the gap to be anything other than intentional.

When Mr Haringa entered the room, he strode to the desk, removed his jacket and hung it on the back of his chair, loosened the knot of his tie, pulled it from his neck, draped it over the jacket, and unbuttoned the top button of his shirt. Had he appeared stark naked, the students could not have been more shocked. He extracted the pocket watch from the waistcoat and opened it. Although gold, or gold-plated, its surface was scratched and dented. With his left hand, he gave the crown a succession of quick turns. Roused to life, the timepiece emitted a loud, sharp ticking. Watch in hand, Mr Haringa said, "Anyone who wants to leave is free to do so. For next class, please be sure to read 'Sailing to Byzantium' and be prepared to discuss it."

The students exchanged glances. Mr Haringa offering them the opportunity to depart class before the bell—after one or two minutes past the bell—was almost as startling as the scarlet waistcoat, the removal of his jacket and tie. One of the better students raised her hand. Mr Haringa nodded at her. She cleared her throat and said, "Are you serious? We can go?" The class tensed at the directness of the question, ready for it to provoke their teacher's notorious sarcasm.

But his razored wit remained in its scabbard; instead, he said, "Yes, Ashley, I'm serious. If you want to leave, you may."

Another student raised his hand. "What happens if we stay?"

"You'll have to wait to find out."

In the end, slightly less than half the class accepted the offer. Once the door had closed on the last student's departure, Mr Haringa closed the watch and returned it to its pocket. "Aidan," he said, "would you get the lights?"

For an instant the classroom was plunged into darkness. Someone laughed nervously. There was a click, and a series of lights sprang on around the room's perimeter. Positioned at the base of the walls, each cast upward a crimson light whose long oval shape suggested a window. A trick of their placement made the lights appear to hover ever so slightly in front of the painted brick. A couple of the students wondered when Mr Haringa had been in to set up so elaborate a display. They had watched him walk to his car yesterday afternoon, and they had seen him exiting it this morning. Not to mention the teacher had not impressed them as especially proficient in technology. Perhaps another faculty member had helped him? Mr Baillie, maybe?

Despite the fabric enveloping it, the pocket watch was louder in the crimson space, every tick opening into a tock. Yet when Mr Haringa spoke, his voice, though low, was clear. "You will recall," he said, "that, following his trip up what was then the Congo River, Joseph Conrad became ill. As does Marlow, yes. Unlike Marlow, Conrad went to a spa in Switzerland the year after his trip, to continue his recovery. He was suffering from a variety of complaints, including gout, which likely was unrelated to his time on the Congo, recurrent malaria, which likely was related to his months on the river, and pain in his right arm, which may or may not have been connected to his recent activities. Oh, and there was something wrong with his hands too, a strange swelling. To put it mildly, he was not in good shape.

"The spa he went to overlooked a mountain lake. A small steamboat, not unlike the one Conrad had captained on the Congo, ferried passengers to and from the spa to a modest town on the opposite shore. From his chair on the spa's front porch, Conrad could watch it chug across the lake's smooth blue surface. He found the sight simultaneously comforting and unnerving. Eventually, once he was feeling well enough, he left his chair, ventured down to the landing, and bought a ticket for the crossing. When the boat reached the town, he did not disembark; instead, he remained on board as the vessel took on a fresh load of passengers and set off for the spa. At the dock, he stepped off and made his way up to the spa.

"Conrad repeated this trip the next day, and the one after that, and every day thereafter for a week and a half. Finally, the steamboat's captain introduced himself to him. His name was Heuvelt. He was from Amsterdam, originally, had commanded a merchant vessel in the Dutch East Indies for twenty years before retiring to the Swiss mountains, where he had established the steamboat service and was now as busy as he had ever been. He was approximately ten, fifteen years older than

Conrad, late forties to early fifties. In a letter Conrad described him as weather-beaten to handsomeness. The two of them had a pleasant exchange. Conrad complimented Heuvelt on his vessel. Heuvelt invited him to try the wheel. Conrad declined, politely, but he and Heuvelt continued their conversation over the course of their next several visits, trading stories of their respective ocean voyages. According to everyone who knew him, Conrad was an accomplished raconteur, and apparently Heuvelt was reasonably gifted as well. Their daily meetings, Conrad wrote, did as much to restore him to well-being as any of the spa's therapies. Eventually, he accepted Heuvelt's offer to steer the boat, to the irritation of the young local whose job it was. Heuvelt was impressed with Conrad's handling of the boat, and soon this became part of their daily routine. Conrad would board the steamboat, assume the wheel, and he and Heuvelt would converse while he guided the boat back and forth across the lake.

"After another couple of weeks, Heuvelt asked Conrad if he would be interested in joining him on board that evening, around sunset. There was something he wished to show Conrad, a peculiarity of the lake Heuvelt thought he would find of interest. Conrad agreed, and a few hours later was waiting alone on the landing as the steamboat pulled up to it. To his surprise, Heuvelt had the wheel, his young man nowhere to be found. 'This is not for him,' Heuvelt said, which sounds more odd, and even ominous, to us than it did to Conrad: ship captains are notorious for keeping secrets from their crew, no matter that the crew consists of a single man. Whatever their destination, Conrad understood Heuvelt was trusting him to keep it to himself.

"Heuvelt turned the boat toward the other end of the lake, which was hemmed in by steep mountains. About halfway to their destination, the sun set, leaving in its wake a crimson sky. The water caught the light, and it was as if,

Conrad wrote, they were steaming across a tide of blood, beneath a bloody firmament."

For an instant, a handful of students had the impression that the light saturating the classroom was in motion, as if they were seated on the steamboat with the writer and his friend. The tick-tock of Mr Haringa's pocket watch echoed like an enormous grandfather clock. The students shook their heads and returned their attentions to the teacher. A couple of them noticed that, despite the red filter laid over everything, Mr Haringa's waistcoat remained visible as its own distinct shade of the colour, but did not know what, if any, significance to ascribe to this.

His words still audible through the pocket watch's see-sawing progress (perhaps he was wearing a microphone?), Mr Haringa proceeded: "With the sun setting, the mountains ahead grew shadowed. As the boat drew closer to them, Conrad saw that what he had taken for a recess among the peaks was in fact a steep valley, through which a surprisingly wide river rushed into the lake. Heuvelt turned the wheel to bring the prow in line with the river, and started them up it. To either side, thick walls rose, reducing the sky to a single red strip. There was a light on the boat, but Heuvelt made no move toward it. Conrad wondered if the man was attempting to impress him. If so, he was succeeding. While the river was sufficiently broad to admit the steamboat's passage, rocks and clusters of rocks pushed up through its current every few yards, requiring a skill at navigation Conrad did not think he would have been able to summon. He assumed Heuvelt was steering them toward another lake, because he could see no way for the boat to turn around in the river, but he did not want to distract Heuvelt from his task by asking him to verify his assumption.

"They rounded a bend in the river, and there in front of them a great tree stood in the midst of the water. Easily a hundred feet high, a third that in girth, it was like no tree Conrad had seen anywhere on his travels, which, as you know, had been considerable. Deep grooves ran up its bark, clumps of moss and small plants filling the channels. Pale lichen tattooed the tops of the ridges. High overhead, thick branches formed a crown like a vast umbrella, from which a network of vines hung in loops and lines. To show him such a thing might well have been Heuvelt's intent, but the steamboat showed no signs of stopping, so Conrad assumed there was more to come. In order to circumvent the enormous obstacle, Heuvelt had to steer perilously close to its vast trunk, an arm's length away, less, and this close, Conrad could feel the tree's age. This was an ancient of its kind; when the Romans were laying roads across their empire, the tree must already have stood proud. Conrad stretched out a hand to touch the hide of so venerable a being, only to be warned off completing the act by a shake of Heuvelt's head.

"On the other side of the tree, the river spread out dramatically. Dozens of trees, each the same species and dimensions as the one they had passed, reared from the water, a flooded forest. In the twilight the trees reminded Conrad of great beasts, a herd of prehistoric animals gathered in the water to relieve the heat of the day. It was an astonishing sight, which had not been so much as hinted at during Conrad's time at the spa. This strained belief. Surely, he thought, a location as remarkable as the one into which the steamboat was sailing should be the pride of its location, should it not?"

Within each of the red lights around the classroom, a darker form appeared, a thick column suggestive of the trunk of a tree, viewed from a distance. While Mr Haringa's pocket watch counted its time, the shapes to the class's left became larger, the light on that side dimmer, as if the students were sailing this way. A handful of them felt the floor shift under the soles of their shoes, rising and falling as it would were they on the deck of a boat pushing up a river.

Although he had not changed his position in front of his desk, Mr Haringa's voice sounded closer; eyes closed, each student might have believed their teacher was seated beside them. As he continued with his narrative, the shadowy forms bisecting the rest of the red lights expanded, until it seemed the immense trees of his story surrounded the class. He said, "Employing signposts Conrad could not identify, Heuvelt sailed a winding course through the forest. Although he considered himself possessed of a superior sense of direction, Conrad soon lost track of which way they were travelling. Thinking he would regain his bearings by checking the stars already visible overhead, he leaned out from under the boat's roof. But he recognized none of the constellations burning in the sky from which the last traces of red had yet to vanish. This was impossible, of course, and he wondered if the crowns of the trees spreading between him and the stars were in some way distorting his view, which was not much more likely, but preferable to the other explanations available. He retreated beneath the roof and saw Heuvelt watching him, the expression on the man's face an indication that he knew and had shared Conrad's observation. Such confirmation was almost too much to bear, Conrad later wrote; rather than acknowledge it, he asked Heuvelt if their destination had a name.

"In reply Heuvelt said, '*Haak.*' During his years at sea, Conrad had picked up a smattering of Dutch, but this word was unfamiliar to him. He started to ask for a translation when the steamboat chugged out of the trees into a wide pool in which sat the wreck of a great ship. It was a Spanish galleon, what you or I might imagine as an old-fashioned pirate ship, with three masts for its sails, a raised deck at its rear, and square windows perforating the sides for its cannons. Centuries had passed since such vessels had been in widespread use. The ship was tilted to the right, its wood blackened with age. Gaping holes in its left flank exposed its ribs. Its foremast had broken near the base and tipped into the water. The mainmast and mizzenmast were intact, the ragged remains of their sails and rigging draped from them like faded bunting. Amidst the tattered canvas, Conrad picked out shapes dangling from the masts, the corpses of a score of men, their flesh desiccated, their clothing rotted. They had been hanged, their hands tied behind their backs."

Now the darker columns within the red lights faded, to be replaced by a variety of shapes. At the front of the room, shadowy arcs suggested a ship's ribbing, while thick diagonal lines to either side of the students stood in for the tilted masts. Interspersed among these shapes were the silhouettes of men at one end of a heavy rope, their necks crooked. Only the lights at the back of the class were absent any form, and the glow they cast forward highlighted Mr Haringa in a hellish luminescence through which the waistcoat was visible in its own scarlet hue. The pocket watch had increased in volume to the point its TICK-TOCK shuddered the students' desks, and not a few of them wondered how much longer it would be until a teacher in one of the neighbouring rooms stuck their head in the door to request Mr Haringa turn down the noise.

His voice in each student's ear, Mr Haringa said, "Conrad was stunned. As if a flooded forest in the Swiss mountains was not fantastic enough, the wreck of a huge, ocean–going ship in its midst defied explanation. There was no river large enough to have borne the galleon anywhere within fifty miles of the place. In his time at sea, Conrad had heard sailors relate glimpses of islands not on any maps, of vessels from centuries gone by. He was enough of a rationalist to ascribe the majority of these accounts to old and incomplete maps, to the confusion of distance and poor eyesight, but he was also enough of a sailor himself, to recognize that the immensity of the ocean held room for all manner of things. Although he had thought them far from the sea, it appeared the sea was not far from them. Combined with the unfamiliar constellations overhead, the remains of the ship indicated Heuvelt had taken them into one of those strange countries whose coastlines he had heard described.

"Heuvelt guided them around to the galleon's top side, keeping a wide distance between the steamboat and the masts with their tangle of sails. Throughout the trip so far, he had maintained a more or less constant speed, which he reduced as they circled the wreck. One eye on the ship, one on their course around it, he said, 'You have heard of the Armada, yes? The great fleet the Spanish king sent to invade England when Elizabeth was her queen. One hundred and thirty ships, it was said. It was defeated by the English Navy's ships, which were smaller and faster, and its tactics, which were superior. There is no one as ruthless as an Englishman. The Spanish captains chose to flee up the English and Scottish coast. Their enemies pursued them all the way. North of the Orkney Islands, the Spaniards turned west, intending to sail down the western side of Scotland into the Irish Sea. As they entered the open Atlantic, however, a ferocious storm greeted them. All along northwest Scotland and northeast Ireland, Spanish sailors were shipwrecked and came ashore. Many were killed by the populace. A few were given shelter by those Britons unfriendly to their queen.

"'There was one ship whose captain sought to escape the catastrophe of the Armada by sailing directly into the storm. He trusted his ability to navigate the wind and waves, and his crew to follow his commands. The English captains saw him heading toward the gale and allowed him to go, sure the Spaniard would not outlive his disastrous choice.

"'You know what it is like on a ship during a storm. The English were not wrong to let the Spanish vessel escape; they must have assumed the captain was choosing to die in this fashion, rather than at the edges of their swords. They were not familiar with this commander, Diego de la Castille, who was new to the responsibility of a ship but was a gifted sailor and inspiring leader. Although Poseidon struggled mightily to bring the vessel and its crew to his watery halls, the captain outmanoeuvred him, and exited the other side of the storm.

"'Perhaps the old god had the last laugh, though, because when the wind quieted and the waves calmed, the ship was in a location not even the most seasoned hand recognized.'

"Conrad said, 'This place.'

"'Yes,' Heuvelt said, 'this place of great trees rising from the water, of a hundred scattered islets.' The steamboat had drawn opposite the tip of the mainmast. So distracted had Conrad become by Heuvelt's story that he did not notice the boy crouched on the end of the mast until he uttered an exultant, blood-curdling whoop and leapt toward them. Heuvelt had kept a good fifteen yards between their boat and the mast, but the child crossed the distance effortlessly. He landed on the steamboat's roof with a solid bang, scurried along it to the front of the boat, and dropped onto the deck before the men. Only Heuvelt's raised hand restrained Conrad from fleeing the short sword whose tip was suddenly pointed at his throat. Already Heuvelt was speaking, a patois of Spanish and another tongue Conrad recognized as Greek, but of an older, a much older, form. From what Conrad could understand, the man was urging calm to the child aiming his blade at the base of Conrad's neck. Panos, Heuvelt called the boy, who was perhaps ten or eleven, his long hair sun-bleached, his bronzed forearms and legs bare, latticed with white scars. He was wearing a scarlet coat, whose sleeves had been hacked off above the elbows, and whose ragged hem hung down to his calves; despite the antique style, Conrad saw its gold brocade and knew it at once as the garment of a ship's captain. Underneath the coat, the child was dressed in a tunic stitched together from large yellowed leaves. A worn strip of leather served him as a necklace for a steel hook, of the kind a man might substitute for a hand lost to violence. Conrad recalled the name Heuvelt had given this place and said, 'This is *Haak*?'

"Without pausing his speech to the boy, Heuvelt nodded. He was slowing the boat to a crawl. The child's weapon was wavering, but was still far too close to Conrad's skin for him to feel free to move. Its tapered blade was notched, scratched, a record of many campaigns. The design reminded Conrad of illustrations he had seen in books on the ancient world. How strange it would be, he thought, to die on the point of such a sword now, at the end of the nineteenth century, with all its marvels and advances.

"As Heuvelt continued urging the boy to calm, he reached into his coat and withdrew from it a gold pocket watch. The child's eyes widened at the sight of it. Heuvelt wound the timepiece, then held it out. 'Go on,' he said, 'take it.' He'd brought it for the child. Quicker than Conrad could follow, the boy dropped the blade from his neck, leapt across the deck to Heuvelt, snatched the watch from his hand, and retreated with it to the prow. While the child hunched over the pocket watch, pressing it to one ear, then the other, Heuvelt said to Conrad, 'You have heard of the Roman captain who was sailing near Gibraltar when a loud voice declared, "The Great God Pan is dead." The captain sent word of this to the Emperor, who decreed three weeks of mourning for the passing of so important a deity. He was one of the old gods, Pan, foster-brother to Zeus. Now he is pictured as a dainty faun, but he was nothing of the kind. He was wild, savage, the cause of sudden panic in the forest. How could such a one die, eh? He did not. He withdrew into himself, made of his form a place in which he could retreat. Or perhaps that place was always what he had been, and the face he showed the other gods was a mask he put on for them. Either way, he left the society of gods and men. Who can say why? He remained undisturbed for a thousand years, more, long even as a god measures time.'

"Conrad was an experienced enough storyteller to recognize where Heuvelt's tale was headed. He said, 'Until the Spanish captain and his crew arrived to rouse Pan from his slumber.'

"'It is a dangerous thing,' Heuvelt said, 'to wake a god. Pan was both angry at the presumption and intrigued by the sight of these new men on a ship the like of which he had not seen before, dressed in strange clothing, and armed with shining weapons. His curiosity won out, and instead of appearing to them in his full glory, he chose the form of a child.'

"Conrad started. He had expected Heuvelt to declare the boy an orphaned descendant of the Spaniards. He said, 'Do you mean to say—'

"'Of course,' Heuvelt said, 'Pan did not reveal his identity to the strangers. They took the child who stared at them from a rocky islet in this unfamiliar place as another castaway. They brought him on board their ship. A man of some learning, the captain knew enough classical Greek to converse with the boy. Over the next several days, he asked him how he had come to this location, if he knew its name, if he was alone. But the only information the child would offer was that he had been here many years. The captain concluded the child had been shipwrecked with his parents as an infant, and his father and mother subsequently died. Why the boy spoke antique Greek was a mystery, but already the men were teaching him Spanish, and the child was showing them locations of fresh water, and fruit, and game, so the captain decided to allow the mystery to remain unsolved. As for Pan, whom the men had named Pedro: after a millennium of solitude, he found he enjoyed the company of men much more than he would have anticipated.'

"'Obviously,' Conrad said, nodding at the wreck, the corpses dangling from its masts, 'something changed.'

"'There lived in the waters of this place a great beast, a crocodile, such as you may have seen sunning themselves on the banks of the Nile, though bigger by far than any of those. This was an old man, a grandfather croc, veteran of a hundred battles with his kind and others. Blind in one eye, scarred the length of his thick body, he was as cunning as he was ferocious. Their first days here, one of the sailors had sighted him, surveying the ship from a distance, and his size had amazed the crew. A few of the men suggested hunting him, but the captain forbade it, cautious of the risk of such an enterprise. As the monster gave them a wide berth, his command was easily followed.

"'A few weeks after that, the crocodile capsized one of the ship's boats and devoured three of the crew. It may be that the attack was unprovoked, that the beast had been studying the sailors, stalking them. Or it may be that the sailors had disobeyed their captain's order and gone in search of grandfather croc. Well. Either way, they found him, much to their sorrow. The survivors fled to the ship, where they relayed the tale of their attack to their fellows. As you can imagine, the crew cried out for vengeance, a demand the captain gave in to. He led the hunt for the monster, and when the sailors found the crocodile, engaging him in a contest that lasted a full day, it was the Captain who struck the killing blow, at the cost of his good right hand. The sailors towed the carcass to the ship, where they butchered it and made a feast of the meat, draping the hide over the bowsprit as a trophy.

"'Pan was not on the ship for any of this. He would leave the company of the Spaniards for a day or two to wander his home. He would visit the sirens who lived in a hole in the base of one of the great trees, and who sang of the days when they drew ships to break themselves on their rocky traps, so that they might dine on the flesh of drowned sailors with their needle teeth. Or he might watch the Cimmerians, who lived on a rocky island on the far side of the trees, and whose time was spent fighting the crab men who crept from the water to carry away the weak and infirm. Or he would seek out the islet in whose crevice was the living head of a demigod who had offended Pan and been torn asunder by a pair of boars as a consequence. Oh yes, this place is large and full of strange and wonderful things.

"'Wherever the god had been, when he returned to the ship and saw the crocodile's skin hanging from its front, his wrath was immediate. Grandfather croc had been sacred to Pan, and to kill him was a terrible trespass, no matter how many of the men he had eaten. Pan stood in the midst of the sailors feasting on the crocodile's meat and declared war on the vessel and its captain, pledging to kill them to the man. You can appreciate, the crew saw a child threatening them, and if a few were annoyed at his presumption, the majority was amused. The captain chided him for speaking to his friends so rudely, and offered him some of the wine he had uncorked for the celebration. Pan slapped the goblet away and fled the ship.

"'The next time the Spaniards saw the god, he was armed with the blade you have inspected so closely. As one of the ship's boats was returning from collecting fresh fruit, it passed beneath the limb of a great tree where Pan was waiting. He dropped into the middle of the boat and ran through the men at its oars. The rest scrambled for their weapons, but even confined to such a modest form, Pan was more than their equal. He ducked their swings, avoided their thrusts. He slashed this man's throat, opened that man's belly. Once the crew was dealt with, he threw the food they had gathered overboard and left.

"'As it happened, though, one of the first men Pan stabbed

was not dead, the sword having missed his heart by a hair's breadth. Still grievously wounded, this sailor nonetheless was able to bring the boat and its cargo of corpses back to the ship, where he lived for enough time to describe Pan's attack. The crew were outraged at the deaths of their mates, as was the captain, but he was as concerned at the loss of the fruit the men had been transporting.

"'The following day he sent out two boats, one to carry what food could be found, the other to guard it. Before they had reached the islet that was their destination, the men sighted Pan curled in a hollow in one of the trees, apparently asleep. Thinking this a chance to avenge their fellows, they rowed toward him. As they drew closer, the Spaniards heard voices, women's voices, singing a song of surpassing loveliness. They searched the trees, but saw no one. One of the men looked into the water and directed the others to do likewise. Floating below the surface were the sirens, their limbs wrapped in long trains of silk. Pan liked them to sing of his life as it had been, when he and his foster-brother, great Zeus, had spent their days roaming the beaches of Crete, peering into the pools the tide left, on their guard for Kronos's spies. The approach of the boats distracted the sirens from their duty. Long years had passed since they had tasted the flesh of any man but the Cimmerians. From the shores of Crete, their song changed to the delights awaiting the sailors under the water. Wasting no time, one of the younger men leapt to join them. He was followed by all his fellows save one, an old hand mostly deaf from decades manning the cannons. To him, the sirens' song was a distant, pleasant music. He was the one who would return to the ship to relate the fates of the others. He would describe the sirens darting around the men, keeping just out of reach. Like many sailors of the time, none of those who had pursued the sirens could swim; not that it would have made much difference in this case. Maybe they would not have drowned so quickly. That was bad, but what was worse was when the sirens began to feed. Their song ceased, and the old hand who had watched his mates die saw that their beautiful robes were in fact long fins growing from their arms and legs, and that their pretty mouths were full of sharp, sharp teeth. So frightened was the sailor that he forgot about Pan until he was fleeing. Then he saw the god awake, on his hands and knees, leaning forward to watch the water grow cloudy with blood.

"'If the captain grieved the loss of his men, and so soon after the deaths of the others, he regretted the loss of the second boat almost as much. He was aware, too, that for a second day the ship's larder had not been replenished. The vessel had provisions enough for this not to be of immediate concern, but you know the importance of well-fed men, especially on a ship lost in a strange place.

"'First, though, there were the sirens to be dealt with. An expedition to the spot was out of the question. The old sailor's report of the creatures had terrified the men. The captain suggested borrowing a trick from Homer and stopping their ears, but the crew would have none of it. Rather than risk rebellion, the captain ordered the ship's cannons loaded and trained on the sirens' location. Three volleys the Spaniards fired at the creatures. Their cannonballs felled two of the great trees, and stripped limbs from and struck holes in ten more. While the smoke still rolled on the water, the captain and four of his bravest men stuffed their ears with rags and boarded the remaining boat, which they rowed toward the sirens quickly. Upon reaching the spot, they found two of the creatures floating dead, the limbs of a third between them. A fourth swam in a slow circle, right beneath the water's surface, gravely wounded. The captain dispatched her with his sword, then had the men retrieve her body and those of her sisters. They towed the sirens' remains to the ship, where the captain instructed the crew to hang them from the mainmast.

"'Certain that an attack by Pan was forthcoming, flushed with his victory over the sirens, the captain prepared for battle. The armoury was opened, the cannons were loaded, watches were posted. On the ship's forge, the smith crafted a hook to replace the captain's lost hand. All of this for a boy, eh? Yes, the Spaniards did not know Pan's true identity, but they had realized he was no normal child. His immunity to the sirens' music marked him as a supernatural being himself. Many of the crew were sure he was a devil and this Hell. The superstitions of sailors are legendary, and the captain, who worried about Pan more than his station would allow him to admit, did not want the men's fears to undermine the ship's order. He pointed to grandfather croc's hide, to the bodies of the sirens, and told the crew that if this was Hell, then they would make the devils fear them. Brave words, and had Pan appeared at that moment, the sailors would have thrown themselves at him with all the ferocity they had reserved for the English.

"'During the days to come the ship was the model of discipline. The men did not see Pan, but they had no doubt he was preparing his assault. The days became a week. The lookouts saw nothing in the great trees but brightly coloured birds. One week became two. There was no hint of Pan. The crew grew restless. The captain wondered if the child had been struck by a cannonball and killed, but was reluctant to chance his remaining boat to investigate the speculation. With each passing day, the ship's provisions diminished, and this became as great a concern for the captain as Pan's skill with the sword. Hunger leads to desperation, desperation to mutiny, for sailors, at least. For those in command, desperation is brother to recklessness, and the arrival of one foretells the arrival of the other. As the second week of the ship's vigil tipped into the third, the captain called on his four best men and joined them in the boat. Together, they set out to look for Pan.

"'Their search took them to the place he had been seen last, the lair of the sirens. The Spaniards had blocked their ears, but there was no need: the spot was deserted. From that location, they rowed to every one Pan had showed them, from a rocky islet where grew a grove of lemon trees to a long sandbar whose grass fed a herd of goats. Nowhere was the god visible. They came within view of the rugged home of the Cimmerians, which Pan had cautioned them to avoid. Through his spyglass, the captain surveyed the island's huts, but could see neither the child nor the Cimmerians. A terrible suspicion seized him, which was borne out a moment later, when an explosion sounded from the ship's direction.

"'You can imagine, the men rowed with all the speed they could summon. When they reached the ship, they saw her canted to port, a column of thick smoke rising from the hole in her starboard side. A fierce fight was underway on the sloping deck between the sailors and a small army of men and women. They were bone white, these people, armoured in the shells of the crab men they had slain, which proved little match for the Spaniards' steel. But their weapons, spears with fire-hardened tips, axes with sharpened rock heads, were no less deadly when they found their mark, and there were more, many, many more, of the Cimmerians than there were of the crew. Dancing across the bloody boards, Pan stabbed this man in the leg, cut the hamstrings of another, jabbed a third in the back. The air was full of the grunts and cries of the sailors, the cracks of their swords on the shell-armour, and the battle song of the Cimmerians, which is a low, ghostly thing.

"'Once the boat was within reach of the deck, the captain leapt onto it, his blade at the ready. A swordsman of no small repute, he cut a path to the spot where Pan was engaged in a duel with the first mate, who had succeeded in scoring his opponent's legs and forearms with the tip of his sword. Just as the captain reached them, Pan jumped over the mate's swing and drove his blade into the man's chest. Enraged, the captain lunged at the god, but the blood of his lieutenant betrayed him, causing his foot to slip and him to lose his balance. A kick from Pan sent him tumbling down the deck, into the water.

"'Unlike the crew, the captain could swim. He was hindered, though, by his fine coat, whose fabric drank the water thirstily, dragging him deeper. Clenching his sword between his teeth, he used his hand to pull the garment from him. He was almost free of it when the right sleeve caught on his hook. Try as he might, the captain could not extract his arm from the coat; nor was he able to loosen the straps securing the hook. What air remained in his lungs was almost spent. There was no choice for him but to haul the coat with him, as if he were pulling a drowning man to safety.

"'By the time he climbed onto the ship, the battle was done. The crew was dead or dying. They had acquitted themselves well against their attackers, but the Cimmerians had the advantage of overwhelming numbers and the assistance of a god. The captain found that deity's sword pointed at him, together with a dozen spears. However skilled he was with his own weapon, he was a realist who recognized defeat when it confronted him. He lowered his blade, reversed it, and offered it to Pan, telling him the ship was his.

"'If he was expecting his surrender to result in mercy, the captain was disappointed. Pan had sworn death to all the Spaniards, and a god will not break his oath. At his signal, the Cimmerians seized the captain's arms. A pair of them tore the coat from his hook, then used their stone knives to cut the bindings of the hook. They sliced away the captain's garments until he stood naked. They forced him to the deck, and held him there by the elbows and knees while an old woman pressed a sharpened shell to his thigh and began the laborious work of removing his skin.

"'She was skilled at her work, but the process took the rest of the afternoon. The captain struggled not to cry out, to endure his torture with dignity, but who can maintain his resolve when his skin is being peeled from the muscle? The captain screamed, and once he had done so, continued to, until his throat was as bloody as the strips of his flesh spread out to either side of him. Occasionally, the old woman would pause to exchange one shell for another, and the captain would survey the ruination fallen upon his vessel. The Cimmerians had taken the crew's weapons and select items of their clothing, scarves, belts, and boots. Already, they had cut down the sirens' remains and were hanging Spanish corpses in their place. Grandfather croc's hide had been gathered from the bowsprit and folded into a mat, which Pan sat upon as he watched the Cimmerian woman part the captain's skin from him. He had donned the captain's fine coat, waterlogged as it was, and was holding the hook, turning it over in his hands as if it were a new, fascinating toy. Every so often, he would raise his right hand, his index finger curved in imitation of the metal question mark, and grin.

"'As the day was coming to an end, the old woman completed the last of her task, the careful work of separating the Captain from his face. He had not died, which is astonishing, nor had he gone mad, which is no less amazing. Pan stood from his crocodile mat and approached him. In his right hand, he gripped the captain's hook. He knelt beside the man and uttered words the captain did not understand. He placed the point of the hook below the captain's breastbone and dug it into him. With no great speed, the god dragged the hook past the man's navel. Leaving it stuck there, Pan released the hook and plunged his hand into the captain's chest, up under the ribs to where the man's heart galloped. The god took hold of the slippery organ and wrenched it from its place. This must have killed the captain instantly, but if any spark of consciousness flickered behind his eyes, he would have seen Pan slide his heart from him, raise it to his mouth, and bite into it.'"

Mr Haringa paused. The assortment of dark shapes within the crimson lights faded, brightening the room. The pocket watch dropped in volume, its tick-tock merely loud. When the teacher spoke, his voice no longer seemed to nestle in each student's ear. He said, "In his years at sea, Conrad had heard tales that were no less fantastical than this one. He had taken them with enough salt to flavour his meals for the remainder of his life. His inclination was to do the same with the narrative Heuvelt had unfolded, admire its construction though he might. The very location in which Heuvelt delivered it, however, argued for its veracity with brute simplicity. All the same, Conrad found it difficult to accept that the boy who had seated himself at the front of the boat, where he had succeeded in prying open the pocket watch and was studying its hands, was the avatar of a god. He expressed his doubt to Heuvelt, who said, 'You know the story of Tantalus? The king who served his son as a meal for the gods? Why, eh? Some of the poets say he was inspired by piety, others by blasphemy. It does not matter. What matters is that one of the gods, Demeter, ate the boy's shoulder before Zeus understood what was on the table in front of them. A god may not taste the flesh of man or woman. To do so confuses their natures. Zeus forced Demeter to vomit the portion she had eaten, and he hurled Tantalus into Tartarus, where Hades was happy to devise a suitable torment for his presumption. Demeter had been duped, but Pan sank his teeth into the captain's heart with full awareness of what he was doing. Nor did he stop after the organ was a bloody smear on his lips. He dined on the captain's liver and tongue and used the hook to crack the skull to allow him to sample the brain. Sated, he fell into a deep slumber beside the remains of Diego de la Castille, captain in the Navy of his majesty, Phillip II of Spain.

"'In the days after, Pan changed. The Cimmerians had departed the ship once the god was asleep, taking with them the captain's skin, whose pieces they would tan and stitch into a pouch to carry their infants. Alone, Pan roamed the ship, dressed still in the captain's scarlet coat. He loosened the hook from its collar, cut a strip of leather from a crew member's belt, and fashioned a necklace for himself. The captain's remains he propped against the mainmast and sat beside, engaging in long, one-sided conversations with the corpse. He was becoming split from himself, you see, this'—Heuvelt gestured at the child—'separated from this.' He swept his hand to encompass their surroundings. 'The Cimmerians, who had faithfully followed the god into a battle that had winnowed their numbers by a third, grew to fear the sight of him rowing toward them in the ship's remaining boat, a strange tune, half-hymn, half-sea shanty on his lips. He was as likely to charge them with his sword out, hacking at any whose misfortune it was to be within reach of its edge, as he was to sit down to a meal with their elders. The sirens, too, learned to flee his approach, after he lured one of them to the ship, caught her in a trap made from its sails, and dragged her onto the deck. There, he lashed her beside the captain's corpse and commanded her to sing for him. But the words that once had pleased the god now tormented him, and in a rage, he slew the siren. He loaded the captain's body into the stern of the boat and roamed the islets of this place. He chased the herd of goats in and out of the water until they were exhausted and drowned. He hunted the flocks of bright birds roosting in the trees and decorated his locks with bloody clumps of their feathers. He piled stones on top of the rock opening in which he had tucked the head of the dismembered demigod, entombing him.

"'The transformation that overtook Pan's form as man affected his form as nature, as well. In days gone by, the routes here were few. A fierce storm might permit access, as might the proper sacrifices, offered in locations once sacred to the god. Now the place floated loose in space. Its trees would be visible off the coast of Sumatra or in a valley in the Pyrenees. Rarely were those who ventured into the strange forest seen again, and the few who did return told of their pursuit by a devil in a red coat rowing a boat with a corpse for its crew.'

"'And you,' Conrad said. 'How did you come here?'

"'An accident,' Heuvelt said. 'The boiler had been giving me trouble, to the point of almost stranding me in the middle of the lake with a full load of passengers. Not very good for business. Compared to the trials I had faced on the open sea, it was modest, but a difficulty will grow to fit as much room as there is for it. I laboured over the boiler until I was sure I had addressed the fault, and then took the boat out. I should have stayed in. There was a heavy fog on the water. But so obsessed had I become with the problem that I could not wait to test its solution. I flattered myself that my skill at the wheel was more than sufficient to keep me from harm.

"'Harm, I avoided, but I stumbled into this place, instead. You will appreciate my wonder and my confusion. I spied our young friend balanced on the ship's bowsprit, and when he challenged me, I knew enough of Greek and enough of Spanish to speak with him. Of course, I took him for an orphan (which from a certain point of view he was, abandoned by himself). Only later did I understand the peril I had been in. Our first exchange, halting as it was, gave me the sense that there was more to this boy than was apparent to my eye. When I left, I offered to take him with me, but he refused. For the gift of my conversation, though, Pan permitted me to depart unharmed.

"'Thereafter, I might have avoided the western end of the

lake. Whether I judged my experience a waking dream or a visit to fairyland, I might have decided not to repeat it. As you can see, I abandoned prudence in favour of the swiftest return I could manage. I half-expected the way to be closed: I had made inquiries of several of my passengers the next day, and no one expressed any knowledge of strange rivers amongst the mountains. Yet when I searched for it that night, the passage was open. More, my young friend was eager to see me. Since then, I have visited whenever the opportunity has presented itself. I have learned my way around the tongue Pan and the Spaniards cobbled together. As I have done so, I have had his story, a piece at a time, in no order. The majority of these fragments, I have assembled into the tale you have heard; though there remain incidents whose relation to the whole I have yet to establish.

"'From the beginning, I had the conviction I must save this child, I must rescue him from this place. My own son died of a fever shortly after he learned to walk, while I was away at sea. I understood the influence this sad event exerted on my sentiments, but the awareness did nothing to diminish them. Each time I voyaged here, I brought candy, cakes, toys, whatever I guessed might tempt the boy away. After I understood what he was—as much as any man could—I continued my efforts to bring him with me. For if it is accounted a good deed to help a child out of misfortune, what would it mean to come to the assistance of a god?

"'Only the timepiece,' Heuvelt nodded at it, 'has continued to interest him. Every time I remove it from my pocket, it is as if he sees it anew. It fascinates him. Occasionally, I believe it frightens him. I have told him that, should he come with me, I will make a gift of it to him. The lure of the watch is strong, but not yet greater than the fear of venturing forth from his home. I think he will choose to accompany me into the world of men. It is why I have been able to travel the waters here so often. For the trespass he committed against his divinity, he must atone.'

"'What form would such a thing take?' Conrad said.

"'I do not know,' Heuvelt said. 'Perhaps he would live as a mortal, resolve the conflict in his being by walking the path we tread all the way down to the grave. Or perhaps he would require more than a single lifespan. How long is needed for a god to atone to himself? He might spend centuries on the effort.'

"There was a clatter from the front of the steamboat. Conrad glanced in that direction to see the child leap onto the railing and from there up to the roof. Another astonishing jump carried him from the boat to the tip of the ship's mainmast, which he caught one-handed and used to swing onto the mast. While he was running down the spar to the ship, Heuvelt brought the boat's speed up and turned the wheel in the direction of home. The child had left the watch on the deck; Conrad retrieved it and handed it to Heuvelt, who tucked it into his coat with a sigh. 'The next visit,' he said, 'or the one after that, perhaps.'

"Although Conrad remained at the Swiss spa another two weeks, and continued to take the ferry every day, he and Heuvelt did not discuss their voyage to the wrecked galleon and their encounter with the figure Heuvelt claimed was a god gone mad. He understood that the man had given him a gift, shared with him a secret mysterious and profound. But there was too much to say about all of it for him to know where or how to begin, and as Heuvelt did not broach the topic, Conrad chose to follow his example. Heuvelt did not invite him on a second expedition.

"Nor would Conrad speak or write of the trip until the last years of his life, when he spent fifteen pages of a notebook detailing it, more or less as I've related it to you. By then he had been contacted by a number of critics, each of whom wanted to know about the sources of his fiction. He'd never made any secret of his life on the sea, but many of the letters he received sought to connect his biography to his writing in a way that stripped the art from it. He grumbled to his friends, but he answered the inquiries. He also recorded his experience in the Swiss mountains. Once he was finished, he turned to a fresh page and listed the titles and dates of a handful of narratives: 'The Great God Pan' (1890), 'The Story of a Panic' (1902), *The Little White Bird* (1902), *The Wind in the Willows* (1908), *Peter and Wendy* (1911). Under these, he wrote, 'A coincidence, or a sign Heuvelt at last succeeded in his quest, and delivered the god to his long exile?' Not long after writing these words, Conrad died.

"In the interest of scholarly integrity, I should add that the majority of Conrad scholars consider the notebook story a bizarre forgery. Even those few who accept it as Conrad's work dismiss it as a five-finger exercise. It's an understandable response. How could such a tale be anything other than pure invention?"

The pocket watch stopped. With a click, the crimson lights switched off, flooding the classroom with darkness. Something vast seemed to crowd the space with the students. Mr Haringa's voice said, "Aidan, would you get the lights?"

After the dark (which took a fraction of a second too long to disperse), the fluorescent lights were harsh, prompting most of the students to turn their heads aside, or lift their hands against it. By the time their eyes had adjusted, Mr Haringa was behind his desk, shuffling through the folders in which he kept his selection of relevant newspaper clippings. Without looking up, he said, "All right, people, you're free to go. Thank you for indulging me. Don't forget, next class we're starting Yeats's 'Sailing to Byzantium'. Anyone who feels particularly ambitious can take a look at 'Byzantium', which is a different poem."

Still half in a daze, the students rose from their desks and headed for the door, some shaking their heads, some mumbling, "What *was* that?" A pair of students, the girls who competed for the highest grades in the class, paused in front of the teacher's desk. One cleared her throat; the other said, "Mr Haringa?"

"Yes?" Mr Haringa said.

"We were wondering: what do you think happened? To Pan? What did the Dutch guy do with him?"

Mr Haringa straightened in his chair, crossing his arms over his scarlet waistcoat. "What do you think?"

"We don't know."

"You have no idea whatsoever?"

"Can you just tell us, please? We have to get to Pre-Calc."

"All right," Mr Haringa said. "We know Heuvelt was using the watch to lure Pan out of his world and into ours. The question is, once you have him here, how do you keep him here? Or—that's not it, exactly. It's more a matter of, how do you accommodate him to this place, with all its strangeness? I'd say the answer lies in language, story, poetry, song. He knew some Spanish, so you might begin by reading him *Don Quixote*, a little bit at a time. As his fluency improved, you could introduce him to Lope de Vega, who wrote a long poem about the Spanish Armada. Yes, the same one the galleon had been part of. Maybe you would move on to Bécquer, his *Rimas y legendas*. Then—you get the idea. You teach him other languages: French, Italian, Dutch, English. You introduce him to Racine, Boccaccio, van den Vondel, Shakespeare. You bind him to our world with narrative, loop figures of speech around him, weight him with allusions. Does this answer your questions?"

"Kind of."

"Kind of?"

"Didn't you say Pan would have to atone for eating the captain?"

"Ah." Mr Haringa paused. "To be honest, I've wondered that myself. I have no idea. I'm not sure how the god would figure out what he had to do, especially if he was cut off from himself, from that fullness of being he had known before his trespass. I can picture him telling and retelling the story of that event in an effort to discover whether the answer lay somewhere in its details. In this case, your guess is just about as good as mine."

"Um, okay. Thank you."

"Yeah, thanks, Mr H. See you tomorrow."

After the class, Mr Haringa had a free period. Once the hallway outside his room had grown quiet, he crossed to the door and turned the lock. Returning to his desk, he unbuttoned the scarlet waistcoat and shrugged it from his shoulders, draping it on the back of his chair. He opened the white dress shirt underneath down to his navel. A raised white scar ran up the centre of his breastbone. His eyes focused on some distant internal image, Mr Haringa traced the ridge with the fingers of his right hand. Slowly, he dug his fingertips into the scar, grimacing as the toughened flesh resisted the tear of his nails. As his skin parted, he brought up his left hand to widen the opening. His sternum cracked and rustled. There was surprisingly little blood.

The hook was slippery in Mr Haringa's grasp. Exhaling sharply, he slid it from his chest. He swayed, gripping the chair with his left hand to steady himself. Tears flooded his vision; he blinked them away, raising the hook to view. Stained and discoloured with blood and age, the metal reflected Mr Haringa's features imperfectly. The point of the implement had retained its sharpness. Mr Haringa brought the hook to his mouth and pressed its tip into his lower lip. He remembered the bitter taste of the captain's heart, its chewiness.

Si les dieux ne font rien d'inconvenant, c'est alors qu'ils ne sont plus dieux du tout
—Mallarmé

For Fiona, and of course, for Jack

THE DEAD THING
Paul Tremblay

It's Thursday and instead of walking with Stacey to the skate park (it's next to the high school so it isn't a good place for people (especially seventh grade people (especially seventh grade girls people)) who aren't in high school to go to unless you like the smell of weed, rape jokes, and getting cigarette filters and lit matches thrown at you), and instead of walking down the train tracks behind the driving school and to the combo gas station Honey Dew Donuts that this late in the day only has plain bagels and stale donut holes left, I decide to go straight home. I feel like I have to go even if I don't want to because I worry something bad (or worse (worse than the bad that is everyday)) has happened or will happen to Owen, because the elementary school gets out fifteen minutes before the middle school and Owen is probably home and sitting on the couch and burning through another bag of sunflower seeds (eating seeds is how Owen deals with everything and he deals with a lot because he's too young to know anything or understand like I do so he eats seeds because Dad figured out if Owen had a mouthful of seeds he couldn't ask about Mom or cry as much so, yeah, sunflower seeds, the ones baseball players eat and spit, and Owen eats so many seeds most days he's not hungry for dinner or breakfast or whatever food you try to put in front of him, and the kid is getting smaller instead of growing bigger, I swear), and what if Owen is watching TV and he accidentally swallows some of the seed shells (I've seen him swallow and scratch at his throat like he was dying and then be okay two seconds later and back with a mouth of seeds, my baby brother the world's saddest gerbil) instead of spitting the shells into a cup or an empty (or half-empty) can of soda and he's choking for real, and Dad is passed out next to him on the couch or maybe he didn't even make it to the couch today, so I'm going home because that feeling of something *worse* is stuck down in me. Stacey wants to come with me but I told her she can't and it's this joke between us how she never gets to go to my house when I go to hers all the time. She only jokes about it with me, which is why she's the only one I'm totally honest with. I've told her why she can't come. She says she gets it but I don't think she totally gets it, and it's not her fault because she hasn't seen the house, and I mean the inside of the house because her parents have dropped me off so they've all seen the outside which is bad (blue paint is fine but the window frames' white paint is coming apart and the yard is all overgrown) but like a normal bad. Maybe I should let her come home with me once and I can give her a tour and I'd start with the kitchen and tell her, hey, yeah, that's the sink full of nasty dishes and flies as big as grapes and I keep two bowls (one for me and one for Owen) clean in my room, and don't open the fridge, you won't like it, but then I'd point at the walls, which is what she'd probably see first anyway, and using a fancy tour voice tell her that this is where Mom tore all the wallpaper off the walls because she was drunk or high or both, and Dad tried to stop her but she told him, don't worry, I'll put up new wallpaper and it'll be great, and she said that to him while standing on the stained and splintery plywood, which would be the same plywood we're standing on during the tour because a few months before she ripped down the wallpaper she jacked up all the linoleum tile because home improvement, right?, it was going to be a big project and make our kitchen look like the ones they show on those home improvement shows, and while in tour mode I'd whisper so no one else could hear me that Mom was super-drunk or high or both (and I could tell because her eyes would be red and big and she'd breathe only out of her mouth so it sounded like she was laughing and puking at the same time, and she looked like that when I saw her for the last time or the most recent last time because I don't know yet if it's a forever last time), so yeah, it was makeover time for the kitchen, and Dad was drunk or high or both (and I can tell with him because his face and body sags like he's a human beanbag chair and he huffs more than speaks so the words come out of his nose) and Dad tried (not very hard, in fact, he sucked at trying) to stop Mom from buzzing through the floor tile but she told him to shut his assy mouth (that's a direct quote) and that she'd put in the new laminate flooring herself and without his worthless assy ass because he was too lazy to do it, and I wouldn't yell like they yelled while on the tour but I could do perfect impersonations of them fighting if I wanted to. I don't know if Stacey would make it past the kitchen on the tour so it's easier just to tell her that she can't come over today, that I have to help Owen with something and I say *something* like it's two different words (some thing) and we both laugh even though it's kind of stupid and she says okay and tells me to FaceTime her after dinner and I can do that when I'm in my room because my room is like a bomb shelter of regular clean in a nuked house. So I walk home by myself listening to music on my phone and I like to pretend that dressed all in black I'm a shadow or a blur or like a smudge of someone that when you drive by you don't really see them. I get home and I can hear the TV through the open front windows (no screens) and it sounds super-loud, louder than normal, and I panic because it sounds too loud and that has to mean something's wrong, or some thing is wrong, so I run inside and drop my backpack and it bass drums on the kitchen floor, and I obstacle course past sagging garbage bags in the hallway to the TV room and Dad is on the couch asleep, passed out, whatever, and sports talking heads are shouting on the TV, but Owen isn't there, maybe he's already in his bedroom. I think about asking Dad where Owen is and I think again. I try to turn down the volume without the remote (because when I got close to the couch Dad grumbled something and there were black dots of seeds and shells all over the cushions and I didn't want him to wake up and blame-yell at me about it) and I can't find the stupid volume buttons on the side of the TV. The back slider off the kitchen crashes open so Owen must've been in the backyard and I somehow didn't see him out there when I got home. I run back down the hallway and I want to yell, where've you been?, and say things to make him cry but I also know that's not me so I swallow all that down to deal with later (I don't eat sunflower seeds but I record messages on my phone and write things down and that's how I deal) and I find him (and I always think that I'm finding him, like he's lost) closing the slider real careful and slow with his foot, which is poked through the screen at the bottom and he shouldn't be doing that because he's making the rip in the screen bigger and we'll get bugs (more bugs) and mice (more mice) in the house, but then I zoom in on what he's carrying. Not that I can see it yet because his back is to me and he's curled around and over whatever it is he's carrying.

Owen, what do you have?
 Nothing.
 Seriously. Tell me.

Nothing.

Don't be a shit. I won't tell Dad.

(nothing)

Did you steal something? You can't be—

I found it.

Where?

Outside.

————————What is it?

(nothing)

It better not be a mouse or a squirrel or something. Or like a shrew? Is it a shrew? You can't keep that in here.

It's not.

What is it? Tell me?

(nothing)

I could rip it out of his hands and look inside, but I won't. I could hit him and then take it away from him but I won't. I don't hit him, not ever, but that awful terrible no-good thought flickers through my brain like someone waving a flashlight in my face (I see myself hitting him and what I see is more bright than what I normally see and then it goes dark in my head when I shake the thought away or say no no no but then it flashes bright again when I see myself hitting him again and again), and maybe because I don't hit him I think about hitting him more (and I'm afraid I'm thinking about it more and more because I'm getting older and I'm afraid that's what goes on in all adults' heads. I'm afraid all they think about is doing violent, terrible no-good things, and especially to the people they're supposed to take care of, I mean all the violence in the world has to start in our heads first, right, and I'm mostly afraid I'm thinking like Dad when he stabbed Owen's Nerf dart gun through the plaster in his bedroom and I'm thinking like Mom when she would tell me what an awful stupid fat-ass daughter I was or like when she wouldn't say anything to me and just stare at me with her mouth closed so tight and I could hear her saying nothing to me). I won't ever hit Owen (I'd chew my own hand off first) but it's hard, it's all so hard, but I can't believe he won't tell me what it is, whatever it is inside the cardboard shoebox that is dark green and doesn't have a logo, which is weird, I mean, everything has a logo on it, so maybe it isn't a shoebox (or sneakerbox, I think they should call them sneakerboxes) and is just a rando box. It's smeared with dirt and mud and there are dark spots on the cover and on the sides, and those dark spots look like the grease spots on the inside cover of a pizza box, so now I'm thinking that whatever is inside the box is nasty and leaking through the cardboard, and I want to tell Owen to wash his hands, but then he's scurrying past me, or trying to, and I block him, tickle his stomach with my left hand (there really isn't any stomach to tickle, only his sticklike ribs) and grab for the box with my right, and it works, kind of, because he flinches and for a second I have the box balanced in my hand, only it isn't very balanced and whatever is inside of it shifts, and whatever it is inside of it feels blob-like, oozy, and it's so gross I might throw up. Actually, it's so gross I'm past throwing up because my stomach turns to goo and sloshes down into my toes, and more gross, the bottom of the box, the underside, feels damp, and then, oh my god, the smell, worse than the smell that comes out of the laundry room on a hot day, worse than the septic tank being pumped, and even worse than opening that garbage bag I didn't realize was full of months-old garbage (because it was sitting in the hall coat closet we never use anymore and I only looked in it because Dad left the doors open and I thought it might be the dolls and toys that manic-phase Mom collected in a "Morgie" bag (and she never told me what Morgie meant or stood for but only that was where your old stuff went to give to the poor people (like us now))), and then Owen whines like a puppy, swats my hand away, and his eyes are all red like he's been crying and they're sunken into his head too, and then he is past me and running down the hall, bouncing between all the bags and junk like a miniparkour pro. I yell after him and then Dad slur-shouts something from the TV room, so I stop running, frozen in place, and I don't want to talk to him now and I tell him to go back to sleep in my head, which I know never really works but it works this time, but it doesn't matter because Owen gets away and locks himself in his room. I wait until Dad is out again and I tiptoe past him down the hall to Owen's closed door and I smell the box's smell (and still feel the box's feel on the tips (and the insides, I swear) of my fingers).

Owen. Come on.
    (nothing)
    Can I see it?
    No.
    Why not?
    (nothing)
    This is stupid. Just let me in.
    No. Go away. Please.
    You can't stay in there forever. I'm gonna get in there and I'm gonna see it.
    (nothing)

I go to my room and shut the door and instead of screaming or crying or trashing everything, I neaten (old-Mom's old word) it some more (the room is already clean, so clean you could eat off it (something Mom, old-Mom, used to say with a smile) so it's like straightening, or picking up stuff and putting it back where it was), and, I'm telling you, *neatening* is something I never did before Mom left, before things got worse-worse. When I was Owen's age my room was a pit and I loved it, owned it and it really was a beautiful pit, but now it isn't. Clothes are in my bureau and hanging up in my closet and books are on the bookshelf and everything has a place (the glass in my two windows are cracked and have pieces missing but you can't really see it (but you can feel it on cold nights) unless you open the curtains, and I would fix it if I could, but I don't know how to unbreak broken glass), and none of it makes me feel better, and it makes me feel anxious because my room is the nexus of the universe (something me and Stacey came up with, or she came up with it because the word *nexus* was in a book she read, she loves to read (I have too much time to read so I don't and I can't stay in my head that long without other stuff creeping in so I draw sometimes but most of the time I shut off my brain watching music videos on YouTube and videos that show ghosts are real even though I think most of them are faking even if I want them not to be), or if I'm not that important to be the nexus of the universe, my room is the nexus of this house, which means I have to keep my room like this or the worse-worse will get even worse (it can always get worse) and everything will come crashing down). I try to FaceTime Stacey but she isn't answering and I hope she isn't mad at me and I think about making my own video to show her what the rest of the house looks like (besides my room, which she sees every night when we talk) but I hear Dad up and creeping around the house like a creep, and the wooden floors creak and groan and are so tired under him, and then it's already dinner time, or what is supposed to be dinner time, and I leave my room (with one of my clean bowls, and I hold it like a shield), and Dad is back on the couch eating Pop Tarts and drinking beer, and we still have these plastic one-serving cups of mac 'n cheese and I make one for myself, three minutes thirty seconds in the microwave and add the radioactive yellow cheese dust, and I pour the stuff into my clean bowl (I won't eat out of the microwaved plastic cup because I don't trust it's not melted) and toss the plastic into the full sink because I don't care if the kitchen is clean or not because the kitchen isn't the nexus. I stand and eat quickly even though the mac 'n cheese lava burns my tongue and the roof of my mouth and I think about making Owen a bowl and bringing it to him because a good big sister would do that, but I don't feel good right now, and I'm going to wait him out of his room, like waiting is some action, a thing that I can throw against his door and break it open, but I don't want to wait, I so don't want to wait I even go into the TV room to talk to Dad.

Owen won't come out of his room for dinner.

I'll take care of it.

He needs to eat.

Worry about yourself.

Dad—

He'll eat when he wants to.

(nothing)

This isn't going to go well because I know, I can feel it, that Owen shouldn't be in his room by himself with whatever it is he found in that box, that dead-smelling thing, and that's all I can imagine is in the box, some dead thing, and why would he save that?, and I picture him just staring into the box at some awful mess that used to be alive, and there's blood and ripped-up fur and pink guts and dark, empty eye sockets (and in my head the eye sockets look like his do now, and then I can't unsee Owen standing there looking into the cardboard box with no eyes, with nothing eyes) and I see him touching it and he's there in his room crying by himself and he's sad for the dead thing because he doesn't really understand what dead means, and I think he thinks it means you simply go away when you're dead because like a week after Mom left he asked if she was dead and Dad laughed and said Why not? So I'm standing here with steam coming out of my mac 'n cheese bowl and it feels like it's coming out of my ears too because I'm so mad and so don't-know-what-to-do and I stomp out of the TV room the way Dad hates, like really hates, and I yell at Owen to come out and bring out the shoebox and I pound on his door, and then Dad comes thundering down the hallway yelling at me, at us, at everything. Normally Dad being Dad would turn me quiet and small but I'm so mad I don't really hear him and it sounds like everything is underwater and I throw my bowl at Owen's bedroom door and it bounces off and shatters on the floor and Dad is too drunk-slow to grab me but it doesn't stop him from wrecking-balling into a wall trying to block my escape, but I easily sidestep him and duck into my own room and lock the door and then he's banging on my door swearing at me and calling me names and saying I'm just like Mom but I don't care about any of that and I let his pounding and yelling be underwater sounds, but I'm crying because I broke the bowl and now there's only one clean one in the whole fucking stupid fucking house.

r u ok Hanna banana?

no

talk?

can't hell hear me

he'll
no facetime tonight
pretending I'm asleep

that bad?

always
I'm sorry Stacey

don't be
can u sneak out and stay over at my house?
Mom wouldn't mind
she says u can stay here whenev

can't

why?

I just can't
Owen brought something weird bad home

???

worried about him
tell u tmorrw at school

k
what about tomorrow night?

???

sleepover my house tomorrow

idk maybe idk
I'll be ok

I wake up and it's the kind of dark that fills you through
more than just your eyes (when I was little I used to ask
my parents about how I slept at night because I didn't like
thinking about me lying there with my mouth open so
anything could go inside and I wouldn't know and I would
get upset and ask them to check on me (this is what they used
to tell me) and push my mouth closed if it was open before
they went to bed and I'd ask them to double and triple check
my mouth if they woke up in the middle of the night to use

the bathroom). The house feels quiet but like a fake kind of quiet, like there are things crouched and waiting to jump out at me and then I realize there are noises in the hallway and they were there when I woke up and I heard them without hearing them which means the sounds were probably there when I was asleep too, and that makes it sound worse now, so I listen and I don't know what is making those wet sounds, not like something dripping, but more like a squish, a wet sponge in a fist, and then maybe that sponge is sliding and slurping across a door, not my door but Owen's. I sneak out of my bed, grab my phone (I fell asleep watching videos and I didn't plug in and charge so there's only three per cent battery left) and sneak across the room and stand with my ear only inches away from my door and I cover my mouth (not because I think something will go inside) to keep from breathing too loudly and keep myself from calling out, not because I think Dad is out there cleaning (yeah, like he'd ever be out there cleaning, ever, never mind the middle of the night when he's likely a case of beer deep into his blackout) but because it must be Owen cleaning up the mac 'n cheese mess, and that means he's out of his room, standing in front of his door and that means his door is not locked and if it's not locked, then I'll be able to get in his room and to the shoebox if I'm quick and I'm careful, and no, forget quick, I don't want to scare him, so I turn the knob slow and hope he doesn't hear the little click that sounds like a crash, and I'm about to open the door when I notice there's no light coming from the hallway, and I used to always go to bed with the hall light on and I'd stare at that glowing line under my door until I fell asleep, so, okay, that's really weird, right?, I mean, why would Owen be out there cleaning up in the dark (he hates the dark more than I ever did and he usually sleeps with a light on in his room)? He must really be trying to not wake me or Dad up, and if he doesn't want to wake

me it's because he doesn't want me going into his room, and
it's like he's making me and Dad out to be the same person,
and we're so not, and I want to cry and instead I open the
door and start to tell Owen that I'm sorry I was all over him
earlier and that I grabbed the box away from him and that I
won't make him do anything he doesn't want me to do or
see and maybe I can help him clean up the mess and then
I'm worrying he's out in his bare feet and there are probably
still big shards of broken cereal bowl on the floor (when I
was seven I cut my wrist and had to get stitches after falling
on a broken coffee mug and the scar is a fat red worm or a
slug curling down my wrist), and then my door is wide open
and the hallway is so dark and empty, and it's hard to tell but
there's no outline of Owen standing in front of his door at
the end of the hallway, but I think the door is open, and, yes,
it is and it's open into more darkness. I'm standing there in
the hallway and the wet sounds have stopped and I hear my
ears trying to hear in the silence and there's a small, muffled
clap from down the hall, near the collection of dark lumps
that is the broken cereal bowl, at least I think it's the cereal
bowl, and I turn on my phone's flashlight app, and the light
it throws is a weird white, like bones on an X-ray, and on the
floor is Owen's shoebox, all by itself, I mean there's no cereal
bowl and the mac 'n cheese mess is all gone, just the shoebox,
and it looks bigger than I remember it, way bigger actually,
like it almost stretches from wall to wall in the hallway, and
is it a different box? Its colour is hard to tell in the flashlight,
but I can see some of those damp spots on the cover, and it's
a few feet away from Owen's door and I can't smell it, but I
know if I get closer I would, so do I get closer? This is my
chance to see inside of it, yeah? Instead I stand there and
listen and there's only the electric hum of the fridge coming
from the kitchen, and I whisper Owen's name, and he must
be in his room because I don't hear him in the bathroom

or in the kitchen or anywhere, I mean, he was just out here cleaning up the mess, right? That's what I heard, I swear, and I don't know why he'd leave the box on the floor and his door open, and my feet finally shuffle forward and then the phone flashlight dies and it's like the house and the world and everything went away and left me floating in darkness, and I blink my eyelids as fast as a hummingbird's wings trying to adjust, and I say Owen's name again, a little louder and a little less braver, and instead of the shoebox I look where his open door is and I can sorta make out the doorframe and then within that dark I see something move, or I think I do, sliding around the corner, coming out from Owen's room, or more like the shape is expanding, like how a balloon fills up, and it's big, or tall, and it's not Owen, way too big for Owen, so it's Dad, but that's me putting the math of who's in the house together to come up with *it's Dad* because I swear it doesn't feel like it's Dad and I know middle-of-the-night-stuff is always weird and wrong and off but I'm totally awake and totally aware, like super-aware, like an animal instinct aware, right, and I can't see Dad, and he doesn't say anything to me, which is whatever because he's probably drunk, but again this doesn't seem like what's going on, and now his breathing sounds broken down and not in rhythm, and like real underwater sounds, and he must've knocked the box over (not that I hear it) because the dead thing smell takes over the hallway and I cough and I back up and go into my room and shut the door and run to my bed and go under the covers and I leave the light off because I don't want him to know I'm awake, if he's drunk enough he'll forget or not bother, and I'm always dying and surviving because of his not-bother, and the hallway floor creaks with his weight then the creaking stops, and it didn't stop in front of my door, and there's a long nothing, the longest nothing, and my mouth is covered and I breathe through my nose just in case, and then I hear the cardboard box sliding on the hallway floor, slowly, sliding away down the hall, away from my door, and in my head I see Owen (not Dad) dragging the box across the floor and into his room because it's now too heavy for him to carry.

The sun is bright in my room and I bolt upright in bed and I'm in a panic because I can't miss school, not because I love it (I hate it (and I hate almost everything and everyone there except for Stacey and few other kids and Ms Whiting is cool too, I guess) and my stomach turns into a stinging ball of pain when I'm there most days) but because I stupidly hope doing well in that awful school is my only chance, which isn't much of a chance at all, and I have no idea what time it is and how could I have slept through my alarm? Then I look at my phone and it's dead and I remember last night and the hallway and it seems far away and at the same time it's still there in the room with me because the rest of the house is still and quiet even if I'm running around my room slamming drawers and putting clothes on. Why didn't Owen wake me up? He's usually awake before me and watching TV (the morning is pretty much his only chance to have the TV to himself) and then I make him and me breakfast with the two clean bowls and I walk him to the bus stop and it's all fine because Dad isn't there to yell at us or do nothing. I go out into the hallway hoping that Owen is out there waiting for me (maybe he didn't come in to wake me up because he was afraid I'd get mad he was coming into my room when he doesn't let me go into his), and the hallway and the house is quieter than it was last night, and I tiptoe (afraid to disturb something, and maybe I still should be asleep, like I woke up during some secret hour or time I shouldn't see, that no one should see) into the TV room and no one is there (just empty beer cans on the floor and chip bags and sunflower seed bags on the couch) and then I dance around the big trash bags and into the kitchen and no one is there (just more trash and dish piles and open and empty cabinets), and then I go back to the hallway, our hallway and the floor near Owen's door is clear (no broken cereal bowl, no mac 'n cheese, no shoebox) and his door is open halfway, so I walk toward it, and my stomach is in that ball of pain, and I don't want to go in his room now that it's open. I whisper-yell.

Owen? You still asleep?
(nothing)
It's time to get up. We don't want to miss school.
(nothing)
We'll get in trouble.
(nothing)
I'm coming in. Okay?
(nothing)

I stand there, listening. Maybe I can hear Owen breathing or turning in the covers if I listen hard enough, and the weakest saddest scardest lost-est youngest part of me screams at me to go get Dad, go get Dad, but I will not, no matter what, and I shimmy through the open door, careful to not make contact with the wood (as my face passes by, I notice there's no evidence of last night's mac 'n cheese explosion) and I can't remember the last time I've been in Owen's room and by the looks of it, maybe it has been since Mom left, maybe it's been for as long as he's been alive, and I start crying because as bad as the kitchen is and the rest of the house is, his room is worse, because it smells like an unchanged hamster cage and it smells like a dead thing, and I can't see the floor through a sea of trash and toys and torn up books and clothes and stained underwear and seeds and seeds and seeds, empty shells spit out everywhere, and half-full plastic cups and over-full cups on the windowsill and seeds and smaller seed-shaped pellets that I'm afraid aren't seeds and are mouse poops (I've seen plenty of those throughout the house) and water stains on the wallpaper, and his elevated bed frame has no box spring and mattress (they must be on the floor under everything else) and there are cans of Coke on the platform where the mattress used to be and some cans are on their sides and caked in seeds and there's one can upside down stuck in the corner of the bed frame, and I can follow the syrupy stain leading down the frame and splashed black on the walls, and I turn away and I see his closet behind me and it has no door and it's full of trash and I see empty beer cans and maybe full ones (does Dad hide them in here? Does Owen hide them from Dad?), and I can't possibly see it all, and now all I'm thinking is that I'm going to pull Owen out of here no matter what it takes and not let him back in this place, and then the smell again, like in the kitchen when he brought in the shoebox and last night in the hallway, and I wade through the room whispering Owen's name, and to where I think the box spring and mattress must be underneath the pile of bedding and I pull away the blankets and it's the shoebox but now it's the size of the mattress and it's the same colour with the same stains, but it can't be the same, it can't be, and without thinking I scream for Dad.

(nothing)

And there's rustling inside the giant box and so I open the cover, and the cover is heavy but I can handle it and it feels wet and damp and cold, and that cold gets under the skin of my hands, and I hate touching it but I don't let go, and inside is darkness, is all the darkness collected and saved, and way down inside I can hear noises and they are faint but I can hear the slurping, sloshing, wet noises I heard when I held the box and in the hallway last night, the dead thing noises, and I hold the cover open over my head and look down and down and down.

Owen? Are you in there?
(nothing)
Please, Owen?
(nothing)
We'll go away, okay? We'll run away to someplace better? We'll be okay there.
(nothing)
We won't get in trouble. I promise.
(nothing)
I'm coming in. Okay?
(nothing)

THE SKETCH
Alison Moore

Ailsa moved into the light. She held the drawing close to the bedroom window and studied it. She had found it inside her old portfolio case, which she had opened today for the first time since her youth. The rest of the work—a collection of self-portraits and still lifes—was familiar, recognisable as her own, but *this* piece—she would swear on the Bible—she had never seen before, not until just a minute ago when she had turned over an unfinished head and found this strange thing underneath.

As a girl, she'd had her heart set on art school, on nothing less than the Slade; she had hoped to become an artist, perhaps an illustrator. In the event, further education had not been a possibility, due to her mother's illness. "You can get that idea out of your head," her father had told her. The portfolio had been put away then and had not been opened again while her father was alive, although Ailsa had taken it with her when she married Peter, and again when they moved out of their first house and into this flat. She was supposed to have thrown things out *before* the move, but she had been finding it hard. In the end, she had brought much of it with her, promising Peter that she would, when she'd had a chance to think about it, keep only what was absolutely necessary; she would be brutal.

Now the portfolio lay unzipped and wide open on the unmade bed. The drawing's heavy pencil lines captured the likeness of some kind of troll or sprite, some devilish-looking creature. This was not something *she* had drawn, surely. Her own work had been much more conventional. She did not remember making this picture; it did not look like her work. She touched it, as if she might be able to feel those textures suggested by the pencil lines: the roughness, the hairiness. When she looked very closely, at details rather than at the whole thing in one go, perhaps there *was* something familiar about it; and whether or not it had come out of her, it did speak to her in some way.

The graphite had come away on her fingers; her fingerprints made an ellipsis at the edge of the paper.

Her father's funeral took place on a Wednesday. Peter could not be there as he had to be at work, and it was necessary for Ailsa to take the baby with her to the crematorium. Peter needed the car, and anyway, he did not like her to drive it: she had once scraped a wing, scratched the paintwork, and she had a bad habit of letting the windscreen washer reservoir run dry. He accused her of not looking after it properly. Ailsa thought he was being unfair. In recent years, she had taken a car maintenance class for beginners, and she had been a good student—she had paid attention and made careful notes, which she kept in order in a ring binder. On the other hand, it was true that she was sometimes careless with that old car of his.

She caught the bus to the crematorium, with the baby strapped to her chest. It was a cold midwinter day, but fresh and rather lovely, and as she walked through the gates of the crematorium the sun emerged briefly.

She sat at the front, and as the curtains closed around the coffin a distant relative leaned close, laid a hand on Ailsa's and said, as if to soothe her, though she was not crying, "That's just his body going. He doesn't want it any more. He's free now." Ailsa looked at the relative's hand pressing down on her own; it looked like her father's.

"Out," said Peter. He reached back into the cardboard box. "Out." The discard pile in the flat's narrow hallway reminded Ailsa of the bonfires they used to have in their back garden when she was little. She always made a Guy to put on top of it, with an old pillowcase for a face and her mother's tights for limbs, all stuffed with her father's newspaper. Her father, approaching the bonfire with a box of matches, said that if any hedgehogs were hibernating in there they'd better get out now, and then he lit the twists of paper he'd screwed into the gaps, and Ailsa watched the Guy. She imagined, as the flames rose higher, the Guy's felt-tipped face turning towards her, seeking her out in the dark, in the firelight, his overlong limbs twitching and shifting away from the heat. Then the nylon and the paper would catch and the Guy would flare and—so soon, so quickly, considering the time and care that had been put into making him—be gone, apart from the fragments that, still burning, blew towards her, and she had to step back so that she would not get holes in her winter coat.

"Keep," said Peter, putting aside the canvas of tiny handprints and footprints, done when Bella was only a few weeks old.

"Out," said Peter. He was holding Ailsa's portfolio. It had not sounded like a question, but Ailsa said, as she came forward and took the portfolio from his hands, "I'm not sure."

"You can't hang on to all this stuff," he said. "We don't have space for it here."

"I don't see how we're going to manage in this little flat," said Ailsa. "Not with the baby."

"We have no choice," said Peter. "You know that. We have to downsize."

"All my drawings are in here," she said.

"But what would you need to keep them for?" asked Peter.

"I might want to look at them," said Ailsa.

Peter, delving back into the box, adding sheaves of old paperwork to the pile, said, "You haven't looked at them in twenty years."

"I looked at them yesterday," said Ailsa. "There was one drawing in there that I don't even remember doing. It's nothing like the others. It's peculiar, rather horrid, but I think in a way it's better—more vivid and realistic and affecting—than anything else I've done. It looked like if I touched it, I'd be able to feel the textures—dirty hair and stubble and ragged nails. And its eyes look right back at you, I swear they do. I'm going to show you." She went to the kitchen table, moving the baby's things to make space for her portfolio. She opened it up. "It's here," she said, "in amongst the self-portraits, just under these heads."

Peter came and stood at her shoulder, waiting.

"It's here," she said again, "somewhere…"

"Ailsa," said Peter.

She rummaged through the sheets of paper, going all the way down to the bottom of the pile. "It was…"

"Ailsa," said Peter. "We're all having to make sacrifices. Even Bella is having to make sacrifices. She'll have to manage with less stuff, less space, no garden."

Ailsa looked at Bella, who everyone said had her eyes, but the baby's eyes were blue while Ailsa's were dark. Perhaps the baby's eyes would change; Ailsa expected that they would, in due course. Bella was still so young—too young, Ailsa thought, to even see her across a room, to see anything more than a murky blur where Ailsa was standing.

The picture of the troll, the sprite—the devilish-looking

whatever-it-was—was not there. She would swear that she had put it back inside the portfolio, but now it was gone. In between the heads and the fruit, she found a sheet of paper that was blank except for the fingerprints at the edge, one so clear that you could see the pattern, like ripples in water. She tried to match it to her own. The others were just smudges.

Ailsa saw Peter's face contort; she watched him spit his tea back into his mug. Holding it at a distance, he said, "Is there *salt* in this?"

"There shouldn't be," she said.

"I know there *shouldn't* be," he said, "but *is* there?"

"Mine's fine," said Ailsa, but she did not take sugar anyway; she drank her tea black, with lemon. "Perhaps the sugar and salt got mixed up during the move."

"And the mug's dirty," complained Peter, putting it down heavily and pushing himself away from the kitchen table. Ailsa looked and saw that the mug was indeed dirty: there was a smudge on the side, just where it said BEST DAD. She wondered who had bought that mug. *She* had not bought it for him, and of course the baby had not; had he bought it for himself? As a joke, perhaps.

When she had cleared the breakfast table and given Bella her milk, she went to look for her portfolio. She had to make some decisions today; she had to decide which of her belongings to keep and which to discard. She called to Peter, "Where's my portfolio?"

"I put it out," said Peter.

Ailsa looked at the pile that remained in the hallway. "Out where?"

"I put it out for the dustmen," said Peter.

Still in her dressing gown, Ailsa hurried out of the flat and down the stairs. At the bottom, she pushed open the front door. The world was bitterly cold.

The bins had been emptied. Ailsa heard the distant screech of the bin lorry.

There was a lot of work to be done on the flat, to make it habitable. The kitchen in particular was disgusting. Ailsa remembered her mother saying that the kitchen was the most important room in a home; the kitchen was its heart.

Ailsa sat the baby in a rocker in the doorway and set to tearing up the old lino, which she despised—it looked like a vast and foul chessboard. She was halfway through the task before it struck her that the tiles revealed beneath were just the same as they'd had at home when she was young. For a moment, looking at these childhood tiles, it was as if it might be possible to go back and start over again, make a fresh start, have another go. Then she saw the dirty marks on the doorframe, and she thought of her father, home from the workshop, slouching in the doorway, a small man with grime on his hands, in the whorls of his skin, oil under his fingernails.

When Peter came home from work, he stopped in the kitchen doorway and looked at her. Looking back at him with red-rimmed eyes, she told him, "I don't want to live here," but her voice seemed thin, whispery, and she was not sure he heard her.

"You're a state," he said. "Some women are like this after having a baby." He reached down and lifted Bella out of the rocker. "Sssh…" he said to her. "Sssh…" To Ailsa, he said, "Do you think you should see a doctor?"

Ailsa was often woken at night by Peter's snoring. When it reached a crescendo, his breathing seemed to stop altogether, before starting again. But this was different. Ailsa had woken to find Peter lying there with his hands around his own throat; she had been woken by the choking noises he was making. His eyes—she saw, as she got herself up onto her elbows to see what was going on—were very wide. As she turned on the bedside lamp, he finally managed to draw in a breath, a desperate, shallow gulp of air, and then another. When he could speak again, he whispered, "I couldn't breathe."

"I expect it's this flat," she said. "All the old dirt and dust has got into your lungs."

"It felt like something was sitting on my chest," he said.

In the lamplight, Ailsa looked at his chest, but the T-shirt that he wore in bed was black—there was no evidence that anything had been there; she could see no tell-tale marks.

When it happened again, she said to him, "Do you think you should see a doctor?"

The doctor found nothing wrong. "He says I'm in good shape," said Peter.

Ailsa washed the T-shirt. She spring-cleaned the flat, with the windows wide open, even though it was winter. When she found grimy streaks low down on walls that she knew she had cleaned, she supposed that they might just be scuff marks from Peter's polished shoes. When she found the same marks down near the bottom of the baby's bedroom door, she began to get up in the night whether or not she could hear Bella crying; a silence was more worrying. Every few hours she was out in the hallway, going into Bella's room, turning on the overhead light to look for grubby prints on the bedding or on the babygro or on Panda, who had been Ailsa's own favourite cuddly toy when she was small.

"I've been moving the furniture," said Ailsa.

"I can see that," said Peter. He stood in the doorway of the baby's room, blocking the light from the hallway, the toes of his shoes on Bella's carpet. "But—" He looked at the thigh-high wall of furniture that Ailsa had built around the cot, inside which the baby lay prone. "But whatever for?" said Peter. "Bella can't even sit up yet, let alone climb out of her cot."

"It's not to keep Bella *in*," said Ailsa.

"Then what?" said Peter, but Ailsa did not reply; she was busy lashing the piano stool to the fireguard. These were both things that were not supposed to have come with them to the flat: they had no fireplace here, and no space for the piano, and even if there had been space they would not have been able to get it up all the stairs. The piano had belonged to Ailsa's mother, whose repertoire of fey little tunes had never seemed to make use of the lower notes. For equilibrium, Ailsa had made a point of only ever playing the lower notes, until her mother complained, after which Ailsa was forbidden to touch the piano at all. Nonetheless, the piano had come to her when her father went into the home, and then Peter had got rid of it because it would not fit into the flat.

When Peter had arrived home from the bank with the news that they would have to move out of their house and into this flat, the piano had been Ailsa's first concern. She objected to its loss. She told him that when she was a child she had loved the piano; she had longed to touch its forbidden keys. Peter agreed that it was good for a child to learn a musical instrument, but said that Bella would just have to learn something smaller, like the flute. "It doesn't really matter," said Peter. "It just has to be something small."

Peter stepped into the baby's room now, coming closer to the wall that Ailsa had built around the cot. "How are we supposed to get to Bella?" he asked.

Ailsa straightened up. "I can climb over it," she said. "I'm tall enough."

Peter made an appointment at the surgery for Ailsa, and dropped her off on his way to work. When the mid-afternoon bus brought her back, she saw—as she made her way from the bus stop on the corner, with the baby in a sling—the furniture out on the street, and Peter opening the boot of his car. He picked up the piano stool and put it in. As Ailsa walked past him, he picked up the fireguard.

Still in her coat, still bearing the baby, she stood looking into Bella's room. She went back out to where Peter was busy fitting everything into the back of his car. As he slammed the boot down, Ailsa said to him, "What have you done?"

"I've taken all that crap out of Bella's room," said Peter.

"I can see that," said Ailsa. "But whatever for?"

"I'm taking it to the tip," said Peter. He checked that the boot was secure and moved towards the front of the car. "What did the doctor say?" he asked.

"I need more fresh air and exercise," said Ailsa. "And a hobby."

"A hobby?" said Peter.

"A hobby," said Ailsa. "You know, like drawing. I might find a class to go to, pick up the still life again. Or perhaps not still life. I'm tempted to experiment, to try for that texture again. That hair was so realistic."

"Are you still going on about that bloody sketch?" said Peter.

Sketch. She disliked the word. Sketch, like scratch, like retch, like etch. *Would you like to come and see my etchings?* A man—a friend of her father's—had actually said this to her once, a long time ago, and she had gone with him, this man she had known only slightly; she had actually gone with him to see his etchings, sketchings, scratchings, retchings, and she should not have done. Her father, when she got home, shaking and tearful, and told him, had looked at her, looked her up and down. "Well, what did you expect," he said, "going home with him, and dressed like that?" And then, within the week, this friend of her father's was at their door, coming into the kitchen and joining them at their table as if nothing had happened, as if his being there—at their kitchen table with his fingers on their crockery—were in no way extraordinary.

"Why don't you decorate the baby's bedroom?" suggested Peter. "It could do with brightening up. There's plenty for you to do here. You don't need to go out to a class. Find a hobby you can do at home."

She had also liked reading, but since the baby had come along she had not so much as picked up a book, with the exception of baby books. Bella's books had no words in them, just stark black-and-white patterns.

At some point during her mother's illness, her father's friend—whose name Ailsa could barely recall now, whose name she had no desire to bring to mind—came to live with them for a while. When he sat with the family in their living room, Ailsa made sure always to have a book in front of her, one that was many hundreds of pages thick, the thickness of a door, or a thousand pages thick, the thickness of a wall. She learnt how to be in his company for hours at a time, day after day, and hardly see him. But at the same time, he had learnt how to get around her, for example by challenging her to a game—he would go to the games cupboard and make a show of choosing something, and her father would insist that their guest be indulged. When Ailsa went up to bed and closed her door, she wedged a chair under the handle before turning out the light. One morning, she threw out his shoes. Now she saw that this had been topsy-turvy thinking, as if throwing out his shoes could make him leave. Anyway, by the end of the day, the shoes were back in their place on the shoe rack and nothing was said, and she began to wonder if she had really done it at all or only thought about it.

Peter got into the driver's seat and slammed the door, and

Ailsa stood and watched as he struggled with the engine. When he finally got it started, he pulled away angrily, leaving filthy exhaust fumes clouding the air. The car looked like a wreck but it could still get up speed on an open road, especially when Peter was cross and put his foot down too hard.

By the time he returned, Ailsa was sweeping the hallway with a dustpan and brush.

"What's that?" asked Peter, pointing at the baby's bedroom door.

"It's a padlock," said Ailsa.

Peter opened his mouth; he shook his head. He followed Ailsa into the kitchen, watched her as she emptied the dustpan into the bin beneath the sink and put the dustpan and brush away in the cupboard. She undid the locket around her neck, with her mother in one half and her father in the other, both of them in black and white; she threaded the padlock key onto the chain and returned the locket to its place around her neck.

"This has to stop," said Peter.

"Yes," said Ailsa, looking up at the ceiling, at the grubby marks around the light fitting.

When Ailsa had put the baby to bed and locked the bedroom door, she ran herself a bubble bath and then went to bed herself. She felt terribly tired and yet found it difficult to settle and slept lightly until she was woken by an eerie quiet.

She got out of bed and went into the hallway. At the baby's door, she had to bend down so that the key on the chain around her neck could reach the lock. As she entered Bella's room, she snapped on the overhead light, so that nothing could hide in the dark; nothing, she thought, could sneak unseen beneath the furniture.

She approached the sleeping baby, and saw—in spite of the lock—filth on the bars of the cot. She carried the baby to the chair in the corner of the room and sat awake all night while Bella slept in her arms.

Peter found her there in the morning, with the bulb still burning. "What are you doing there?" he asked. "How long have you been sitting there? You look awful, Ailsa, absolutely awful."

"This is your fault," she whispered. The baby stirred on her chest. "He's out and I can't put him back—there's nowhere for him to go back to."

"What are you talking about?" asked Peter.

"The portfolio," said Ailsa. "I needed that portfolio but you threw it out."

"I haven't got time for this," said Peter. "I've got work." He went into the kitchen and ate a bowl of cereal standing up in front of the fridge. It was still dark outside when he left. The door slammed behind him.

Every morning Peter drove north for twenty miles, and every evening he drove south again. Ailsa thought he drove too fast, always a little bit faster than the road allowed, overtaking everyone else as if he had more of a right to the road than they did. He would arrive home in a temper, fuming over some bad driver, some cyclist, always something, something that wasn't his fault, fuming at Ailsa as if it were *her* fault, as if *she* had cut him up, as if *she* had overlooked his right of way.

Ailsa washed the dishes and wiped the table, scrubbing at a stubborn stain that had got into the grain of the wood. She looked for the place mats. Peter disliked them—he thought them feminine—but they protected the table. She found them in the pile in the hallway; and right at the bottom, in the middle, just where she imagined the hedgehogs used to hide in the bonfire, Ailsa found the grey ring binder that she had used for evening classes in the years between her father going into the home and the baby being born. She sat and leafed through it, singing a tune that she'd learnt to play on the piano a long time ago.

"It's not too late," said Ailsa. "We can explain to the people in the house that we want it back, that the flat is too small for us, that we miss our garden. We can't possibly be happy here."

Peter, taking off his shoes, said, "But we can't afford the house any more."

"There might be some money, though," said Ailsa. "He might have left me something in his will."

"And he might not have done," said Peter. "There might have been nothing left to leave. The home might have sucked him dry."

Ailsa looked at Bella playing with her toys in the narrow hallway. "But the flat is just too small," she said, "for the two of us and a baby."

"Bella hardly counts," said Peter. "She's only little."

"For now," said Ailsa. "But she's going to grow. She'll grow big. She'll be a young woman with size six feet and a will of her own."

Peter looked down at Bella. He said to her, "Is my baby going to have size six feet? Is she? Is she? I don't think so! No, I don't think so! Daddy loves her little feet! Little itsy bitsy feet! Yes, he does!"

"He keeps interfering with things," said Ailsa.

"Who does?" asked Peter.

Ailsa did not know what to call him, and she'd rather avoid naming him anyway, for fear it would somehow make him more real. But he was real enough: he'd been tampering, so that things that had worked when they'd first moved in had become temperamental or had broken down altogether. First the boiler had gone, and then the television: while Peter was down at the pub, getting to know the locals, Ailsa sat down to watch something and the screen went black. He tampered with the electrics, so that sometimes the lights did not work and she had to make do with what little daylight came in through the mean windows. And she kept finding—down at knee-height and underneath things and in tight corners that she had to peer at with a torch—those sooty streaks, those grey-black smears. The thought got into her head that if those dirty marks appeared on Panda's black limbs, she would not be able to see them. She put Panda into the wash, just to be sure that all the baby's things were clean.

He was just concerned about her, he said; she could do with a little rest, a few days without Bella to take care of. His mum would have her for the weekend; it was all arranged. In the morning, she should pack a bag of baby things, and when he got back from work he would drive Bella over to his mother's.

"But your mother's flat is even smaller than this one," said Ailsa. "She only has one bedroom."

"Mum will manage just fine," said Peter.

"But Bella needs more space," said Ailsa.

"Perhaps," said Peter, "while Bella's at Mum's, you could go and see the doctor again."

At night, while Ailsa slept ever more lightly and woke ever more frequently, Peter slept soundly, unless his own snoring or struggling to breathe woke him up. Only Ailsa was ever up and about in the night, in the baby's room, or sometimes out at the front of the flats, in between the flats and the road, looking at the moon or at a moonless sky, or at one of the very few people walking by, or at the cars that zipped past, and at their own car parked by the kerb. She stood there smoking the roll-ups that she was not supposed to have any more because of the baby, but which she liked because they cleared her head, they helped her to think.

She did not like to think of Bella going to Peter's mother's cramped and painfully quiet little flat. She did not want Peter taking Bella out in that crappy old car, driving so fast. With Bella here, in her own room, Ailsa could keep checking for smudgy marks on Bella's clothes or on her bedding. She considered the car, thinking of the engine, the underside, the parts that were already grimy, oily; how would one ever notice some small smudgy fingerprints on a vital part, such as a brake cable? If something were to happen, it might be impossible to say exactly how it had occurred.

In the morning, at breakfast, Peter commented on the dark smudges under Ailsa's eyes. "Did you sleep?" he asked.

"A bit," said Ailsa. Although she had been up for most of the night, she had slept quite well in the final few hours.

Peter finished his cereal, put his bowl down near the sink and said, "I'll be back after lunch to take Bella to Mum's. Get her bag ready. Remember to put in her formula."

Ailsa nodded. She listened to Peter closing the door behind him. She stood and went to the window and looked down at him getting into his car and driving away. She watched him accelerating into the gloom, heading for the bypass.

She did not hurry to pack up the baby's things. Instead, while Bella sat in her high chair playing with her first solid food, Ailsa sat down and lit a roll-up. The charcoal-grey ring binder was still on the kitchen table. The pages of careful notes and neat diagrams from the car maintenance class were dirty at the edges. It could go out for the dustmen now.

When her roll-up had almost burnt down to her grubby fingertips, she used the smouldering end to light another one. She might have all day now to sit and think about what to do next.

PIGS DON'T SQUEAL IN TIGERTOWN
Bracken MacLeod

FRIDAY

The muzzle flash lit up Raymond's mouth and nose like that jack-o'-lantern trick kids play with a lit match behind their teeth. Light spilled out from his lips and nostrils and it all seemed like a joke in the half second between him pulling the trigger and the top of his head spreading against the dusky wallpaper like a red fireworks fountain bought from a plywood shed on the roadside. Except, instead of sparks, his head showered blood and brains and bone around the room. Just like the Fourth of July, the air smelled of smoke and sulphur and the scents of bodies too long in the sun waiting for dusk to come.

The second before Raymond stuck the pistol in his mouth, he said, "Nature don't give a shit about fairness." Immediately before that he'd said, "Fuck you and fuck the Dead Soldiers too." Before Orrin had thought to warn Raymond about watching what he said, his heart skipped a beat and he'd told the man that if he didn't want to have it shoved up his ass, he needed to put that gun away. And prior to that, he told Raymond that if he thought the motorcycle club was being unfair about his debt, he could take it up with the club president, Bunker. All those seconds in time, from Orrin banging on the door, to the creaking of his Chippewa boots on the steps, and the rumble of his 2,294cc engine at the end of the driveway to Tigertown were gone in silence, as though they never existed—just like the back of Raymond's head and his memories and all of his dreams. And all that remained was the thrum of Orrin's heart and the ring of his concussed eardrums.

Before he'd driven his Triumph under the WELCOME TO TIGERTOWN sign hanging from a gallows arm over the access road entrance, he'd read the hand-painted markers along the side of the state highway spaced out like old Burma Shave ads.

OTHER ZOO'S

YOU MIGHT OF PAST

BUT TIGERTOWN

IS WORTH IT!

THE MEMORIES WILL LAST!

½ MILE ON YOUR LEFT

Even though he'd seen them on his other visits to Raymond and his old lady, there was something about the visual rhythm of them passing by as he sped up the road, throbbing in his eyes like a dull strobe. They commanded his attention and he read each one of them every single time, as if the visit before and the one before that and the third and second and first didn't matter. He needed reminding. Yes, this way to Tigertown. The memories will last.

Before he took the turn for Route 30, Orrin glanced at the plywood board affixed with rusted baling wire to the EXIT 42 marker that read:

TIGERTOWN NEXT EXIT — 2 MI. EAST

Before that were the entrance ramp and the city streets in Bannock Falls and the driveway of the Dead Soldiers MC clubhouse. Setting all these future memories in motion was President Bunker sitting on a barstool smoking an American Spirit unfiltered and saying, "You tell him, if he couldn't afford the interest, he never shoulda taken out the loan."

The movement of time seemed to still while Orrin existed in a ghost world of memories. If he hadn't bought his first bike, if he hadn't met "Demon" Langan in The Rising Phoenix bar, if he hadn't become a Prospect and earned his rocker patches, if he hadn't been loyal and dependable and stood for the vote to be Sergeant at Arms, if he hadn't had the day off of work and gone into the clubhouse for a whiskey and a few laughs, everything might've turned out differently.

If.

But none of that had gone differently. These were the choices he'd made. The collection of decisions that brought him to the present moment where he sat in a straight-backed chair in a rundown ex-farmhouse turned roadside attraction halfway to Vulcan Hot Springs trying not to puke at the sight of brains and the smell of blood and gun smoke.

The distant clack of the hand cannon dropping onto the glass table top, and the sharp crack of it giving way and spilling hot steel and shards into the floor below set time moving forward again. Reality surged into motion and flowed around Orrin as his legs spasmed straight, trying to propel him away from the blast that was already long gone. His chair tipped and he went over, falling backwards, sprawling gracelessly on his back as the ancient boxy television on the entertainment centre behind him wobbled and threatened to mash his own brains into the deep-pile carpet.

Orrin scrambled to his feet, his head swimming and lungs struggling for fresh air while all he breathed was the stench of the piss and shit filling Raymond's Wranglers intermingling with the other odours of squalor. He bent down and put his hands on his knees, panting, trying to slow the beat of his heart. He was fluent in the language of violence—it had been taught to him early—but ever since his fourteenth year when he grew taller than his old man, it had always been uttered in *his* voice. He guided the hand that determined when and where and how that language was recorded and what message was sent. He'd done terrible things to living men before, but he'd never seen anyone blow his *own* head off. That troubled him in a deep place he didn't know existed until now. A place of uncertainty and loss of control. Writ on the wall in front of him was an accusation in someone else's script, an indictment he couldn't answer, but one he might be held to account for anyway. His command over the situation had been wrenched away, and he couldn't see what was coming next any better than Raymond could see anything anymore.

It was time to go.

He tugged his riding gloves up tighter, assuring himself he was still wearing them and didn't have to wipe any fingerprints off of the chair or the doorknobs. His hearing slowly came back to life and he heard the ambient sounds of a house return. The refrigerator was running. A fan in the window struggled to move the summer heat around. He was repeating, "Aw fuck, aw fuck, aw fuck," and hadn't noticed that he'd been speaking until that moment. He backed up and pawed blindly at the door handle, unwilling to turn his back on the corpse, knowing it couldn't get up to follow him, but still too unnerved to look away. The latch clicked and released and he pulled the door open and pushed against the screen with his ass. The hinges shrieked, and behind him he heard a low huff and growl.

He turned and saw the thing a hundred yards away, sniffing at the seat of his bike. He owned the largest, loudest motorcycle in the club. His brothers joked about it, asking if Triple A would send a crane to help him pick it up if it got knocked over in the parking lot. But the thing standing next to it, the tiger, was bigger than the bike.

The screen door slammed shut behind him with a loud bang. The animal raised its massive head and looked at him, its eyes full of intelligence and intention. It opened its mouth and growled. Since the club had discovered Tigertown, seeing big cats was as common for Orrin as spying cows in fields along the highway. But, unlike a cow, he'd never seen a tiger with nothing in between him and it but distance. And that's all that separated them now: a frighteningly short distance. No cage, no moat. Just open space.

He grasped at the door, desperate to rejoin a dead man and get back inside. Behind him, he heard the footfalls of a perfect predator making short work of maybe twenty-five yards. Fifteen. Five. The screen swung open, and Orrin leaped into the house, flinging the solid front door shut behind him. It slammed as he heard the beast land on the porch, yowling its frustration. He threw his back against the wood and twisted the deadbolt, squinting his eyes shut, waiting for the feeling of the door and six hundred pounds of hungry beast falling on top of him. Instead, he heard the creature pacing back and forth on the boards outside. It roared. The sound scared Orrin worse than the report of Raymond's forty-five, worse than anything he'd ever heard.

He jerked his pistol out of its holster, aiming it at the door with a quivering hand. For the first time in his life, it felt perfectly impotent in his grip. He hadn't had a chance to draw it when Raymond had pulled his piece from between the sofa cushions.

Worthless then.

And the tiger between him and his bike was waiting on the other side of a door without a window. He couldn't see it to even *try* to get a shot off.

Worthless now.

He stepped away from the door, crouched low, and crept to the window to get a look out onto the deck. Though he couldn't see the tiger, he could hear it walking away from him on the creaky boards. He imagined it was searching for another way in. It roared again, and Orrin's pulse thrummed in his ears both faster and louder.

He had no idea if his piece even packed the kind of punch to kill a tiger. The thought of such a thing had never even occurred to him; his handgun was made for killing men. To him, tigers were the sort of animal that seemed untouchable. Like some kind of creature from myth that existed in the liminal spaces between light and dark and only stepped out to take what *they* wanted. Of course he knew they weren't mythical creatures. He'd seen them often enough right here in Tigertown.

Orrin had toured the "zoo" with the rest of the Dead Soldiers a couple of times. The cages were made of chicken wire stretched around scrap wood from pallets and who knew what else. He assumed, like everyone else, that the cages, however ramshackle they appeared, were sturdy and secure. He'd thought, *Raymond and Val wouldn't live here if they weren't. Right?* But then, he knew people who did stupid, self-destructive shit all the time. They rode in the rain, they shot smack, they borrowed money from the Dead Soldiers, and they visited places like Tigertown off of Route 30, halfway to Vulcan Hot Springs. Of course one of the cats had broken free; it was an inevitability. And it was his bad luck that he happened to be here when it happened. Not luck. *Bunker.* Bunker had sent him instead of coming himself because he wanted to send Raymond a message. I don't come when you call, like a dog.

The sound of the big cat's steps on the porch grew louder, and for a brief moment, out of the corner of his eye, he caught a glimpse of an orange-and-black blur in the window. He aimed, and it was gone. He thought maybe if he went *upstairs*, he could lean out and try to get it from above, taking his shots from a safe position. He reckoned, whether or not his piece was capable of killing one, a mag full of nine mil rounds would discourage it at least—but only *if* he could hit it. His hand was shaking so badly he was uncertain he could even hit the door right in front of him. His gaze returned to Raymond's gun resting in the mess of glass on the carpet. It held fewer rounds, but packed a bigger punch. If he could kill the thing with five bullets, then he could put the piece back where he found it, and maybe it'd look like Raymond had greased himself in despair over having to off one of his precious cats. He slipped his own pistol back into its holster and reached through the chrome table frame to pick up the Taurus revolver. It felt better, heavier, in his hand. He tightened his grip and walked out of the front room.

But before that.

TUESDAY

The Fort Basin County Sheriff parked her truck in the driveway a few yards from the front door and killed the engine. She sat for a moment, listening, waiting for the proprietor to come out like he always did when someone first arrived at Tigertown, waving like an idiot and welcoming them to "The best safari this far from Darkest Africa!" Pat had brought her kids here once and instantly regretted it when she saw the condition of the cages holding the animals.

They were cramped and ramshackle and, worst of all, filthy. She led her boys through the tour, pretending everything was all right, but feeling fearful and increasingly angry at the people who kept the animals in these conditions. Before that, the kids had been so excited to see tigers they'd practically jumped out of the car and run up ahead as she eased up the driveway, afraid of hitting another visitor or wrecking the already struggling suspension on the deep frost heaves and ruts in the road. Kyle and Patrick had seen big cats before at the Salt Lake City Zoo, but they'd heard stories from their friends about *this* place. About how close you could get. About how many tigers there were. They were as excited as she'd ever seen them, and couldn't turn around without losing the little credibility she worked to establish with young boys embarrassed to have a cop for a mom. They were good kids, though, and were as disappointed and disgusted at the state of the place as she was.

Now, she held the papers in her hand and felt a tinge of satisfaction at the idea that she was starting something that might lead to better lives for the animals behind the house. She pushed open the truck door. It creaked loudly on rusting hinges and she winced. While the city PD an hour up the highway was getting all sorts of secondhand military equipment from the Feds, the County still had her rolling around in an old Bronco with a hundred and fifty thousand miles and a rebuilt engine. She left the door hanging open and crunched through the gravel on the way to the front porch. Before she got to the steps, Raymond burst out the front door, tucking in his denim shirt and looking like he had just woken up. Pat checked her watch. A quarter to eleven.

Raymond nodded at her with his chin and spat on the porch. "What're ya' after, Officer?"

"That's Sheriff Trudell, Mr Pawlaczuk. I'm here on official business."

"Mr *Pawlaczuk?*" Raymond said his own name with contempt, as if being called anything other than Raymond was an insult to his age. Pat herself did the same thing anytime someone called her Mrs Trudell. She'd reply with a folksy, *Aw hell. My* grandmother *is Mrs Trudell. I'm Patricia. Pat for short.* Her grandmother was now twenty years in the ground, and Pat was in her late forties. There was no arguing she wasn't the elder Trudell woman in Fort Basin County. On top of it, her husband had died more than five years ago in Afghanistan. She wasn't Mrs Anyone. All her affectations of youth were falling away with the passing days. Still, Raymond had at least twenty years on her. Maybe more.

She held the twin envelopes out. He refused to reach for them or even come down the steps. She took a step up onto the first riser. "That's just far enough, Sheriff. Whatcha got there?"

"An order to cease and desist all operations on this… *animal preserve*, and a notice of foreclosure from the county. This zoo is operating illegally without permits or any of the licensure a man'd need to keep exotic animals. The conditions are a violation of county and state health requirements for both humans and livestock. And the county had condemned this house as well." She failed at suppressing a smile. "You're out, Raymond. We're closing you down."

FRIDAY

The stench grew stronger as he made his way deeper into the house. Competing smells of unwashed dishes and old garbage hovered on top of the scent of wild animal seeping in from outside. Just standing in this place made Orrin feel filthy.

Turning the corner on his way to the stairs, he passed the kitchen and half expected to see an orange-and-black monster sitting at the dinner table, licking its lips, wearing a barbecue bib, with a knife and fork clutched in its paws. Instead, all he saw was last night's dishes and a pile of junk mail on the table. Beyond that, the back door. He crossed the room and checked the lock. He knew a tiger couldn't turn a knob, but still, it made him feel slightly better to know the deadbolt was thrown.

The oppressive heat muddied his already jangled thoughts. He stared out the window in the kitchen door, and tried to remember the layout of the property, wondering if there was a way to flank the animal the long way around and get to his bike. While he'd toured the "zoo" a few times, it had been with his brothers along, distracting him. They'd laughed and talked shit and paid no attention to anything around them because they were the Dead Soldiers and the world stepped aside when they rode or strode through. Exit strategies and future plans weren't anything they bothered with. A man, especially a Dead Soldier, walked out the same door he walked in. Except, Orrin was *merely* a man. And— one percenter or not—he couldn't outfight a fucking tiger. His bike was parked in front, and that was his only way out. He had to outsmart the animal.

He went back out of the kitchen and found the stairs to the second floor. He took them three at a time. Somehow, it smelled worse upstairs than down. He approached the door on the south-facing side of the hallway. It was closed. His hand hovered by the knob as he imagined Raymond's old lady, Val, waiting inside with a shotgun in her lap ready to cut him in half, leaving him to die like his father, bleeding out on the floor of a strange woman's bedroom. He assured himself that Val wasn't on the other side. If she was, she would've come running when Raymond checked out. He reached for the knob, and as soon as he cracked the door, he knew she was right where he feared he'd find her. Except, instead of sitting on the edge of the bed, waiting for him with a twelve-gauge, she was laid out, arms folded across her chest, face pale, a dark red stain under her hands. The high-pitched drone of flies buzzing in the room was maddening. He steadied himself against the doorjamb and tried to breathe, but the smell of her invaded his nostrils, made him feel like smothering, like he was being drowned in filth. He breathed her in and gagged. How long had she been lying there dead, waiting to be found? How long had Raymond been planning this?

Orrin recalled Bunker telling him to go to Tigertown. "That fucker Raymond's been calling for two goddamn days," he'd said. "You go find out what the fuck he wants and give him a reminder that he doesn't get to demand a meet with me. I'll talk to him when *I* want, not when *he* fuckin' feels like it."

Two days. She's been in here two days.

Summer in Tigertown stank. The heat baked the dry dirt outside like a kiln and the smell of sun-cooked tiger piss hovered, pungent, in the air. And under that, there was rot. Raymond and Val tossed sides of beef, whole chickens, pigs and whatever else they could get their hands on into the cages to keep a dozen big cats alive. But they didn't pick up after them, and whatever the cats didn't eat sat in the sun, swarmed by flies and growing ever rank with decay. Compared to the bedroom, though, the cages smelled like the Yankee Candle shop in the mall.

Orrin put a hand over his mouth. The effect was minimal, merely adding a hint of leather to the fetor of the room. He pressed harder with the back of his glove, held his gorge, and staggered toward the window next to the bed.

The window fought him as he tried to yank it open with his left hand. The frame was old and neglected and it got stuck at an odd angle halfway open. He wanted to smash it. The sound of recalcitrant things breaking was often how Orrin measured compliance. Wood, glass… bones. But shattering the window wasn't going to help him get away without leaving a trace. When the police finally showed up, he didn't want them to find any sign the Dead Soldiers had been here. He put the pistol on the sill, held his breath, and slid the window down before lifting it open again more gently with both hands. This time it rose without sticking. He pushed the screen out, letting it clatter to the ground, leaned through and took a deep breath of merely distasteful air.

He looked down and muttered, "Fuuuck me." The eaves below the window blocked his view of the porch and the tiger. He couldn't hear it anymore either. Had it just stopped moving or had it moved on? He'd half expected to see it react to the falling screen, but it wasn't a housecat. He didn't figure he was about to distract it with a ball of yarn or a laser pointer.

In the distance, his motorcycle gleamed in the sunlight like an oasis. Shimmering in the hot air distortion as if it would vanish if he got too close. While the path from the house to his Triumph looked clear from up where he stood, he knew that was the real illusion.

Then he saw it.

The animal was stalking away from the house into the tall weeds on the other side of his bike. He watched it turn and crouch down. A shiver passed through Orrin as he realized the thing was lying in wait for him. Hunting. But the cat's pelt was brighter than the dry brush in which it hid. He had it dead to rights.

He knelt down in front of the open window and took aim. His hand trembled with adrenaline and the unfamiliar weight of Raymond's hand-cannon. The thing wasn't right below him anymore. At this distance, he'd be better off trying to get the shot with a deer rifle. Raymond almost definitely had a thirty-aught somewhere in the house. He knew the old bastard had to be poaching deer to feed the cats. There was no way he could afford to buy enough meat from the butcher for his zoo. Not the way he kept coming to the Dead Soldiers for money. But Orrin had the tiger in his sights *right now* and didn't want to risk losing that advantage while he went looking for a better weapon. He aimed, let out a slow breath, and squeezed the trigger.

The report of the gun deadened his ears. The fucking thing was loud. His own pistol made demure little *pop pop pops* compared to this one.

A small cloud of dust kicked up from the ground where the slug hit yards away from his target. He blinked in the bright daylight and tried to re-aim, but couldn't see where the tiger had gone. It moved so fast. And now, instead of knowing where it was, he was blind to it again. *I should've waited. Fucking stupid.* If he'd had any illusion about what his role in predator and prey was, it was dispelled.

He stared at his bike. He reckoned the distance between the front door and his ride wasn't one he could cross before the tiger cut him off. Even though the animal was probably half-starved from its keepers' neglect, it could see, hear, run and kill better than he could on his very best day. The damn thing had almost got him when all he was sprinting for was the door at his ass. He had to find the rifle. He needed more power, and a scope. Hunt it like they did in Africa or India or whereeverthefuck a tiger like that was from. He ducked inside and immediately wanted back out again.

Orrin breathed through his mouth, trying not to smell the rot breaking down Val's body. She smelled worse than the carcasses they threw in the animals' cages. Of course she did. She was whole, guts and all. She was human.

That was his way out.

But before that.

TUESDAY

Raymond asked, "So, you're the lawyer for the county now too?"

"Nosir. I'm just doing my job. You asked and I told you. And since you're here looking me face to face, it doesn't matter if I put these in your hand or toss 'em at your feet. You been duly served as I see it." She held the papers out and waited another couple of seconds. Raymond reached over and snatched them out of her hand with a sound like "Fuck you" beneath the rattle of the envelopes, but definitely not a clear "Fuck you," or else Pat would have been inclined to take another step or two up onto the porch after him.

"Unconstitutional!" he shouted. "It's my goddamned property, and I can do what I want with it."

"Tell it to the judge. Afternoon, Raymond." Pat didn't need to stick around to watch him open the envelope. She'd done her duty. Though she wanted the extra pleasure of seeing the results of her effort play out on his face, it would only aggravate him more to linger. Her job was to deescalate conflict. So, she tipped her hat and turned to leave. Pat stepped down and started back toward her truck. She heard the sound of paper being balled up, but didn't care. If Raymond ignored the summons and they issued a bench warrant for his arrest, all the better. She'd be happy to come out again and gaffle him up personally. She'd even do it on her day off. Hell's sake, she'd do it on Christmas if it meant shuttering Tigertown for good. It wasn't until she heard the sound of something hard sliding against leather that she realized she shouldn't have turned her back on the man. She spun around, flipping the leather tab off the hammer of her revolver and tried to draw. The bullet from Raymond's gun caught her in the thigh and sent her sprawling. She lost hold of her gun and it bounced out of her hand and slid away in the dirt. Heavy footsteps raced toward her as she tried to scramble for it. But the broken bone and screaming hole in the back of her leg kept her from reaching it in time. A shadow fell on her and she turned over, holding up her hands.

Raymond loomed over her, his expression dark and angry. He hadn't had time to regret what he'd done yet, but it would come. His face would change when he realized what a terrible mistake this was.

"It's a fucking injustice and I won't stand for it. This is *my* property and this is still America."

"S-stop. Stop this. The D-deputy Sheriff knows I'm here. Everyone... knows. Th-this is... is official business. It's not personal," she lied. She hadn't told anyone she was coming out to Tigertown. She'd seen the envelopes awaiting service and, instead of handing them on to her deputy, had taken them herself. She wanted to see his expression when she served him. Because it *was* personal.

Raymond's face fell. Fury changed to fear and the realization that he'd just lost everything. His house, his farm, the cats, and now his freedom. Maybe, eventually, his life at the end of a needle. No matter what, he was going away. Pat felt a hint of satisfaction at the idea of it. But while the day was hot, she was starting to feel cold and tired and satisfaction soon became fear and realization. *Oh, shit. I'm bleeding out.*

She tried to reach for the radio transmitter on her epaulette. Raymond stepped on her arm and bore down. It hurt less than her leg, but still, it hurt goddamn bad. She couldn't help it and cried out in a way she never had done on the job. The only female sheriff in all the state's forty-six counties, she didn't have the luxury of a high-pitched cry. In her own ears, she sounded like one of her sons. The seven-year-old had a way of keening high at his hurts. Pat thought she sounded like him just then.

She thought of her sons.

Raymond reached down and yanked the transmitter

cable out of her radio. He took the whole thing and threw it back up toward the porch. It squawked once and was silent. "Pigs don't squeal in Tigertown, Sheriff. It gets the cats too excited."

FRIDAY

Orrin found the gun locker in a room downstairs. It might have been a dining room once, some place for the family that built this house to gather at the end of a long day of honest work and eat together. Orrin knew hard work, though he wasn't sure he could call much of it honest. And if his family had ever taken a meal together, it was before he was old enough to hold on to such a memory. In the corner stood an oak gun cabinet like the one his grandfather had owned. The glass door and tiny lock wouldn't keep anyone from getting their hands on anything inside—it wasn't a safe, it was a china hutch for rifles. And Raymond had a collection. Any other time, Orrin would be considering taking the lot of them home with him. There was a pump shotgun, a pair of .22 calibre rifles, and exactly what he was looking for: a Remington bolt-action .30-06 with a scope. He tried the door and wasn't surprised to find it unlocked. He grabbed the thirty-aught and considered taking the shotgun as well. He could only fire one rifle at a time, though, and if his plan worked, he wouldn't need the shotgun at all. Still, while he'd have to leave the deer rifle behind to make it look like Raymond had put down the cat before taking himself out, the Mossberg was going to be Orrin's reward for having to endure this mess of shit.

He pulled out the drawer underneath the cabinet. Boxes of ammunition were stacked neatly inside. It seemed to him the only space in the house that had any order. He dug through until he found the right calibre and took the box. He loaded four long rounds into the rifle, stuffed the remainder, still in the box, into his jacket pocket and returned upstairs.

His stomach did a hard flip in the doorway to the bedroom and he gagged again. Time in the house wasn't doing anything to help him get used to the smell. He set the rifle by the door and shrugged out of his leather jacket, letting it drop to the floor. The buckle on the kidney belt made a loud clank as it hit the hardwood and he flinched a little. He pulled off his T-shirt and wrapped it around his face the way he'd seen kids playing in his neighbourhood do, pretending to be ninjas. He tied the short sleeves behind his head. The shirt was sweaty and smelled like his body odour and engine grease. Though the house was stifling and breathing through the cloth only made him feel hotter, the smell of it was soothing in its familiarity. Those were the aromas of sitting in his garage working on his bike, smoking a little weed and drinking a beer. They were the smells of normality and peace. Still, there was much more than a hint of Val's stench getting through. He'd heard stories of how the smell of a dead body never came out of things. That you could smell it in a house for years afterward. He could burn his clothes and buy himself brand new ones, all except for the denim cut-off jacket he wore over his leathers—his kutte. He couldn't replace that or the club patches sewn on it. He'd slice off the tattoo over his heart and throw that in the fire first. His kutte was therefore destined to always stink. If he survived this, he'd happily smell like a corpse. But first he needed to get out with both it and his skin intact.

Orrin took a deep breath through his mouth and approached the bed. Val's skin was grey and mottled with long purple streaks, like her veins were swollen with dark ink. Her lips were the same purple and starting to blacken on the inside. Touching her felt like a very bad idea, even with his gloves on. As if death itself might rub off onto him. Bacteria was eating her up from the inside. He knew it couldn't hurt him. He could wash up and everything would be fine. Still, he felt a powerful repulsion at the idea of getting too close to her, like the prehistoric fear of death he'd inherited from his most distant ancestor, calling out to him from across millennia: *this is unclean. This is a* bad *thing.* But he couldn't listen to that voice. Moving Val was the only plan he'd come up with, and nothing else was springing to mind.

He grabbed her wrist and yanked. He'd expected her to be stiff with rigor mortis, but she wasn't. Her body was loose, and he pulled harder than he meant to, jerking her to the edge of the mattress. Moving her made the smell worse and a wave of stench hit him like a fist even through the shirt covering his face. He looked at the mattress where she had been, and though there was an indentation, there was no bloodstain. The bullet that killed her hadn't exited out her back. He was thankful for small miracles. He bent over, slid an arm behind her shoulders, the other under her knees, and lifted her off the mattress. She was skinny and light, though her limp body was uncooperative. He had to hold her tightly and close. She was dressed for summer in a crop top and a pair of shorts. The feel of her cool skin against his naked belly made him feel ill. He hadn't thought to put his coat back on and zip it up, and now it was too late. They were skin to skin, and he didn't want to prolong it. He kept breathing through his mouth and walked out of the room holding the dead woman.

He carried her down the stairs and into the front room where her old man still sat cooling on the sofa. Orrin felt angry and wanted to kick the shit out of the fucker. Even if he was dead and couldn't feel it, at least *he'd* know Raymond was getting the beating he deserved. He left the dead man alone and looked outside. There was no sign of the tiger that he could see. Just the porch and the drive and his bike.

At the door, he dipped down like he was curtsying to

twist the deadbolt latch. Val's head lolled around and he reflexively squeezed tighter to keep from dropping her. Like it would matter if he did. The feeling of her body giving in his arms broke him a little. She was soft and felt like a person. There was something wet on his arm. He tried not to think about it. Pulling the door open, he waited for a second, ready to kick it closed if he saw the blur of a big cat racing toward him. When nothing came running out of the weeds, he let out a breath he didn't know he was holding, and pushed at the screen door with Val's hip. It opened with a pop and a loud creak. He stepped outside.

The stairs groaned beneath his weight as he descended. The sound made his back tense and his heart beat a little quicker. At the bottom, he stopped and listened. He couldn't hear much above the breeze and his own breathing in the makeshift mask. He hazarded a glance back at the porch. Though there hadn't been anything there a moment ago, he wanted—*needed*—to be certain he could get back inside. It was one thing to run a few feet into the house, but if it cut him off and he had to run the other direction, it was all over. It was a comfort to see nothing in between him and the front door. He took a few more steps out into the open and knelt down to lay her body in the dirt. He looked over his shoulder at the window to the second-storey bedroom. Crouched where he was, the window was clear of the eaves. Good enough.

Sunlight glinted off the rear-view mirror of his motorcycle, and with no sign of the animal around, the urge to sprint toward it pulled at him like a hook in his flesh. *But my fuckin' kutte's in the house.* Orrin chided himself for leaving it behind. Stress and fear were going to kill him as sure as an escaped tiger. He needed to get his shit together if he wanted to ride away from this place.

He stood and began walking quietly, but quickly, back to the house. Behind him he heard the rustle of the tall weeds.

It might have been the breeze. Or it might have been a beast. Either way, his bladder almost let go and he sprinted for the front door.

He leaped up the stairs, nearly falling as he cleared the bottom four, but not the last two. He scrambled across the deck and ripped open the screen. It banged against the side of the house, and Orrin was inside and slamming the front door before the screen swung back into place.

"FUCK! YOU!" he screamed, ashamed at his naked terror. He shook and slammed a fist into the door. Pain reached up from his knuckles into his wrist, but he didn't care, and he punched it again, shouting out his frustration. Taking a deep breath, he looked at his hand while he flexed it. It wasn't broken. Sprained maybe, but as long as he could hold a throttle it'd be fine. More importantly, he felt sure he could still pull a trigger.

A soft sliding sound and a muted thump made Orrin jump again. He spun around, arms up in front of his face.

Raymond's corpse had slumped over on the sofa. Whether it had been the reverberations of Orrin's violence or simply gravity, the result was the same: Orrin's chest felt tight and he was breathless. His vision blurred as he tried to keep from hyperventilating. "I hope you're sweating in Hell, motherfucker!" he hissed from between clenched teeth. He went to the window and looked outside. If the tiger had been behind him, it wasn't there now. He was beginning to feel like the animal was a dream. Raymond had drugged him somehow and he was hallucinating everything. Except, he could see Val out there dead in the road, and Raymond was spilling what was left of his brains onto the couch behind him. And this was still Tigertown. He wasn't hallucinating. Somewhere out there, death was waiting, tooth and claw.

He stumbled into the kitchen and searched the cupboards until he finally found what he wanted in the one above the refrigerator. A big plastic jug of tequila stood next to a smaller bottle of cheap margarita mix with a woman wearing fruit on her head on the label. He grabbed the tequila, twisted off the cap, and took a healthy couple of gulps to settle his nerves. He forced himself to stop, replaced the cap and then the bottle. Just enough to give him the Dutch courage he needed.

He stomped upstairs, snatching his jacket off the floor and slinging it on without untying the T-shirt from around his face. He grabbed the rifle and went to wait at the window.

Earlier.

WEDNESDAY

Val stood in the doorway watching Raymond pull his stained shirt up over his head. He dropped it on the floor. She picked it up to throw in the fire pit along with the Sheriff's uniform. "Did you get through? Did you try calling again?"

He shook his head. "Nope. They ain't answerin'. I can't imagine what the Soldiers can do to help, anyways. With what we already owe 'em too? There's nothin' in it for them."

"Horseshit. They won't get *any* of their money if we go to jail. Cats're already takin' care of the bitch. We throw this in the burn pit with her uniform," she said, holding up his shirt, "and all we got left to do is get rid of the truck in the barn. Choppin' a truck is the least bad thing those sons a bitches get up to. It don't cost them a thing."

Raymond stepped out of his pants. His tight, off-white underwear sagged off of a skinny ass that was twenty-five years past firmness. He looked at his wife with tired eyes and said, "We're fucked up way past fixin'. You ought to pack a bag and go. I reckon they'll be out tomorrow at the latest lookin' for her. I'll say you went to see your sister up in Mercy Lake and you weren't here when she came by to give me the papers. Takes a whole day to get there, so nobody'll be able to say for sure just when you hit the road. Evelyn'll vouch for you."

"And what are you going to do?" Her eyes went wide and her mouth dropped open. "You're not gonna…"

"Go grab your bag." He stepped into a pair of jeans he pulled off the top of the overflowing hamper. "Pack up what you need and get on the road. No sense in both of us getting caught up in this."

Val didn't say anything as he walked out of the room. She didn't ask him to come back, or offer a better plan. She just let him go.

When he returned, she had the bag on the bed and was stuffing clothes into it. She looked up from what she was doing. Her brow knitted as she saw the gun in his hand. "Are they here already?"

He raised the pistol and fired.

FRIDAY

Sweat moistened the shirt on his head, but the cloth kept it from dripping in his eyes while he watched the road. He'd scanned the weeds and the far edges of the property with the rifle scope, but he wasn't catching sight of the tiger. He'd thought for certain Val's body and the promise of an easy meal would lure it out, but it had been forty minutes and it hadn't taken the bait. He wondered whether it had wandered off, looking for other prey. There was no shortage of horses and cattle in the countryside around the county. Sheep and a few alpacas too. He decided he'd give it another twenty minutes, and then he was going to try sneaking out to get away. And then he saw it.

It was stalking around the opposite side of the house by

the barn, instead of where he'd seen it when he tried to take the shot with the pistol. His heart thumped harder at the sight of it. The thing was big and moved like liquid. It was beautiful and terrifying. A perfect thing. He almost regretted having to kill it.

The tiger slowed its pace and lowered its head as it came closer to Val's body, sniffing at her. Orrin centred the crosshairs on the top of its skull and waited.

What are you waiting for? Dig in.

The animal looked around as if it was trying to figure out where Val had come from. It reached out with a paw and grabbed at her. Val's body jerked like it was a child's doll and the tiger bit down on her neck and quickly started to drag her back the way it had come. At the edge of the road near the weeds, it plopped down and tore off a long strip of her flesh.

Bile burbled up Orrin's throat, stinging and threatening to choke him.

He swallowed, re-aimed, and squeezed the trigger.

The sound in the bedroom was deafening and he thought he might have let out a yelp of pain, though he didn't hear it if he did. His ears were dead and ringing; his head hurt a little. He pushed past all of that to pull back on the bolt handle and eject the spent casing. He shoved the bolt back into place and chambered a new round. Through the scope he saw the tiger lying next to Val. A pool of dark blood was spreading from its skull and muddying up the dirt. He contemplated putting another round in it, but deaf or not, the rifle was loud, and he didn't want to risk attracting any more attention than that shot might've already. Even this far out in the boonies people didn't like hearing rifle reports near where their kids got off the bus, or where they were grazing their livestock.

He stood up and shook out his legs. His knees and his fist ached. The ride home was going to be long. But it didn't matter. It was going to be the best ride of his life. He'd just killed a fucking tiger. None of his brothers were ever going to be able to top that no matter how many points the next buck had. He just had to trade rifles and he could get on his way.

Earlier in the day.

FRIDAY

Raymond ran out the back as soon as he heard the motorcycle pulling up the drive. He'd just about given up hope that Bunker was coming. He pulled the keys out of his pocket and looked at his zoo. He thought that he'd miss his cats. But then, probably not.

"Time to raise hell."

FRIDAY

Orrin stepped out onto the porch, pulling the door shut behind him and took a deep breath of fresh air. He walked down the steps, not looking over at where he'd shot the tiger. He'd made sure it was dead before he came down from his roost. He'd put the rifle back in the gun cabinet and took the Mossberg along with the ammo. It wouldn't do for the cops to find shells for a shotgun that wasn't in the house. He wrapped the box of shells in his T-shirt and stuffed that into his saddlebag. The shotgun he tied to the side of the bike with bungee cords. It wasn't perfect, but it'd get him home.

He swung a leg over the bike and turned the key. The engine roared to life and he twisted the throttle. His hearing was coming back slowly, but it was still muffled. Between that and his pipes, he never heard the animal behind him.

When it pulled him off the seat into the tall grass he had no idea what was happening until he was already on his back.

Everything was a blur. He felt claws puncturing his jacket and his flesh underneath. He felt its hot breath, and then the thing's teeth biting down on his neck. Orrin wanted to reach for his pistol, but it was under him in the holster at the small of his back. He beat uselessly against the animal with his fists. He struggled and kicked but the tiger knelt down on its elbows and held him there. He tried to gasp for breath, but the jaws holding him were tight and he couldn't breathe.

He felt a hard tug at his leg and a searing pain as his leathers ripped open and a long muscle tore away from his bone. Another tug. The tiger that had taken him down tightened its hold on his neck. The sound of his spine breaking echoed inside his own skull like when he'd bite down on a piece of gristle. It was a vibration from *inside* his body, not a sound outside.

The bright day grew dim, even though the sun wouldn't be going down for hours. And he slipped away while the other hungry tigers ate him, leaving nothing left in his life to come.

Before that, he had been a man who would have liked to have taken a last ride.

Long before that, he had been a boy who loved his bicycle, and the feeling like flying when he rode it down the tall hill behind his house and took his hands off the handlebars.

And earlier still, he was a child and occasionally his mother held him and whispered to him, her breath tickling his ear like a warm bourbon breeze.

And before that, he wasn't yet born and was exactly like he was now.

Gone in silence, as though he never existed.

BIOGRAPHIES

Priya Sharma's fiction has appeared in such publications as *Interzone*, *Black Static*, *Albedo One*, *Nightmare Magazine*, *The Dark*, *Mithila Review* and on *Tor.com*. Her work has been anthologised in several volumes of Ellen Datlow's *Best Horror of the Year*, in Paula Guran's *Year's Best Dark Fantasy & Horror*, in Jonathan Strahan's *The Best Science Fiction & Fantasy 2014*, Steve Haynes' *Best British Fantasy 2014* and Johnny Main's *Best British Horror 2015*. Her stories have also been on many of Locus's Recommended Reading Lists. Her story "Fabulous Beasts" was a Shirley Jackson Award finalist and won a British Fantasy Award for Short Fiction. A collection of her short fiction, *All the Fabulous Beasts*, is available from Undertow Publications.

Website: *priyasharmafiction.wordpress.com*

Stephen Volk is probably best known for the notorious BBC drama *Ghostwatch* (called by some the most terrifying drama ever seen on TV) and as creator and lead writer of the award-winning ITV drama series *Afterlife* starring Andrew Lincoln and Lesley Sharp. He wrote ITV's three-part chiller *Midwinter of the Spirit* starring Anna Maxwell Martin and David Threlfall, and has penned numerous feature screenplays, including ghost story *The Awakening* starring

Rebecca Hall and Dominic West, and Ken Russell's *Gothic*, while his other TV work includes Channel 4's *Shockers*. His play *The Chapel of Unrest* premiered at the Bush Theatre starring Jim Broadbent and Reece Shearsmith. He is the winner of two British Fantasy Awards and a BAFTA. His stories are collected in *Dark Corners*, *Monsters in the Heart* and *The Parts We Play*. His three novellas comprising The Dark Masters trilogy (*Whitstable*, *Leytonstone* and *Netherwood*) will be published by PS in late 2018.

Robert Shearman has written five short story collections, and between them they have won the World Fantasy Award, the Shirley Jackson Award, the Edge Hill Readers Prize, and three British Fantasy Awards. He began his career in the theatre, and was resident dramatist at the Northcott Theatre in Exeter, and regular writer for Alan Ayckbourn at the Stephen Joseph Theatre in Scarborough; his plays have won the *Sunday Times* Playwriting Award, the World Drama Trust Award, and the Guinness Award for Ingenuity in association with the Royal National Theatre. A regular writer for BBC Radio, his own interactive drama series *The Chain Gang* has won two Sony Awards. But he is probably best known for his work on *Doctor Who*, bringing back the Daleks for the BAFTA-winning first series in an episode nominated for a Hugo Award. His latest book, *We All Hear Stories in the Dark*, is to be released by PS Publishing next year.

Trained as a journalist, **Gemma Files** has also been a teacher, screenwriter and film critic. She broke onto the horror scene when her story "The Emperor's Old Bones" won the 1999 International Horror Guild Award for Best Short Fiction. She is the author of the *Hexslinger* series (*A Book of Tongues*, *A Rope of Thorns* and *A Tree of Bones*), *We Will All Go Down Together: Stories of the Five-Family Coven* and *Experimental Film*, which won both the 2016 Shirley Jackson Award and 2016 Sunburst Award for Best Novel. She has also published two collections of short fiction and two chapbooks of speculative poetry, and will soon add three more short fiction collections to that list—two (*Spectral Evidence* and *Drawn Up From Deep Places*) from Trepidatio Publishing, one (*Dark Is Better*) from Cemetery Dance Graveyard Editions. Five of her stories were adapted as episodes of *The Hunger*, an erotic horror anthology TV series from Ridley and Tony Scott's Scott Free production company.

Kit Power lives in Milton Keynes and writes dark genre fiction. These two facts may or may not be connected. His novel, *GodBomb!*, and novella collection, *Breaking Point*, have been published by The Sinister Horror Company, and he blogs regularly for *Gingernuts of Horror*. He's also a serial podcaster. His debut collection *A WARNING ABOUT YOUR FUTURE ENSLAVEMENT THAT YOU WILL DISMISS AS A COLLECTION OF SHORT FICTION AND ESSAYS BY KIT POWER* is now available.

Tim Lebbon is a *New York Times* bestselling author of over forty novels. Recent books include *Relics*, *The Family Man*, *The Silence* and the *Rage War* trilogy of Alien/Predator novels. He has won four British Fantasy Awards, a Bram Stoker Award and a Scribe Award. The movie of his story *Pay the Ghost*, starring Nicolas Cage, was released Halloween 2015. *The Silence*, starring Stanley Tucci and Kiernan Shipka, is due for release in 2018. Several other movie projects are in development in the US and UK.

Website: *www.timlebbon.net*

Benjamin Percy is the author of four novels—most recently *The Dark Net*—as well as two short story collections and a book of essays. He writes for DC Comics (*Green Arrow, Teen Titans*) and Dynamite Entertainment (*James Bond*), and his fiction and non-fiction have been published in *Esquire, Time, GQ* and the *Paris Review*. His honours include the Whiting Award, the Plimpton Prize, an NEA fellowship, two Pushcart Prizes, and inclusion in *Best American Short Stories* and *Best American Comics*.

Mild-mannered laboratory technician by day, **Laura Mauro** was born in south-east London and currently lives in Essex under extreme duress. Her work has appeared in *Black Static, Interzone, Shadows & Tall Trees* and a variety of anthologies. Her debut novella, *Naming the Bones*, was published in 2017. She is currently studying towards a Master's in Modern and Contemporary Literature, which mostly involves pretending to have read James Joyce's *Ulysses*. In her spare time she collects tattoos, dyes her hair strange colours and blogs sporadically at *www.lauramauro.com*.

Ray Cluley's short fiction has appeared in various magazines and anthologies and has been reprinted in Ellen Datlow's *Best Horror of the Year* series, Steve Berman's *Wilde Stories 2013: The Year's Best Gay Speculative Fiction*, and in Benoît Domis's *Ténèbres* series. He has been translated into French, Polish, Hungarian and Chinese. He won a British Fantasy Award for Best Short Story and has since been nominated for Best Novella and Best Collection. That collection, *Probably Monsters*, is available from ChiZine Press.

Tim Lucas is the author of two well-received novels, *Throat Sprockets* (1994) and *The Book of Renfield: A Gospel of Dracula* (2005), as well as the Saturn Award-winning *Mario Bava: All the Colors of the Dark* (2007) and *Studies in the Horror Film: Videodrome* (2008). Since the early 1970s he has written for nearly all the major magazines devoted to fantastic cinema, as well as *Film Comment, Cahiers du Cinéma* and *Sight & Sound,* for which he wrote a monthly column for nearly a decade. He also edited and co-published 184 issues and two Special Editions of *Video Watchdog: The Perfectionist's Guide to Fantastic Video* (1990–2017), which raised the bar for critical and journalistic standards in genre film writing. In October 2016, at the Vista Theatre in Los Angeles, Joe Dante directed a live table reading of his as-yet-unproduced Roger Corman biopic script *The Man with Kaleidoscope Eyes,* starring Bill Hader as Corman (with a special appearance by Corman himself)—an event billed as "The Greatest Film Never Made". A prolific audio commentator for DVD and Blu-ray discs, his forthcoming publications include *The Secret Life of Love Songs* (a novella) and a monograph on the 1968 Poe anthology film *Spirits of the Dead.*

Brian Hodge is one of those people who always has to be making something. So far, he's made thirteen novels, around 130 shorter works, and five full-length collections. He'll have three new books out in 2018 and early 2019: *The Immaculate Void,* a novel of cosmic horror; *A Song of Eagles,* a grimdark fantasy; and *Skidding Into Oblivion,* his next collection. He lives in Colorado, where he also likes to make music and photographs; loves everything about organic gardening except the thieving squirrels; and trains in Krav Maga and kickboxing, which are of no use at all against the squirrels. Connect through his web site

(www.brianhodge.net),

Twitter

(@BHodgeAuthor),

or Facebook

(www.facebook.com/brianhodgewriter).

Catriona Ward was born in Washington, DC, and grew up in the United States, Kenya, Madagascar, Yemen and Morocco. She read English at St Edmund Hall, Oxford, and is a graduate of the Creative Writing Masters at the University of East Anglia. Her debut novel, *Rawblood* (Weidenfeld & Nicolson, 2015), won Best Horror Novel at the 2016 British Fantasy Awards, was shortlisted for the Author's Club Best First Novel Award and was selected as a Winter 2016 Fresh Talent title by WHSmith. *Rawblood* is published in the US and Canada as *The Girl from Rawblood* (Sourcebooks, 2017). She works for a human rights foundation and lives in London. Her second novel, *Little Eve*, was published by Weidenfeld & Nicolson in July 2018.

V.H. Leslie's stories have appeared in many publications, including *Black Static*, *Interzone* and *Shadows & Tall Trees*, and have been reprinted in several *Year's Best* anthologies. Her fiction has been nominated for the World Fantasy Award, the British Fantasy Award and the Shirley Jackson Award, and she won the Lightship International First Chapter Prize. Her non-fiction has appeared in *History Today*, *Gramarye*, *Thresholds* and *The Victorianist*. She has also been awarded Fellowships at Hawthornden in Scotland and the Saari Institute in Finland and is currently studying for her PhD in English and Creative Writing at the University of Chichester.

Rio Youers is the British Fantasy Award–nominated author of *Point Hollow* and *The Forgotten Girl*. His short fiction has been published in many notable anthologies, and his novel *Westlake Soul* was nominated for Canada's prestigious Sunburst Award. He has been favourably reviewed in such publications as *Publishers Weekly*, *Booklist* and *The National Post*. His new novel, *Halcyon*, was released by Macmillan/St. Martin's Press in July 2018.

Brian Evenson is the author of a dozen books of fiction, most recently the story collection *A Collapse of Horses* (Coffee House Press, 2016) and the novella *The Warren* (Tor.com, 2016). His fiction has been a finalist for the Shirley Jackson Award and the Edgar Award, and he has won the International Horror Guild Award and the ALA–RUSA Award. He received a 2017 Guggenheim Fellowship. His work has been translated into Czech, French, Italian, Greek, Spanish, Japanese, Persian and Slovenian. He lives in Los Angeles and teaches in the Critical Studies Program at CalArts.

Steve Rasnic Tem is a past winner of the Bram Stoker, World Fantasy and British Fantasy Awards. His latest novel, *Ubo* (Solaris, February 2017), is a dark science fictional tale about violence and its origins, featuring such historical viewpoint characters as Jack the Ripper, Stalin and Heinrich Himmler. *Yours To Tell: Dialogues on the Art & Practice of Writing*, written with his late wife, Melanie, also appeared in 2017 from Apex Books. New for 2018 from Valancourt Books is *Figures Unseen*, a volume of his selected stories, as well as *The Mask Shop of Doctor Blaack*, a middle grade novel about Halloween from Hex Publishers.

Aliya Whiteley was born in Devon in 1974 and currently lives in West Sussex. She writes novels, short stories and non-fiction and has been published in periodicals such as *The Guardian, Interzone, Black Static* and *Strange Horizons*, and anthologies such as Fox Spirit's *European Monsters* and Lonely Planet's *Better than Fiction I and II*. Her recent novellas, *The Beauty* and *The Arrival of Missives*, have been shortlisted between them for a Shirley Jackson Award, the James Tiptree Jr. Award, the BSFA and BFS Awards, and the John W. Campbell Memorial Award. She blogs at aliyawhiteley. wordpress.com and she can be found on Twitter as @AliyaWhiteley.

John Langan is the author of two novels, *The Fisherman* and *House of Windows*, and three collections of stories, *Sefira and Other Betrayals*, *The Wide, Carnivorous Sky and Other Monstrous Geographies* and *Mr. Gaunt and Other Uneasy Encounters*. With Paul Tremblay, he co-edited *Creatures: Thirty Years of Monsters*. One of the founders of the Shirley Jackson Awards, he served as a juror for its first three years. Currently he reviews horror and dark fantasy for *Locus* magazine. He lives in New York's Hudson Valley with his wife, younger son and the sound of guitars.

Paul Tremblay is the British Fantasy Award–winning author of seven novels including *The Cabin at the End of the World*, *A Head Full of Ghosts*, *Disappearance at Devil's Rock* and *The Little Sleep*. He is currently a member of the board of directors of the Shirley Jackson Awards, and his essays and short fiction have appeared in the *Los Angeles Times*, *Entertainment Weekly. com*, and numerous *Year's Best* anthologies. He has a master's degree in mathematics and lives outside Boston with his wife and two children.

Alison Moore's first novel, *The Lighthouse*, was shortlisted for the Man Booker Prize and the National Book Awards (New Writer of the Year), winning the McKitterick Prize. Both *The Lighthouse* and her second novel, *He Wants*, were *Observer* Books of the Year. Reviews of her third novel, *Death and the Seaside*, referred to her as the "talented creator of a new English grotesque" (Isabel Berwick, *The Financial Times*) and as "one of the most gifted and interesting writers of weird fiction in Britain today" (Nina Allan, *The Spider's House*). Her fourth novel, *Missing*, is out now. Her short fiction has been included in *Best British Short Stories* and *Best British Horror* anthologies, broadcast on BBC Radio 4 Extra and collected in *The Pre-War House and Other*

Stories, whose title story won a novella prize. Her first book for children, *Sunny and the Ghosts*, will be published in 2019. Born in Manchester in 1971, Alison lives in a village on the Leicestershire-Nottinghamshire border with her husband and son and is an honorary lecturer in the School of English at the University of Nottingham.

Website: *www.alison-moore.com*

Bracken MacLeod has worked as a martial arts teacher, a university philosophy instructor, for a children's non-profit organisation, and as a trial attorney. He is the author of a collection of short fiction titled *13 Views of the Suicide Woods* and the novels *Mountain Home, Come to Dust* and *Stranded*, which was a finalist for the Bram Stoker Award. He lives outside of Boston with his wife and son, where he is at work on his next novel.

For more fantastic fiction, author events, exclusive
excerpts, competitions, limited editions and more

VISIT OUR WEBSITE
titanbooks.com

LIKE US ON FACEBOOK
facebook.com/titanbooks

FOLLOW US ON TWITTER
@TitanBooks

EMAIL US
readerfeedback@titanemail.com